THE Ruby AIRSHIP

by SHARON GOSLING

SWITCH
PRESS

THE RUBY AIRSHIP IS PUBLISHED IN 2015 BY SWITCH PRESS,
A CAPSTONE IMPRINT
1710 ROE CREST DRIVE
NORTH MANKATO, MINNESOTA 56003
WWW.SWITCHPRESS.COM

FIRST PUBLISHED IN 2013 BY CURIOUS FOX,
AN IMPRINT OF CAPSTONE GLOBAL LIBRARY LIMITED,
7 PILGRIM STREET, LONDON, EC4V 6LB
REGISTERED COMPANY NUMBER 6695582
WWW.CURIOUS-FOX.COM

LIBRARY OF CONGRESS CATALOGING-IN-PUBLICATION DATA IS AVAILABLE ON
THE LIBRARY OF CONGRESS WEBSITE.

ISBN: 978-1-63079-004-2 (HARDCOVER)

SUMMARY:
RÉMY HAS LEFT THE CIRCUS AND HER LIFE AS A THIEF, BUT SHE DOUBTS THAT
DETECTIVE THADDEUS REC WILL EVER TRULY TRUST HER.

DESIGNER:
KAY FRASER

COVER ILLUSTRATION:
LIAM PETERS

IMAGE CREDIT:
SHUTTERSTOCK © LYNEA

PRINTED IN CANADA.
092014   008478FRS15

For my mum and dad, with love –
a ruby airship for your ruby wedding year.

{Chapter 1}

THE OPAL'S CURSE

*I*t was late, or — depending on your point of view — perhaps very early. Outside the theater, the streets of Shoreditch were cast in deep shadow. Rémy slipped out of the Albert Saloon's stage door and stopped for a moment, looking up. The moon was curved and yellow, like a hard heel of cheese discarded against the tablecloth of the London sky. From somewhere close by came a rattling clatter, followed by the unholy racket of two alley cats doing battle.

Rémy loved this time of night. She liked it in any town or village, but when she walked the streets of London after midnight it felt as if she were seeing a different world. It was a fairy-tale world: magical, but as cruel as it was enchanting. London by night was a reflection of itself. The people living in it were different, as dark as their surroundings. Rémy enjoyed the danger of walking among them, seen but untouched. She had been one of them, once; plotting dark deeds by the light of only a candle and the meager moon. But that had been before. Now, she was free, as long as she was careful . . . as long as certain parts of the law didn't find her.

She set off for Limehouse Basin, still energized by her recent performance. Less than twenty minutes ago, Rémy had still been on the stage. It was Saturday: payday. The coins jangled in Rémy's pocket as she pulled up the black hood of her heavy cloak against the early bite of frost. She was heading home, back to the Professor's old workshop.

They'd been there three months now, she and J — after all, it seemed a pity to let the old place go to ruin when they were both homeless. Rémy had taken over the Professor's private study as her bedroom, and J — on the rare occasion that the boy slept — had the use of a small anteroom off the main floor. So she hadn't been alone since the circus had left London, even if a certain young policeman's visits had become less frequent than she might have once hoped.

She quickened her step, replacing thoughts of Thaddeus Rec with thoughts of food and hoping that J had left her something on the stove. Ahead of her, a carriage rattled along the narrow road before turning a corner, disappearing through the tame halo of light thrown down by a gas lamp. In her head, Rémy tried to rehearse the new routine she'd been formulating for the past week or so. The problem with being a permanent fixture at a theater instead of in a touring circus was thinking up enough new tricks to keep the audiences coming back.

A piercing shriek shattered the gloom. There came another and then another. It wasn't cats this time, it was something even more chilling. There were shouts, men's voices overlaid by the whinnying of terrified horses and a series of sharp bangs that sounded like someone hammering against wood with fist or foot. Then more screams, echoing through the gaslight, shivering along the road toward her like ghosts.

Rémy ran to the corner of the street. The unlit road beyond was very dark, cast in such blackness that it was almost impossible to see what was happening. Quickly, Rémy reached into a pocket and pulled out the night glasses she'd borrowed from J, slipping them on. The world immediately took on a faint green tinge, but at least she was no longer blind. The carriage that had passed Rémy a few moments before stood in the middle of the road at a skewed angle. The petrified horses reared between the shafts, screaming as only a scared animal can. Rémy looked for the driver and spotted a figure lying slumped and still against the curb. Two men were hammering at the door of the carriage, their voices menacingly loud in the dark.

"Open up, lady!"

"No need to fear us, lovely — all we want are those sparklers."

"Tha's right. Hand 'em over, and you'll be right as rain. Make it difficult, and we'll . . ."

Rémy looked around, but the streets were deserted. More screams came from inside the carriage as the two ruffians began to rock it, tilting it on its thin wheels. The horses were going crazy, and Rémy couldn't understand why they hadn't bolted. Then she saw the scrawny boy standing bravely between them, holding on to their reigns as if his life depended on it, which it probably did. She strained to hear any other male voices, but there were none. The woman — and there was only one, she thought — must have been traveling alone. That was unusual, not to mention dangerous, especially at this time and in this part of the city.

Rémy bit her lip. How did she get herself into these things? She slipped off her cloak. Beneath it, she was dressed in her everyday clothes, which were not the sort the folk of London were used to seeing on a young woman. She wore a black corset with a loose black shirt underneath, open at the neck. Around her waist was a wide leather utility belt that had a place for everything from her lock-picks to her night glasses. Rémy's slim, agile legs were clad in black breeches, tucked into tall, black leather boots. Her dark hair was still up from being on the wire, twisted into a coil and pinned neatly against the back of her head. Rémy also hadn't removed her stage mask, the iridescent black bird that she had taken to painting over her eyes, nose, and lips to disguise her face. On the wire, it was spell-binding — on the dark streets of night-London, it was fearful.

She ran out of the shadows and into the street. Surprise was the best tactic — if she could take one of them out before the other realized what was happening, they'd be one-to-one before the fight even began. A few yards before she reached the melee, Rémy pirouetted, launching herself into the air in a quick spin and kicking out at the back of the first man's right leg. He crumpled like a sack of potatoes as her toes connected, his knees hitting the slabs below so hard that he screeched in pain. Rémy was already deep into another turn, yanking herself around so fast that the street became a blur. This blow was aimed higher, and by the time her free foot landed back on solid ground, the man was out cold, sprawled headlong over the filth of the broken cobbles.

The second man realized what was happening just as his companion lost consciousness. He lunged at her. Rémy sprang sideways and then, in two nimble leaps, was on top of the carriage, eliciting another series of screams from the woman inside. The lumbering brute tried to reach her, but Rémy side-stepped and brought the heel of her boot down on his fat fingers. He yelled, jerking backward and almost stumbling over the inert figure of his colleague.

Rémy leaped again, head-height to the scoundrel as she sailed out of the dark, her knee cracking into his chin and then, once she'd landed, her third spin-and-kick leveled at his crotch. He folded in half like a cheap penknife, winded and cursing. She stood in front of him and lifted one foot to push against his shoulder. He slumped to the ground.

The horses bolted, let loose as the boy who'd been holding them scarpered. The animals lurched along the street, no longer in step with each other and completely without regard for the carriage harnessed behind them. The screams from the woman inside grew even more frantic as the two animals tried to escape. The carriage careened erratically down the road and away.

Rémy ran after it, splashing through the stinking, murky puddles to draw level with the foam-flecked gelding in the leftmost shaft. His neck was stretched; his head down and pushed forward, his ears back. She tried to grab at the reigns, but the horse, its eyes rolling in fear, jerked its head up and away from her hand. Rémy ran on, the muscles of her legs burning as they came to a corner. For one terrifying moment she thought the two horses were going to choose different directions, but then the second followed the first and crashed right, almost upturning the carriage as they slewed it against one of the ragged houses lining the street.

There was nothing for it. If she wanted to stop them, Rémy was going to have to take the driver's place. She dropped back slightly and then leaped at the front of the carriage, her feet hitting the running board as she flung herself across the driver's footrest. The screams from inside the carriage rose again like an orchestra reaching a crescendo, as Rémy scrambled up, first to her knees, then to her feet, grabbing the reigns.

Rémy stood on the driver's seat of the carriage. Feeling it tilt and move beneath her, she kept her knees unlocked to help her balance. The horses strained against her as she pulled back on the reigns. Then they began to slow, responding first to the bit and then to the familiarity of having a driver. Eventually, they found pace with each other, and then, finally, with her.

Rémy brought them to a stop, pulling the carriage in against the curb and taking a breath.

"Hey there," she called to the occupant of the carriage. "If you will tell me where to go, I will take you home. I can't let go of the horses or they may bolt again."

There was a moment's silence. Rémy pushed her night glasses up into her hair and spoke to the trembling, exhausted horses in the way she'd learned from the horsemen of the circus — *Breathe through your nose, Rémy, with horses you must always breathe through your nose* — trying to keep them calm. Then there came the sound of wood rubbing against wood as the carriage's window opened. Rémy twisted around to see an elegant woman peering up at her, her hair coiled elaborately atop her head.

"H-Hello?"

"Good evening, mademoiselle," said Rémy. "Are you well?"

"Sh-shaken, but mostly unharmed — thanks to you. I owe you my life. Th-thank you."

"You are welcome, mademoiselle —"

"I am Lady Sarah Valentine."

"You are welcome, Lady Sarah," Rémy adjusted. "I will take you home, if you will tell me your address?"

"Hanover Square, Miss — it is Miss, isn't it? Who are you?"

Rémy smiled, suddenly remembering the grease-paint still covering her face. "Sit back and calm your nerves, my lady. I will have you home quick-smart." She turned back to the horses and, a second later, heard the window grind shut again.

"Hey — you!" Rémy called as a shoeless little boy in tattered trousers slunk out of an alleyway beside them. "Want to earn your breakfast?"

He nodded eagerly and came closer. His expression changed as she came into better view — the black bird on her face cast a shadow of fear over him. Rémy dug a coin from her pocket and dropped it into his outstretched hand. "The driver of this carriage is injured. He's lying against the curb in Worship Street. See that he's taken care of. And see this?" She pointed to her face and the mask painted there. "Cheat me and this will come looking for you. *D'accord?*"

The boy nodded and then, in the space of a shattered second, was gone into the night.

The rest of the journey was uneventful as Rémy drove the carriage from the shadowy murk of the East End into the richer, though hardly cleaner, parts of London. As soon as she'd turned into Hanover Square, a group of men started toward the carriage. They'd obviously been waiting anxiously for the return of Lady Sarah.

"Who the devil are you?" asked one, as Rémy drew to a halt before the grand house.

"Lady Sarah met with some . . . misfortune on her journey this evening," Rémy explained. "I was able to assist her."

"Were you, by Jove," said the man as a liveried footman darted past him to open the carriage door. "And what the blazes have you done with Evans, my driver?"

Lady Sarah appeared, helped down from the carriage by the servant, and for the first time Rémy saw her full finery. She wore a dress of sky blue, edged and embroidered in fine gold thread. At her throat was a sapphire of a matching hue, large enough to take Rémy's breath away. It was Lady Sarah's fingers, though, that truly made Rémy's heart thump. Each was adorned with a ring bearing an enormous precious stone, and none spoke louder to the former jewel thief than the huge ruby on her index finger. She realized that Lady Sarah was looking at her intently as she spoke to the man, who appeared to be her husband.

"Charles, do show this young lady some manners. She single-handedly saw off a bunch of ruffians who accosted me and then tamed the horses before the carriage could fall to pieces. I owe her my life, or if not my life, then at the very least my jewels."

Charles peered over her shoulder. "Where's your feckless brother? Weren't you under his protection?"

Lady Sarah glanced down at her hands. "He left me during the intermission. He's probably at the gaming tables as we speak."

Charles made a disgusted sound in his throat, and then glanced angrily up at Rémy. "Well, I am in your debt, whoever you are . . . if you were indeed Lady Sarah's savior and not part of the plot."

"Charles!"

Rémy jumped from the driver's seat to the ground in one fluid movement to stand before them both.

"I am sorry, my dear," began Lady Sarah, "for my husband's rudeness. I know I am greatly indebted to you. How can I repay your efforts?"

Rémy shook her head. "I need nothing, Lady Sarah. I will leave you now. Good night."

She began to walk away, but Lady Sarah stopped her with a hand on her arm. When Rémy turned back, she saw that the woman was pulling the ruby ring from her slender finger.

"Here," said Lady Sarah, "please, take it. I saw how your gaze was drawn to it."

Rémy stared at the glittering jewel in the palm of Lady Sarah's hand. "No, my Lady, really —"

"Take it," the woman ordered. "As you see, I have many jewels. And how many does one woman need? Besides, I heard you pay the boy to help poor Evans, and so you are out of pocket, too. Take it as a token of my thanks."

Rémy did as she was told. The ruby was warm, as if the jewel contained a miniature fire, burning safely in its belly. Lady Sarah smiled once more, and then turned to join her husband, sweeping up the steps of her fine home and into the comfort beyond.

★ ★ ★

By the time Rémy finally made it back to Limehouse Basin and the Professor's workshop, it was so late that the sky over the river was beginning to take on the pink tinge of dawn. Weary and starving, she pushed open the door to find the cluttered space empty and still, save for the flickering of embers in the fireplace grate. Rémy sighed, trying not to feel the disappointment that weighed upon her heart. She had half-hoped that Thaddeus would be there, waiting for her to get home, as he used to in the weeks after she and J had first moved in. She wondered where he was and whether he was thinking of her at all.

{*Chapter 2*}

UNPLEASANT
DUTIES

"*Y*ou realize, of course," said Lord Falconer from over the candelabra at the other end of the table, "that the situation in India is not merely one of economics, but of ideology, too."

There was a general murmuring of assent. Or perhaps it was dissent — Thaddeus Rec couldn't be sure. He stared down at the shallow dish of soup that had appeared before him. It was green and had the aroma of peas. The policeman — Detective Inspector now, no less — had been dreading the soup course ever since he had learned that he would have to attend this dinner. Soup generally ended up down his front instead of in his mouth. And this one was green, for goodness' sake! Thaddeus blinked, imagining the horror of tipping food down his only good white shirt in front of the assorted gentry around Sir Henry Strong's elegant dinner table. The thought made him feel faintly sick.

The conversation about the state of the Empire rumbled on around him. Thaddeus wondered again, for the millionth time, just how he had ended up in such eminent company. He'd be happier down by the docks, clearing out the opium dens of the city's lost souls or chasing pickpockets through Whitechapel. But ever since the affair of the Shah of Persia's diamond, Thaddeus had been no ordinary London policeman. He had been held up as a shining example of good policing by Queen Victoria herself, which is how the boy from the East End had ended up as the youngest detective inspector in her Majesty's constabulary. At the time, Thaddeus hadn't realized that his promotion would mean less actual police work and more fiddling about at evenings such as this. Apparently, though, it came with the territory.

Everyone else was beginning to eat. Thaddeus glanced down at his enemy, the spoon, and noticed that the cuff of his shirt was poking out from beneath his black jacket. It was frayed, betraying its age. He'd borrowed the dinner suit from the Professor's stash of disguises, but he hadn't been able to find a decent white shirt to go beneath it. Buying a new one was out of the question. An inspector's salary, it turned out, wasn't that much more than a constable's.

"Perhaps the young monsieur has an — how you say? — insight on the situation? He must surely come across similar during his duties as one of 'er Majesty's police?"

It took Thaddeus a moment to register that the speaker was addressing him. He looked up to find the eyes of the entire table trained in his direction. Opposite, the man who had spoken — the Comte de Cantal — was watching him with calculating eyes and an unfriendly smile. The ladies present obviously found the Comte handsome, as they had been twittering behind their hands about him ever since he had stepped into the room earlier that evening. To Thaddeus, the man seemed strangely snake-like. An unusually thin, curling scar stood out on his left cheek, and all his movements were sly and darting. If he'd been dressed in street garb, Thaddeus would have pegged him for a pickpocket.

"Forgive me," the man said, flicking his cool gaze away with a lazy shrug. "I have neglected — I should address you as Lord, no doubt?"

Thaddeus's fingers twitched away from the spoon. "Er — no."

"Ah," said the stranger, his soft French accent caressing the English words with undue care, as if to make them hang around longer than necessary. "Sir, then. Sir — I'm sorry, what is your name?"

Thaddeus clenched his jaw. Sir Henry had introduced everyone upon their arrival, and there were not so many present that it was difficult to remember who was who. Particularly since Thaddeus was the only guest with no honorific title. The Comte de Cantal knew full well the policeman's name and that nothing went in front of it. Which was, the policeman surmised, the reason the nobleman had drawn attention to him with such cunning mockery. It wasn't the first time that someone had chosen to point out his true station in life among polite company. For Thaddeus, it had become just another tedious aspect of his promotion.

"Neither am I a Sir, Comte," Thaddeus said, with a faint smile of his own. "I am merely Thaddeus Rec, born and bred of London town."

"Come now, Rec," spluttered their host, Sir Henry, from his seat at the table's head. "There's no 'merely' about it, my boy. Rec is the very future of the force,

Comte, the very future! We are lucky that he has found time to grace our little soiree, what?"

The Comte's handsome, angular face momentarily twisted into a grimace but was just as quickly forced back into a grin as he looked directly at Thaddeus. "The future, yes," he said, "and how bright the future must be, no? If even one such as yourself may prosper in the glow."

Thaddeus understood. Just a year ago, he would have been nothing to most of these people. Born on the streets of the East End, parentless, homeless, Thaddeus Rec had clawed his way up out of the gutter. There were plenty of those, such as the Comte, who wished he had not. For how many other commoners might decide they had the right to follow in his footsteps?

Thaddeus forced a pleasant smile on to his face and was about to reply when Sir Henry stepped in again.

"Perhaps you did not hear, Comte," Sir Henry began, "about the shocking events surrounding the theft of the Shah of Persia's diamond. It is called the Ocean of Light, you know — quite the biggest in the world, excepting her Majesty's own stone, the Mountain of Light, of course. Well, if not for Rec here, it would have disappeared into the clutches of a circus brat — one of your countrywomen, in fact, now I come to think of it. She was rather famous in your parts, I believe. Now, what was her name? Something flighty, something — well, you know — typically French."

Thaddeus made no reply, but his stomach churned at the thought of Rémy's stage name being mentioned in connection with the crime. She was still a wanted criminal, still in London — and he knew exactly where she was.

"Le Petit Moineau," murmured the Comte. "In English, I believe you call her Little Bird." Thaddeus found the Frenchman looking at him with renewed interest, though his gaze was no friendlier. "She has been wanted in France for some years, as you say, Sir Henry, but she always seems to slip the net. Well, well, well. So this is the man who thwarted the best jewel thief in Europe. Or almost, at least, no? I congratulate you, Monsieur Rec. An achievement indeed."

Thankfully, at that point the conversation moved on, although Thaddeus had not missed the Comte's final jibe. Neither was he ignorant of the Frenchman's inquisitive gaze as the evening continued. Thaddeus survived the soup course and the fish course, too. They were embarking on the meat course — a huge hunk of beef that had been broiled with onions — when the Comte spoke again. This time his words were only for Thaddeus's ears.

"Tell me, Rec," he said softly, "the time of the theft of the Darye-ye Noor and your subsequent investigation. That was also when Lord Abernathy disappeared so mysteriously from London, yes?"

The Comte's casual mention of Abernathy in connection with the diamond's theft almost made Thaddeus choke on his food. He forced himself to stay calm, looking at the Frenchman with a deliberately puzzled frown.

"I'm sorry, Comte? Lord who?"

Something unpleasant flickered in the Comte's dark eyes. He leaned back, pausing before he spoke again. "You do not remember the case? Strange, for I believe the Lord in question was present when the jewel first disappeared. I thought I heard tell that he had even been the one to help the girl thief into the Tower of London on the night the diamond was stolen."

"Ah," said Thaddeus, pretending to remember. "Indeed, you are right, of course. I did not know, however, that Lord Abernathy was said to have disappeared. You mean no one has seen him recently? I am afraid I was so busy during that investigation —"

"But of course," the Comte whispered, with a rather mocking nod. "You were . . . busy."

Thaddeus picked up his champagne glass and took a sip. "Lord Abernathy was an elderly gentleman, wasn't he? I am not certain that he disappeared so much as . . ."

"Died?" The Comte de Cantal supplied the word with a sharp tongue and shot Thaddeus a piercing look. "It is possible, I suppose. Although for that to happen with no one to hear about it . . . Strange, do you not think?"

The policeman felt sweat begin to prick at his brow and cursed himself, hoping that this strange Frenchman could not see his discomfort. Thaddeus had a terrible feeling about this man. Did he know something about the truth of what had happened beneath the streets of London? What Abernathy had sought to bring about through his army of infernal machines? Surely not. Abernathy and his men had died, thanks to Rémy's own willingness to sacrifice herself. Only she, Thaddeus, Desai, and J knew the truth of what had happened.

He was trying to come up with an appropriate reply to the Comte's question when a butler entered the room and spoke to his master.

"Comte," said Sir Henry a moment later, "there is a messenger outside for you. He insists on speaking to you in person. Rec, there is a message for you, too. Go on, Jackson, give it to him, don't delay!"

The Comte stood, dabbing his mouth with his napkin in an elaborate show of delicacy. He bowed to the table. "My apologies, dear friends, for this interruption. Please excuse me for a moment."

Thaddeus watched the Frenchman as he departed the table, but the Comte did not look at him. Jackson appeared at Thaddeus's shoulder, proffering a silver tray that held one small sealed envelope with his name scrawled untidily upon it. The policeman recognized the hand at once — it was from his sergeant, Collins. Tearing open the envelope, Thaddeus read the enclosed note and grimaced.

"A problem, Rec?" Sir Henry asked.

"I am afraid so, Sir Henry," Thaddeus told him, standing. "I am sorry, but I must take my leave. Police business."

"Not another darned burglary, Rec?" Sir Henry demanded. "Lord Theakston's hopping mad, you know. Lost his grandmother's pearls in his, by Jove."

"I'm not at liberty to say, Sir Henry," said Thaddeus, smoothly, "but my attendance is needed. Can you please excuse me, with many thanks for this excellent meal?"

"Yes, yes, Rec, of course. Come, I will walk you out." With effort, the considerable bulk of Sir Henry stood and ushered Rec from the room. Once outside, the kindly old gent placed a hand on the policeman's shoulder. "Now look here, Rec," he said. "You're not to mind that fool Cantal. He may be aristocracy, but he's not got two pennies to rub together, and he's sure as heck not fit enough to lick your boots. So chin up, young chap. Understand?"

Thaddeus smiled. "Thank you, Sir Henry. And I am truly sorry to break up your party."

"Pish," said the gent, with a wave of his hand. "Enough of that. Bunch of useless windbags, the lot of them. Now be off with you. Save us from the rabble, Rec. Save us from the rabble."

Outside, the night had congealed into a mess of gray clouds tinged a sickly yellow by the weak moon beyond. Thaddeus pulled the collar of his old leather overcoat up around his ears and ran down the steps from Sir Henry's townhouse. There had indeed been another burglary, and Collins had called him to the scene. It wasn't far. Thaddeus began to walk, crossing the square and heading into the streets.

He was passing a shaded alley when a noise caught his attention. He glanced in its direction to see two men standing in the buttery glow of a gas lamp, talking quietly. He recognized one as the Comte de Cantal. The other's face was half-hidden in the murky shadows. He was a young man, with a high forehead and a thin nose. He was dressed in a dark tailcoat, a top hat clutched in one hand. The stranger glanced toward him as Thaddeus passed, sharp eyes looking out of a sharp face. Then he turned away into shadow, passing out of the policeman's sight as if he had never been there at all.

Thaddeus walked quickly onward, shivering slightly in the evening chill. For him, at least, it was going to be a long night.

{Chapter 3}

AN OLD FRIEND

At noon the next day, Rémy woke to the familiar sound of tinny hammering coming from J's room. The boy had been hard at work on something for weeks now, but he hadn't said a word about it. In fact, Rémy had hardly seen him for days. She wondered what he was doing but knew better than to ask. The explanation would likely be as confusing as whatever contraption J was trying to cobble together. Since moving in to the Professor's workshop, he'd become obsessed with the various mechanical marvels — or, more accurately, bits of mechanical marvels — that were scattered around the building. Still, at least it kept him out of trouble.

She washed and dressed quickly and then stepped out into the chaos of the main workshop. Everywhere there were piles of bits and pieces — clockwork watch parts here, strange, half-assembled masks there; listening devices; power gauges; odd-looking boxes that held who-knew-what . . .

Every time Rémy tried to look at it all, it made her dizzy. The one relatively tidy part of the room was just in front of the great fireplace, where a semi-circle of old leather sofas and chairs had been arranged. She picked her way toward it, spying a tray of bread and cheese that J had thoughtfully left out for her after his own breakfast. As she ate, she looked around, hoping to see a pile of post. But, as had been the case with the past three weeks, there was nothing. Anxious, Rémy sat down, drawing her legs up under her.

It was now almost a month since she had heard from her oldest friend, even though they had promised to write to each other every week when Claudette departed for France. Claudette Anjou, once a talented pickpocket and fortune-teller, had taken over running the circus that had been Rémy's only home when its canny and criminal owner, Gustave, had finally received his just desserts. Claudette had changed the name from Le Cirque de la Lune to Le Cirque des

Secrets — The Circus of Secrets — and had taken it back to France to begin anew. Rémy, though, had decided to stay behind in London. It had been a difficult decision, but going back to France would have meant never seeing Thaddeus Rec again. At the time, that had somehow seemed unthinkable.

He'd said he loved her.

Rémy shivered slightly as the memory surfaced.

A deep chasm had been between them, and she'd thought she was going to die a watery death, alone, because it was the right thing to do and only she could do it. Thaddeus had stood there, shouting over the abyss, and convinced her to let him cross. To be with her, no matter what happened, as they tried to save the city from Abernathy's dastardly plot. Because he loved her.

That was why she was still in London. That was why she hadn't gone back with Claudette. It was all for Thaddeus and that moment. Yet they hadn't spoken of it since, not once.

Rémy felt her opal pendant shift slightly against her skin — a small, mystical sliver of stone with a life of its own. Most of the time she wasn't aware of it, but every now and then, it would make itself known. There would be something like a tingle, a tiny, insignificant buzzing in her head. And then, filtering like new mortar through the bricks of her thoughts, there would be others. Thoughts that weren't hers; the thoughts of people passing in the street, of J in his sleep . . . of Thaddeus, trying to find something to say to her and mentally crossing out every sentence before it even got to his lips. His eyes, that odd mixture of one blue and one brown, clouding with a confusion that she wanted to understand but couldn't bring herself to talk about.

She stood, shaking off this sudden, unsettling feeling with a flick of her shoulders. She hadn't seen Thaddeus for days. The last time he had visited, it hadn't even been to see her. He'd been looking for J, as he always seemed to be now that the boy was his unofficial eyes and ears on the ground in the East End. She and Thaddeus had stood in front of the fire together, awkwardly, neither quite meeting the other's eye. They talked of nothing at all, because all the things they should have been talking about had flooded the space between them and turned it into a fathomless, impassable ocean.

And that, she thought, *was what I abandoned my oldest friend for? Where are you, Claudette? Why don't you write to me?*

To occupy her mind, Rémy decided to go to the theater and practice her new routine. She wasn't due on stage that evening, which was just as well. After the exertions of the previous night, Rémy knew she wouldn't be at her best. But she needed something to distract her, both from her worries about Claudette and from thoughts of Thaddeus, and there was nothing better for that than mastering a new trick. J was still hammering frantically behind the closed door of his room as she stepped from the noise of the workshop into the roar of Limehouse.

When Rémy had first begun living at the workshop, she'd tried to work out what time of day the dock was busiest but had soon given up. The place never seemed to settle; there was always work to be done. That morning a clipper had arrived, traveling up the Thames on the morning tide from whatever far-off place it had begun its journey — India, perhaps, or maybe even farther.

Now the ship's sails stood furled as men of all sizes and colors rushed up and down her gangplanks, hauling crate after crate back down onto the solid, wet-sluiced stone of the dockside. Rémy paused beside one of the wooden boxes, wondering what was inside. Tea? Spices? Silk? Everything came through

Limehouse, though little of it stayed. It was for richer folk in richer places than this.

The bustle danced to a different tune as she turned onto Whitechapel Road and began heading north. The rooming houses had turned out their penny-chair renters hours ago, and now the scramble to earn enough to find a warm place for tonight was in full swing. The pickpockets were on the lookout for the unwary; the women who could do no better were trying to find men with which they could do worse. Under the pale, miserable London sun, the stink of the streets was rising to meet the stink of the people who lived there. Rémy had grown used to it over the months. She knew this place now, and she knew that what the people did, they did because they had no choice. Take J, for example — their chance encounter had been driven by his need to steal her bag, but at the first chance he'd been given, he'd dropped all that thievery and become a model citizen. He'd even traveled as far as some of those clippers, to India and back with their friend Desai.

The East End was a strange place, a wild place, a dangerous place, and sometimes even a kind place. It was the sort of place that someone like Rémy found very easy to make home.

The theater was quiet, its lights dimmed for the daytime. The old doorman let her in with a black-toothed smile that was really more of a leer. She slipped up the stairs to the dressing rooms to change before heading for the stage, only to find that it was already occupied. The surprise performer was a magician. Rémy could tell that even from where she stood in the wings — he was wearing the ubiquitous black top hat-and-tails combination that workers of stage magic seemed to favor. There was only one person in the audience — Mr. Richards, the owner of the theater, was sitting in the stalls, three rows back so as to get the best view. He had obviously offered the magician a chance to try out for a coveted spot on the playlist.

"Come on then, lad," Richards bellowed at the tall young man on stage. "Show me what you've got, and be quick about it. I haven't got all day, y'know."

"As you wish, monsieur," said the magician, with a French accent as elegant as his outfit. "Since your audience will be unacquainted with the Magnificent Yannick and his astounding talents, it would be best to start with —"

At the sound of his name, Rémy's mouth fell open in astonishment.

"*Mon dieu* — Yannick?" she exclaimed, the words

bursting from her lips before she'd even thought them. "Yannick! Is that really you?"

The magician turned sharply toward her. His face was partially cast in shadow by the rim of his hat, but Rémy would have known her childhood friend anywhere.

"Good gracious!" Yannick exclaimed, whipping off his hat to let a flash of white-blonde hair free. "If it isn't the very excellent Rémy Brunel! Where on earth did you spring from?"

Rémy laughed, dancing forward onto the stage to pull The Magnificent Yannick into a hug. "I perform here, you idiot! Three times a week. I'm the star attraction!"

"Ahem." They both turned toward Richards, who was on his feet, looking at them both with raised eyebrows. "That is a matter for debate, Miss Brunel," he said, "and in that debate, I will always have the deciding vote. Perhaps you'd both like to stop wasting my time so that I can see whether Yannick is as 'magnificent' as he'd have us all believe?"

Rémy bit her lip, nodding as she retreated to the wings again. She watched as Yannick got into his part with gusto, laughing quietly and willing him on. He was better than she remembered, with more stage presence and a nice turn in tricks. He'd even added in some hypnosis. Richards evidently thought he was good, too. Not that he clapped once Yannick was done, but he did book the magician for a trial week, which was even better.

They embraced again once Yannick came off stage, Rémy's face fixed in the permanent grin she had worn since she'd first realized who he was. It had been so long since she'd seen anyone from home — anyone from that life.

Yannick pulled back from the hug to look at her, though he didn't let her go. His bright blue eyes were twinkling, just the way they always had. "I wondered what had happened to you," he said. "I heard that Gustave had . . . how shall we say it? Got his come-uppance, at last."

Rémy smiled grimly at the memory of her old circus master, the devil who had forced her parents into a curse that tore them apart and made her into his pet jewel thief. "*Oui.* Well, he had it coming, wouldn't you agree?"

Yannick laughed. "Oh, I would . . . I would, Little Bird."

Rémy felt a jolt at the sound of her old circus name. No one called her by it now, not in her new life in London, and she realized that she missed it. And with that she also realized that it wasn't just the name she missed. A wave of homesickness rolled over her as she thought of Claudette and Amélie, of her pony Dominique, of the whole company helping to put up the circus tent at each new place they visited, of nights around the circus fire, laughing and eating and just . . . being together. She swallowed, hard, to stop the memories engulfing her heart.

"Hey, what's the matter?" Yannick asked, his hands still on her arms.

Rémy stepped back and smiled a watery smile. "Oh, nothing. Nothing at all! It's just so good to see you, and such a surprise! What are you doing in London?"

Yannick glanced at the toes of his shiny black shoes and shrugged. "The circuit in France wasn't what it used to be. I thought I'd try my luck here. Cross your fingers for me, Little Bird."

Rémy grinned again. "Ach, you'll be fine. The Magnificent Yannick always falls on his feet, isn't that right?"

Yannick grinned back, and Rémy realized with another shock that he had grown up since she had seen him last. He wasn't the floppy-haired, awkward boy she'd known when they were both small and trying to learn their trade. He was a man now, and he was handsome with it. She wondered for a moment what Yannick saw when he looked back at her and suddenly wished that she'd thought to brush her hair instead of just scrunching it all up into a ball to get it out of the way.

"Where are you staying?" she asked, to pull herself away from the unexpected thought. "Not too far away, I hope? We must catch up, Yannick!"

"Ah, well," the magician said, ruefully, turning to point at a battered old suitcase that was propped against the wing. "In that respect, I'll take any advice you care to give me, Rémy. As long as it's cheap, that is."

"Oh, well, if you don't have anywhere, you must come and stay with us," Rémy blurted, almost before she'd even realized she'd been thinking the words.

Yannick raised a quizzical eyebrow at her. "Us?"

"Yes — J and I live in a place in Limehouse Basin. It's huge, big enough for you too, of course, if you've still got your bedroll and aren't too proud to sleep on the floor!"

Yannick looked doubtful, and also a little curious. "And this . . . J . . . won't mind my intrusion into your . . . lives?"

Rémy laughed, "No, of course he won't." Then she realized what Yannick had really been asking, and laughed again. "J's just a boy, Yannick, a street boy who needed a home, just like me. It's a long story, but now we're friends and we share an old workshop. Come and stay there with us, at least until you find those famous feet of yours again. It'll be fun — like old times!"

Yannick grinned along with her, and nodded. "*D'accord*. Okay, I will."

{Chapter 4}

NEW TROUBLE

*I*t was early evening when Rémy and Yannick walked back to the warehouse, winding through the throngs of people who crowded the East End streets. Yannick had swapped his elaborate stage clothes for a plain pair of brown trousers and a rough cream shirt, topped off by a cap that made him look far younger and much more like the boy he'd been when they'd first known each other. As they chatted, Rémy thought back to those days, when life with the circus had seemed to be one long, hot summer of fun that would never end. That was before Gustave had realized her talent for stealing jewels, before her life had been as much about breaking into houses as it was about performing on the trapeze. She laughed at another of Yannick's circus tales and realized that, in his company, she was completely relaxed. Even better, the opal hadn't twitched once, so her mind was clear of anything but her own thoughts. It was refreshing, for sure. *This, thought Rémy, is how all friendship should be — easy and undemanding.*

"Do you remember that time outside Rouen," Yannick said, laughing even as he remembered, "when Marta the elephant took fright and went on the rampage, right into that woman's vegetable patch? I thought Gustave was going to have a fit!"

Rémy laughed, "I do remember! She only calmed down because of you. You were always so good with the animals. Marta loved you."

"I felt sorry for her. She shouldn't have spent so much time in that leg iron." He scowled for a minute. "Gustave never understood that she would have stayed of her own accord, as long as we showed her love. He always preferred that animals — and people — obeyed him through fear. He was a fool."

"He was," Rémy agreed, "but he is gone now, and we make our own lives, at last. Look, here we are!"

They had arrived outside the workshop, which, seen through Yannick's fresh eyes, she realized seemed rather a corner of nothing. It was just a rotten old wooden door beside a stinking, salty lock. But of course that was what the Professor had always intended it to seem, to disguise what was hidden beyond.

Inside, the fire that burned fiercely in the big fireplace had warmed the space, and the room smelled of fresh cooking.

"Aha," Rémy said, cheerily. "Looks as if someone was ready for us, Yannick. J's been cooking stew again!"

"Wot do you mean, again?" asked J, sticking his head around the door to his room. The boy's face almost completely hidden by a large contraption that looked at bit like a metal globe. He wore it as a hat, making his unruly fair hair stick out all over the place. It seemed to be combined with a pair of the Professor's night glasses and two sets of conjoined compasses that met in the center of the wearer's head. It jangled slightly as the boy pulled it off. "You want something else, you only 'ave to say so, Rémy."

"I wouldn't dream of it," she said, seeing J look Yannick up and down.

"Oo's this then?" The boy asked, putting down the device and shuffling into the room.

"J, I'd like to you meet an old friend of mine, from back in my circus days in France. Yannick, this is J, a very good new friend of mine."

"It's wonderful to meet you, J," said Yannick, offering an opulent bow and holding out a hand for the boy to shake.

J looked a little bowled over by the elegant greeting and flushed as he grasped Yannick's hand. "Er, likewise, I'm sure," he said. "You stayin' for dinner?"

"Actually, J, if you don't mind, Yannick's going to stay not just for dinner, but for a few nights. He's on trial at the Albert Saloon, you see. I said it would be all right. It is, isn't it?"

"Oh," said J, a tad awkwardly. "Yeah, o'course it is. Any friend, et cetera. You'd better be happy bunking on the floor, though."

"You are very kind," said Yannick, smiling. "I cannot tell you what a relief it is to find a friendly face — more than one — in a new city such as this. I am in your debt."

"Ah, well, none o' that," J muttered, turning back to retrieve his spoon. "Dinner'll be ready in a mo. Make yourself at home, like."

There was a knock at the door. With barely a pause, it creaked open on its old hinges to reveal Thaddeus

Rec, his battered hat under one arm and a bunch of bright yellow daffodils in the other. The first person he saw as he stepped into the room was Yannick. He stopped dead.

"Oh," he said, after a moment of silence. The policeman's eyes flicked from Yannick to Rémy and back again. "My apologies. I didn't realize you had visitors."

"He ain't a visitor. He's a friend," J said, raising his eyebrows significantly as he stirred the pot. "Just like you are, Mister Rec. Come on in, grub's nearly up."

Thaddeus continued to stare at Yannick. Yannick stared back. Rémy, confused by the sudden and unexpected hostility that had entered the room, took a step between them.

"Ah, Thaddeus Rec, this is my old friend, Yannick. We used to be in the circus together. He's a magician — he's just arrived in London and has got a spot at the Albert Saloon. Isn't that amazing? We're going to be colleagues again!"

Thaddeus nodded curtly at Yannick, but didn't relax for a second. At a loss for something else to say, Rémy pointed at the flowers. She'd never seen Thaddeus with any such thing before.

"You are visiting family later?"

"What?" Thaddeus tore his gaze away from Yannick and looked at her for the first time. Then he looked at the flowers, still clutched in his hand. His cheeks flushed a little. "Oh. No. These . . . these were . . . are . . . for you, actually."

It was Rémy's turn to blush. Flowers! No one had ever given her flowers before.

"Ah," said Yannick, a knowing smile in his voice. "So you are the type of girl who likes flowers now, *oui?*"

Rémy flushed deeper, embarrassed as she saw the amused look on her old friend's face. Beside her, she felt Thaddeus tense even more and knew he had taken Yannick's jibe as if it were aimed at him. It wasn't — Yannick had always teased her in the past and it looked as if the present would be no different.

"You don't have to have them if you don't want them," Thaddeus said with a carelessness he obviously didn't feel, dropping the daffodils and his hat on a nearby table. "They're a shameless bribe, really. I'm — " he cleared his throat, "I'm on official police business. Well, in a manner of speaking, anyway."

"Police business?" Rémy asked. "Then you'll want to talk to J, I suppose. Thaddeus is an Inspector with Scotland Yard, Yannick," she explained.

Yannick's eyebrows shot up into his fair hair.

"A policeman!" he said. "Well, you really are moving in exalted circles now, Rémy Brunel. I will really have to — what is it you English say? — mind my Ps and Qs." He strolled toward the fireplace and sank into one of the armchairs that flanked it. "Isn't that so, Mr. Policeman?"

Thaddeus glanced at him, an expression of annoyance briefly passing across his face. "That depends on what you've done that I might be interested in, Mr. . . . Yannick, is it?" he said coolly. Then he turned back to Rémy again. "Actually, it's not J I wanted to talk to this time. I was hoping you might help me. I need a fresh pair of eyes on this case, and I can't think of anyone better. You know, given your . . . previous, um . . . occupation."

Thaddeus seemed to suddenly realize what he was saying and looked away, embarrassed. Her criminal past as a jewel thief was something else they never, ever talked about.

"Well, don't mind us," said Yannick, apparently oblivious to Thaddeus's discomfort. "I'm just going to sit here quietly and wait for J's delicious-smelling stew."

Thaddeus frowned. "Perhaps we can talk privately?" He suggested to Rémy.

"Anything you have to say you can say in front of Yannick, Thaddeus," she said, with a touch of irritation. "I've known him for many years. He is completely trustworthy."

Rémy saw Thaddeus's eyebrows flick up slightly. He looked at Yannick again. "Have we met before?" he asked suddenly. "You seem familiar, somehow."

Yannick shrugged. "Not that I know of. Perhaps we passed in the street once."

"Perhaps." Thaddeus frowned, and then turned back to Rémy. "There's been a burglary, a strange one, and the second of its kind. It happened last night — well, early this morning, really. One of the big houses in the West End. Hanover Square, to be exact. Jewels taken from a locked safe in a locked room that's only accessible through the gentleman's locked study."

"Hanover Square?"

"Yes. It's a very well-to-do place. Lots of Lords and Ladies live there. You wouldn't believe the way they live on that side of town."

Rémy nodded. "Little men in uniform to open doors for you . . . more jewelry than clothes..."

Thaddeus looked at her curiously. "How do you know what it's like? You've never been there . . . have you?"

The opal tickled, moving against her chest almost as if in warning, just as Rémy saw the policeman's gaze fall upon the huge ruby ring given her by Lady Sarah. She loved the red stone so much that she hadn't taken it off since.

"Where did you get that?"

And there it was, clear as day, his doubting voice in her head . . .

Where did that come from? Could Rémy be the thief?

And then, just as quickly . . .

No. No, she wouldn't do that. She's changed . . .

But the damage was done.

Rémy leaped toward him. She only came up to Thaddeus's shoulder, but even so, he took a step back in the face of her towering anger.

"You think it was me!"

"What?" Thaddeus asked, holding up his hands, "No, of course I don't! I just wondered where the ring came from, that's all!"

"And you assumed I must have stolen it! As if I am still a thief! As if I hadn't done enough to prove myself to you!"

"Rémy, wait! That's not what I meant!"

"But it's what you thought! Isn't it?"

"No! No — not really."

"And here I thought you actually wanted my help, but no, you just wanted to find someone to pin your case on. That would be so easy, wouldn't it?"

Rémy saw the anger flicker into Thaddeus's eyes, the brown and blue darkening as if thunder had rolled into the room. His jaw tightened, and he shook his head.

"How can you say that? How can you even think that after everything? Do you even understand how difficult this entire situation is for me? You're still a wanted criminal, Rémy! I am a Detective Inspector of the Metropolitan Police! Do you know what would happen if they found out —"

"Then what are you doing here at all, little policeman? Why associate yourself with a disgusting criminal like me? Eh?"

"I don't think you're disgusting. Of course I don't — you know I don't!"

"But I am a thief, yes? And you are sworn to put people like me in jail. Why else would you be here, eh?"

"I came because I thought you could help me," Thaddeus said. "I thought, stupidly, that you might want to help me solve this case. I thought — God knows why — I thought we might work well together."

"How can we work together when you think I am the criminal you are searching for?" Rémy yelled back.

"I don't! I never even said that!"

"You didn't have to!"

The both stopped, breathing hard, staring at each other through seething eyes. Something electric sparked between them, and just for a second, Rémy remembered the kiss they had shared, all those long months ago. Thanks to the opal, she couldn't work out if she was the one thinking about it or if he was.

"Ahem . . ." The discreet sound came from Yannick, still seated in the chair across the room. It cut through the tense silence in the room like the crack of a whip.

Thaddeus jumped, as if he'd forgotten that they were not alone. He stepped away, scowling as he took a deep breath.

"I am sorry," he said, in a cold voice, "that I intruded on your reunion with such unimportant matters. Good evening. J, I'll see you soon."

He turned on his heel and stalked to the door, snatching up his hat with such violence that the discarded bouquet tumbled to the floor. A moment later he was gone, but Rémy was too angry to let Thaddeus get away so easily. She followed him.

"That's it?" She hissed, incensed, catching him

outside on the street. "You're going to walk into my home, accuse me of theft, and simply leave?"

Thaddeus spun around to face her, his features just as angry. "I did not," he said in a harsh whisper, "accuse you of theft." He paused for a moment, as if hesitating over something.

"What?" Rémy asked, jutting out her chin and crossing her arms. "What now?"

"Does he have to stay here? With you, at the workshop?"

Rémy frowned. "Yannick? Why shouldn't he?"

Thaddeus made an annoyed sound in his throat. "I don't trust him. I don't think you should either. And besides . . ."

"Besides — what?" Rémy asked as he trailed off.

Thaddeus shook his head again. "I just don't like it."

"You don't like it?" Rémy asked, her voice rising in annoyance. "You want me to turn a friend out on the street because you don't like it?"

"He was a friend, Rémy. How long is it since you've seen him? When you were both children? Who knows what kind of man he is now? I've seen his face somewhere before. I can't place where, but it worries me."

Rémy stepped away from Thaddeus, angry. "Only an Englishman could demand I turn an old friend out on the street when he has nowhere else to go. How can you ask me such a thing? First you accuse me of theft —"

"I. Did. Not," Thaddeus hissed.

"And now you try to tell me who I should keep as my friends. Well, you have no right! You have no right, and I will not listen to you. Go back to work, little policeman. You are not wanted here."

She watched as Thaddeus set his jaw, gritting his teeth. "Fine," he said, his voice stony cold. Then he turned on his heel and was gone, disappearing into the nighttime murk almost at once.

{Chapter 5}

CATCHING UP

$\mathcal{B}$ack inside the warmth of the workshop, Yannick was attempting to regale a somewhat downcast J with a tale of their shared past. The boy stood up as soon as she stepped back inside.

"I fink I'll go to bed meself," he muttered. "Lots to do in the morning."

Rémy nodded. "Night, J."

"A pleasure to meet you, J," said Yannick with his warmest smile. "And thank you for letting me stay."

J half-shrugged a response. The next moment, the door to his room was closing behind him. Rémy expected the sound of hammering to start up again, but all was silent.

"Well," said Yannick wryly, "that's two of your friends I seem to have upset already, and with only one evening gone. Perhaps tomorrow I should make more of an effort and try for three?"

Rémy sighed as she sat down opposite him in front of the fire. "It's just that Thaddeus and J are really the only friends I have here in London. The three of us have become very close over the past few months," said Rémy. "We've been through a lot together."

"Really?" asked Yannick. "You wouldn't know it from the way that policeman of yours spoke to you. Let me guess, in that little chat you two had out there, he warned you that I shouldn't be staying here with you. Am I right?"

Rémy scrubbed her short thumbnail against the frayed material of the chair's arm. "Something like that. He says I don't really know you anymore. I suppose he's right, though."

"Tsk!" exclaimed Yannick. "What rubbish! I know you better than some English boy you met just a few months ago, Rémy Brunel. How many years were we on the road together? Can I really have changed so much?"

Rémy raised her eyebrows at him. "I hope so. You used to be so clumsy you'd fall over your own feet."

Yannick laughed, and then she did too, and Rémy's discomfort at Thaddeus's words faded into the background. They had only spent an evening together, but already she felt more at home, more comfortable, with Yannick than she ever had with Thaddeus. Yannick put her at her ease, whereas Rémy always felt as if she had to be better than she ever could be around Thaddeus.

"I don't know why you put up with him coming around here," Yannick said, almost as if he knew what she was thinking. "That sort are never good news."

"Thaddeus is a good man, really. He's — it's just not . . . I don't . . ." Rémy sighed and tried again. "It's difficult, that's all. Anyway, I don't want to talk about Thaddeus. I need news, Yannick. Tell me what has been happening in France."

"Well, of course everyone's excited about the Jamboree," Yannick told her. "Or had you forgotten that it was this year? It's this week, you know."

Rémy stared into the fire, imagining the gathering. Once every four years, circus troupes from all over France — and sometimes beyond — gathered in one place, just outside Paris. It was a chance to catch up with old friends and make new acquaintances, to learn news, and for some, to change jobs. When she was younger, it had always been what she looked forward to, a week-long festival of noise, magic, fire, and fun. Yet this year, she'd hardly thought about it. London was her home and where she was meant to be now. Or so she'd thought.

"I suppose Claudette and the circus will be living it up there, won't they?"

"I don't know." Rémy rubbed a hand over her face. "I'm sure it's nothing, Yannick, but I haven't had a letter from Claudette for ages. We were supposed to write to each other every week, but . . . she hasn't returned word for a while."

Yannick stared into the fire. "That seems a little strange, doesn't it? I always remember you two being so close."

The well of unease that had been flooding Rémy's stomach bubbled a little. "I know. To tell you the truth, I am worried. But I don't know what to do. I can't keep writing if I don't know where she is."

Yannick sighed. "Ah, Claudette. I will not lie to you, Rémy — when I was a boy, I had a little crush on her. She's so . . . so different from the rest of us circus folk. Isn't she?"

Rémy laughed faintly, thinking of her friend's beautiful face and chestnut hair, of her way with languages and her ability to write, which was almost unheard of in circus life. "She is. She was beginning to teach Amélie to read when they went back to France. You never met her daughter, did you?"

"No," said Yannick, "though I heard about her. Poor Claudette and the baby — to be left like that. The man must have been a monster."

Rémy thought back to those months before Amélie had been born. Once Antoine had gone, Claudette refused to speak his name. Her belly had swollen along with her grief, and then Amélie had been born as beautiful as her mother, but as mute as a swan. Though Claudette never said it, Rémy knew her friend blamed herself. Claudette thought that somehow, her grief had poisoned the baby in her womb. Not once had Amélie spoken, in all her six years, not until the day Rémy's opal had woken and allowed her to hear the little girl's thoughts in her head. But Rémy hadn't told Claudette about the opal's powers. She hadn't known how to, and while Rémy was still trying to find the right words to explain, they had both gone back to France.

She and Yannick were silent for a moment, both staring into the flames as the memories swallowed them both. The feeling of homesickness overcame Rémy again as she thought of her friend, so far away.

London suddenly seemed a very strange place for her to be.

"I'm sorry, my dear friend," said Yannick, his face full of concern. "I did not mean to make you think of worrying things. If it helps, I do have word of a more jolly nature."

"Oh?"

"Indeed. It seems as if the fabled Lost Comtesse may actually be found at last."

"Really?" asked Rémy, genuinely surprised. "No, surely not? I thought that was just a silly story, a fairy tale that parents told their children. You know — 'Don't run off, you know what happens to naughty children who run off . . . You'll end up like the Lost Comtesse' . . ."

Yannick shook his head. "It's not just a story. Bits of it might have been made up, but she's out there somewhere, for real."

Rémy blew out a breath. "*Mon dieu*. And she's been found, you say?"

"Well, not yet, no, but soon, I think. The new Comte Cantal de Saint-Cernin has issued a reward, and he says he's determined to find her once and for all. He says he has studied his family's records and she is his cousin. So now that his father is dead and he's the new head of the family, he thinks it's time he put all his efforts into finding her."

Rémy shook her head, thinking about the old story. It was one all circus children grew up knowing, because it was what marked them out from the rest of the world. In it, circus people were a bad lot, kidnapping unwary children who strayed into their path. The story went that there was once an old circus couple who were desperate to have a child but, year after year, the wife remained barren. This saddened her beyond measure, and the husband could not bear to see his beloved wife bowed double by the grief of her childlessness.

One day, the rich governor of a city gave a huge party for his wife's birthday. The entire city turned out for the celebration, which attracted many performers and circuses from miles around and continued late into the night. The governor had a daughter, a young girl who did not go to bed as she had been ordered, but begged her maid to take her down into the town instead. The maid was persuaded but then became distracted and forgot her charge, just for a moment. The little girl wandered off, straight into the path of the old circus performer, who snatched her up at once and gave her to his wife, making her the daughter they couldn't have. The girl had never been seen since, and was said to still be with a circus somewhere.

"The story never really made sense to me, even when I was a child," said Rémy. "Surely the girl could have screamed as they dragged her away. And it's not as if they could have kept her locked in their caravan forever — she would have been able to run away at some point. So why didn't she?"

Yannick shrugged. "Not every girl is as able as you are, Little Bird. I heard tell that they'd built a tall tower in a secret forest and locked the child in it. They bricked up the door so there was no exit except for a high window that was too far from the ground to escape."

Rémy laughed. "That's the fairy tale of Rapunzel, you idiot!"

"Ah," said Yannick, waggling his eyebrows and making her laugh even more. "But is it? Seriously, though, Rémy. Imagine being the Lost Comtesse. Imagine having that entire inheritance sitting there, just waiting for you to remember who you were and come forward. How extraordinary would that be?"

Rémy smiled. "Very," she said.

They were silent for a while, staring at the fire and thinking their own thoughts. Rémy's homesickness returned, and she wondered again where Claudette and Amélie were and what they were doing at that moment. Yannick sighed and stretched his legs out toward the fire, his face pensive and a little sad, as if remembering all their childhood adventures and wishing it were possible to relive them all.

"Are you sure this is where you belong, Rémy?" he said at last. "What are you doing here, in London? What — who — is keeping you here?"

Rémy stared at the fire.

"I don't know," she said finally, in a whisper. "I don't know anymore."

{*Chapter 6*}

AN IMPOSSIBLE CASE

$\mathcal{T}$haddeus sat at his desk, his notes on the case spread out in front of him. None of what he had read, over and over, made sense. Two burglaries, both of jewels, each as inexplicable as the other. Both Lord Theakston's and Lord Bolsover's valuables should have been as safe as . . . well, he wouldn't ever use the saying "as safe as the crown jewels" ever again, not after what had happened a few months ago, but they were as safe as a very safe thing. As he had told Rémy, they seemed to have been taken from locked strongboxes in locked rooms, which had remained locked even after the thefts. Now both men were demanding that London's police force find the culprit and return their jewels as quickly as possible. Thaddeus had no idea even of where to start. The more he turned the facts over in his mind, the more impossible both events seemed to be. After his argument with Rémy, Thaddeus had known he wouldn't sleep. So he'd gone back to his desk instead and tried to work it all out in his own head. He'd been sitting there all night.

Lord Theakston had taken his wife and daughter out to the Adelphi theater. Two of the servants had been granted the night off, but the rest of the household had remained at the residence. All of the servants had exemplary records of service, and neither Lord Theakston nor Lady Theakston would believe that any of their houschold would steal from them. Indeed, it seemed a remarkably happy home, both upstairs and downstairs. Thaddeus was beginning to agree that the thief must have been an outsider, which only served to make the policeman's job all the harder.

As for Lord Bolsover, that case was even more difficult. Those jewels had also been within a safe in a locked room, this time one with no windows and only a single door, which opened into Lord Bolsover's private study, and for which only he had the keys. And as with Lord Theakston, Bolsover swore blind that those keys had never been out of his sight, not even long enough for an enterprising thief to have made an impression of them.

How do you steal a jewel through three locked doors? Twice?

The more he thought about it, the more Thaddeus was convinced that the only person who could truly help him solve the case was Rémy Brunel.

As her face floated into his mind for the millionth time that morning, the policeman sighed and rubbed a hand over his eyes. His Rémy Brunel. At least, he'd thought she was at one point, but now . . . now they could barely be in the same room together. Every time he tried to say something about what had happened in that cave — about what he'd said to her when he'd thought she was about to die — something passed through her eyes that made him think he'd be better not saying anything at all. And now, after last night . . .

Thaddeus stood up and began to pace. There was something just not right about that Yannick fellow turning up out of the blue. Besides, the policeman was sure he'd seen the man's face somewhere before, and until he could place it, he wouldn't be happy. And of course Thaddeus hadn't really thought that Rémy could be the thief he was searching for. Had he? No, not really. It was only that she'd suddenly been wearing that ring — a ruby that, if sold, could buy the workshop and everything in it several times over. It was natural that he should be a little suspicious, wasn't it? After how they had met and what her life had been like with the circus? But he'd never seriously suspected her. He believed her, unreservedly, when she'd protested it wasn't her. He'd just wanted her help.

Because how do you steal a jewel through three locked doors, as if by magic?

Thaddeus blinked, staring at the mass of notes on his desk. A cog turned in his head. A switch flicked.

Magic.

* * *

Rémy woke with an ache in her head that echoed an even more painful one in her heart. Getting up, she looked in the mirror and saw dark circles beneath her eyes. It wasn't just the worry about Claudette, or the homesickness that had enveloped her since meeting Yannick again. It was the argument with Thaddeus. Their bitter words had rolled around and around in her head all night. If only she'd not heard what he was thinking in that split second. If only she'd just been able to listen to what he actually had to say — I thought we might work well together.

But how? she thought. *How would we ever be able to do that, when you think I'm still capable of being the thing you most despise?*

Her fingers went to the opal. It hung on a thin gold chain around her neck, just as it always had, ever since Claudette had given it to her as a child, saying it was a gift from the mother she'd never known. *The gift has turned into a curse,* she thought. Not for the first time, Rémy wished she'd found the time to talk to Claudette about what her newly woken opal could do. Before they'd come to London, it had just been a talisman given in love. Now it was something entirely different — no, not different, but more. Rémy didn't know how to deal with it.

Reaching for the clasp, Rémy took the necklace from around her neck and coiled it into her palm. The opal glinted, a thousand threads of color in a milky sea of white on either side of the great split that had been there ever since the night she had almost died. She had never taken it off before. Without it she felt naked, and yet with it came such a burden now that it was almost a relief to be free. Reaching out, Rémy opened the drawer of the old dresser and hid it carefully in an old matchbox.

★ ★ ★

When Rémy left her room, it was to discover that Yannick had already gone out. J didn't know where and didn't seem particularly bothered by the fact.

"You don't mind him staying, do you, J?" Rémy asked as they shared some bread and cheese over a subdued breakfast.

J shrugged. "I s'pose not. It's a bit of a coincidence though, innit? Him finding you in the whole of London, like. Some might say he knew what he was about, going to the very theater you perform in, eh?"

Rémy frowned. "You sound as suspicious as Thaddeus."

J sighed. "I'm not suspicious. Well, no more than usual, any case. I just don't like seeing you and Thaddeus fight, that's all. And I's got a feeling that if Mr. Yannick stays around, there'll be a lot more fighting."

Rémy shrugged. "Well, Thaddeus has only got himself to blame for that."

J put down his chunk of bread and leaned over the table toward her. "Now, why would you go and say a thing like that? What's Thaddeus to blame for? Ain't 'e helped us both out? Ain't 'e been the best mate we both could have asked for?"

"Yes, J, he has helped us out — a lot. But he's still a policeman. And policemen and people like us never mix. Not really. We're like oil and water. You can swirl us around and it'll seem like we're one. But we always separate eventually. That's just the way of the world."

"Bollocks!" scoffed J. "That's total rubbish, that is. I never heard such tripe, truly I ain't. You and Thaddeus, you're two of a kind. Or you were, before that Mr. Yannick turned up. Why are you so angry at Thaddeus? What do you fink 'e's done? Cos I bet it ain't what you think it is. No way. He'd walk over hot coals for you, Rémy, and no mistake."

For a moment, Rémy thought about her discarded opal and wondered whether to tell J about it — about what she'd heard Thaddeus thinking. But she dismissed the idea almost immediately. Best to leave those worms to squirm beneath the ground where they belonged.

"You wouldn't understand, J," she said instead. "And as for Yannick, he's my friend. He's always been my friend, ever since we first met. And that's more than I can say about Thaddeus, isn't it?"

J set his jaw in the stubborn line Rémy had become used to and shook his head. "Well, you know best, Rémy. But, well, I don't know what's up with you two. Honestly, after all that stuff that happened in Abernathy's caves, you'd think —"

Rémy covered her face with her hands. "Not now, J. *D'accord?*"

"All right, all right. You've got to admit, though — that's some whopper you've got there. Ain't really surprising Thaddeus thought it might be nicked, is it?"

Rémy dropped her hands and saw that the boy was pointing at Lady Sarah's ruby, still sitting heavily on her index finger.

"That's a right beauty, that is."

She shrugged. "That's what I thought, too. Now I think I'll throw it in the Thames."

"Don't do that! It's just what I need. Can I borrow it for a bit? I'll give it back, promise."

Rémy pulled the ring from her finger and threw it to him. J caught it one-handed, staring into the red jewel with wide eyes. "Keep it," she told him. "I wish I'd never seen the damned thing."

* * *

Thaddeus spent most of the day following a hunch that took him deep into London's West End. Once there, he called at the Adelphi theater, where Lord Theakston and his wife and daughter had spent the evening before the jewels had disappeared. Once he had taken a look at the playbill and spoken to the establishment's owner, he moved on to another theater called The Vaudeville, where, he had discovered upon checking, Lord Bolsover had visited the night of his robbery. There he looked again at the playbill and spoke to that theater owner, too. By the time he had completed these tasks, Thaddeus felt not only that his hunch was proving itself to be a solid line of inquiry, but also that where it was leading him was uncomfortably close to home.

He returned to his office, foot-sore and not a little perturbed. Sitting down, he spread his notes out across his desk again and tried to find a clear path to follow through the fragments.

He was still deep in thought when a strong knock sounded at his office door. Thaddeus glanced at the clock to find with surprise that it was after six p.m., and the police station was almost empty. He stood and opened the door to see his friend Maandhata Desai standing patiently outside. Thaddeus smiled as he bid him come in, noting the slight frown on his friend's face.

"Desai," said Thaddeus in greeting. "It's good to see you."

"And you, Thaddeus," said the older man, his floor-length cloak rustling as he took a seat. The cloak was a rich, dark blue, embroidered at the edges with foreign flowers that made Thaddeus's drab office seem even duller than usual. Desai pulled the hood down to his shoulders, and the young policeman saw a new touch of gray in his friend's long hair and beard.

"You look worried," Thaddeus observed. "Something I should know about?"

"I am afraid so, my friend, and worse than you will be expecting." Desai let out a sigh, his eyes troubled.

Thaddeus and Desai had first met during the Abernathy affair, when Desai's men had rescued the policeman from the belly of one of the mad Lord's malfunctioning machines. Thaddeus had heard Desai's name whispered before that, though, and had assumed that he was just another gang lord making money from the misfortunes of the poorest in the East End. This had turned out to be far from the truth, and Desai had proven to be a great ally in helping Rémy and Thaddeus thwart Abernathy's insane plans to destroy London.

Afterward, he had taken J under his wing, even going so far as to let the boy accompany him to his native homeland of India to release Rémy from her family curse. Since he'd been back in London, Thaddeus had found Desai a great help in keeping an eye on the criminal workings of the city.

"Well, tell me," said Thaddeus, beginning to tidy his desk of his notes on the robbery. "Perhaps it is something that, together, we can put right."

Desai smiled. "My young friend, your optimism and positive spirit are a valuable gem in these injurious times." He leaned forward. "You know that my men have been, as you would say, keeping an eye on the rivers?"

Thaddeus frowned, alert at once. "Yes, I do, of course. Why? Has something come of it?"

Abernathy's plan had been to attack London from below, using terrifying mechanical machines of war that could navigate the city's submerged rivers. The would-be despot had died trapped inside one such contraption. It and the others had sunk into the silt deep below the streets when Rémy's heroic efforts to disable their power source had been successful, and they were still there now. Desai had made it his mission to see that these machines never again saw the light of day.

Desai nodded. "At first my scouts believed they were interrupting salvage seekers who had simply stumbled on some remains by accident. But now I am convinced otherwise. Over the past month, we have tracked three or four larger-scale operations that have specifically targeted the Black Ditch, where Abernathy's largest machines lie."

"'Specifically targeted'?" Thaddeus repeated. "But . . . how can that be? That would mean that someone else — someone other than us or Abernathy and his army — knew what he was doing."

Desai nodded grimly. "Indeed, my friend. As I said, worse than you were expecting, no doubt."

"But how?" Thaddeus asked. "How could anyone know?"

The other man pulled a folded piece of paper from his pocket and passed it to the policeman. Thaddeus smoothed it out. The paper bore two columns of neat handwriting — Desai's own pen had made these lists. One was of names, the other a list of countries.

"What's this?"

Desai leaned back in his chair, steepling his fingers. "What I have not told you up until now, my dear friend, is that besides monitoring the rivers, I have also been examining Abernathy's past. It started when I returned to India — I took the opportunity to begin tracing his path onward from that first fateful meeting with the Professor. My inquiries have turned up several disturbing facts, the chief among them being that Abernathy was not alone in his insanity. He had friends. The names you hold there in your hand are his consorts, his abettors, his encouragers, and, I am sorry to say . . . his investors."

Thaddeus stared at the note again, feeling a sick chill beginning to churn in his stomach. Among the names listed were counts and princes, noblemen all. Their countries ranged from Bavaria to France, from Turkmenistan to China and even beyond. He shook his head, reeling in a revelation he was only just beginning to grasp.

"Are you saying that these men may also have the machines the Professor designed?" he asked hoarsely, through a mouth grown suddenly dry. "What could they possibly want them for? War?"

Desai unsteepled his fingers to raise his palms. "This I do not know. What I do know is that at least one of them has been trying to recover what he can from the scene of Abernathy's failure."

Thaddeus looked up. "Surely that's a good sign? Perhaps it means that they have also failed in their own attempts and are clutching at anything."

Desai smiled wryly. "We can but hope. Alas, I think it more likely that at least one of these men is eager to see a return on an investment that is surely to have been far heavier than he expected."

Thaddeus shook his head, staring again at the paper. "But what can we do? These men are powerful, and so spread out. Who can we approach for help? How do we build proof? Where do we even start?"

Desai sighed, a soft sound that filled the room with melancholy. "Ah, Thaddeus, this is where I must burden you further. For whatever must be done, must be done by you alone, at least in the immediate future."

"What do you mean?" the policeman asked with a frown.

"I am imparting this knowledge to you," explained Desai, "as I cannot be a vessel for it myself any longer. I must return to my homeland to deal with a problem I had thought long quelled."

"But — you've only just come back."

"I know, my friend. But there are things about my past you are unaware of; ancient responsibilities that, when they call, cannot be ignored."

"What problem?" Thaddeus asked. "What is it?"

The older man smiled, his face creasing into a harmony of fine lines around his eyes and mouth. "Nothing that you should burden yourself with, my friend. The Sapphire Cutlass is a worry for me alone."

He reached out a hand, grasping Thaddeus's own firmly. "I am sorry to leave you at such a time and with such a burden in your heart and mind. But in my absence, I wanted you to be aware. In case I do not come back —"

"What do you mean, in case you don't come back?"

"In case I do not come back, my men have been ordered to report to you. In fact," Desai added, "I am informed that one of these men —" he pointed to the paper Thaddeus still held, "is to meet with the salvage hawkers tonight. We do not know which, but finding out is vital. I feel it would be prudent for you to attend yourself, since I cannot. Inconspicuously, of course."

"Tonight?" Thaddeus asked, looking at his watch. The evening was already drawing on. "You must leave that soon?"

"I am afraid I must. If you had plans this evening, I apologize my friend, but —"

"It's nothing like that," Thaddeus interrupted quickly. "But a case I am working on — a difficult case . . . I finally have a lead, and I cannot afford to let the trail go cold. From what you have told me, this, I am sure, is more important, but..."

"But your superiors do not know of it and therefore, would not care. I understand."

"What time is the meeting?" Thaddeus asked, glancing at his watch again. "If it is late, as I'm sure it must be . . ."

"It is late, indeed," agreed Desai, "for who conducts nefarious deeds in daylight? We believe the meeting is set for close to midnight — though, of course, it would be prudent to be in place beforehand in order to observe."

The policeman shut his eyes briefly. He had hoped never again to have to enter the dank underworld that lurked beneath the city. But it seemed he had no choice.

"I should be free from ten o'clock," he said quietly.

"Excellent." Desai stood up. "Where shall I have my man meet you?"

Thaddeus stood, too, his stomach churning. "Outside the Albert Saloon theater, in Britannia Fields."

"Very well." Desai dipped his head, a slow gesture full of dignity. "And now, Thaddeus, I must leave you. I am truly sorry for this abrupt departure, and that I must leave at all. With any luck, I will return swiftly and with a better plan of how to proceed, aided by the information you will gather tonight. But for now, I must take my leave."

Once Desai had gone, Thaddeus sank back into his

chair, chilled. He'd thought Abernathy's madness to be far in the past, but now it seemed that what they had battled was in fact only the tip of the iceberg. He stared at the list of names Desai had given him. One drew his attention more than the others. Comte Cantal de Saint-Cernin. That name rang a bell. Where had he heard it, or something like it, before?

Thaddeus glanced at the clock again and, after another moment's thought, stood and reached for his coat. Desai's problem was not the only issue he had to deal with. Tonight he would come closer to finding out if his hunch about the "impossible" burglaries were indeed more than a hunch.

Chapter 7

DARK DEEDS

*Y*annick was already on stage when Rémy arrived at the theater that evening. Even without seeing them, she could tell from the buzz of the crowd that they loved his act. But that wasn't surprising — she'd always known Yannick was going to be a great magician once he'd honed his craft, in the same way that he'd always told her she was going to be an amazing trapeze artist.

Rémy stood in the wings and watched. "Is there someone out there willing to volunteer?" Yannick was saying, standing at the front of the stage and addressing the audience. "I need someone of strong mind, someone not easily swayed."

There was a chorus of calls from the seats before

him. Rémy peeked out from the curtain to see a flurry of hands — mostly men, though a few women were also brave enough. Yannick picked a fat old wheezing man in a black dinner jacket who struggled slowly to the stage with the help of a carved, dog-headed cane.

"Welcome to the stage Mr. . . . ." Yannick greeted him, his voice carrying sharply through the auditorium.

"Sir," said the fat old man, coughing slightly. "I am Sir Johnson."

"Sir Johnson, it is an honor to have you as my guest this fair night," corrected Yannick, smoothly. "Now sir, I ask you again — are you of strong mind? This next part of my act requires a strong mind. If you are not, I fear . . ."

"Oh, I have a strong mind, damn you," boomed Sir Johnson. "Do your worst, trickster, you'll see you can't fox your betters. Stuff and nonsense, hypnosis — it'll only work on the weak. Not me, my boy, not me!"

Rémy smiled. So that was why Yannick needed the old goat — to hypnotize him! A smart move, because unlike other tricks, hypnosis performed by one truly skilled in the art was no illusion — it was real, and it worked best on those who swore blind they would never be controlled by it. Just as Sir Johnson had done. It was what made the turn so hilarious for the rest of the audience and why they loved it. There was nothing better than seeing the pompous taken down a peg — or a dozen.

Rémy scanned the audience as Yannick prepared his hapless helper. They were animated, interested, excited, and it made her smile. Good. That meant that when Rémy herself took the stage to finish off the night, the audience would be nicely warmed up and ready for —

Rémy froze, her gaze falling on a familiar figure in the fifth row. Oh, he was without his battered top hat, but she'd know that face anywhere. Thaddeus! What was he doing here? Had he come to see her perform? Because if he had, it was a sweet gesture, but it wouldn't . . .Then it hit her. No, he wasn't here to see her. He was watching Yannick too intently for that, his sharp policeman's eyes following everything her friend did, taking it all in, filing it all away.

Thaddeus suspected Yannick! He still couldn't find the real culprit behind his blasted burglaries, and since he couldn't pin it on her — because she was innocent — he was going for the next best thing: Yannick, whom he'd hated on sight.

Rémy was instantly furious. How dared he? How dared he? Was Thaddeus going to pursue all her friends from now on? Was it enough to be a former circus act for the great and pure Thaddeus Rec of Her Majesty's Police to assume that you were a criminal and treat you as such?

Rémy didn't see the rest of Yannick's act — she was too blind and deaf with rage. It bubbled in her ears, an angry roar that didn't diminish even when the audience exploded with applause as the curtain came down on a humiliated Sir Johnson. By the time Yannick had finished, she was pacing like a caged tiger, up and down, up and down, so fast that the magician almost collided with her as he stepped from the stage.

"Rémy? What on earth's the matter?" Yannick's face showed alarm as he put out his arms to steady her. He gripped her shoulders. "What is it? Tell me! You look as if the fires of hell itself burn behind your eyes this evening!"

"They might as well, too," Rémy hissed. "Yannick — we're not wanted here. We don't belong here. Not in this theater, not on this stage, not in this stinking, godforsaken city. Let's go back to France."

"Rémy — what's happened?" Yannick asked, puzzled, rubbing her arms in an attempt to calm her down. "You can't go out on the trapeze like this, you're too tense. You'll do yourself a mischief."

"I'm not going on," Rémy hissed. "Not here, not ever again. Let's go back to France. Right now. We can get the last train from Waterloo and be on the first boat back home in the morning."

"But —" Yannick began.

"I mean it, Yannick," said Rémy. "We're not welcome here. And I can't leave you here — don't ask me why, but I know something bad will happen to you if I do. We've got to go. Now."

Yannick stared into her eyes for a moment, and then away at the wall, frowning seriously as he considered her words. *"D'accord,"* he said, finally. "Let's do it. Just give me a moment — I have an errand I must attend to."

He stepped away from her, motioning to one of the backstage boys who was lurking in the shadows. They conversed in low voices for a moment. Then the boy nodded once before vanishing back into the shadows.

"Right," said Yannick, returning to her. "Let's go."

They left the theater quickly and quietly, slipping through the night as eels would through the murky sediments of the Thames.

★ ★ ★

Thaddeus did not stay for Rémy's performance. Instead, he left as soon as Yannick had exited the stage, having first noted the name of Sir Johnson on the notepad he had tucked into his top pocket. That line of inquiry would have to wait for tomorrow for him to follow up, however. For now, he had even darker deeds to observe.

Desai's man fell into step with the policeman as soon as he left the theater's main doors. He was, as all of the Indian's attendants seemed to be, hugely tall and broad shouldered, with his dark hair swathed in a deep blue turban. As the policeman had expected, his escort had little to say, merely introducing himself as Satu.

"Follow," Satu said, and then he took off at a brisk pace to lead Thaddeus back east.

What Thaddeus had not expected was to find himself on the path beside Regent's Canal, heading toward Mile End. As they passed St Anne's, a vague suspicion of just how they would enter the remains of Abernathy's underworld began to occur to him.

"Wait," he said, pausing as a bridge loomed out of the darkness ahead. "I know where this is. We're not — we can't be . . ."

Desai's man turned to look at the policeman,

smiling slightly. "Please," he said, his deep voice rumbling in the darkness. "We are not far now."

Thaddeus began walking again, though reluctantly. He knew they weren't far away, because he had traveled this route before. He'd been in the company of Desai's men then, too, as well as Desai himself. Rémy had been there, wounded by a gunshot and a terrible fall, and J, too. They'd all been prisoners of Abernathy's thugs, who had dragged them down into the darkness.

As they reached the bridge, there was a rustle in the undergrowth to his left. Thaddeus started as two eyes blinked out at him, but Satu seemed unperturbed. He nodded silently to the watcher, who nodded back and melted back into the verge once again. *A sentry,* Thaddeus thought. *One of Desai's own.*

His escort pulled an ancient, heavy key from beneath his dark robes and fitted it to the rusted lock of an old door set in the side of the bridge. The door looked so old and disused that Thaddeus imagined most passers-by failed to even glance at it. But for those in the know . . .

The key turned and the door swung inward. Beyond was an inky darkness that made Thaddeus shiver from the memory of the last time he'd been here. Desai's man did not hesitate, stepping over the threshold and disappearing from view almost immediately. Thaddeus swallowed hard and then followed him, pushing the door shut and casting them both into pitch darkness.

There was the sound of a match being struck. A second later a yellow flame bloomed as Satu lit two sturdy candles and handed one to Thaddeus.

The dim candlelight revealed a set of wooden steps that twisted down and out of sight. With the door to the outside world shut fast, Thaddeus felt as if he'd been thrust into the dank belly of the earth itself. From somewhere there came the slow, incessant *drip-drip-drip* of moisture, and the air reeked thick with rot. They began to make their way down the stairs, one at a time, for they were slippery and as degenerate as the air around them. As they reached the bottom, his guide turned to him, his face sallow in the weak candlelight.

"Be careful," he said. "The way here is difficult. Watch your feet."

Satu was right. Thaddeus could feel slime beneath his shoes, and here the stink of old water was far worse than he remembered. The drip had become a modest trickle — a remnant, no doubt, of the flood that had burst the underground banks of London's Black Ditch.

The policeman was beginning to think that they would walk forever when Satu stopped abruptly. Desai's man appeared to listen intently for a moment, and then turned to him.

"Thaddeus Rec," Satu said in a low voice. "You must trust me now. Place your hand here." He turned his back to the policeman and patted his shoulder. When Thaddeus had done as instructed, Satu blew out his candle. "You, too, please."

Thaddeus hesitated for a moment, and then snuffed out their one remaining light. The darkness was instant and cloying, and he had to take a breath to steady himself. He felt Satu step forward, and followed — after all, the only alternative was to be left entirely alone in that dank passageway.

His guide continued to walk, without light, for what felt like ages. They turned corners several times, which Satu did without hesitation. Thaddeus lost all sense of how far they had come and what direction they had taken. His initial bout of panic had subsided. He was just beginning to think that his eyes had adjusted to the incessant gloom when he realized that, in fact, there was a light somewhere far ahead of them. It was tinged greenish-blue, eerie and dim, but it was definitely a light.

Satu stopped at the mouth of another turn. The light had grown strong enough that Thaddeus could see ahead now, and he dropped his hand from his guide's shoulder.

"You see?" Satu asked, nodding toward what lay ahead.

Thaddeus did indeed see. Beyond the tunnel in which they stood, the passageway opened out, dropping several feet to form a wide, shallow cave. It was lit with torches that burned not with fire, but with a substance that gave off the strange green light that cast the place in peculiar, flickering shadows. Through this cavern cut a fast-running channel of water, formed with wide banks of stone on either side. It was what was in the water, though, that gave the policeman pause.

"That's one of Abernathy's underwater boats," he whispered, making sure that his voice didn't carry.

Satu nodded grimly. "It was found two nights ago. Whenever they salvage something like this, they bring it here. It is . . . a marketplace, of sorts."

Thaddeus rubbed his face, weary and worried. He'd only ever seen one of these machines before, but that had been enough to etch it into his memory. Its bottom half was almost like the normal hull of a boat, though it had been hammered from gleaming golden metal rather than wood.

Above the level of what would have been the deck, however, the contraption was encased in glass, so that it looked a little like a supernaturally strong bubble. The entire machine could be submerged. Abernathy had built several of them as war machines, intending to attack London from below, via the city's underground rivers.

"It's not in good shape," Thaddeus observed. The machine's glass was cracked. It's once-shining metal was dented and dull. The policeman wondered what had happened to the men who had crewed it, but thought the answer was probably obvious. He shivered. Thaddeus had thought he was going to drown the night he's last been in the caverns, and that had been bad enough, but to have been stuck inside one of those things . . .

A noise echoed up from the cave, interrupting his dour thoughts. Satu crouched beside the wall, pulling Thaddeus down with him. Voices drifted up from below, along with the sound of echoing footsteps as a group of people entered the cavern.

There were five of them, the leader a small, wiry man with ragged trousers and a dirty shirt. At his right hand was an individual who Thaddeus guessed was a bodyguard, for his size would be enough to make anyone considering violence think twice, let alone the large pistol he could see jammed into the man's belt.

These two were a pair of the kind Thaddeus had seen many times in the East End, but the remaining three were something different. He instantly recognized the first as the Comte de Cantal, who had mocked him so mercilessly at Sir Henry Strong's table. *Of course*, Thaddeus thought. His name had even been on the list Desai had given him earlier — his *full* name, Comte Cantal de Saint-Cernin.

The Comte was tall and stood straight, his chin raised, his figure exuding a swagger that had nothing to do with movement and everything to do with expectation. This man was used to being obeyed. The Comte was dressed in a richly tailored suit matched with a long, dark coat of fine wool. In one hand he held a thin walking stick, which Thaddeus had no doubt concealed a razor-sharp sword.

The party stopped beside the wreck of Abernathy's wondrous ship.

"Well?" said the thin man who had led them in, whom Thaddeus assumed to be the seller. "Told you the truth, didn't I? Didn't I say I'd hit the jackpot this time?"

The Comte regarded the contraption for a moment. He made a show of walking this way and that, looking it up and down.

"It is damaged," he observed, in his cool French accent.

"That ain't my fault, is it?" said the seller. "Not my concern, neither."

After another moment, the Comte nodded slowly. "I will give you two thousand pounds for it."

Thaddeus couldn't help drawing in a sharp breath. Two thousand pounds? That was more than he'd earn in years. It was an insane amount of money.

But the seller simply laughed. "You must think I were born yesterday," he said. "I won't take a shilling less than four thousand."

The Comte de Cantal made a disgusted sound in his throat. "Obscene. I will give you two thousand five hundred, and you will be grateful for it."

The seller shook his head firmly. "This ain't a nego-tiation, mister," he said. "I got another buyer, ain't I? And he's already agreed to the four thousand, like I asked for. Problem is, he's a bit far away, like, so I'd have to wait a few months for him to get to me with 'is payment. So if you stump up the cash sharpish, you can have it. If not, say toodle-pip to the find of a life-time. Your call, yer lordship."

"Don't call me that, you impertinent whelp," said the Frenchman through gritted teeth. "I will get you the money."

"When?" the seller asked. "Cos I got fees, you know. I got expenses. I can't be hanging around for the likes of you forever."

In a flash, the Comte had drawn his sword-stick and was holding it at the seller's throat. He'd moved so quickly that the thick-necked bodyguard had had no time to react.

"Listen to me, you low-bred scoundrel," the Comte hissed, his angry voice echoing around the cave. "By rights I should not need to pay you at all. By rights, I should slit your throat and take this and everything else you have for nothing, for I have already paid. Paid, and paid, and paid. But, because I am a fair man, a good man, I will —"

The sound of running footsteps interrupted the man's flow. A boy, dressed all in black, entered the cave, out of breath and puffing hard. He went up to one of the Comte's men, who bent down so that the child could whisper in his ear.

"Well?" asked the Comte, his blade still at the man's sweating throat. "What is it?"

The boy vanished again, his footsteps echoing back the way he had come.

"A message, sir." He stepped forward and whispered in the Comte's ear.

There was a moment of silence. The Comte's face changed, relaxing as it lost all hint of the fury that had dogged it just a moment before. Abruptly, he dropped his sword arm, releasing the seller to cough and splutter, supported by his useless bodyguard.

"Well," said the Comte, his voice soft and full of danger. "Well, well, well. How . . . unexpected."

He contemplated for another few moments, seemingly lost in his own thoughts. Then he laughed coldly, the unexpected sound bouncing around the chamber.

"It is your lucky day, it seems," he said to the seller, who was still recovering. "How about this, eh? Five thousand. I will give you five thousand, payable in cash. But you must wait for a month. Understand? In one month, I will have the money. Perhaps sooner. But you will wait, yes? You. Will. Wait."

The seller nodded. "All right, mister. I'll wait. But remember what we agreed on. Five thousand. We've got witnesses here, see?"

The Comte laughed again, the sound grating against the stone walls like nails down a blackboard. He sheathed his sword-stick with a flourish. A moment later, he swept from the cave, the rest of them following in his wake.

{Chapter 8}

FLIGHT FROM LONDON

$\mathcal{R}$émy hadn't spent much time on boats, but she liked them. She liked the feel of something solid under her feet that could still move however it pleased. It wasn't unlike being on the trapeze, but with less chance of falling. She stood at the boat's stern, watching the white chalk cliffs of England fade into the low cloud and mist of early morning. Above the boat wheeled a flock of screeching, whooping gulls, a mocking fanfare chasing her home.

Yannick was off somewhere, finding them something for breakfast. The crossing would take them a few hours and they wouldn't reach the port of Calais before lunchtime. They were both already hungry, having forgone supper the night before. Rémy should have been feeling pleased that her plan had worked so smoothly — they'd caught the last train out of Waterloo station by the skin of their teeth and stepped off in Dover at about one in the morning. Then all they'd had to do was wait until the first boat left the harbor at six o'clock.

At first it had been exciting — Rémy had spent all her life on the move, much of it in a mad dash to run away from the law — and fleeing so suddenly and without forethought had felt exhilarating and familiar. But now, as she stood watching the shores of England draw away from her, Rémy couldn't escape the feeling that she was leaving something behind.

That "something," of course, was the family she'd built from the ruins of Abernathy's lair — Thaddeus and J, and in some ways Desai, too. Rémy knew that it was unlikely that she'd ever see any of them again, and though she was accustomed to leaving places behind, she was used to taking the people she loved with her on the journey.

Rémy pushed her melancholy thoughts away with a shrug. She just had to get over it. She had thought there was something for her in London — she had thought there was something for her with

Thaddeus — but it had just turned out not to be the case, that was all. Rémy had given it a try and nothing had come of it — no harm in that. Now it was time to return to her real family, the circus, and to make sure that Claudette and Amélie were safe and sound.

She took the sheaf of letters from her pocket — the ones that Claudette had sent her before her long and worrying silence — and was rereading them as Yannick returned.

"There wasn't much on offer, I'm afraid," he said, holding up a cloth-wrapped loaf and two battered-looking apples.

"It's fine," Rémy told him with a faint smile, taking one of the apples as he tore the bread in half.

They sat on the deck with their backs against the rails, facing the distant shores of France with the wind whipping around them. "What have you got there?" Yannick asked around a mouthful of bread.

"Claudette's letters. I thought that maybe she'd said something I hadn't noticed the first time, or that there might have been a hint that something was wrong, but . . ." Rémy shrugged and shook her head. "I can't find anything."

Yannick patted her on the shoulder. "I'm sure she's fine," he said, smiling at her. "Claudette always struck me as someone who could look after herself. Like you."

Rémy smiled at the compliment. "Thanks, though Claudette is about a million times smarter than I am."

"I don't believe that for a second," Yannick told her. "Although — there was always something . . . I don't know, a little mysterious about Claudette, wasn't there?"

Rémy took a bite of her apple. "What do you mean?"

Yannick shrugged. "She always seemed far too well-educated for the circus, for one thing, don't you think? All those languages she could speak." He waved at the bunch of papers in Rémy's hand, "And how many of us can write the way she can? Apart from you, obviously — and that was only because she taught you, isn't that right? Where did she learn all that?"

Rémy shook her head. She couldn't pretend she'd never wondered the same thing herself. Claudette was unusual for a circus woman, Yannick was right. It wasn't just her knowledge of languages and history. It was the way she carried herself, her elegance and poise. Rémy had asked her about where she came from once, but Claudette had dodged the question with one of her quiet smiles. With a jolt, Rémy realized now that she didn't even know where Claudette had been born, or anything about her parents. Were they also part of a circus somewhere?

"What are you thinking about?" Yannick asked, watching Rémy's face with open curiosity. "Claudette?"

"Yes," Rémy said with a sigh.

The magician nodded, moving to sit up slightly taller. "I have been too, you know. And the more I think about her, the more I think . . ."

"What?" Rémy asked, frowning at the intense look on Yannick's face.

"Well," he said. "You're going to think I'm mad, but . . . All those strange things about her — all those things that make her different — they'd make sense if she were the Lost Comtesse. Wouldn't they?"

Rémy nearly choked on her bread. She laughed outright. "What — Claudette? *My* Claudette?"

"Why is it such a funny idea, Rémy?" Yannick asked, leaning forward earnestly. "Think about it. What do we know about her, really, other than the fact that she's educated far too highly for a circus brat? She's always vague when you ask her about her parents . . ."

"You asked her?" Rémy said in surprise. She hadn't known Yannick and Claudette had been that close when he'd been with the circus as a child.

Yannick shrugged, looking away. "A couple of times, you know, just in passing. A long time ago. Anyway, she never really answered. And you remember the story — wasn't the old woman who raised the princess supposed to be a palm-reader? Well, Claudette's a fortune-teller as well as a pickpocket, isn't she? She could have learned that from the old woman — the woman she thought was her mother, but really wasn't."

Rémy shook her head. "Claudette might have learned pickpocketing at the circus, but the fortune telling isn't a trick. She can really do it. I've seen it happen. She sees things. No, I don't mean see, really. It's more as if she feels them. It's part of her, not something she learned."

Yannick leaned back, looking up at the gathering dawn above them. "Ah, well. It was just an idea. Wishful thinking. It would be great to think that one of us lot was the Lost Comtesse, wouldn't it? Just think of it — all that money, just waiting to be claimed . . ."

Rémy stared at her bread, the idea turning her mouth dry. Yannick was right. Claudette had always been different. "She can't be the Lost Comtesse," she muttered, as much to herself as to him. "She'd have told me."

"If she is the one, she probably doesn't know,"

Yannick pointed out. "If she did, she wouldn't be lost, would she? Who in their right mind would carry on scraping a living in the circus when they're heir to that fortune?"

"I suppose you're right," murmured Rémy. "But still . . ."

"You haven't ever noticed a birthmark? The Lost Comtesse is supposed to have one isn't she?"

"Oh, yes, that's right. A dark mark that looks like a sea serpent, isn't that right? Well, there you go then," Rémy said, her relief taking her by surprise. "Claudette has no such mark."

"No?" Yannick asked. "You're sure? It was supposed to be on the child's back, wasn't it? Would you have definitely seen it?"

"Well — yes," said Rémy, frowning, although now that she thought about it, she wasn't sure if she'd ever seen her friend's back properly. Now that she thought about it, Claudette had a habit of keeping a long garment on, even when swimming. It was to protect her arms from cold, she said, and Rémy had never questioned it. "I mean — I must have. At some time . . ."

"Ah well — I suppose when we get to the Jamboree and you find the Circus of Secrets, you can ask her, eh?"

"I don't think Claudette will take the Circus of Secrets to the Jamboree this year," said Rémy as she shooed away a gull that was a little too interested in their breakfast.

Yannick sat up with a frown. "Oh? Why not?"

"She never really liked it," said Rémy. "Claudette was always reluctant to go with Le Cirque de la Lune, and when it was on, she usually stayed in her caravan or at least didn't stray far from it. I'm surprised you don't remember. I asked her why once, and she said she didn't see the point of swapping tricks. What makes people want to see a circus is originality, she said, so why dilute that with ideas they may have seen somewhere else? I can see her point, I suppose. And now that she's the circus master, and Le Cirque des Secrets is such a new company . . . I think she'd probably want to stay away. Besides, I've been looking at the postmarks of the towns these were sent from. Claudette seemed to be working her way south, away from Paris, not toward it as she would have done if she were planning on joining the Jamboree."

Yannick brushed the crumbs from his fingers before reaching for the letters. "May I?"

Rémy passed them over, and he went through them one by one, studying the stamps and marks. "Which was the last one you received? This one?" He held one up.

"Yes," she said. "It was posted from Moulidars."

The magician nodded with a smile. "Well then," he declared, "that is where we shall start, Little Bird. We'll go there, and then follow the trail until we find the Circus of Secrets. We'll catch up with them in no time!"

"But—I thought you'd want to go to the Jamboree," said Rémy. "Don't you want to find a place with a new circus?"

"Yes," said Yannick, "although to tell the truth, Rémy, I'm hoping that my new circus might turn out to be my old one." He grinned at her raised eyebrows. "Wouldn't it be great if I could join the Circus of Secrets? It'd be just like old times. Just like when we were children."

Rémy laughed. "Except that we're much older. And wiser," she added.

"Yes," agreed Yannick, watching the hopeful gulls still darting into the boat's wake. "Yes, that we are."

Chapter 9

A RUDE AWAKENING

Thaddeus had finally reached his bed as the clock was touching one in the morning and so was asleep when J arrived at his lodgings a few short hours later. The first he knew about the visit was a distant banging disturbing his dreams. Then a loud, poisonous voice invaded too, and the bubble of sleep was broken. He opened his eyes to see the door to his room vibrating on its hinges as Mrs. Carmichael pounded at it, yelling at him to "wake up, damn you!"

Thaddeus dragged himself blearily out of bed and pulled on his dressing gown before opening the door to his landlady.

"For goodness' sake, Mr. Rec," she snarled, her

coarse gray hair beginning to escape the hairnet with which she nightly tried to subdue it. "I will not be having these goings on in this respectable establishment! I simply will not!"

"I apologize, Mrs. Carmichael," Thaddeus said, automatically. "May I ask to which goings on you are referring?"

"There is . . . there is a . . . a street urchin," the woman said, her lips curling around the word as if it were filth itself sticking between her crooked teeth. "He's downstairs. I tried to shoo him away, but he won't go. I even threatened to call the police, but the little monster still won't budge."

Thaddeus stepped into the shabby hallway outside his room. "Perhaps because I am, in fact, the police, Mrs. Carmichael?" he suggested mildly. "I think I know the boy you mean. He must have good reason to call at," he looked at the clock, surprised to find the hour barely touching five, "such a disagreeable time."

His landlady followed him down the stairs. "It's not on, Mr. Rec," she said. "It's just not on. I don't know what you think you're playing at, all this so-called police work that puts honest, decent folk into such hassles."

Thaddeus stopped on the bottom step and turned

to her. "I could find other lodgings, Mrs. Carmichael. If that would suit better?" He raised an eyebrow, though he already knew her response. Whatever her gripes, Mrs. Carmichael had by far the most respectable tenant she could hope for in Thaddeus.

"Less of your lip, if you please. I'm the owner of this house, not a washerwoman or such." She pushed him out of the way and headed back to her own room, grumbling.

"Oh, Thaddeus," said a breathless J, as soon as Thaddeus opened the door. "Something right awful's happened! Something right awful!"

"It's all right, J — whatever it is, we can sort it out. Tell me."

"It's Rémy. She's gone!"

Something like a millstone thumped into Thaddeus's stomach and rested there. He said nothing for a moment and then nodded once. "J, I'm going to get dressed. Give me two minutes. Then we'll go and get breakfast."

* * *

Twenty minutes later, they were seated in the murky bow window of The Grapes, each with a plate of ham and eggs and a pint of strong, hot tea in front of them.

Neither of them, however, seemed to have much of an appetite.

"They must've left last night," J said miserably. "I didn't hear 'em go. They must 'ave got back from the theater early, like, when I was still working, and just — upped and went."

Thaddeus stared at the brief note, written in Rémy's haphazard handwriting.

I'll miss you, J. I'm sorry not to say goodbye in person, but I don't think I can stay in England any longer. I will remember you always. Take care of yourself and be good.

Rémy

There was no mention of Thaddeus at all. He wondered for a moment if she might have left him his own note, at the police station perhaps, but dismissed that notion as soon as it arose. He already knew she hadn't. Why would she, when he was what she was running from?

"This was all they left?" Thaddeus asked.

"Nearly, but not quite," J said, thrusting a hand into his bag to pull out a crumpled roll of paper. "They forgot to take this with 'em."

Thaddeus took the sorry scroll and unfurled it. It was a poster, proclaiming in large red and yellow letters that something called a Jamboree was about to happen. The images depicted all manner of circus performers, from high-wire walkers to elephant riders.

"It's some big circus event that's going on in Paris right now," J said eagerly.

"Right," said Thaddeus heavily, letting the scroll roll back into itself and dropping it onto the table.

"Don't you see?" J asked. "It's where they'll be going. It's where we'll find 'em!"

Thaddeus picked up his mug of tea and stared into it. "We won't be going to find them, J."

"Why not? It'll be easy! Piece o' cake, that's what it'll be. They're two circus folks, heading back to the circus. Where else would they go?"

Thaddeus shook his head. "That may be so, but there's the little thing of getting there. I don't have any money. Do you? Certainly not enough for the train and then the boat that we'd need to take, not to mention the fact that I wouldn't even know how to buy a ticket for the train we'd need once we got to France. And say we do get there — say we do find them. Then what? What do we do then?"

J stared at Thaddeus as if the policeman had lost his

mind. "We get her back, Thaddeus." he said slowly, as if he were talking to a simpleton. "You get her back."

Thaddeus sighed. "I don't see why she'd be willing to listen to me, J," he said. "She never has before."

"Yeah, she has," said J, staring at Thaddeus intently. "That time you told her you loved her. I was there, 'member? She listened to you then, didn't she?"

The policeman felt his cheeks go red at J's words. "That was . . . those were extreme circumstances, J. It's not —"

"It ain't what? It ain't true?" J made a disgusted sound in his throat. "Poppycock. You ain't pulling that one, Thaddeus. I know you love 'er. Just like I know she loves you, even if she ain't smart enough to sort that out in her own head yet. I don't know what you two've been playing at over the past few months, honest I don't. I thought, once you'd found her again, you'd be happy — both o' yer. But yer've been dancing around each other like two fish in the net."

"J —" Thaddeus began, uncomfortable.

"Don't you 'J' me," said the boy, warming to his theme. "You's both as pig-headed as the other. And then this Yannick bloke comes along and catches you napping, and now he's carried 'er off and you're just going to let 'im get away wif it?"

Thaddeus laughed at the notion of anyone carrying Rémy off. "J, you know as well as I do that Rémy never does anything she doesn't want to. If she's gone back to France, it's because it's where she wants to be, and if she's gone with Yannick, it's because she wants to be with him. I'm not sure what you think I can do about that."

"Sumfin'!" J exclaimed, thumping his hand on the table and causing his uneaten fried eggs to wobble wildly on the plate. "Sumfin', instead of nuffin'! How can you just let her go, especially with him? He's as dodgy as the pope's cloak is long, and what's more, I think you know it. Don't yer?"

Thaddeus grimaced. "Yes, J, I think he might be."

"And yet you're going to let the girl you love go off into the night wiv him, just like that?"

"I don't have any proof, J!" Thaddeus exclaimed. "All I've got are theories and a hunch. I told her I didn't trust him, and she took no notice of me. What else can I do?"

"Why don't you trust him?" J asked. "What is it you fink 'e's done?"

Thaddeus glanced out the window at the busy high road. "There hasn't been time to investigate properly. And now I can't."

"Come on," J insisted. "Out wiv it. No other beggar's going to listen to yer, are they?"

Thaddeus laughed, though there wasn't much mirth in it. "All right, then. These robberies — there've been two of them now. Impossible thievery, right through locked doors. Tell me, J, how do you do the impossible? How do you steal something through several locked doors when the key holder swears the keys never left his sight?"

J shrugged. "Can't see how you would do it, to tell you the truth. I surely wouldn't try, that's for sure."

"Exactly. Because it's impossible. And yet it happened. So what does that tell us?"

"Yer've got me there. What?"

Thaddeus leaned back, his breakfast forgotten. "You don't do it, J. You don't."

J stared at the policeman for a moment, and then blinked. "Have I missed something? Cos —"

"J, the only way those jewels got out of those strongboxes and through those locked doors is if the key holders either never put them in there in the first place, or they took them out themselves. Nothing else makes sense. You can't do the impossible; therefore, what happened wasn't impossible, and the two explanations I've just given are the only logical answers."

J stabbed a piece of burnt toast with the point of his knife and shoved it into his mouth, chewing thoughtfully. "You saying these rich fellers stole their own baubles? For the insurance or sumfin'? Cos I can't see that theory going down too well."

Thaddeus shook his head. "No. No, I think whatever they did, they did without realizing, and willingly. That's why there's no sign of a break-in in either case — because there wasn't one."

J looked perplexed. "You're talking too smart for me. I've got no idea what you're on about."

Thaddeus sighed. "Well, anyway, it's irrelevant. It's just a theory, and I don't have any way to prove it."

"But you fink it was Mr. Fancy-Pants magician, right? Yannick, you fink 'e was behind it?"

Thaddeus stared into his rapidly cooling tea. "I don't know what I think, J. I'm pretty sure that he's been in town longer than he let us assume. I spoke to two theater owners who each say they've employed a hypnotizing magician with a French accent over the past month. Both of them had different names, but they fit Yannick's description and both burglary victims visited those theaters on the nights their crimes were committed. I was planning to prove my hunch one way or another, but now I won't know if there wasn't another burglary because Yannick's not my man, or because he left town before he could complete the third. None of that proves anything, anyway. Maybe I just want it to be him. Maybe me suspecting The Magnificent Yannick has nothing to do with police instinct and everything to do with me being . . ." he trailed off.

"Jealous?" J prompted shrewdly. When Thaddeus didn't reply, he went on, "Well, what about the Frenchie coppers? Can't you check in with them, tell them about your worries and what-not, find out a bit more about 'im? If he's got form on that side o' the water too, stands to reason they'd know about it. If they've got gripes as well, they might give us a bit of help tracking him and Rémy down, like. You won't even have to go yourself. Problem solved."

Thaddeus looked at J seriously. "Yes J, they might help . . . you're right there."

"There we go then! Sorted! What are we waiting for?" J, raring to go, made to stand up, but Thaddeus stopped him.

"What about Rémy, J?"

"What about Rémy? This is perfect — the police'll go looking for Yannick and lead us straight to her."

"Exactly. Come on, be smart. Rémy's hardly what

you'd call a clean character, is she? I know for a fact that the police here have told them they want her for the Tower of London theft, not to mention for breaking out of custody. She's a wanted woman, J, most likely in every country in Europe. And you want to send the gendarme after her?"

J sat down again, his face glum. "That's a good point."

Thaddeus nodded. "There's something else, too," he said after a moment's hesitation. "Desai came to visit me yesterday."

J's eyebrows shot up at the sound of his mentor's name. "Oh? Why? More trouble?"

Thaddeus sighed. "You could say that." He quietly outlined what their friend had told him about the list of names, adding a description of his late-night visit into the bowels of the city and Thaddeus's realization that the Comte de Cantal was both the buyer and one of the names on Desai's list. J's face paled as Thaddeus went on, the boy's fingers gripping his knife and fork until they turned white.

"Blimey," J muttered when Thaddeus was done. "That's not good. That's not good at all."

"The thing is, J," Thaddeus added. "You remember when I first met Yannick, and I asked him if we'd met before? Well, when I saw him last night, on stage in his top hat and tails, I realized where I'd seen him. He was the man who brought the Comte a message during Sir Henry's dinner. He was talking to the Comte as I left."

"'Ang about," hissed J. "You're telling me that rotter Yannick is mixed up with Abernathy's lot?"

"I don't know that exactly, but . . ."

"Wait, wait, wait," said J. "Go back a mo. You mentioned this Comte feller, that he needs money, right? And you reckon Yannick's in league wiv 'im, on top o' which, you fink Yannick's the one's been nicking all these jewels and such. See where I'm going 'ere? What if that's what the connection is? This bloke the Comte has gone and got himself a way of picking up all the money he wants — he just gets his tame hypnotist to nick him a new bauble to flog every time he needs the cash, right?"

"Right," said Thaddeus. "That does make sense, because otherwise it'd be Yannick who was living it up like a prince, instead of bunking down with you and Rémy at the docks."

"Yeah," said J, raising his eyebrows. "Unless there was a partic-alar reason 'e was looking for the greatest jewel thief in Europe. Come on, Thaddeus, don't be a fool. Rémy doesn't have an inklin' what Yannick's like.

She got away from that Gustave bloke, but I bet there are loads out there just like him who'd kill to have a pet jewel thief as good as she is. How much money do you fink it'd take for Yannick to be willing to hand her over to one o' them, eh? Like this feller, the Comte?"

Thaddeus stared at him, the cogs whirring around in his mind. "The Comte told the seller of Abernathy's submarine that he'd have five thousand pounds for him within a month."

J speared a piece of ham and stuffed it into his mouth. "Sure sounds like he needs someone who can nick 'im something big in a hurry, don't it? Bigger than some beggar's pearls. We know anyone who fits the bill, d'ya fink?"

Thoughts whirled in Thaddeus's head. He'd always seen Rémy as a free spirit, strong-willed, able to do whatever she wanted. But he hadn't known her before, when she'd been part of that circus of villains, all kept on a leash held in the hand of one nasty kingpin.

"That'd be awful, wouldn't it?" J probed. "If that's what Yannick's about? And you know what'll be even more awful? The fact that if you don't go after her, you'll never know. Will yer?"

The boy was right. Thaddeus knew he was right. And, moreover, Thaddeus wanted to go after her — he did. Of course he did! How could he live the rest of his life without her in it? How could he let the Comte de Cantal use her to become the kind of threat he would be with one of Abernathy's awful machines? But it was no good.

Thaddeus shook his head, staring at the congealed mess of his wasted breakfast. "There's no way to get there, J. I just don't have the money."

J grinned. "Tell you what, I might be able to help you there." The boy leaped up. "Meet me at the workshop tonight. Late. The later the better. And be ready to leave on the biggest adventure of your life!"

"J," Thaddeus began, but the boy was already halfway to the door, weaving between the tables and away. "J . . . wait! What —"

"See you later!" J shouted, just before the door banged shut behind him.

{Chapter 10}

HOME AGAIN

$\mathcal{R}$émy and Yannick reached Calais at midday, stepping from the ferry and into sunshine. Rémy was momentarily flummoxed to find herself surrounded by people speaking her native tongue. It had been so long since she'd spoken French properly that for a few moments it felt strange to hear the lilt of it everywhere, instead of the blunt vowels of English curled around the cockney tongues of the East End.

"It's good to be home, isn't it?" said Yannick, watching her with a smile. "Smell that bread! See that sun! Good God, Rémy, what on earth were we thinking when we left this for decrepit little England?"

Rémy laughed along with him, but still she felt a

brief pang in her heart. She wondered what Thaddeus was doing at that moment. J must have found the note and told him of their departure by now. Rémy had thought about leaving one for Thaddeus, but what could she have said? At the time she'd been so angry about seeing him there in the theater, blatantly lining up her friend as his next target, that she'd not even wanted to say goodbye. And now . . .

"Rémy!"

She jolted out of her reverie to discover that Yannick was no longer by her side. Instead, he was standing under the sign that pointed to the train station.

"What are you doing?" she asked as she hurried over to him.

"Train, Rémy. We need to catch a train. If we take it as far as Angoulême, we'll be pretty close to Moulidars, the last place we know the Circus of Secrets stopped."

Rémy shook her head. "I can't afford a train ticket, Yannick! I used most of my money to get us this far. I was thinking we could hitch a lift — you know, find a cart or something going in that direction . . ."

Yannick shook his head firmly. "It'll take too long. Leave it to me. I've got a little saved. I put it aside in case England wasn't as fruitful as I'd hoped."

"But you said . . ."

Yannick held up a hand. "Stay here. With any luck, we won't have to wait too long for the next train."

He vanished into the crowds before Rémy had a chance to say anything else, reappearing a few minutes later with two thick tickets in his hand.

"We're out of luck, I'm afraid — there's an hour's wait until the next one."

Rémy shrugged. "It doesn't matter. Yannick, listen. Thank you, so much —"

He cut her off with another smile. "Rémy, it's nothing. Really. Once we find the Circus of Secrets, money won't even matter, will it?"

Rémy laughed at his optimism. "I'm not sure about that," she said. "It's not as if the circus life is a way to get rich, is it? But I'm sure we'll get by. We always have before, isn't that so?"

Yannick offered a crooked smile, looking away to scan the crowds. "Something will come along," he said. "Come on. Let's go and wait on the platform. I think it'll be quieter there."

The station at Calais had only two platforms. They fought their way through the crowds to platform two, Yannick showing their tickets to the blue-uniformed guard waiting by the entrance. He scrutinized their tickets before waving them through. Beyond the barriers, the platform was almost empty, though on the other side stood an engine just arrived from Paris. It gleamed red in the midday sun, disgorging a final stream of hissing steam into the cloudless blue sky as passengers spilled out of its doors. Rémy watched them scurrying about, hauling bags, gripping hats, calling for children in danger of being lost in the fray. It reminded her of an audience at the end of a performance, hurrying home, and another wave of homesickness struck her. Whatever she had left behind in England, Rémy was looking forward to being back with Claudette and the circus. The farther away she got from London, the more those six months felt like a strange, unearthly dream.

"Rémy?" asked Yannick from the bench he'd found. "You are far away again."

She smiled. "Sorry," she said. "Just a lot to —"

She stopped dead as she saw the poster. It was pinned to the post behind the bench, there for any disembarking passengers to see.

"What is it?" Yannick said, the look on her face making him leap to his feet. Together they stared at the poster. A sharp sketch of Rémy's face stared back at them. The words below the picture read WANTED FOR THE THEFT OF JEWELS. Below that there were more details, and a reward for her capture. It was a hefty one, at that.

A thousand francs, Rémy thought, in shock. *All of that, just to catch me.*

"Ah," said Yannick.

Rémy dipped her head and pulled her hair around her face, glancing quickly around them. "Someone's going to see me! We have to get out of here."

Yannick laid a hand on her shoulder. "Don't panic, Little Bird. There's no one here at the moment except us and the chubby guard who let us in, and he didn't even look at our faces. When our train arrives, people will be too busy with their own affairs to even notice us, and once we're aboard, we'll find a quiet carriage and keep ourselves to ourselves. There is nothing to worry about."

His reassurances did nothing for Rémy. "We should never have chosen the train," she muttered. "It would have been safer by road."

"And slower," he reminded her. "Really, Rémy . . ."

She looked around, spying a sign for a ladies-only restroom. "I'll be back," she told Yannick, before walking quickly toward it.

Inside, Rémy locked the door. *Stupid*, she thought. *How could you forget that you are a wanted girl here in*

France, as well as in England? Welcome home indeed, Little Bird!

With one quick tug, Rémy let her hair fall down around her shoulders, and then opened her bag, searching for the nail scissors she had found in the Professor's workshop and always carried with her. They most definitely weren't for cutting hair, but this was an emergency and they were all she had. Taking a breath, Rémy grasped the first strands and snipped.

* * *

She emerged as their train pulled into the station. It wreathed the platform in thick white steam that billowed around her as she headed toward Yannick. He was examining something in his hand, and only glanced at her when he first looked up. A second later he looked back, his eyebrows raised, with a slight smile on his face.

"You never were one for doing things by halves, were you, Rémy Brunel?" he said.

Rémy ran her fingers through her newly short hair. "Different enough?" she asked.

"Different, but still beautiful," he told her. "As always, of course."

Rémy flushed at the compliment and how easily

it had been given. Wouldn't life be simpler if all men could say what they were thinking just as easily? Pushing away the turn of her thoughts, she looked up at the poster of herself. It had gone.

Yannick moved closer to her as the passengers began to disembark around them in a cloud almost as thick as the engine's smoke. He showed her what was in his hands — the poster.

"So no one else sees," he told her. "Everything will be fine, Rémy. Trust me."

She was about to reach for it, to tear it into pieces so small that no one would ever be able to tell it had been her face that was drawn there, but before she could, Yannick moved. He turned toward their train as he folded the paper, tucking it into his pocket before looking back at her.

"Shall we, Little Bird?" he asked, offering her his arm.

Chapter 11

AN UNEXPECTED DEPARTURE

*I*t was well after eleven o'clock that evening when Thaddeus headed for Limehouse and the Professor's workshop. As he walked, he wondered how long they would continue to call it that. It seemed to have stuck, despite the man being dead these six months now, and also despite Thaddeus being the only one of the three that had ever really known him. Or at least, Thaddeus reflected, he had thought he'd known the Professor.

The workshop was in darkness when he finally reached it, the door firmly locked. Thaddeus pulled out the key the Professor had cut for him, back when he'd thought they'd both been working together for the betterment of the police force. It turned easily, and the door swung inward with a familiar rusty squeal.

"J?" Thaddeus called into the room beyond. The fire had burned to embers and the dinner table was empty. He tried not to look toward the door to Rémy's room but failed. It was half-open, as if she'd just stepped out for a moment and would be back. "J," he called again, turning away. "Where are you?"

Neither he nor Rémy had ever been inside J's bedroom. They understood that the street-boy, never having had a home before, desperately wanted his own private place. Thaddeus was about to knock on his door, when it opened. J's face appeared around it, speckled with grime and grease and wearing a pair of over-sized glasses with metal surrounds, rather like the Professor's revolutionary night-vision goggles, but far more substantial.

"There you is," said J with a sigh of relief. "When I said late, I didn't mean tomorrer."

"Sorry," said Thaddeus. "There was a lot I had to do at the station."

In truth, Thaddeus hadn't known how to leave. J had seemed convinced — though Thaddeus couldn't imagine how — that they would be setting off for France tonight. For Thaddeus to take a sudden leave of absence in the middle of such a difficult case was impossible, so in the end he'd just left two notes on his desk for Collins to find in the morning. One was a list of tasks for the sergeant to get on with while he was gone, and the other simply saying, "Following urgent leads. May be away a few days. Will be in touch when I can."

At least two of those three sentences were lies, though Thaddeus tried not to think about which they were. If he had a chance of saving Rémy and thereby thwarting the Comte's plans for Abernathy's submersible, what other choice did he have but to abandon his post? With any luck, he'd also be able to reveal Yannick as the perpetrator of the robberies and thus return with the case solved and the criminal in custody.

"Ah, well," said J with a shrug. "You're here now. Best come in then, hadn't yer?"

Thaddeus frowned. "Into your bedroom? Whatever for?"

The boy's face took on the kind of grin he always got just before food arrived on the table. "For a copper you ain't always very observant, are yer? You ever see me sleep in 'ere, 'ave yer?"

"Er, no. But —"

J disappeared for a second, and there was the

sound of a winch being turned, the faint squeak of rope winding over upon rope. And then, much to Thaddeus's astonishment, the wall of J's room began to fold back on itself. It seemed to work like a concertina. What he had always assumed to be solid walls of wood turned out to be as moveable as a cart. They zigzagged together, moving along cunning metal tracks embedded in the floor and ceiling, until the whole wall had neatly removed itself to one side.

It was what was in the room beyond, though, that made Thaddeus's mouth fall open and his eyes bulge in naked shock.

"So then, Mr. Rec," said J in a theatrical voice, clearly enjoying the policeman's reaction. "What do you fink of the Professor's greatest invention?"

It took Thaddeus a moment to move, and even longer to draw his next breath. Inside the now open room was another workshop. It was as cluttered as the main room of the warehouse, but a space had been cleared right in the center of the floor. And it was what stood there that had caused the policeman to stare.

The huge structure looked a little like the hull of a boat, though it was like no boat Thaddeus had ever seen, apart, perhaps, from those monstrous contraptions that Lord Abernathy had secreted in the underground rivers of London. This one, though, was a mite smaller, and had been made of wood as well as of scraps of metal, riveted together roughly to form a whole. When Thaddeus thought of the hull of a boat, he thought of something almost cup-shaped, semi-circular and open to the skies, but this vessel looked like a large, sealed tube with two smaller tubes connected at either side. Small round windows had been cut into the wall of the main cylinder, three lined up along its length, with circular wooden shutters that fastened to close them. There was a door, too, or at least a hatch, as curved as the sides of the boat on either side of it and currently sealed firmly shut. At one end of the vessel — which Thaddeus took to be the front — was a semi-circular window. Below this, pointing out like the sharp nose of a deep-sea creature, was a twisted spindle of metal that tapered to a lethal-looking point. At the other end — the boat's rear — were fixed several small but powerful-looking propellers.

"J," said Thaddeus, walking forward in slow wonder. "What on earth is it?"

"It's a ship," the boy said with unmistakable pride. "But it ain't any old sail boat, oh no. This here is an airship."

Thaddeus turned to look at J in astonishment. "An airship? What do you mean?"

"It flies, Thaddeus!" J said proudly. "Now d'yer see what I meant earlier? We don't need no train or boat to get us to France! We can just take off right from here and fly ourselves there."

Thaddeus blinked. "Fly to France?"

"Aye, of course. What could be easier?"

"But — how? I've heard of balloons crossing over to the continent, J, but this isn't a balloon, is it? And even if it was — it's too solid, too heavy, surely."

Chuckling at Thaddeus's bemused state, J beckoned him over to a cluttered workbench that ran along the left wall. The only part of the bench not buried by bits and bobs was right in the center. An oil lamp had been lit and was burning gently, illuminating the pages of a large book that lay open to its center.

"See this?" J said, pointing to it. "This here book has got all the Professor's inventions in it — all his ideas, whether he got around to making them or not. I found it the first week me and Rémy moved in and I've been trying to work it all out ever since. Take a look."

Thaddeus did as he was told, turning the pages slowly and taking in the intricate sketches and scrawled notes. There were detailed plans for everything, from the night glasses that the Professor had given them so as to be able to see in the pitch dark, to the terrifying mechanical armor that Abernathy had put his hired thugs into. There were other plans, too — Thaddeus recognized the strange contraption that had swallowed him whole when they'd first stumbled into the mad Lord's lair. It looked just as he remembered it — like a strange hollow cone with a sharp nose at one end and sturdy metal feet at the other. For some reason the Professor had drawn it surrounded by stars.

"I thought you might be interested by that one," said J, peering over his shoulder. "Look at where he's scribbled out loads of notes around it, over and over, like there was something he couldn't get right."

Thaddeus nodded, turning the page to see another version of the mechanical armor. He stared at the helmet, which seemed to have no space for a human head. Beside him, J shuddered.

"Now, these I'm glad he never made," said the boy. "Look, 'e's scribbled out all the words around 'em, which far as I can make out meant he never managed to get somefin' to work. These would 'ave been nasty blighters, and no mistake. Best as I can work out, they're metal soldiers with clockwork bits inside, instead of brains. Imagine that! A soldier who don't even 'ave to think. Can't get scared, can't stop, doesn't feel 'urt. Just goes and goes, and is stronger than an ox." He shuddered again.

The policeman shook his head, turning another page to yet another scrawl of scribbled words and pictures. "How on earth did you manage to decipher all this, J?"

The boy huffed a little. "Just cos I was raised on the street don't mean I'm silly in the 'ead. You should know that right enough. The Sally Ann, they used to teach me my letters a bit — after they'd read the Good Book, o'course. And then Mr. Desai, he taught me some more. The rest I've just been working out for meself. It ain't that hard once you's got the hang of it."

Thaddeus patted the boy on the shoulder. "I didn't mean the reading part, J," he said, soothingly. "I meant, how did you understand all this? It doesn't make a whit of sense to me!"

"Ah, well," said J conspiratorially. "It don't always make sense to me, neither, and that's the truth. You might say there's been a fair bit of trial and error, like. That's why I never showed you and Rémy this before. I wanted to get it right. I wanted you both to see that I ain't a waste of space, or nuffin'. I wanted to do somefin' on my own, like."

"You'd never be a waste of space, J," Thaddeus said, but the boy had already moved on.

"Anyways, I was struggling with like what you said — how this thing flies," he said, waving at the airship. "Far as I could make out from the pictures, it needed some big jewel to power it. For a while I thought the pictures meant it needed one of those diamonds that you and Rémy took out of Abernathy's place. Cos if that were the case, I'd be well and truly scuppered, wouldn't I? But then, couple o' nights ago, Rémy came home with that big old ruby on her finger, and it all came together."

"What did?" Thaddeus asked, trying not to remember what had happened when he'd seen that ring for the first time. The thought of it was still bitter.

"Watch," said J with another grin. He went to the hatch in the side of the vessel and pulled a wooden lever in the side to open it. The hatch eased down, slowly, to reveal a small flight of wooden steps built on the inner side. Once fully open and braced against the workshop floor, the steps led up into the ship. Thaddeus made to follow J as he went up them, but the boy waved him back.

"No," he said. "You stay there and watch. You's got to see this from the outside."

Thaddeus stepped back and waited. A couple of minutes went by, and nothing happened.

"J?" he called. "I can't see anything."

"Hold your horse feathers, why don't yer!" came back a muffled cry from inside the great contraption. "Give an airship 'alf a chance!"

Then, slowly, something began to happen. There was a hissing sound, faint at first but then louder. A moment later, something began to rise from the top of the ship. At first Thaddeus couldn't work out what it was — it seemed to be a sail that had been packed away somewhere out of sight — but then he realized. It was a balloon. A great oval balloon was slowly rising above the roof of the airship. It was bigger than the ship itself, and as Thaddeus watched, it eventually began to press against the workshop's ceiling.

"There," said J, appearing beside Thaddeus and looking up at the swelling balloon with his hands on his hips. "Pretty amazin', huh?"

"It really is," agreed Thaddeus. "But —"

"Hang on a mo. I'll just stop that there balloon filling for a bit so it don't get caught on them rafters, like." The boy was about to disappear into the airship's interior when he turned to wink at the policeman. "About time you saw inside, don't you fink?"

Thaddeus didn't need a second invitation. He climbed the narrow wooden steps, ducking to avoid bashing his head on the low lintel at the top. Inside, the curved walls enclosed a space that seemed far smaller than had been suggested from outside. Thaddeus found that he couldn't stand up straight except for in the very center of the room, or else his head would press against the wood. The craft was rounded in all directions, although the bottom curve of the structure was hidden from his view by a floor, pieced together from mismatched wooden planks. Thaddeus spied pine, oak and bits of beech among the uneven lengths — there was even some mahogany, as well as many others, all lovingly polished to a high shine.

At one end of the airship were four narrow bunks, two on each side, one above the other. Each had a thin straw mattress, and one of the lower ones had obviously already been claimed by J, as it also had a pillow and a crumpled blanket atop it. At the other end of the airship was the window that Thaddeus had seen from outside. Set in front of this viewpoint, reaching up from the floor and to about halfway up this window, was a cabinet overlaid by and riveted together with brass. It was semicircular in shape and tilted at an angle like a writing desk. Into its golden surface were set various knobs, levers and handles, all currently being manned by J. The boy sat in front of the controls on a small wooden chair that had been connected to a spindle so that it could pivot in a circle. He was busily whirling a handle. The hissing that had filled the cabin slowed and then eventually stopped.

"There," said J with a sigh of a relief and a beam of pride as the chair swung around to face the policeman. "Well?" he asked. "What do you fink?"

Thaddeus continued to look around. There were basic wooden cabinets for storage, small oil lamps for light, and a barrel three-quarters full of water. The walls were bare, apart from the portholes and, on one side, a stepladder leading up to another hatch that would open onto the roof. Then he spotted something else.

"J," he said uncertainly. "There are three pigeons in here, did you know that?"

"Oh, yeah," said the boy, jumping up from his seat and coming to stand beside him. They watched the three birds pecking their way merrily around the floor. "They were here when I found it. I've tried shooing them away, but they always come back. I fink they were the Professor's pets. 'E even built them a roosting place up there, look."

J pointed to the ceiling at the rear of the ship. Sure enough, Thaddeus could see a small coop with three separate compartments wedged into the narrow space where the wall met the curving roof. Stranger still, each segment of this coop seemed to have a small circular device hanging below it, attached by a hook. With difficulty, Thaddeus reached up and unhooked one for a closer look. The device was set into a pocket watch casing, but the dial had been altered and in the center was a blue faceted stone.

"Don't ask me what that is," said J, "cos I ain't got a clue. I've looked for a hint in the Professor's book, and there's none. I don't fink 'e had a chance to write it down, whatever 'e was playing at wiv 'em."

One of the pigeons waddled over, cooing gently. It reached Thaddeus's shoe and tapped it with its beak. The policeman bent down and picked it up.

"Friendly beggars, ain't they?" said J.

"It's wearing a collar," said Thaddeus. "Look."

"Well, I'll be," exclaimed J, peering at the little leather contraption. "I ain't never noticed that before, but then I ain't never picked one up, neither."

The policeman ran his fingers along the strip of leather. Embedded into it was a blue stone that matched the device he'd taken from the bird's roosting box. *What were you up to here, Professor?* Thaddeus thought. *You always did love your surprises, didn't you?*

"In the end I let 'em stay," said J, as Thaddeus put the pigeon down. "They're no trouble. Quite good company too, sometimes. Soothing, like. Anyway, enough chin-wagging. What do you reckon? Shall we make for France?"

Thaddeus shook his head. "All of this is amazing, J. But I'm sorry — even with that great balloon, I can't see this thing ever lifting off. It's so heavy."

"Ah," said the boy, holding up a finger. "But you see, that balloon ain't just filled with air."

"It isn't?"

"Nope. That's where the ruby comes in, see?"

Thaddeus shook his head. "You've lost me, J."

J headed back toward the control panel and then knelt on the floor in front of it. "You know what the old Professor was like. He had that thing about precious stones, didn't he?" said the boy as he heaved up another hatch, this one set in the floor. "He believed they had powers. Like the ones Abernathy was trying to use for himself, right? Well, I remembered that, you see, which was just as well, because not all of 'is notes were as clear as they might 'ave been, to tell the truth. Take a look," he advised, shuffling back to make room.

Thaddeus knelt and stuck his head into the hole. There was just enough light for him to see a complicated tangle of glass tubes and copper wires. They led to and from a central apparatus — a larger glass canister full of a filigree of copper, enclosed at one end and open at the other with another glass pipe connected to it at the midpoint. Above its open end hovered a clamp, and held by the clamp was Rémy's ruby ring.

"Watch this," said J, standing up and reaching for the ship's controls. He pulled one lever and then wound the circular handle he'd undone just moments before.

Thaddeus watched as the connections aligned. The ring lowered slowly, pushing into the glass canister until it was only millimeters from the copper filaments. The filaments began to vibrate, faster and faster, until they were moving so fast that Thaddeus could hardly see them. The ruby began to glow, and then, as if by magic, a reaction occurred in the canister. Pale green smoke, almost too thin to see at first, began to coalesce against the glass. It filled the canister and began to billow up the connecting pipe before disappearing in the tangle of tubes.

The hissing returned, growing louder and more insistent as the ruby glowed even brighter.

"And there you 'ave it," said J, shutting down the reaction again. The ruby retracted on its tiny winch, its bright cherry glow fading slowly. "It ain't air in that balloon at all. It's stuff that came straight out of the Professor's brain, and that's good enough for me."

{Chapter 12}

TREADING AIR

$\mathcal{T}$haddeus stood up as J closed the hatch back over the ruby's encasement. He shook his head. "This whole contraption is astonishing, J. But we're inside a workshop. Even if you did trust it to fly, how would you ever get it out of the room?"

J grinned, heading for the hatch and leaping down the steps to the floor in one bound. "Ain't you learned yet? The Professor thought of everything, so he did."

Thaddeus followed as J disappeared around the airship to the other side of the room. There came the sound of metal being forced against metal, and rope crossing over rope — another winch, bigger this time.

There was a moment of silence, and then, from far above them, came a long, slow, creak.

"I could do wiv a bit of a hand here, Thaddeus," came J's voice, breathless from exertion.

Thaddeus ducked under the ship's hull and saw J turning a huge wooden handle that was housed against the far wall. He gripped the opposite side and together they heaved. The creaking continued.

"That's it," yelled J. "She's working — she's working!"

Suddenly Thaddeus felt a draft. Then it was more than a draft — it was a wave, the cold night air crashing over his shoulders. He looked up to see a gap in the ceiling, open to the night skies wide enough to see the North Star.

"What in God's name —" And then he saw it — he saw one of the roof panels flop back on itself, just like the wall had done. The whole roof was folding back, ready to let the airship take off.

"Brilliant, ain't it?" yelled J over the slow squeak and squeal of the moving roof. "Now, just a little more, like . . ."

The final panel fell back with a *whump*, and J's bedroom-come-private-workshop was entirely open to the air.

"Well, I'll be . . ." muttered Thaddeus, turning around below the festival of stars he could now see through the dissipating London smog.

"See? The old Professor, he thought of everything. There's even a switch I can throw to shut it behind us again once we're out and about. Right, then. Ready to go, are yer?"

Thaddeus looked at the boy. "Now? Right now, just like that?"

J shrugged. "Why not? How else are we going to get there? Come on now — quick sharp! We'd best get going, before some smart Joe outside comes to see what all the noise is about. Don't want to cause more of a kerfuffle than we needs to, do we?"

"But —"

J disappeared around the hull, Thaddeus following as he made his way up the airship's short gangplank.

"J, wait," Thaddeus began, as the boy turned the handle that would inflate the balloon with the ruby's mysterious gas. The sound of hissing returned. It seemed even louder than before, and this time, some-how more insistent. "J, now just hold on a minute . . ."

J turned to him with both eyebrows raised. "What's the matter? Didn't bring enough spare undies? I did tell you to be prepared, didn't I?"

"Yes, J, you did, but . . ."

"Oops," said J, as the ship shuddered slightly. "Hey, look — the pigeons 'ave got the right idea!"

As they watched, all three birds flew up to their roosting place, settling into their hutch.

"Before you do the same, Thaddeus, I'm going to need your help. You saw the ropes tying us down, right?"

The airship gave another judder, this time rising a few inches off the ground. Thaddeus reached for the wall to brace himself. "What, outside?"

"Yeah. They need cutting. Do the honors could yer?" J pointed to a small axe secured against the wall by wooden pegs. "No need to be dainty or nuffin'. Just chop 'em off, and we'll be ready to go, like."

"Hold on," said Thaddeus, "If I'm outside when we cast off, how do I get back in? Can you stop the ship from rising?"

"Ah," said J, "I don't think so, no."

"You don't think so?"

"It'll be fine," yelled J over the hissing gas. "Just be quick, and you'll make it to the gangplank, no problem. Just pretend you's apprehending a criminal, like. Better do it now, though," prompted the boy, as the ship lurched and bounced, "cos she's fair raring to go!"

Thaddeus shook his head and grabbed the axe before heading for the gangplank. The wooden stairs were already a few inches off the ground, and he hesitated before taking a deep breath and jumping to the floor. He ran for the aft tethers first, striking the rising rope close to the floor, where it was pulling hard against its restraints. The axe was sharp and sliced through with just one strike. The airship immediately pulled upward, its nose still tethered to the ground, but the stern swinging upward to the open roof.

"That's the stuff," yelled J's muffled voice from inside the ship. "Quick now — gotta cut the other one before she does 'erself a mischief!"

The airship was lurching from one side to the other, knocking into the crowded walls of the workshop. There was a crashing, clattering noise as he ran for the other rope — one of the ship's fins had caught the edge of an over-piled shelf, sending its contents smashing to the floor. He chopped at the second rope, but missed as the ship slewed away from him.

"Hold it steady, J," he shouted.

"I'm trying!" came J's voice back again. "Hurry up!"

Thaddeus's second blow missed again, but the third was enough. The rope broke with a twang and the ship immediately lifted off, so fast that Thaddeus had no time to make it to the gangplank. He grabbed for the rope instead, clinging on for dear life as the airship made a bid for freedom through the open ceiling.

"Thaddeus!" J shouted from within. "Where are you?"

"Put her down, J!" Thaddeus yelled, as the airship continued to rise. Every second took him higher, and he looked down to see he was already several feet from the ground.

"I can't do that!" said J. "The ruby will be all used up if I do! It'd take hours for it to charge again!"

Thaddeus looked around wildly, trying to work out what to do. The gangplank was still hanging open, moving slightly as the ship bumped its way skyward. They were almost out of the workshop now, the balloon already fully clear and the airship's hull rising fast behind it. Thaddeus twisted on the rope to look over his shoulder and saw the edge of the open roof looming nearer. He swung toward it, his weight enough to jerk the airship.

"Watch it!" J cried as the nose dipped, but Thaddeus ignored him. He swung the rope again toward the roof. His feet connected with it, just long enough for him to brace against the edge and spring away. The leverage gave him enough momentum to reach the gangplank. Thaddeus crashed against it, letting go of the rope to cling to the wood, feeling it creak and groan beneath his weight.

"J!" he shouted, "I really need some help!"

The airship lifted ever higher as Thaddeus held on for dear life.

"Bleedin' 'eck," J proclaimed as Thaddeus appeared in the doorway. He turned away for a moment, grabbing a rope and throwing one end of it to the policeman. "There's a hook," he shouted over the roar of the air around them. "It's on the end of the hatch. It'll be somewhere under your belly right now. Loop this through it and throw the end back. Come on, Thaddeus, you can do it!"

It took the young policeman a moment to gather the strength. The air around them was astonishingly cold, and they were still rising. From the corner of his eye Thaddeus could see Limehouse spiraling away beneath them at an alarming speed. Then he rolled sideways, letting one arm take all the weight as he grabbed J's rope and did as he was told.

"Good man!" shouted J as the rope came back to him. He threaded it through another hook and pulled on it. Thaddeus, hanging helplessly on the gangplank like a fish being landed, saw the boy dangling all his weight on the rope, drawing the walkway up, bit by bit.

Eventually Thaddeus tipped down it, rolling untidily into the airship's hold to lie, gasping, on the patchwork wooden floor.

"Blimey," puffed J, bent double to catch his breath. "That were a close one."

{*Chapter 13*}

SUSPICIONS

$\mathcal{T}$he train was less crowded than Rémy had expected, and so she and Yannick were able to find an empty carriage to make their own. This seemed the height of luxury to the trapeze artist, who was used to traveling at best in rickety caravans, at worst on foot for hours on end. She was more than happy to relax against soft, comfortable cushions as they steamed through the countryside. Yannick, however, seemed distracted. Several times he checked his watch and then glanced out of their carriage into the corridor.

"What's the matter, Yannick?" she asked. "Expecting someone?"

She had meant is as a joke, but when he looked at

her, Yannick's gaze was sharp. Then his face softened into a smile and he laughed.

"You know me, Rémy. I'm a circus boy at heart — happier plodding along on the road than traveling like this. The speed makes me nervous."

"We could have gone by road, or even by water," Rémy pointed out. "It would have been far cheaper. I still don't think you should have spent all this money. Not on my account, anyway. I thought you were lacking in funds?"

"Is that what I made you think?" Yannick asked, with another smile. "Well, the truth is I don't have a lot, but I do have some savings put aside. For emergencies, such as this."

"Is this an emergency?" Rémy asked with a frown, looking out over fields of corn that shone like pure gold in the light of the setting sun.

"I thought you wanted to make sure that Claudette was all right?" Yannick asked, sounding a bit hurt. "You seemed quite worried, back in London."

"I am," she agreed.

"Well, there we are," said Yannick, leaning back, satisfied, and closing his eyes as the train rocked a little. "If I can help an old friend in the way that she helped me, so be it."

"How did I help you?" The memory of Thaddeus's face in the crowd at the theater flitted through her mind, along with another question, one she didn't really want answered. Yannick had been poor in London, or at least he'd said he was. And now he wasn't. Why? How?

Yannick opened his eyes again. "By giving me somewhere to stay in London, of course. What else?"

"Oh," said Rémy. "But that was nothing . . ."

Yannick smiled again. "Not to me, it wasn't," he told her gently. "Finding such a friend when I most needed one meant a lot, Little Bird."

But you told me then that you had to live cheaply, Rémy thought to herself. *And now it turns out you didn't have to at all. Why?*

"It might be best to sleep while we can," Yannick said, oblivious to her thoughts. "Once we reach the end of this line, we will have to do the rest of the journey by less comfortable means."

Rémy pushed her troubled thoughts away. Why would he keep the truth from her? It was she who had wanted to return to France, after all. She settled back against the cushions and let the train rock her slowly to sleep.

She woke sometime later to find the carriage in

darkness, the sun having finally slipped below the horizon for the night. Yannick was gone, and she was alone. Disoriented, Rémy stood up, stretching. She rubbed one hand across her eyes. Her brain felt fogged, her thoughts rolling thickly in her head.

Rémy pushed open the door and looked out into the corridor. It was empty. The rest of the passengers, she supposed, were long since asleep. She slipped out, shutting the door behind her, and headed for the restaurant car. To get there, she had to go through two other carriages, and as she approached the door to the first, she saw Yannick through the window. He looked as if he were deep in conversation with a man dressed in an elegant black frock coat, a white dress shirt, and polished black shoes. His dark hair was oiled and neatly coiffed, even at this late hour. The man nodded at something Yannick said, and the dim overhead light of the carriage gilded his cheek for a second. Across it snaked a thin, pale scar. To Rémy, this man looked entirely too richly dressed to be someone who would know a lowly stage performer such as Yannick. And yet they were standing very close, the way friends would who want to shut out the rest of the world.

As Rémy watched, Yannick took something from his pocket — a dark-colored cloth with something wrapped inside it — and passed it to the stranger, who immediately tucked the package inside his coat. There was something about the entire encounter that made the hairs at the back of Rémy's neck prickle. She slid open the compartment door.

Yannick saw her and immediately walked away from the stranger, who moved in the opposite direction as if they had not been talking at all.

"Aha," said Yannick, with a smile. "How was your sleep? Do you feel rested?"

"Who was that?" Rémy asked.

"Who?" Yannick glanced back down the corridor. The man in black had vanished into the next carriage. "Oh, no one. We just had the misfortune of reaching the same point in the carriage at the same time. They are so very narrow, these trains, aren't they?" He shuddered slightly. "Another reason I shall be relieved when this one stops."

Rémy nodded, slowly. Yannick walked past her with a smile, and she followed him back to their own compartment. She was unsettled and suddenly felt oddly wary of him.

"Yannick, have you got that 'Wanted' poster? The one of me? I'd like to see it."

"Oh, that," he said. "I tore it up, Little Bird, and

threw it out of the window while you were asleep. The fair countryside of France is home to it now! I thought it for the best. Don't you?"

Rémy did not sleep again. Instead, she watched the dark landscape pass the window and thought hard while Yannick snored gently in his seat. A sense of foreboding had settled over her again. She thought she'd pushed it away, but it had seeped back into her mind since observing the peculiar exchange between Yannick and the other man. She played it over and over in her mind. Perhaps her discomfort simply came from a lack of sleep. But she hadn't imagined it — Yannick had passed something to the man he had said was a stranger. What was it, who was the man, and more importantly, why had Yannick lied to her so blatantly? The more she looked at him, the less Rémy believed she knew him as well as she thought she had back in London. The Yannick she'd known would never have lied to her as this one just had. And what about the money for this trip? In London, he'd been as poor as she was, but suddenly he had enough money for train tickets? Had he just been lying to her about that, as well? Or had something happened that meant he now had the resources to travel how he liked? *Thaddeus was right*, she told herself. *He is not the boy you knew.*

Glancing at Yannick's sleeping face, Rémy reached for the secret pocket she'd added to her corset a few weeks ago. She'd sewn it herself — inexpertly, but she'd done it well enough, thanks to Claudette's insistent tutoring. It was tucked above the hem so that it sat securely above her navel, only big enough to store something very small within. In this case, it was her opal necklace, coiled inside a fold of paper. Rémy took it out and looked at her talisman in the dawn light. It seemed duller than usual, and she wondered if not wearing it was somehow damaging the jewel. She couldn't bear if that were true. It broke Rémy's heart not to wear it, to reject the only gift her mother had been able to give her.

Well, Little Bird, perhaps now is the right time to wear it. And to use its powers, too . . .

Before the thought had even had time to echo in her mind, Rémy reached up and fastened the opal around her neck, straightening it so that the gem fell against the skin at her throat. It was almost as if the stone was connected to her heart somehow. The opal possessed a pulse that Rémy had felt so often she had forgotten it even existed. Now it was there again, passing between the stone and her body like electricity.

She sat still for a few moments, feeling the rocking of the train over the tracks and letting the opal settle. Then Rémy allowed her mind open and tried to read what was in Yannick's. She looked at him, with no real idea of how this should work. She had never deliberately attempted to direct the opal's powers before — hearing other people's thoughts had always been accidental; an intrusion, rather than something she welcomed. But now the opal could be the key to knowing whether she could truly trust Yannick or not . . .

Something swelled in her mind, like the flame of a candle bursting into life for the first time. There was something there, something below the surface. She tried to follow where the opal was leading her, down a path into Yannick's mind, yet something wasn't right. Usually she heard a person's thoughts straightaway. Yannick's were muffled, as if behind a veil that the opal was trying to break through, but...

Yannick opened his eyes. He was staring straight at her, wide awake, as if he'd not been asleep at all. The flame Rémy felt in her mind was snuffed out, the opal quaking suddenly against her skin before falling still. There was silence.

"Aha," said Yannick, with a wide smile that had

been absent just a second before. He nodded at her throat. "So there's your opal! It's what I remember most about you from when we were children — how you never, ever took it off. I wondered where it was. I was worried to ask, in case it had been lost."

Rémy breathed hard, feeling sick to her stomach but trying to hide it. The moment was confusion upon confusion. The opal had not been able to let her into Yannick's thoughts, but not only that — had the effort she had made woken him? If so, did that mean he had known that she was trying to see into his mind? Or was it just that the shock of him waking had thrown the opal back? How she hoped the latter was the case.

"Rémy? Are you all right?" Yannick asked, and she realized he was watching her with what appeared to be simple concern.

"Sorry. Yes, I'm fine," she managed with a smile, as the train began to slow. "Oh — I think we must be coming to a station. Is this our stop?"

As he stood to look out, she unfastened the opal and hid it away once again, tucking it quickly into the pouch beneath her corset hem.

{Chapter 14}

IN PURSUIT

"*H*ow are you supposed to steer this thing?" Thaddeus asked, once he had recovered enough.

J had returned to his seat at the front of the ship, closing off the gas and dulling the hiss. The airship ceased its rise, drifting over the night sky of London like a concentrated cloud.

"'S got propellers," J said, standing on tiptoe to reach another circular control at the very top of the control desk. "Didn't you see 'em? At the back, like. Rudders, too, one left and one right. Sorry, I mean, one starboard and one port. Right nifty, this is — watch."

He turned the handle slowly. The cabin filled with a whirring sound and the ship's movement took on a purpose, nosing forward over the murky waters of Limehouse. Thaddeus got to his feet, feeling the gentle rocking of the aircraft, and leaned over J's chair, looking out the window at his first view of London from the air. It was an extraordinary sight, despite the darkness. The sparse gas lamps of the east end were burning brightly, illuminating splashes of the surrounding streets with the curdled yellow of too-old milk.

"There's The Grapes," J pointed. "Here, looks like they're havin' a lock-in. And they didn't even invite us, cheeky beggars!"

"J, mind the paper mill," Thaddeus said. "It's coming up on your right."

"Don't worry yourself," said J, with a confidence Thaddeus didn't share. "All's I need to do is twist this handle here . . ."

J thumbed a lever on his left. The airship began to turn to the right — straight toward the tower of the biggest factory in Limehouse.

"J!" Thaddeus barked, "Left! We need to go left, not right!"

"Oops," J muttered.

"Turn us the other way!"

"I'm trying," J insisted, frantically yanking on

another of the levers. "This one seems to be a bit stiff, that's all! Give me a minute . . ."

"We don't have a minute," Thaddeus yelled, gripping the back of the chair as the mill loomed like a dark behemoth through the glass. "We're going to hit it!"

"Hang about a tick," J muttered, concentrating hard as he pulled the lever again. The ship tilted left. "There! Come on, me old girl, you can do it!"

The boy yanked the lever down again and the airship continued to move left. Thaddeus held his breath as the red bricks of the factory tower came close enough to count.

"Yes!" yelled J in triumph as they cleared the building with mere inches to spare. "That's got her, all right!"

"J," said Thaddeus, rubbing an anxious hand over his face. "Please tell me you know what you're doing in this thing."

"I do, Thaddeus. I absolutely, truly do," said J. "And what I don't know, I can read in the Professor's book."

"But have you ever flown this thing before?"

"Not as such, no. It's kind of hard to do that without the balloon fully functional, like, which it wasn't until today. But I have practiced, I promise."

"How have you practiced, J?"

"Well, I've sat here in this very seat and done exactly what I'm doing now. It was just — on the ground, like."

Thaddeus stared at the meager offering of control levers set into the panel. "Right," he said weakly as they headed out over the Thames.

"Sorry," said J, a tad on the defensive. "But I wasn't to know there'd be an urgent call to use her so soon after I'd finished putting her together, was I? Otherwise I might 'ave 'ad a chance to do a proper test and all."

Thaddeus blinked. "After you'd finished . . . putting her together?"

J glanced up at the policeman with a frown. "Yeah. I only finished greasing in the last propeller earlier today, y'see. And up until yesterday I was still trying to get the ruby mechanism to work."

Thaddeus suddenly felt the need to sit down, which was unfortunate, since there was a distinct lack of chairs. He settled for staggering to one of the bunks, instead. "J, are you telling me . . . that you built this?"

"Well, not exactly, no. Like I said, I just finished her. The Professor, he must have got her started, because when I found her, the metal bits had been done. To tell you the truth, I think the Professor had in mind that the ship would be all metal, but obviously I didn't have any o' the right stuff."

"Obviously," Thaddeus echoed weakly.

"I figure all o' what 'e was going to use went down with old Lord Abernathy," J explained. "So I decided to use wood for the rest. Snaffled it from around Limehouse, I did. There's bits of about a hundred boats from a hundred countries in this tub." He rubbed the control desk affectionately.

"Right," said Thaddeus, rubbing his eyes again. "So we're sailing over London in what amounts to a pile of firewood."

"Well, technically," said J, "we ain't actually over London any more."

Thaddeus stood up and looked and saw that the boy was right. They had left behind the dark conglomeration of the city and were heading out toward the leafy, unlit countryside, the Thames on their starboard side, reflecting the hard glint of the stars above.

"So," said J. "Next stop France then, eh?"

"How do you know which way to go?" Thaddeus asked. "Have you got a compass bearing?"

"Sort of," said J, grinning up at him, "but even better." He leaned forward on the control desk to a square of wood that didn't fit in with the rest. The boy pressed the lower edge and it sprang up beneath his touch, rising an inch or so clear of the control panel.

"Sprocket and hinge," J said casually as he flicked up the surface of the square to reveal that it was a tiny wooden door, set on the vertical. Within the raised column was complicated gadget of the like Thaddeus had never seen before.

"What on earth is that?" Thaddeus asked. Whatever it was, it looked as if it had been repurposed from a ship's barometer, and was still in the glass housing of one. The original dial had been removed and repainted, and as Thaddeus leaned closer he could see the Professor's neat handwriting. It marked out regular intervals around the new face, marked with what must have been a minute brush. The words ran from left to right, from the center of the dial, where the barometer's original hands remained, to the outside edge.

Each of the words painted in that tiny hand was the name of a city. At least, that's what Thaddeus assumed they all were as he peered at them, though only because some of the more exotic names he'd never even heard of before were arranged alongside ones that he had. London herself, for example, was flanked on one side by Innsbruck and on the other by somewhere called Katmandu.

"Amazin', innit?" said J. "I mean, have you ever heard of somewhere called Manaus? I surely ain't, but it's there, so it must exist and this ship must be able to reach it. And Karachi, Timbuktu, Kandahar . . . they all sound made up don't they? But I don't fink they are. Anyway, watch this . . ."

J reached over and turned the tiny filigree metal dial in the center. Thaddeus watched as the barometer's hands moved. J adjusted them until one was pointing at "London" and the other at "Paris." Then he pressed the dial in. It clicked, locking into place.

Immediately there was a whirring sound from above them. Thaddeus looked up to see two spindly metal arms descend out of the ceiling above the control desk. Each was hinged in several places to allow maximum movement, and on the end of each was what looked like a single lens from a pair of small round pince-nez. The arms adjusted themselves, whirring happily, until they settled against the glass of the airship's window. J pulled one lever and pushed another, and Thaddeus felt the craft move slightly, turning away from the Thames completely to head out over the open countryside. As they did so, the metal arms readjusted. J kept maneuvering the ship until both lenses were aligned, right in the middle of the window.

"There," J said with a satisfied sigh. "We're on the right track now. All we have to do is keep those two arms dead center, with one lens over the other just like that, and we'll sail right into Paris. Or over it, I should say, eh?" He laughed.

Thaddeus shook his head. "Astounding. It's truly, truly amazing, J. But how do you know how all this works?"

J jerked his thumb over his shoulder to where the Professor's book lay open on his bunk. "It's all in there. Glad I didn't have to build these bits though, and there's the truth. The fiddly scientific fings the Professor had already built. I just had to put 'em all together, like."

"Well, I'd say you've done a pretty good job."

The boy beamed, and then yawned. "Thank you kindly. I'd like to think the old Professor, he might have been proud to see her a-sail on the winds."

"I'm sure he would have been. In fact, I know he would have been." Thaddeus looked out the window, into the night. "Why don't you show me how to fly her, J? Then you can get some rest. It's going to be a long night."

Chapter 15

HOME TRUTHS

$\mathcal{T}$he station that Rémy and Yannick stepped into when they left the train was far less grand than the one in Calais. It was nothing but a raised wooden platform, with a small shack to act as the ticket office. Rémy looked around as they walked the short distance from the station to the town, searching their fellow passengers for the man in black, but she saw no further sign of him. Part of her wondered whether she'd dreamed the entire thing, but then she thought again about the incident with the opal and knew that her misgivings were real.

What was I thinking? she asked herself silently, as Yannick lead her toward a small bakery. *Why was I willing to trust Yannick more than I was Thaddeus? Stupid, stupid, stupid.*

"Come on," Yannick said cheerily, unaware of her thoughts. "I think we need a decent breakfast to set us up for the day ahead."

"I have hardly any coins left, Yannick," Rémy said tiredly. "Just ask for yesterday's bread at the *boulangerie*. I should have enough for that."

"*Tsk*," said Yannick, "that's not enough to travel on, Little Bird. Leave it to me."

"Yannick —" Rémy began, but he cut her off.

"No arguments, eh?" the magician chided. "Let a friend help a friend. Sit at that table while I go inside."

Rémy did as she was told, sitting at a white wooden table outside the bakery in the town's main street. It was a pleasant scene, but her thoughts were increasingly troubled and darkened further when Yannick returns with enough fresh, delicious pastries to feed an army, along with a large pot of good coffee. It wasn't the sort of breakfast circus folk could usually afford — unless, that is, they'd stolen it. But before she could say as much, Yannick started talking, his enthusiasm bubbling through his words like a brook through a forest.

"Good news, Little Bird," he said brightly. "I

thought I'd ask the baker if he'd heard of the Circus of Secrets."

"Oh?"

"How about this? He had," said Yannick, biting into a croissant. "He went to see it two weeks ago when he was visiting his daughter in Périgueux. That's about sixty miles away from Moulidars. That was where Claudette's last letter was sent from wasn't it?"

Rémy leaned forward, a twinge of excitement struggling through her anxiety. "Yes, that's right. Périgueux is south of Moulidars, isn't it?"

Yannick grinned. "It is. The good thing is, now that we know the circus was in Périgueux, we don't have to go all the way right into Moulidars. We can skirt around it and head straight for Périgueux. Assuming that Claudette is moving the circus once every week, we should be able to find it from there. I think we have a trail to follow, Little Bird."

Rémy grimaced. "Not a very good one. And that's a long way away."

"This is true," said Yannick, starting on another pastry. "Which is why I think the next thing we need to find is a map and some horses."

"Horses!" Rémy exclaimed, almost choking on her coffee. "Don't be ridiculous, Yannick! How on earth are we going to find the money to buy horses? We'll hitch a lift on a cart or two. That will be fine."

Yannick shook his head. "And what if there are no carts to be had today? Or tomorrow, or the day after? Or what if they are not going in the right direction?"

"Then — then we'll walk," said Rémy, with a shrug. "I've done it before, I can do it again."

"It'll take too long, Rémy. By the time we get to wherever the Circus of Secrets was, it'll have moved on. And on, and on . . . we'll never catch up on foot. No, we need horses — just leave it to me."

Rémy crossed her arms. "I refuse to believe you have enough money for horses," she said. "I can't even understand how you managed to pay for this," she waved her hand at her half-eaten breakfast. "I couldn't have!"

Yannick narrowed his eyes. "That would never have stopped you in the past, Little Bird."

Rémy set her jaw. "I'd steal instead, you mean? Well, I don't do that anymore. It's not who I am."

"Oh? Why not? Because of your black-hearted policeman?"

"Thaddeus doesn't have a black heart. He's one of the best men I have ever known. Probably the best man."

"Then why are you here, Little Bird?" Yannick asked, his voice suddenly holding an angry challenge. "Why are you here, back in France with me, instead of in London with him?"

Rémy looked down at her hands, her fingers tangled together on her lap. She frowned. "Because I am the one with a black heart," she said quietly. "And I don't know if it can ever be anything else — in his eyes, at least." Rémy looked up, surprised and not a little embarrassed that she had spoken such thoughts aloud. She cleared her throat. "Anyway, it doesn't matter now, does it? Here I am, back in France, trying to get back to my old life. Or part of my old life, at least. But I don't want to be a thief anymore, Yannick. Gustave turned me into one, but it's not who I am."

Yannick sighed, his anger fading. "Well, neither am I."

Rémy made a disgusted sound in her throat. "You must think I'm an idiot, Yannick. No circus performer earns enough to save what it would take for you to spend the way you have done since we left London. Where, I might add, you most definitely didn't have this kind of money."

Yannick sighed. "I didn't steal it, no matter what you might think."

She crossed her arms. "Is that so? Then where did it come from?"

"We both have our talents, Rémy. Yours is on the wire. Mine is . . . different."

"What is that supposed to mean?"

Yannick shrugged. "I am good at . . . persuading people. At making them think they want to help me."

Rémy shook her head. "I knew it! You're using your skill as a hypnotist to steal!" She pushed her plate away. "That's how you could afford this food, is it?"

"No!" Yannick protested. "Go and ask the baker, if you like. I paid him, every centime he asked!"

"Oh, yes?" Rémy said, outraged. "And where did that come from, hey? You still haven't answered me that."

Yannick fell silent again.

"It was you, wasn't it?" Rémy probed.

"What was?"

"The thefts, in London. The jewelry that went missing, the impossible break-ins that Thaddeus was trying to solve. You were behind them."

Yannick rolled his eyes. "Ach, Thaddeus again."

"Yes, Thaddeus again. He worked it out, didn't he? Or he was beginning to."

Yannick shrugged. "So what if he had? It's not

thieving if someone gives you something willingly. Especially if they don't even really need it."

Rémy couldn't believe what she was hearing. "So that's how you did it, is it? Those people came to your show, and you hypnotized them into giving over their jewels? That's what's paying for this journey of ours?"

Yannick stared back at her with angry eyes. "I don't know what you're getting so high and mighty about, Rémy Brunel. I remember you once boasting to me about how you were the best gem thief in Europe — no, in the world, you said. You could break into anywhere and steal any jewel you wanted. And you loved it. What's so different about you and me, eh? And don't pretend you didn't know, anyway. Hypocrite that you are."

"I didn't know!"

"Of course you did! Maybe you didn't want to know, but you knew. You were quick enough to get me out of Thaddeus's reach when he got too inquisitive, weren't you? Why do that if you didn't know what was going on? You wanted to come back to France, and I was a convenient way that you could afford the trip. And I suppose it's better, isn't it? To let someone else do the stealing? That way you can tell yourself you had nothing to do with it."

"I didn't know!" Rémy shouted, though Yannick's words pricked at her like the point of a knife. "He's going to think it was me. He already suspected it, and when J tells him that I ran away with you —"

"Oh, in the name of all that's holy," said Yannick scornfully. "Stop talking about your ridiculous boy policeman. He's long gone. As if you two could have stayed friends, anyway. As if you could ever have been anything to each other. You're a circus rat, Rémy Brunel. You were born one, and it's where you belong. It's the only thing you're good at. What did you think you were going to do? Wed him? Become a respectable little London housewife — hold polite dinner parties under a glass chandelier? Get your little husband to take you to the theater and watch people like us perform like dancing monkeys?"

"Shut up," Rémy said through gritted teeth.

Yannick sat back in his chair with a disgusted shake of his head. "You can look down on me all you want, Rémy," he said. "But at least I don't lie about what I am. At least I don't pretend to be something I'm not. And you know where you belong, really. Isn't that why you came back?"

Rémy stood up, pushing her chair back so angrily that it almost tipped over. "I came back to find

Claudette," she hissed. "And I can do that without you. I don't ever want to see you again, do you understand? This is where we part ways, Yannick."

"No — Rémy — wait!" Yannick said as she stalked away from the table. "I'll help you find Claudette. Don't leave!"

"Don't follow me," Rémy warned, not even looking back.

"I'm sorry," Yannick called after her, his voice suddenly desperate. "Rémy — wait!"

She didn't listen, even when his footsteps began to follow her. Instead she turned a corner into another tiny, quiet street, and then another and another, until the sound of Yannick's footfalls faded away. Rémy paused for a moment, thinking. Yannick hadn't been wrong when he'd said that following Claudette's trail would be long and difficult without horses. Rémy turned out her pockets, almost hoping that by some miracle, she'd find a forgotten stash of money hidden somewhere inside, but of course there was nothing. She had but a few centimes left. Which meant the only way the trapeze artist was going anywhere was by begging — or stealing.

I will not become a thief again, she told herself firmly. *I will not go back to that old life. I will not.*

Determined, Rémy headed for the marketplace, instead. With a bit of luck and some charm, she'd be able to hitch a lift on the back of one of the carts as they headed out of the village. There was no way she'd find one to take her all the way, but anything would be a start.

The market, when she found it, wasn't much busier than the rest of the village. Five or six farmers had driven their carts into the small central square to sell their piles of fruit and vegetables to the townsfolk. Rémy's heart sank as she realized how few people there were to ask. What was the likelihood that any of them would be going in the direction she needed?

She'd just approached the first farmer when a shout went up from the north end of the square. Turning, Rémy saw two men in police uniforms standing next to a fat man in a flour-dusted apron. He was pointing right at her.

"There!" the man cried. "See? She was eating at my bakery, just minutes ago. I tell you it's her. It's the jewel thief from the posters!"

Rémy turned and ran, her nimble feet carrying her swiftly over the uneven cobbles as she headed for another route out of the square. But as she reached it, a group of townsfolk closed it off, unwilling to let her escape. She slid to a stop and then ran again, south this time, scrambling for another narrow street as her ears filled with the shouts of the townspeople and the shrill sound of the gendarme's tin whistles. Someone rolled a barrel at her, trying to slow her down, but Rémy leaped over it and up onto one of the carts, scattering apples in her wake as she plunged off the other side, almost losing her footing on the cobbles in the process.

She dodged one policeman and side-stepped another, but there were too many people trying to stop her and they had closed off every way out. Rémy realized she was surrounded and launched herself at one of the houses that lined the square, trying to claw her way up the stone walls and to the roof. But before she could make it, she felt something clutch her leg. Looking down, she saw that one of the gendarme had caught her by the ankle. He wrenched her backward, and she tumbled to the ground where she lay, winded, on the dirty street. The market people surrounded her, threatening to block out the sky as the policemen looked down at her.

"Ah, *tant pis*, my girl," said the one who had caught her. "You have lost your touch, now, eh?"

Chapter 16

PIGEON POST

J was asleep in his bunk, snoring, when the airship struck out over the channel. Dawn was beginning to rise, a pale blush of pink on the far horizon, and Thaddeus looked out on a rose-colored sea that chinked and guttered like a flame. He was so mesmerized by the tiny waves below that he forgot about keeping their heading steady. The lenses drifted apart, slowly, as the airship's nose turned lazily in a direction of its own making. Thaddeus cursed when he realized and grasped the rudder controls, fighting against a headwind to bring the ship right again. When the ship was in drift, she felt weightless, but in trying to control her, Thaddeus realized the craft was anything but.

He wondered for the first time how long the ruby's gas would last and thought about looking it up in the Professor's book. Then he decided against it — it was probably better not to know.

Something pecked at his feet and he looked down to see one of the pigeons searching for breakfast.

"Hello there," Thaddeus said quietly. "Had a good nap, did you?"

The bird cooed slightly before waddling off back to its box. Thaddeus remembered the curious devices attached to them. He checked the heading of the ship and then got up quickly to detach one. He took it back to the controls, adjusting them slightly to account for the moment of drift, and then settled down to examine the gadget. This one had a green stone set in it, in the center of another dial.

"You really liked your dials, didn't you, Professor?" Thaddeus muttered to himself.

"'Ello," came a sleepy voice from over his shoulder. "You've made yerself a little mate, there."

Thaddeus looked up to see that J was awake, rubbing his eyes, and then down to find the pigeon at his feet again. "I think he's hungry," he said. "Come to think of it, so am I. Did you bring anything to eat? Because I didn't."

J nodded, hopping off the bed with hair even more askew than usual. "Always come prepared, that's my motto," he said through a yawn, before reaching up to a cloth bag that hung on a hook above his bunk. "These are yesterday's, but they'll be better than nuthin'."

Opening the bag, J threw him a slightly stale bread roll. Thaddeus broke off a piece and crumbled it for the pigeon at his feet. The other two shot down from their roosts and a brief tussle ensued.

"Hey," said Thaddeus, "there's enough for all of you!"

To escape the fluttering, he got up and walked to the other bunk, taking a bite of his breakfast as he went.

J laughed. "Well, would you look at that? It's definitely you 'e likes, Thaddeus."

Thaddeus looked down to see the pigeon following him. It even hopped up onto the bunk when Thaddeus sat down. "Oy," said the policeman. "You've got your own — this is my breakfast!" The pigeon pecked experimentally at his leg, and then settled down beside it, as if waiting for something.

"Tha's a bit weird, if you ask me," said J, heading for the controls and taking over the empty seat.

"Yes," said Thaddeus with a puzzled frown. "It is a bit." Putting down his roll, Thaddeus scooped up the pigeon and looked at it. It also wore a little leather collar into which was embedded a green stone, like the one on the dial that was now in Thaddeus's pocket. The policeman thoughtfully took it out and looked at it. "J," he said. "Catch this, would you?"

J turned as the dial sailed through the air, catching it with one hand. The pigeon immediately scrambled up and took flight, sailing in to land on the boy's knee, where it squatted, looking up at him.

"Throw it back again, J," Thaddeus said and duly caught the dial again. With it came the bird, as before.

"Bleedin' 'eck," said J, watching as the pigeon perched on Thaddeus's leg. "What's that all about?"

"Another great invention of the Professor's, I think," said Thaddeus with an amazed shake of his head. "Pigeons are known to be able to find their way home from miles away, isn't that right?"

"Sure," said J. "People race the beggars, don't they? Take 'em off miles away, then let 'em all go to find out which'll get 'ome first."

Thaddeus nodded, holding up the dial. "That must be what these are. Portable 'homes.' The pigeons are trained to go wherever its own dial is. I could give you this device, send you off on a train to — I don't know, Scotland, or somewhere. Then, if I let this bird go, it'd find its way to you, just as long as you kept hold of the dial."

"Blimey," said J, clearly impressed. "What's the point o' that, though? I mean, other than being able to tell people you've got a really clever pigeon. Which, I'll grant you, is a bit nifty, but really —"

"Messages, J. They've all got collars, haven't they? All you need to do is write on a bit of paper, roll it up tight, and tuck it into the collar. Then they'll take it wherever you want the message to go to. They've been doing that from battlefields for centuries. The Professor just worked out how to make it properly useful."

"Cor," said J, "that's —"

His words were drowned out by a noise like screaming. Thaddeus and J were on their feet in an instant. There was a sharp thud and the ship shuddered, and then another thud, and another, as if it were being hit by rocks. The airship juddered and jerked, dropping lower and lower in the sky with each thud. J tried to pull the ship straight, but her nose sank into a dive.

"What is it?" Thaddeus yelled. "What's happening?"

J didn't need to answer. Outside the window, there

came the sudden flurry of small, white bodies. A flock of seagulls came crashing down, spiraling, screeching as they fell, righted themselves, and swooped away.

"Oh, lawks — they must have run straight into the balloon!" J cried, fighting the rudders as the ship continued to fall. The metal steering arms were fluttering wildly, waving about as if in a thunderstorm, the direction lenses clattering against each other. J thumped the directional gauge back into its panel. The arms folded safely back into the ceiling, out of harm's way, which was more than could be said of Thaddeus and J.

"Pull her up," Thaddeus shouted, as they continued to plunge. The sea below had darkened as the sun rose, and now shone blue-black, and the waves that had seemed so tiny just moments ago were rearing up like full-grown horses.

"What the bleedin' 'eck do you fink I'm trying to do?" J yelled back, wrestling with the controls, wrenching them back as the ship bucked away from him. "There's vents that open when you want to deflate the balloon — they let the gas out. A bird must have run right into one. We've lost gas — we're too heavy!"

"What do we do? Can't you re-inflate it?"

"Not mid-flight. Oh no." J's voice could barely be heard above the fierce cacophony that filled the airship, but Thaddeus knew exactly what he was talking about.

Out of the window, directly in front of them now that the ship was taking a nose dive, was another ship. This was the normal variety, one that floated and bore sails rather than a balloon, and it was coming up before them fast.

"If we crash into them, we'll burn," J screeched, still trying to yank the ship back under control.

"What do you mean, burn?" Thaddeus asked, shouting over the growing maelstrom of noise and fear.

"The gas in the balloon," J panted. "It's pretty — what you call it   it burns really easy, like."

"Volatile?"

"That's the one!"

Thaddeus wiped a hand over his face.

"I might just have forgotten to mention that bit during our tour," J managed through gritted teeth.

"Yes," said Thaddeus. "Yes, J, I think you just might have done."

The sailors on the ship below were now fully aware of their predicament. They were all standing on the deck, waving their arms as if to shoo away a giant bird.

{*Chapter 17*}

CAGED

*R*émy shifted uncomfortably against the cold, damp stone floor. Her arms had gone to sleep, thanks to the viciously tight handcuffs the police had insisted on clamping around her wrists. They were fastened behind her back, too, to make it even more difficult for her to move. Rémy's ankles were also chained. The cell they'd left her in was dim, with no windows and only one exit — the locked metal grill they had pushed her in through. All in all, the police who had captured her had made it nearly impossible for her to even contemplate an escape. Little Bird was well and truly caught.

Rémy cursed her stupidity. She should have been

more careful — of course cutting off her hair wasn't enough of a disguise. Still, she was surprised at how quickly the baker had recognized her. And it wasn't as if she'd seen any of the wanted posters that had been at Calais stuck up anywhere around the town. It almost made her wonder if someone had tipped them off. Someone who knew exactly who she was . . .

Her thoughts were cut short by the sound of footsteps echoing along the narrow corridor outside. The jangle of keys told her it was her jailor. He'd obviously been told to check on her every half hour, because he'd dragged his fat form down to her prison cell at least three times already. Despite her predicament, this thought made Rémy smile. That so many men in uniform could be so worried about one small girl in breeches and boots! All she needed was one chance, and she'd be out of here. Unfortunately for Rémy, it didn't seem as if the gendarme here were quite as stupid as most of the ones she'd crossed the paths of before.

The chubby policeman trudged into view. He was puffing with the simple effort of walking, and Rémy cursed her chains. Without them, he'd be no match for her, even with the bars between them. To her surprise, instead of just glancing in to check that she was still there, he stopped and fitted one of the keys to the lock.

"What do you want?" Rémy asked as he pulled open the whining grill and stepped into the cell.

"Lawyer's here to see you," he said gruffly.

"Lawyer?" Rémy repeated, confused.

"Aye. Just behave yourself," the gendarme said as he undid the cuffs around her ankles and pulled the chain out so she could stand. He put one hand on her shoulder and pushed her toward the door.

"What about my wrists?" Rémy said, rattling the cuffs that still bound them behind her back.

"You must be joking," said the policeman with a wheezing half-laugh. "What do you think I am, a half-wit? Go on, get on with you."

Rémy walked along the corridor with him pushing her all the way. Her mind was working overtime. A lawyer? Her? There was neither any way she could afford one, nor any who would come to her aid unasked. So what was all this about? Not that she was complaining — she just needed to use this sudden and unexpected boon to find a way out of these cuffs . . . and then the police station.

They reached a room that was only marginally brighter than the cell she'd just left, but it also held a table and two chairs. Rémy's overweight captor pushed her through the door and slammed it shut behind them. A moment later it opened again, and a man in coattails entered.

Yannick! It was Yannick, dressed in his stage clothes!

Rémy was about to say something when he held up a hand to silence her and turned to the policeman. "Take off her cuffs."

"I'm not —" the man began, but something distracted him and he stopped. Yannick was still holding up his hand, and the gendarme was staring at his long, thin fingers moving slightly in the damp air.

"I'll say that again," Yannick stated calmly. "Undo. Her. Cuffs."

The policeman seemed to sag a little, his eyes losing focus. He shook his head, as if there was something in his ear. Then, without another word, he walked forward, pulling the bunch of keys from his belt. He picked one out and jerked his chin at Rémy, indicating that she should turn around. She did, and a moment later she felt the cuffs loosen.

Rémy Brunel didn't need another chance. Seconds later, she and Yannick were outside the room, slamming the door shut with the silent policeman still inside and his bunch of keys in her hand.

"Quickly," hissed Yannick. "He's not properly under, and I can't hypnotize everyone we meet. We've got to get out of here!"

They ran down the passageway. At the other end, the prison's main door opened into a courtyard paved with broken cobbles. The rest of the police station was built around it, with an arch at one end. Beyond the arch was the rest of the town and freedom. To escape, Rémy and Yannick would have to cross right through the courtyard.

"There are gendarme everywhere," Rémy said in a harsh whisper. "We're never going to get out of here alive!"

"See over there?" Yannick asked, nodding toward the other end of the courtyard, where two sturdy horses waited patiently, still between the shanks of the cart they'd been pulling.

"How are we going to —"

Rémy's question was cut off by the sound of footsteps echoing up the corridor behind them. They both turned to see a uniformed police officer striding toward them. He stopped, hesitating for a moment as he saw them. Before he could reach for his whistle or raise a shout, Yannick had thrown up his arm, walking steadily toward the man as he spoke.

"We should be at the courthouse," the magician ordered calmly, in the same voice he used on stage. "You will take us on the horses out there. You will take us now."

"Yannick," Rémy began, but he cut her off with a flick of his other hand. The policeman didn't even look at her. His gaze was fixed on the magician, who was still holding up one hand.

"You should be at the courthouse now," said the gendarme after a moment, as if Yannick hadn't even spoken. "I must take you there."

The man started to walk again, shaking his head as he passed Rémy without as much as a glance. He strode out into the courtyard beyond.

"Follow him," Yannick told her. "Keep your head down, and your wrists together, as if you are in irons. Come on, we need to look as if he's the one in control."

Yannick pulled her by the arm, walking out into the open courtyard and giving Rémy no choice but to follow.

"They're going to see us," Rémy hissed. There were policemen everywhere.

"Keep going," Yannick whispered. "We just need to get to the horses. A few more minutes, and —"

"Hey! Where do you think you're going?"

The challenge had come from a group of officers who had been sitting at a table, playing cards. One stood up as they others looked around curiously.

"The courthouse," Yannick said, shortly, letting go of Rémy so he could raise his hand. "We —"

A shout echoed up the corridor from the prison, followed by another, and then the sound of running feet.

"The guard," Yannick told her, "it's worn off. Run!"

They went for the horses, barging past their would-be captor as uproar broke out around them. It took precious seconds to unhitch them from the cart, but once the animals were free, Rémy only needed one leap to mount her ride, vaulting over its rear and landing on its bare back. Wheeling the animal around, she made for the open archway, the creature's hooves clattering on the rough flagstones hard enough to send up sparks. Rémy heard Yannick behind her, but didn't turn to look. She was too busy avoiding the policemen brave enough to try to stop a charging horse. One managed to grip her ankle, but she saw him off with a kick that sent him sprawling to the cobbles.

A moment later they were through the arch and into the town beyond. Rémy had no idea where to go. As if he'd heard her thoughts, Yannick shouted for her to follow him. He clattered a sharp left and then a sharp right. Rémy followed him as they wound through the small town, hearing distant shouts and the occasional police whistle as the search for them continued. Eventually they reached the town gate and rode through it at a flat gallop, charging along the dirt roads and into the forest, leaving the town and its police behind them.

{*Chapter 18*}

TERROR IN THE AIR

"*J*!" Thaddeus yelled as the airship began to creak and quiver. "Tell me you've got an idea!"

"B-b-ballast!" J yelled back, his voice vibrating along with the ship as he held on to the shaking controls. "W-w-we've got to u-u-unload some — we've g-g-got to l-l-lose weight — get h-h-higher!"

"Tell me how," Thaddeus ordered, over the now constant noise of wood and metal under strain. It felt as if the entire craft might come apart at the seams at any moment.

"Open the h-h-hatch," J bellowed. "Ch-ch-chuck anythin' out y-y-you's can g-g-get yer hands o-o-on! I'm going to l-l-link up the r-r-ruby again, see if sh-sh-she's got anyfing e-e-else left in 'er. H-h-hurry! They d-d-down there are c-c-comin' up q-q-quick!"

Thaddeus glanced through the shuddering window, seeing that the ship below now filled it entirely. He thought briefly that they were lucky the boat wasn't a frigate, because Thaddeus was pretty sure that if it had been, he and J would have a primed gun trained on them right now.

He wrenched the hatch lever open, but the airship was traveling so fast that, even unfastened, the wind kept it shut. He braced his shoulder against it, fighting against the element outside that whistled and screamed at their violent descent. For a moment his efforts were useless, and then the hatch disappeared from beneath him, torn away so fast that it almost took Thaddeus with it. The air outside sucked at him, trying to drag him out. If he hadn't grabbed at the lintel and held on for dear life, it would have succeeded.

Eyes blinded by a stream of tears, Thaddeus staggered backward against the inner wall beside the open hatch. Through it he could see the gangway hanging in the air, flapping wildly in the current. The ship lurched to one side, favoring its open side.

"The barrel!" J yelled, not even turning around

as he continued to wind the ruby's control. "That's heaviest!"

Thaddeus forced himself away from the door and toward their store of water. Reaching it, he paused to check the seal of the cork in the top before tipping it onto its side and pushing toward the hatch. It was heavy and ungainly, despite the now sloping kilter of the floor. Thaddeus tried in vain to aim it straight toward the gangway, but it crashed into one of the cabinets to the right of the hatch instead. The cupboard splintered like firewood, sending lethal shards of wood flying through the air. One struck him in the cheek. He felt blood as the blankets that had been folded inside rushed toward freedom, taking flight like huge birds and vanishing through the hatch.

"Get it out!" J yelled again. "Yer've got to get it out, or —"

Thaddeus dragged the barrel around, forcing it against the lip of the opening. For a moment it teetered there, as if hesitating before the leap. Then it was gone.

The airship immediately tipped up a little, buoyant without the weight, but it was still dragging to the side thanks to the open hatch. Thaddeus caught the end of the rope that would close it, but it was as

heavy as dragging a dead body from the bottom of the
Thames. He braced all his weight against it and pulled,
the effort sparking lights behind his eyelids. Suddenly
he felt another weight added to his — J had left his post
to help. Together they heaved. At first it seemed as if
nothing was happening, but then the gangplank lifted
into view.

"One more pull, J!" Thaddeus yelled. "On my
count — one, two — THREE!"

Their last effort was enough to put the walkway on
the right side of the gale outside. It slammed shut with
such force that they both crashed to the floor. The airship recovered and lifted a little more.

It wasn't enough. As they scrambled to their feet,
they saw the mast of the ship below them coming up
fast, threatening to hit dead-center to the main window's glass. J swore, lunging for the control panel and
yanking the airship's rudder hard to port. They swung,
nose up at last, but not quite enough — the mast of
the other ship struck them a glancing blow to starboard. They could hear it scraping along the airship's
hull with a noise as vile as chalk dragged hard down a
black-painted board. J pulled at the rudder again, but
still the mast gashed them from stern to aft. Thaddeus
half expected to see it punch a hole right through, but

somehow the airship tore herself free. She flew out over open water.

Neither of them could talk for quite a while after that. They simply stared out of the window as the airship gained altitude again, watching as the coast of France drew ever nearer.

{*Chapter 19*}

BANDIT COUNTRY

*F*or the first few miles of their ride, both Rémy and Yannick were anxious that they may be followed, but they could spy no riders behind them. Neither did they pass anything on the dusty road, which grew steadily steeper as they went on. They hadn't spoken much since their escape — at first, they were both too out of breath. Now, Rémy had no idea what to say.

"Why did you do it?" she asked eventually. "Why did you help me escape?"

Yannick looked over at her. He'd removed his top hat but was still dressed in his stage coattails. The outfit looked rather odd, given that he was riding a thick-legged carthorse. "Do you really think I'd just leave you there?" he asked. "You should know me better than that, at least. We circus people have to stick together, no matter what, isn't that right?"

Rémy smiled wanly. "Well, thank you." Then, after a moment's thought, she added, "Not that I couldn't have got out of there on my own."

Yannick raised his eyebrows. "Of course. You were just . . . waiting for the opportune moment."

"Exactly."

The magician grinned and then raised his face to the sun, breathing in deeply.

"Ah, smell that, Little Bird," he said. "That beats the stink of the East End any day, doesn't it?"

"That I can't deny," she agreed. "This does indeed smell a good deal better than Limehouse."

The magician screwed up his nose. "All those people squashed one upon the other," he said, "the stench of the opium dens, rising up to meet the reek of burning oil and dirty flesh. I am amazed you stayed for as long as you did, Rémy."

She shrugged. "A city is like a circus. It's about more than its parts, Yannick. It's about the whole."

Yannick turned in his saddle to look at her, his eyes shadowed despite the sunlight. "Ahh," he said, "you are thinking of the best man you know again, are you?"

Rémy stayed silent. Yes, she was thinking about Thaddeus. How could she not? She missed him. She wondered what he was doing at that moment, back in London. Rémy could imagine him leaning over his desk, the usual frown of concentration creasing his forehead as he puzzled over some piece of evidence he'd collected. Unexpectedly, she felt tears prick at her eyes and blinked them away. If her last escapade had shown her anything, it was that she could never fit into polite society. There would always be the risk of someone recognizing her as a thief who should be behind bars. *What did you think you were going to do? Wed him? Become a respectable little London housewife?* Yannick's earlier jibe may have stung, but it was no less true for that.

Squaring her shoulders, Rémy urged her pony on. "Do you actually know where we're going?" she asked her companion, who picked up the pace to fall in beside her. "Or are we guessing the way to Périgueux?"

Yannick grinned again. With a flourish, he produced a crumpled map from his pocket. "I've got a compass too," he added. "We'll be fine as long as we stick to the road and don't try to cut through the forest."

Rémy nodded, and they rode on toward the spreading, leafy green horizon of trees ahead. The sun was at its zenith when they turned along a valley ridge, the road loose with pebbles. On one side of the road, a precipice dropped abruptly to the dry riverbed far below. On the other, a band of scrubby young trees lifted over a rocky ridge and into a thicker, deeper forest beyond. Rémy dismounted and picked her way up the incline between the saplings to get a better look. The forest stretched into the foothills of faraway mountains, an impenetrable carpet of green, made all the deeper by the darkness beneath the branches. In the heat of the midday sun, Rémy thought it looked like the perfect place for a break, but Yannick shook his head.

"We should move on as fast as possible," he said. "Who knows what's lurking in there?"

Rémy smiled slightly. "Afraid of monsters, Yannick?"

"Not of the imaginary variety, no," the magician said dryly. "But I'd bet fair money there's plenty of the human sort skulking among that wood."

They trotted off again, the ponies puffing in the heat. Around them, the landscape grew rockier as the road rose higher and higher toward the pass.

"What would you have done?" Rémy asked, sometime later.

"What do you mean?" Yannick asked, puzzled.

"If I'd got away from the gendarme on my own, fled the town before you could get to me," Rémy expanded. "What would you have done? Gone back to Paris, to the Jamboree?"

Yannick was silent for a moment. Then he shook his head. "I would have carried on looking for the Circus of Secrets."

It was Rémy's turn to be puzzled. "Why?" she asked as they turned a sudden corner in the road. Pebbles skittered, falling down the ravine, echoing as they chinked and kinked their way to a new resting place. "You'd have a better chance of a sure position in Paris. What's so special about —?"

Yannick pulled his pony up short, holding his hand up to Rémy for silence. Ahead of them, a large tree lay across the road, blocking their path.

Rémy frowned. "That looks deliberate."

"It is," said Yannick, looking up at the walls of rock surrounding them. The horses pawed nervously, picking up their riders' anxiety. "We have to go back, right now."

There came the sound of footsteps behind them, echoing up the rocky walls like tinny thunder. Rémy and Yannick turned their horses to see five men, burned brown by the sun, blocking the path back to the ridge. Their clothes were worn and shabby, their boots little more than scraps. But they were large, and they each carried a heavy club.

"Time to pay the toll," grated the largest of them.

"What toll?" Rémy asked, keeping her voice level despite the swift thumping of her heart. "I heard of no toll on this road."

"Then you heard wrong," said the beast, stepping forward.

Rémy's pony shied, but she held him steady. "I don't think so," she said, as disgusted by these ruffians as she had been by the thugs who had tried to rob Lady Sarah in London. "Move, and let us pass. Or better yet, move the tree so that we can continue."

There was a burst of laughter from the bandits, who as one moved closer still. "Is that so?" asked their leader, his voice laced with threat. "And who are you to talk to me so, little girl?"

Yannick stirred nervously in his saddle. "Rémy, don't —"

"Not little girl," said Rémy coldly. "Little Bird."

She kicked her heels into her pony's flanks. It reared, and while the animal was still on its hind legs, Rémy pushed it to step forward — not far, not as far as Dominique could have moved in one, but just far enough. The animal's forelegs thrashed the air as they came back to earth, catching the bandit full in the chest. He went down like a sack of flour, crashing to the shale in a spray of blood and spit.

"Ride!" Rémy shouted in the split second before his men had fully realized what had happened. "Yannick — ride!"

She spurred the pony between the gap left open by the fallen man, and then pulled her feet from her stirrups. It was dangerous to try circus tricks on an untrained horse, especially in boots that were meant for the road, but Rémy had no choice. She leaped up, her feet finding a hold as the pony careered on. She almost slipped against the horse's unfamiliar back but regained her balance as one of the men came to his senses and lunged. He swung at her with his club, but Rémy jumped and he missed, the momentum and fury of his swing sending him off balance and tumbling in the dust beside his leader as she brought her feet back down as lightly as possible.

Rémy dropped back into her seat and glanced sideways to see Yannick land a booted kick against the jaw of another of the men, who spun away but managed to right himself. She watched as the thug pulled something free from his belt, and for a moment Rémy was afraid it was a gun. Instead, though, he put it to his lips and blew.

It was a bugle. The thin sound filled the air, a wailing cry that echoed off the rock and down the valley as Rémy and Yannick gained the ridge and fled back down the stony road, the sound still dying against the valley walls.

They'd only got a few hundred feet when more men began to appear, running down through the scrub in answer to their fellows' call. As one they began to walk up the road toward the charging horses, three-deep and as impenetrable as a wall.

"Into the trees!" Yannick shouted, "It's our only chance!"

Rémy drove the piebald right, its shoes churning the dust and scattering stones like shrapnel. They cantered up the slope, slaloming between and over the young trees that dotted the scrub. Cresting it, Yannick charged ahead of her into the forest that had become their only chance of escape.

"Stay clear of the river," she yelled, one arm up to shield her face from the whipping branches. "It's where their camp will be!"

Yannick didn't answer but pulled his pony right, running them parallel to the pass they had failed to cross. Behind them, the sound of the bugle came again, and then again, the shouts of their pursuers matching it as they entered the forest.

"We should separate," Rémy yelled. "Agree to meet at the next town."

"No," Yannick barked. "We stay together."

"But —"

"We stay together," he ordered, his voice curt as they changed direction again, skittering down another short slope in a flurry of churned earth and undergrowth.

They rode as far as they could, dodging between trees and around stumps that looked as ancient as the earth under their feet. Eventually they stopped, dismounting the exhausted horses. The four of them stood together, all breathless and panting.

Rémy listened for a moment. The silence of the forest was as thick as a blanket. "I can't hear them," she said quietly. "I think they've given up."

Yannick bent double, coughed, and nodded. "Let's hope you're right."

Rémy slowed her breathing and looked around as she patted the piebald's quivering nose. "We're completely lost," she said.

"Not completely," said Yannick, taking out a

compass. He looked at it for a moment, watching the spinning, fractious hand as it finally settled. "It's that way," he said, pointing into the deeper forest, away from the road.

Chapter 20

NEW FRIENDS

$\mathcal{T}$he ruby airship sailed over Paris like a jewel of the skies, glinting in the colors of sunset and causing quite a stir on the ground. As Thaddeus and J steered the ship over cafés and bars, restaurants and theaters, people of all sorts looked up and saw her, and began to give chase. The ship's two passengers could see them shouting and waving, knocking on their neighbors' doors to urge them to see this great wonder that owned the air as surely as a ship owned the seas.

"'Ere," said J, a little uneasily. "There's quite a crowd down there, y'know. What are they going to do when we land?"

"I don't know," Thaddeus said, feeling the same anxiety.

J blew out a breath, "Let's just hope they're all friendly, eh? Any sign of the circus field yet?"

Thaddeus squinted into the indigo sky, and then pointed at a glare of rioting light on the very edge of the city. "That must be it, mustn't it? Turn a mite to port, Captain J."

"Aye, aye," said J, pulling the right lever.

They sailed on, descending slowly like a bird on the wing coming into land. The ship headed toward the smudge of light, which as the sky grew ever darker with the onset of night, slowly coalesced into thousands of large white candles. Each was set atop a metal pole that had been driven into the ground at regular intervals to mark out a giant circle. The circle was big enough to encompass the hundreds of caravans that sat inside it, gathered in little clusters and knots but still part of the whole, like the bark of a tree that has grown to adjust for branches. There were circus tents, too, many of them, a myriad of colors melding into the dusky evening light — some were striped, white and red or yellow and blue. Others were studded with cultured stars, and still others were one large block of a glaring hue such as violet or turquoise. Around and between these, people milled, though they were different and, in turn, more wonderful than those who had chased the airship across Paris. There were clowns and stilt-walkers, fire-eaters and jugglers, acrobats and tumblers, all mingling together as if inside the circle was its own fantastical city.

"Better set down inside, if I can," J muttered, a look of concentration on his face. "Got a hunch it'll be safer than leaving this beauty outside."

"Think you can manage it?" Thaddeus asked. "There's not much room."

J nodded but didn't answer aloud, and Thaddeus didn't speak again. The boy continued to let gas out of the balloon in a slow, steady hiss that matched their rate of descent. Thaddeus wondered how long it would take to refill it if they needed to lift off the ground again swiftly for whatever reason but decided not to ask. It was too late to worry now — the airship had lost so much height that he could see the astonished looks on the faces of the circus folk below. Many had stopped what they were doing and were simply staring up at them, mouths agape.

The circus tents seemed bigger now, more like the big top where Thaddeus had first seen and tried to save Rémy all those months ago. He wondered if she was down there now, looking up at them with the same amazement as everyone else. He scanned the astonished crowds, searching for her face, but could not see it. Perhaps she was mid-performance, flying through the air with a grace that made her seem as if she had been born with wings.

"Ah," cried J, "that's right! That chap's got the right idea, look!"

Thaddeus saw that one of the circus men had spotted where J was aiming the airship — a patch of empty ground as wide as two caravans beside a scarlet-colored tent. He was directing the surrounding caravans to move back, making more room.

The owners of the caravans were hitching their horses, pulling the wooden homes away just far enough to make space for the airship. Soon there was an empty gap of land easily bigger than the room in which the ship had been built. This was just as well, as it turned out that landing was a far trickier proposition than taking off.

"Easy," Thaddeus warned as the ship slipped slightly to port, her stern swinging dangerously close to the scarlet marquee.

"I got it, I got it," J muttered, pulling her around even as they sunk lower. They were level with the tops of the caravans now, and a horde of gawkers had gathered, held back by the man who had seen that the ship had needed more space. He was walking back and forth at the edges of the crowd, waving them back just far enough to keep them in line. He was dressed in an elaborate scarlet coat studded with gold buttons that shone in the candlelight and with tails so long they almost trailed in the dust. He carried a whip, coiled about his right hand so comfortably that it seemed a part of him. A circus master, Thaddeus supposed, used to marshaling crowds.

The ship set down with a thump hard enough to judder their teeth. J let out a sigh of relief and rested his sweating forehead against the control desk. Thaddeus thumped him lightly on the back.

"Well done, lad," he said.

"Bleedin' 'eck," J muttered, straightening up and wiping a hand across his face. "I won't be wanting to do that again in a hurry, and that's the truth."

The sound of the crowd was clear to hear now, a great bubble of noise — shouts and whoops, hollers and cries of, "Come out! Let us see you!" The circus master who had directed them to land appeared in front of them, smiling broadly through the glass and tipping his hat to them both and then bowing with a flourish to invite them out. Thaddeus and J nodded and grinned.

"You ain't got that ray gun the Professor used to spring yer that time, 'ave yer?" J asked, as they began to lower the gangplank.

"Afraid not, J."

"Pity," muttered the boy through a large, fixed grin.

The airship's walkway opened to a sudden hush. Thaddeus and J took a step out onto the gangplank.

"Behold!" boomed a voice to their left. "The Magnificent Circus Maximus presents to you, all the way from Great Britain . . . The Caravan of the Air!"

Thaddeus and J looked to see their circus master friend signaling frantically to a scrawny little man pushing through the crowd. The newcomer held a tiny trumpet, and at the master's urging he held it to his lips, emitting a loud, bright fanfare. The crowd exploded with applause and pandemonium took over.

"Circus what?" J asked out of the corner of his mouth, as they both stepped warily to the ground. "Caravan of the where?"

"I think we've been appropriated," Thaddeus muttered back. "How does he know we're British? And why is he speaking English?"

"*Mes amis!* My friends, my friends!" exclaimed

the circus maestro, barreling toward them with out-stretched arms. "What an entrance! What an act! What an amazing contraption!"

"Thank you, Mr. . . . ." Thaddeus began, feeling his hand crushed into a grip that could have been made of iron.

"I am the Great Constanto," declared their new friend extravagantly. "It is my great pleasure to welcome our wonderful English cousins, yes?"

"Yes," said J, "but 'ow in 'eck did you know we was from Britain?"

"Ah — the flag, yes? The . . . how you say . . . Union Jack?"

J and Thaddeus both turned to look at the ship. "What flag?"

The Great Constanto pointed to the underside of the hull. Thaddeus and J both bent down to look. Sure enough, there was a Union Jack in its bright colors of red, white, and blue emblazoned on the underside of the ship, tainted by the jagged scrape of the mast that struck it earlier.

"You never noticed that before?" Thaddeus asked J.

"Never," J admitted. "That bit were already built, weren't it? And it's not like I ever lifted her before, is it?"

"*Mes amis, mes amis,*" the circus master interrupted. "Your public awaits!" He threw his arms wide, indicating the crowd, which whooped and hollered in response.

"Actually," said Thaddeus, "we're just here looking for our friends."

"Then you are circus folk!" Constanto exclaimed. "I knew it! I knew such a marvelous beast of the air could be nothing else!"

"Not exactly circus folk," said J, eyeing the crowd. "But I bet you know our mate. Rémy Brunel?"

"She's a trapeze artist," Thaddeus added. "She sometimes performs as Little Bird?"

"Aha!" said Constanto. "I think you mean Le Petit Moineau. Le Petit Moineau," he shouted to the crowd. "*Oui? Oui?*"

"*Oui!* Le Petit Moineau! Le Petit Moineau!" The crowd roared.

"You see," said Constanto, satisfied. "If you are friends of the great Rémy Brunel, you are friends of ours. Alas, long have I tried to persuade her to join the Circus Maximus, but she would not leave Le Cirque de la Lune without her fortune-teller friend, and I already have one of those. It would not have done to . . . set the cat among the pigeons, you see?"

"Er," said Thaddeus, a little overwhelmed to discover just how well Rémy was known here. "Yes, I see. But — can you take us to her? Is she performing here, somewhere? Her circus is called The Circus of Secrets now."

"Ah, yes, Le Cirque des Secrets," sighed Constanto. "But *non*, they are not here — we are missing them from our number for this Jamboree. It is such a pity, we were all so looking forward to seeing this troupe under a new name, without that stinking cur, Gustave." Constanto spat the name so violently that both Thaddeus and J took a step back.

"They — they ain't here?" J asked.

"Non, my young friend."

"Well then, perhaps Rémy is here without a circus?" Thaddeus suggested. "She was traveling with a friend — a magician called Yannick?"

Constanto frowned and shook his head. "I am sorry, *mes amis*, but I have not heard of her being seen. I cannot believe that Rémy Brunel would come to the Jamboree without some new tricks to show us, and there has been no talk of the girl who can fly without wings. Besides, if it were known that the great Little Bird was no longer traveling with a circus, there isn't a master among us who wouldn't try to buy her talents for themselves. It would be the talk of the circle — but I have heard no word of it. Still, perhaps there is someone who can help you with more news."

"Oh?"

"Yes — I have recently taken on a German violinist, a man by the name of Dorfmann. Until recently he was traveling with the new circus of Claudette Anjou — the Circus of Secrets, as you say. Come, I will take you to him."

J and Thaddeus hesitated, looking back at the airship, unwilling to leave it unattended under the hungry scrutiny of so many unknown people.

"Do not fear, eh?" said Constanto, and put his fingers to his lips. He emitted a piercing whistle, which was answered by two large men who looked for all the world like prizefighters. "They will take care of the Caravan of the Air, you see?"

Constanto made to move off. "Hang on a sec," said J. He looked out at the crowd, and then back at the circus master. "Reckon they'd pay a bit for a squizz inside, like?"

"J?" Thaddeus asked. "What are you doing?"

"If we're going to be here for a bit, we're going to need some readies, ain't we?" he said reasonably. And then, to Constanto: "Two . . . what do you call 'em? Centimes? Two centimes for a peek. We'll split the take wiv you if your blokes make sure they don't touch nuffin'. They ain't to scare the pigeons, neither. Right?"

Constanto grinned. "I like the way you think, young master," he said, before barking a swift order in French to the two men the size of tree trunks who were now standing on either side of the door. "Any time you want a job, you come to the Great Constanto, no?"

{*Chapter 21*}

REAL MAGIC

"What's that?" Rémy asked, pulling up her horse suddenly, sometime later. The forest seemed endless, the trees stretching on as the day lengthened.

Yannick barely paused, urging his steed to plod onward. "I can't hear anything."

"I can," she said. "It's music. Yannick! Listen."

He did as he was told. After a few moments, he shrugged. "It's the bandits, in their camp," he said. "It must be drifting down the valley."

"No," said Rémy. "No, it's not the bandits." She stayed still, listening to the sound, mesmerized.

"Rémy," said Yannick. "Come on — it'll be getting dark soon. We need to keep going."

"I know it," Rémy said, feeling as if she were dreaming. "That music — that tune. I've heard it before." She pulled her horse around, heading in the direction of the sound.

"Rémy," Yannick called after her. "What are you doing?"

"I have to find it," she told him absently. "It's for me. I know it is."

"Don't be ridiculous," said the magician, riding up beside her. He caught hold of her arm and forced her to stop before snapping his fingers in front of her face. Rémy blinked. "I know you're tired, but come on. We've got to find our way out of this forest. Then we can rest for a while."

"Yannick, I'm telling you, I know that music."

"So what if you do? It'll be some tune you've heard in a bar somewhere — or around a campfire late one night."

Rémy frowned. "Yes," she said. "Yes, I think that's exactly where I've heard it. Around a campfire." She nudged the horse onward again, more determined this time.

"Rémy," Yannick tried.

She stopped and turned to him. "Yannick, I want to know who's playing that tune. I swear to you, I know it. It's music I haven't heard for years, music I didn't remember existed until a moment ago, but I recognize it and I have to find out why. Come with me, don't come with me: that's up to you. But I'm finding the player, regardless."

Rémy turned her back on him and continued to wind through the trees. The music was distant, drifting on a rising and falling breeze, but growing stronger. After a few moments, Yannick's horse appeared beside hers. They fell in step and rode on in silence, listening to the sound of the melody that Rémy knew bone-deep. As the music became louder, the trees thinned. Above them, they could see twilight filtering between the branches, a cloudless, starry night settling over the forest.

The music was coming from a caravan. It was wooden, hand-carved in the old Romany style, with a rounded roof and half-paneled door. The cross-planks had been painted cherry red, the mid-panels a yellow as bright as the sun. It was standing in a clearing that almost seemed as if it had been created by the forest itself, as if the trees had bowed and taken a step back to make room for it. Fireflies sheltered in their nooks and crannies, imitating the stars still waking up above. In the center of the clearing was a small blaze, the low, curling flames cooking a scrawny wild chicken on a spit.

An old woman sat on the steps of the caravan, her ancient fingers tangled around a small wooden pipe that wove the tune as she blew through it. She looked wizened enough to be part of the forest herself.

Rémy had never seen the woman before in her life, but she knew that music. She and Yannick stood, watching the old woman and feeling the melody grow into the world like a frond of fern uncurling for the first time. It was at once unexpected and familiar, and when it stopped, Rémy had no idea whether she had been listening for minutes or hours.

The old woman opened her eyes and looked at them as if they had always been there.

"Ah," she said. "The chicken will be done cooked by now. Time for dinner." She looked at Yannick. "You, boy — make yourself useful. Take 'em off the spit. There are bowls yonder," she waved one finger at the fire. "Some tomatoes, too. No greens today, but that's the way of it."

Yannick shrugged and did as he was told. Rémy took a step closer to the old woman. Her face was as creased and cracked as the bark of a tree, but her eyes were bright and blue. She pulled a purple

shawl around her shoulders and shuffled toward
Rémy.

"Ah, and isn't it good to see you again," the old
crone cackled, her voice as scratchy as new wool. She
raised one ancient hand to Rémy's face, patting her
cheek. "Pretty, too, though I knew you were going
to be from the moment you opened that mouth and
bawled."

Rémy shook her head. "I'm sorry, old mother, but
I don't know you."

"I know you don't, girl, but that's no matter. I know
you enough for both of us. Come on, let's sit and eat
afore the chicken goes to waste."

She shuffled toward the fire, Rémy staring after her,
confused. Yannick handed the old woman a bowl and
she settled on her haunches, turning to look at Rémy.
In the firelight she looked even older.

Rémy sat beside her, taking another bowl from
Yannick.

"Can you tell me how you know me?" Rémy said.
"If we have met, I must have been very young, I think?"

The old woman cackled between mouthfuls. "Oh,
yes, you were very young. Next to nothing, in fact.
I remember you, though. Oh, how you and your
brother made your mother howl."

Rémy sighed, her suspicions confirmed. "Ah, old mother. I am sorry, but you have me confused with someone else."

The old woman eyed her with a twinkle of blue. "Have I, now?"

"Yes. I have no brother. My parents had no children other than me."

"Is that so?"

A twitch of annoyance tensed Rémy's shoulders. The old crone's tone was teasing, as if she knew what Rémy herself didn't. "Yes, it is most definitely so."

Abruptly, the old woman put down her bowl, shaking her head. "Ah, what a thing, to go through the world without knowing your own kin."

"I told you," said Rémy, "I don't have any kin. You're confusing me with someone else."

"And I am telling you, Rémy Brunel," said the old woman, in a voice suddenly as clear as day and as straight as a plumb line, "that I remember you, and I remember your brother."

Rémy jumped at the sound of her name on the old woman's lips and drew in a breath. "H-how do you know my name?"

The old woman smiled again, the twinkle back in her eye. "I have birthed babies for the circuses of

France since I was thirteen years old. That is longer than either of you can imagine, and I tell you, my girl, that I never forget one of mine." She smiled again, reaching out to pick up her bowl. "No one expected you, but out you flew, hanging onto your brother's ankle as if you were already performing in the tent." The old woman chuckled. "And what a scrawny little bird you were, and didn't I tell your poor mother so?"

"That's . . . that's what they call me," stuttered Rémy. "That's . . . that's always been my nickname."

The old woman looked at her steadily, the slight smile on her ancient lips telling Rémy that she already knew full well that Rémy Brunel was more usually known as Little Bird.

Rémy stood up, a little shakily, turning away. "I don't have a brother," she said again. "I — I don't. I would know if I did. Wouldn't I?"

The old woman shrugged. "The things we don't know in this world are enough to fill the spaces between stars, are they not?" she said.

Rémy spun to face her. "But . . . if I do, where is he? Why don't I know him? Where is he now?"

"I did not stay long enough to be able to answer all your questions, Little Bird," said the old woman. "I am a midwife. I go where the births are and leave the babies behind me." She looked into the fire, the sparks illuminating a face that had grown sad. "I will tell you this — when I heard of your parents' misfortune, I wept over it. They were good people. I expect their offspring are good people, too."

Rémy sank down again, her food forgotten. Her head was spinning. Had she really had — did she have — a brother, or was this woman just lost in a world of her own making? Even if she was a mid-wife, how could she remember every child she ever helped into the world? And Rémy, have a twin? It was impossible, unthinkable. She was alone in the world, except for Claudette. Gustave had seen to that when he'd forced her parents to steal a jewel that had cursed them both, driving them apart and away from their daughter forever.

Almost as if Yannick had heard what Rémy was thinking, he spoke.

"Tell me, old mother," he said, "if you remember all the babies you have ever birthed, do you remember bringing one into the world called Claudette Anjou?"

Rémy frowned, wondering why Yannick wanted to know. She glanced at the old woman, but she was staring into the fire, her lips set in a determined line as if she were remembering things far in the past.

For a moment Rémy thought she hadn't even heard Yannick's question. And then:

"If there's one thing I can't abide, boy," came her cracked old voice, turning harsher, "it's a question being asked where the answer is already known."

Rémy looked at Yannick. He looked back, uncomfortable, and shrugged.

"You are not wearing your opal," said the old woman suddenly, as she crooked one gnarled twig of a finger at Rémy's neck.

Rémy's hand flew to where she pointed. "How do you know about —? No . . . I did once. Always. I never took it off, but . . ."

Something about the look on the old woman's face told Rémy she didn't need to say any more, that in fact she knew exactly the gift — and the burden — that the opal had bestowed. Rémy felt faint, the blood rushing from her face. If the old woman knew about the opal, then what else did she know?

"Let an old woman see it, eh?" she asked, tipping her head to one side. "It is such a pretty thing, such a perfect thing. It has been a long, long time."

Rémy nodded, slipping her fingers beneath her shirt and finding the corset's hem. She felt for the pocket there, and the pouch within it.

She leaped up. "It's gone!" Rémy cried.

"What has?" Yannick asked, standing up on the other side of the fire in alarm. "Rémy? What's gone?"

"My opal! It was here, in a pocket beneath my corset, but it's gone! It's gone!" She stared at Yannick, her heart turning cold. "You — did you take it?"

"What?" Yannick asked, aghast.

"You heard me, Yannick. Did you steal my opal?"

"How could you even ask me that?" he demanded angrily.

"How?" Rémy asked, with just as much fury. "Oh, well, let's see now. Between the two of us, who last stole something? And what was it, exactly? Remind me again would you, Yannick?"

The magician shook his head in disgust. "I can't believe you," he hissed. "After what I did for you, breaking you out of prison. After what I risked for you."

They both fell silent, staring at each other across the flames. The old woman stayed where she was, watching calmly.

"Anyway, don't you always have it around your neck?" Yannick asked coldly. "Didn't I see it the other day? How would I be able to steal that?"

"I took it off," Rémy said, her voice cracking over the words.

"You took it off?"

Rémy was distraught. How could she have lost the only possession in the world that meant anything at all to her? "I sewed a pocket for it, to keep it safe."

Yannick made a sound in his throat. "Safer than around your neck? You took off your most valuable possession and put it in a pocket, and you're accusing me? Any pickpocket could have got at it, Rémy. It was probably one of those bandits on the road."

"None of them got close enough," Rémy protested. "It wasn't them."

"Really? Check," Yannick ordered. "Has the pocket been sliced?"

"No," said Rémy, pulling up her shirt and turning up the edge of the corset to show the pocket. "I would have felt it. I would have —" She stopped. The corner of the pocket was open, the bottom seam of stitching neatly cut, as if with a knife or pair of scissors. Rémy stared at it in horror. She had been robbed by a pickpocket — she, who had spent her life with the lowest of the low, had been cheated by a common thief.

Rémy covered her face with her hands and sank to the ground, the tears pricking at her eyes. She should have worn it, always. She should have fastened it around her neck so that no one could ever get at it.

Rémy felt something on her shoulder — it was the old woman's hand, squeezing her gently.

"Be of good heart, Little Bird," the old woman whispered in her ear. "The opal has only one true owner, and it will always return home, however long it takes."

Rémy sobbed a little. "Then I will surely, surely never see it again," she said, her heart broken. "Because that wasn't me. My parents stole it, didn't they? From a Rajah in India. They did not own it, they stole it."

"Rémy Brunel, dry your tears and look me in the eye," the old woman demanded, her hand on Rémy's shoulder becoming an iron grip until she did as she was told. Rémy stared into the old woman's eyes, which seemed as deep and as blue as the ocean, and just as old. "Did no one ever tell you that you were an Indian baby? It's as clear as the pretty on your face."

Rémy swallowed her tears, her spine tingling. "Yes," she said. "Yes. Someone did, once. Not long ago. But . . ."

The old woman smiled again, letting go of Rémy's shoulder and straightening up. She said nothing for a moment, just stood beside the dwindling fire, looking up at the stars that pricked the sky, brighter than candlelight.

"It is time for an old woman to sleep," she said, eventually, before beginning to shuffle toward her caravan. "Sometimes we all need to go home."

"But," Rémy began, getting to her feet. "Wait, I need to ask you so many questions. Please!"

The old woman turned to her with a smile. "I am not an oracle, Rémy," she said. "I do not know the world's secrets. I have simply lived a very, very long time and I have seen many, many things. Old women need their sleep, and now I need mine. Good night. Rest, now."

And she turned her back. She walked slowly to her home and up its little wooden steps, shutting the door behind her without another word.

Rémy and Yannick settled beside the dying embers of the campfire, but it took a long, long time before Rémy could sleep. Her mind was full of questions and upset, reproach and anger. She had no one to blame but herself for losing the opal. She should have been wearing it, as she always had, but her cowardice had got the better of her, and just at the moment when it seemed she had met someone who knew about the stone and what it could do.

Rémy thought she would not sleep at all, but eventually the rigors of the day caught up with her. She fell into a fitful slumber. In her dreams, the woods were on fire. She was trying to flee the blaze, stumbling after someone who kept turning to wait for her, despite the flames licking at his feet. Rémy thought it was Yannick, but the only time she managed to glimpse his face, she realized it was Thaddeus.

Chapter 22

TROUBLING NEWS

Thaddeus and J left the storm they had created, following the Great Constanto as he led them toward another circle of light. This one was the halo of a bonfire, burning in the center of a small cluster of caravans. From one floated the haunting sound of a violin. A figure formed through the flickering darkness. It was a large man, sitting in front of the wooden wheel of his caravan with his knees hunched and a violin beneath his chin. The music spun into the night sky, accompanying the crackle and spit of the flames.

"Dorfmann," said Constanto, his voice softer now. "I have brought two people to see you."

The man stopped playing and opened his eyes, which were a deep and melancholy blue. He looked at Thaddeus first, and then at J before settling back on Thaddeus.

"You," he said, his thick German accent making heavy shapes of the English words. "You, I remember. You came to the circus in London, the night that we lost Little Bird. You are policeman, ya?"

"A policeman!" Constanto exclaimed in horror, taking a step back.

Thaddeus held up his hands, eager not to lose the friend they had made. "No — I mean, yes. I am a policeman in London. But not here. Here, I am just trying to find a friend. Have you seen Rémy Brunel?"

Dorfmann looked at him with open suspicion. "You are searching for Little Bird?"

"Yeah," said J, "but for a good reason, nuffin' bad like I reckon you're thinking, mister. We fink she might be in trouble, see. An' more than that, Mr. Rec here, he loves her, like, and . . ."

"J!" said Thaddeus.

"Beg pardon," said J, earnestly, "but we got to tell 'im the truth! Can't you see that? If we don't he'll fink we're hunting her for another reason, 'im knowin' you're a policeman and all. And we ain't. Are we?"

There was a brief silence as Dorfmann watched the discomfort on Thaddeus's face.

"Why did you think she would be here?" the German asked.

"Where else would she be?" said Thaddeus. "Once Yannick had shown her the poster for the Jamboree . . ."

At the magician's name, Dorfmann looked surprised. Then his expression hardened. "Yannick? What do you know of him?"

"He met up with Rémy in London. They came back to France together. You know him?"

Dorfmann stared into the fire, nodding. "That one. He is bad news." The German looked back at Thaddeus with narrowed eyes. "But I think you know that already, ya?"

Thaddeus swallowed, his mouth suddenly dry. "I have my suspicions, yes. What can you tell me about him?"

Dorfmann shrugged. "Up until two weeks ago, I was still with The Circus of Secrets. Until a month ago, Yannick was there, also."

Thaddeus blinked. "What do you mean, Yannick was there?"

"I mean exactly what I say, Englishman. When we

got back to France, some of the acts decided to move on. They were not sure Claudette had it in her to create a new circus from the ashes of the old. We needed new talent. Yannick turned up as we moved toward Paris. He was peddling his worth as a magician, and so Claudette took him on."

"What happened?" J asked.

"Nothing, at first." Dorfmann shrugged. "We went on. We were doing well. Yannick's act was popular. Then one night, I heard an argument. It was between he and Claudette, though do not ask me what it was about, as I do not know. Yannick stayed for a few weeks after that, but Claudette would hardly speak to him. Then he left, and Claudette lost her mind."

"Lost her mind?" Thaddeus repeated. "What do you mean?"

Dorfmann sighed. "We were supposed to be building a new circus, ya? A better one than under Gustave — bigger, stronger. Up until then we were doing well, but to be a big circus you must play the big towns, where there is money, ya? Claudette did the opposite. She avoided the cities and then even the towns. She moved us on to village after village, farther and farther away from where they can afford luxuries like a night at the circus. Then she announced that we would not be going to the Jamboree, which was insanity itself. Instead, she said, we would go south — so far south that we would leave France. She intended to head for the mountains and beyond that — Spain."

"And you think that had something to do with the argument with Yannick?" Thaddeus asked, searching for a clue as to what had happened.

Dorfmann nodded. "I think so, though I have no proof, and I don't know what. Anyway — with regret, I told her I could not stay in The Circus of Secrets, and I left. If money had been no object, I would have stayed, but I could not. So I came back to Paris in time for the Jamboree, to find new work," he said. "Claudette is a good woman, a smart woman. But the summer will not last forever, and the mountains are no place to be when the snows come. Still, if you want my opinion, if you are to find Rémy Brunel, you must find Claudette. Those two are like sisters."

Thaddeus nodded, thinking hard. "Tell me, Dorfmann," he said, "have you ever seen Yannick hypnotize someone to do something against his will?"

The big man laughed, but without mirth. "Of course," he said. "It is the best part of his act. It is also how he takes whatever he wants. Something else I think you know already, ya?"

"Yes," said Thaddeus. "Yes, I do. And this is the man Rémy is alone with."

Dorfmann stood, and then, to Thaddeus's surprise, laid one huge hand on the policeman's shoulder. "Do not worry yourself too much, my friend," he rumbled. "I have never known Little Bird to do anything she did not want to do. A will like that cannot be broken by that of a mewling whelp like Yannick, and God help him when she becomes wise to whatever plan he has. But I do worry for Claudette. She has a darkness following her, with Yannick at its head."

* * *

It was late when Thaddeus and J got back to the airship. The crowds of circus folk had returned to their homes. Constanto's two hulking men nodded at them and then melted away into the night. J paused, looking after them with a wistful look on his face.

"Wish we 'ad the cash to hire those two," he said. "I didn't like what that chap Dorfmann had to say in the slightest, I can tell you. Oh, well. Looks like it's just me and thee." J stumped up the gangplank and into the airship. "Still, we done all right for ourselves before, ain't we? I'm sure we can again."

Inside, they found the ship almost as they'd left it,

save for a cloth bag placed on the control desk. It was full of centimes — their take from the evening.

"Not bad," said J, yawning. "That'll keep us in bread and drippin' for a while, at any rate." He paused with a frown. "Er — do they 'ave drippin' in France?"

Chapter 23

MORE QUESTIONS

$\mathcal{R}$émy woke to birdsong and the dapple of warm sunlight on her face. She sat up and looked around. The horses she and Yannick had stolen were grazing quietly where they had been tethered the night before. A blackbird cocked its head and regarded her from atop a fallen tree, but apart from that she was alone. The old woman, her caravan, and Yannick were gone.

Rémy jumped to her feet. The blanket she'd covered herself in the night before fell around her feet, and with it something heavier. It clunked to the ground and lay still.

It was a cube, golden-cultured and covered in intricate patterns, whorls, and connected circles that swirled across its surface like waves on a turbulent sea. Rémy sat cross-legged on the blanket, turning the cube over and over in her hands. It was small enough to fit into her palm, and it wasn't heavy, though it felt solid. Then she looked closer and saw a series of tiny hinges cleverly hidden among the patterns.

Something else caught her eye, too, discarded among the blanket's folds. It was a scrap of paper, folded roughly. Rémy opened it. A note was scrawled on it in untidy writing.

Show this only to the one you trust the most. Solve the puzzle. Find the truth.

Rémy stared at the words for a moment. Who had written them? Who had left her the box? Surely it must have been the old woman? She stood and looked at the patch of grass where the caravan had stood the night before, but already it seemed to be springing back into place. Even the cooking fire seemed to have sunk into the soft earth. Had the woman really been there at all, or had it all been a dream?

She got to her feet, picking up her pack and hiding the cube deep within it before looking around again. Yannick couldn't be far away — after all, his horse was still there and he wouldn't get far on foot. Rémy looked for an obvious way out of the small clearing and found a faint track. She was fairly sure that it wasn't the one they had used the night before, though it still didn't look wide enough for the caravan to have passed that way. She shouldered her pack and followed it into the forest, glancing behind her. It wouldn't do to get lost out here alone.

Rémy listened out for the sound of running water, thinking that Yannick had perhaps decided to bathe. The forest, though, was quiet apart from the rustle of wind in the leaves above her head and the occasional creak from one of the trees.

Rémy was just beginning to think that it might be best to go back to the clearing and work out a course of action there when she heard voices. She stopped, trying to place where they were coming from, and then realized that actually, there was only one voice. It was low and speaking in short bursts, though the wind made it impossible to hear what the speaker was saying. Rémy followed the sound, stepping as quietly as possible. She wove her way through the trees until, abruptly, they ended. Beyond the tree line was a road, as dusty and pebbled as the one they had been chased from by bandits the day before.

Yannick was crouching in the dust, his back to her. He'd changed out of his stage gear and back into his day clothes.

"Yannick?" Rémy asked.

He stood up quickly, turning to look at her. "Aha!" the magician said with a quick smile. "I was going to come and wake you. Look — we've found the road again!" He was trying to conceal something on the ground behind him, but it was too late — Rémy had already seen it.

"What's that?" she asked, walking around him to see the object more clearly. For a moment she thought he had been left a puzzle box, too. But it wasn't a box — or at least, not of the sort that Rémy had found in her blanket.

"Oh, it's nothing . . ." Yannick said with a shrug, as they both looked down at the small device.

Rémy bent down and picked it up. It was made of silver-gray metal — an oblong with a rotating cylinder set inside it and wand-like antennae sticking out of it. She looked at Yannick with a frown. "I've seen this — or something like it — before," she said. "It's one of the Professor's communication devices."

"Oh, is that what it is!" Yannick laughed, though to Rémy it sounded forced.

"Did you take this from the workshop?"

Yannick made a face. "Rémy . . ."

"You stole it?"

"I'm sorry," he said. "But there were so many things there — so many fascinating things. I couldn't resist. I didn't think you'd ever notice. And it's not as if it's worth anything, is it? It's just a pile of junk, like the rest of the things in that place."

"Who were you talking to, just now?" Rémy asked, still frowning.

Yannick looked confused. "Talking to? What do you mean?"

"I heard you, Yannick. You were using this to send a message."

The magician held up his hands. "Rémy, I didn't even know what it was for until you told me just now."

Rémy set her jaw and stared at him. "Don't lie to me, Yannick."

"I'm not! I swear! Come on — as if this little thing could be anything other than a useless pile of junk anyway! Now, that really would be magic." He laughed again, and then said, "Look, it's going to make me sound stupid, but what you heard was just me talking to myself. It's a habit — I don't even realize I'm doing it. When I concentrate, I end up muttering things, telling myself what to do. That's all. That's what you heard, not me trying to send a message. Who would I be sending it to, anyway?"

Rémy stared at him for another moment before opening her pack and putting the Professor's device inside. "I can't believe you stole from me," she said. "I thought you'd said you'd never do that?"

Yannick sighed impatiently. "I didn't steal from you. I stole from the Professor. Who I thought was dead, anyway. He's not going to miss it, is he?"

Rémy slung her pack over her shoulder and looked at him seriously. "Look, Yannick. I don't think it's a good idea for us to carry on together. I'm grateful for what you did, breaking me out of that prison. But I don't think you're a good fit for The Circus of Secrets. Claudette wants it to be within the law. I know she does — she told me so. And you . . . I don't think you can help yourself, Yannick. You see an opportunity to steal, and you don't think anything of taking advantage of that opportunity. You always find a way of justifying what you've done. I don't think you even see it as wrong. And that's just not what Claudette wants. So I think it'd be best if we part ways, here and now. *D'accord?*"

Yannick looked away for a minute, staring down the

road and at the dusty horizon beyond. Then he looked at her and shrugged. The magician lifted one hand to rub it through his hair and opened his mouth as if he was about to say something, but then felt better of it.

Rémy felt a buzzing in her ears. She shook her head to clear it. Everything suddenly seemed a little distant. She felt tired — her sleep obviously hadn't been as sound as she'd first thought.

"Come on," she said with a sigh. "Let's get the horses and go. We'll never catch up with Claudette and the circus at this rate."

{Chapter 24}

SOUTHWARD

$\mathcal{T}$haddeus slept little, disturbed by more than just the snatches of music and raucous laughter that drifted on the shifting breeze. In the morning, he took one of the Professor's devices from the row of pigeon roosts, closing the door of the hutch so the bird with the corresponding stone on its collar would not immediately follow its signal. Then he went to find Dorfmann again.

The overgrown camp was all a-bustle with the business of morning, full of laughter and chatter as the circus folk prepared for another day of performance. Thaddeus tried to imagine what it would be like to have such a life — to be always moving on, always thinking ahead. He concluded that it was probably something you could not imagine unless you had lived it yourself. That was why circus folk always stuck together — only another circus performer could truly understand the nature of this life. Thaddeus stopped for a moment, thinking about Rémy. She'd abandoned all that when she chose to stay in London. At the time he'd not given it much thought. But somehow he had just assumed that it would be better than a life on the road. Now, he realized that perhaps that was not the case. He felt guilty. Had he taken her decision to stay in London for granted? Maybe he had, he realized now.

Sighing, he raised his head. Thaddeus's eye was caught by a poster nailed to a fence post. It was so colorful that no one could miss it, the paper having been stained yellow, and printed with bright blue lettering.

REWARD

BY ORDER OF COMTE CANTAL DE SAINT-CERNIN

FOR THE SAFE RETURN OF THE "LOST COMTESSE" ARIETTE DE CANTAL.

BRING THE COMTESSE HOME!

Thaddeus moved closer, frowning as a sudden chill washed over him at the sight of the Comte de Cantal's name. He pulled the poster from its nail and read it over again as he continued on his way.

Dorfmann looked as if he'd been up for hours. He was tying down the guide rope of a new tent that had miraculously appeared, like a mushroom, since the night before. He nodded at the policeman as he approached. "I've got something for you," Thaddeus said, holding out the homing device.

"What is this?" asked the German, as he turned it over in his giant palm, the green stone glinting in the morning sun.

"Where we're going, we may need all the friends we can get," Thaddeus said. "At the moment, in this place, that's you. If I ever have to send you a message, this is how it'll reach you. Don't lose it."

Dorfmann nodded. "I'll help if I can, Englishman."

Thaddeus held up the poster. "What can you tell me about this?"

The German shrugged. "What do you want to know? The missing girl, it is an old wives' tale, made to scare misbehaving children. The Comte . . ." Dorffman made a hawking sound in his throat, as if he was about to spit. "Whoever she is, real or not, she'd do best to stay away from him."

Thaddeus nodded. "I agree."

Dorfmann raised an eyebrow. "You know of the Comte?"

"Our paths have crossed. Back in London. And —" He hesitated. "And I think Yannick is working for him. Thieving. We think that's why Yannick's with Rémy — they're going to use her to steal something really big sometime in the next few weeks."

Dorfmann frowned. "What is it they will take?"

Thaddeus shrugged, a little helplessly. "We don't know. That's why we want to find her — before they can force her back into her old life."

The German watched Thaddeus silently for a moment, and then nodded. "So the Comte de Cantal needs money, ya? That explains the search." He waved a finger at the poster.

"Oh? Why?"

"The story goes that the old Comte and his Comtesse settled everything on their missing daughter," Dorfmann explained. "All their money is still sitting in a vault somewhere. It has been for decades. It will not be released to any descendant, until she turns up and claims it, or unless someone can prove without doubt that she's dead."

Another chill passed through Thaddeus as he looked again at the poster. "So the Comte . . ."

Dorfmann gave a short laugh. "I would say that this search is more about proving she's dead than finding her alive, eh? Then he can inherit."

"What happens if he finds her alive?" Thaddeus asked.

"Then she will inherit, and he will get nothing." The German shrugged. "What fools these rich folk are, eh, Englishman? What a tangle they do make of their lives. For me, I am always happier poor. And now, I must get on with my work, or I will be too poor even for me."

"Sorry — yes," said Thaddeus. "Thank you, Dorfmann."

The German nodded, patting the pocket he had slipped the homing device into. "Get me a message, Rec, and I will come if I can."

Back at the airship, J was up and about, readying her for takeoff. Thaddeus could already hear the faint hiss as the ruby, recharged from a night of rest, did its job.

"Wondered where you'd got to," the boy said as Thaddeus came aboard. "Didn't stop to get breakfast, did you, by any chance? No? Never mind, I'll pop out myself and grab some of those curly bread things the Frenchies are so partial to."

"Croissants, J," said Thaddeus absently, still thinking about the poster. "They're pastry, not bread."

"Whatever they is, I like 'em," said J. "A nice bit of bacon and eggs would be better, but they'll do . . . 'Ere," he said, concerned. "What's up?"

Thaddeus sat down on one of the bunks, holding out the poster to J, who took it.

"What's this all about?" the boy asked. "I mean, I know this involves the Comte, and whatnot, but what has this got to do with us?"

"J," Thaddeus said, after he'd briefly explained what Dorfmann had told him. "What if we're wrong about why Cantal wants Rémy?"

The boy blinked. "You ain't saying you fink Rémy's this Lost Comtesse, are yer? She's too young, ain't she?"

Thaddeus shook his head. "It can't be Rémy. We know the story of her parents, and Desai knew it too, so that's not in dispute. But what about Rémy's friend? What about Claudette? Think about it, J — Dorfmann said she and Yannick quarreled, and then after that, she started avoiding the cities and going south, almost as if she was running from something. And we know that the other thing the German said was true — that they're like sisters."

"Rémy ain't had a letter from 'er for weeks," J said. "They was s'posed to write each other all the time, but Rémy's been worried lately cos she ain't 'ad one."

"And then Yannick turns up," said Thaddeus, "out of the blue, just like that, and persuades Rémy to go back to France. None of them are here. What if Yannick's using Rémy to find Claudette?"

They were both silent for a moment, thinking it all through.

"Why would she not want to be found?" J asked. "If she was this missing girl, like, and she could prove it, why wouldn't she want to do that? She'd be in for a shed load of money, wouldn't she?"

"Yes. I don't know the answer to that," said Thaddeus.

J sighed. "It don't change nuffin' for us right now, do it?" he said. "I mean, we still got to find Rémy. Maybe now it's for a different reason, but either way . . ."

Thaddeus nodded. "Exactly."

"Well, then," J said grimly. "Better get on wiv it then, 'adn't we?"

Another crowd gathered to watch the airship take off, drawn by the hissing of the ruby's gas as the balloon billowed and swelled skyward. There was a great cheer as they lifted away. J waved through the window at the enchanted spectators, who slowly shrunk to the size of ants as the airship rose higher and higher.

"Come on, old girl," J muttered, wrestling slightly with the controls.

"What's the matter?"

J shook his head with a slight frown. "Prolly nothin'. Just seems to be something off, that's all. Feels like she's listing a bit — like she's trailing something under her. You didn't see nothin' caught, did yer? None of that circus bunting, or a bit o' tent?"

Thaddeus shook his head. "Nothing. We're probably just getting used to how she moves, J."

J nodded. "Right enough. She seems to be all right, anyway. It should even out once we're up. So then, where'd Dorfmann say we needed to head?"

Thaddeus spread out the map Constanto had given them and found the name of the town on the map. "Périgueux. That's where the circus was when Dorfmann left it. The circus will have moved on by now, but it's a start."

"And that's south of here, that's what he said, right?" said J. "The Professor's dial ain't no good for anything but big cities, so we'll have to navigate our way there ourselves."

"Not to worry, J," said Thaddeus. "I'm sure we'll be fine. I've read a map before."

The ship tipped as J turned her into the prevailing wind, moving in a graceful curve over the city to bring her around. There was a clunk and the sound of something rolling, briefly, bouncing across wood. Thaddeus and J both jerked around to look, but there was nothing in the cabin.

"What the bleedin' 'eck was that?" J asked.

"I don't know." Thaddeus went to the other end of the ship, searching for any sign of something coming loose, but there was nothing. "I can't see anything."

"It were under the floor, in the ruby chamber," J said. "Better take a look. If we've got a problem, we'll need to put down quick-sharp."

Thaddeus went to the hatch and pulled it up. There was nothing wrong with the ruby assembly — it sat peacefully in its coupling, glowing slightly from the exertion of filling the balloon. Everything else seemed to be in its rightful place, too. He leaned in farther, peering into the gloom of the small space beyond. Was there something there, at the back? He couldn't make it out.

"Well?" J called over his shoulder. "See anything?"

"I don't know," Thaddeus said, straightening up and

feeling the blood rush from his head in a whoosh. He blinked. "It's too dark, J."

"Hang on," J said, a determined look on his face. "Give me two ticks, then take another look."

The boy began to bank the ship again, hauling her around in a tight circle that forced Thaddeus to grip the edge of the hatch to stop himself sliding the length of the cabin. From below, there was another clunk. He ducked his head into the hole again as J continued to turn the ship as sharply as he could. Through the darkness, Thaddeus saw something move, thrown to the other side of the airship's hold as J pulled her in the opposite direction.

"There's definitely something there!"

"Can you see what?"

Thaddeus straightened again. "Not a chance. It's just too dark. And I can't fit down there."

"Any idea where it's come loose from?" J asked, "I can't think of nothin' that could break down there. It should be empty 'cept for the ruby and its fittings. 'Ere — you take the controls, I'll have a look."

Thaddeus swapped places with him and watched as the boy stuck his head into the hole. He wriggled down so far that he disappeared up to his waist. Thaddeus half expected J to vanish completely, but after a moment, he gave a muffled yell and scrambled backward.

"'Ere," said J, pulling his head out of the hole and staring with outright indignation at Thaddeus. "You won't believe this!"

"What?"

"We've only got ourselves a bleedin' stowaway!"

"What?" Thaddeus exclaimed, but the boy had already scrambled back under the floorboards, this time disappearing completely.

"Oy!" J shouted, as angry as Thaddeus had ever heard him. "You! Come 'ere! Think you can make this ship your own, do yer? Well you've got another fing coming, and no mistake!"

There came the sounds of a scuffle. The ship juddered slightly.

"J," Thaddeus shouted, trying to hold the airship steady. "Take it easy, would you? Whoever's down there, we're all in the same boat — literally!"

There came a faint, muffled scream from below as J ignored him.

"Aha! Got you now, ain't I?" came J's triumphant yell. "Right — out you come, sunshine!"

Thaddeus looked over his shoulder as, with great effort and not a little yelling, J hauled a tangled bundle of rags out of the hatch. He dumped it on the floor.

"There," J said, still scuffling with the bundle. "Let's see what we've caught, shall we?"

The bundle threw out an arm, tossing away the ragged old blanket it had wrapped itself in.

There was a moment of silence.

"It's . . . it's a . . . girl!" J exclaimed in horror.

And so it was. Their stowaway was a thin child, not much older or younger than J himself. Her hair was a mass of tight, jet black curls. From beneath this mop, angry green eyes stared from a bronzed face. She jumped sharply to her feet, scolding J in broken English.

"Stupid *bengel*!" she shouted with a strongly German accent. "You ruin my blanket! You owe me."

"Like hell I do!" J retorted, to which the girl responded by stepping forward and slapping him smartly across the face. J's shocked mouth formed a perfect O as she stepped back.

"For language, *blasphemiker*," she announced stoutly.

"She — she —!" J spluttered, when he found his voice, holding one hand to his reddening cheek. "She hit me! God darn it, I'll —"

He took a step toward her.

"J," Thaddeus warned.

"Fine," said the boy. "Set the ship down, Thaddeus — let's get rid of her, right now." J stared angrily at the girl, who was standing with her chin jutting out in defiance and her arms crossed.

"We can't, J. How long did the ruby take to recharge last time — it was all night, wasn't it? We can't waste another day waiting."

"Oh, well, nothing for it then," said J. "I'll just open the gangplank and chuck 'er out as we go."

The girl took a step back, wary and scared despite her defiance.

"J, we both know you're not going to do that. Let's just all calm down, shall we?" Thaddeus checked that they were heading in the right direction and stood up. "Come and sit down," he said to the girl. "Tell us who you are and why you did this."

J made an outraged grumbling sound in his throat, but Thaddeus held up his hand for quiet. The girl watched them both suspiciously.

"Please," said the policeman, indicating his bunk. "J, sit. We'll talk this out like civilized people. Understand?"

After another moment of complaint, J did as Thaddeus asked. They both sat side-by-side on J's bunk. Their stowaway looked around the cabin for a moment, as if deciding whether there was some way to escape. Having decided there wasn't, she walked slowly to the bunk opposite and sat down.

She was small, Thaddeus realized — smaller than J. When she sat on the bunk, her bare brown feet didn't reach the ground. She still held the torn blanket around her shoulders. Beneath it she was dressed in a tattered dress that may once have been black, but had faded to gray. It looked a little too small, even for her. The sleeves, which would once have been wrist-length, were now hovering around her elbows.

"Good," said Thaddeus. "Well, that's progress of sorts, I suppose. Hello. My name is Thaddeus Rec, and this is J. What's your name?"

The girl set her jaw, as if she was about to refuse to speak and then apparently changed her mind. She sighed and shrugged, still with her arms crossed. "Dita," she said. "I am Dita."

"Dita!" J mocked with a howl of laughter. "I never heard nothin' so daft in my life!"

"Oh, yes?" Dita spat back. "And what kind of name is 'J'? Nothing, ya? Because you came from nowhere and have nowhere to go. Yes?"

"Stop it, both of you," Thaddeus ordered, before

they could start another argument. "It looks as if we're stuck with each other for the time being, so at least try to be pleasant. Dita, why did you do this? Why did you stow away on this airship?"

Dita didn't answer for a moment, looking around her. Then she shrugged again. "I wanted to see. Then I wanted to fly." She paused. "It is *herrlich*. Magnificent."

"Yeah, it is," chipped in J. "And it's mine."

"Yours," Dita scoffed. "*Pfft*. How can it belong to a dirty boy?"

"I ain't dirty, I 'ad a bath last week," J retorted. "And the ship's mine cos I built 'er, that's why, and that's more than you could do, useless hellcat that you are!"

"J," Thaddeus said, "please!"

A look of surprise had settled on the girl's face. "You built this? The truth?"

"Yeah, truly," growled J, and then he added, "Well . . . bits of it."

Dita shrugged. "Okay for a smelly boy like you."

"Dita," Thaddeus said, before the fighting could begin again. "Where we're going, it's not —"

"I know. I heard you talk to Herr Dorfmann."

"You know him?"

She nodded. "He is good man. Kind to me, got me work at Circus Maximus." Dita wrinkled her nose at the thought. "Cleaning after the elephants. Not a good job, but —"

J hooted with derision, pointing at the girl and slapping his leg. "A dung sweeper! The girl's a dung sweeper, and she calls me smelly!"

Dita glowered. "Better than to starve, dirty boy. Not that you know what that means."

J stopped laughing and scowled. "I've been starving more often than you've had years of your life," he growled. "And proper starving too, like there's something eating your bones and —"

"Enough!" Thaddeus shouted, smacking his hand against the wooden bulkhead above him. "Stop squabbling, this minute, or I'll gag you both, do you understand?" J and Dita looked at him with faint reproach but nodded. "Right. J, you will refrain from speaking until Dita has finished her explanation. Dita, what was it about our conversation with Dorfmann that made up your mind?"

Dita bit her lip. "You are going south. I want to go south. My father was German but my mother, Spanish. Andalucia. I want to go to her village. My grandmother is there, and maybe other . . . *sippe*." The girl looked down at her feet, which were bare. "I want . . . *nach hause*. In English — home."

There was a brief silence. Thaddeus nodded. "I don't suppose the circus pays enough for you to travel there with money you have saved, eh?"

The girl shook her head, her ringlets flying. "And alone — it would be *riskant*. But this wonderful machine . . ." She shook her head. "Anyway, I can be useful to you. I can pay my way."

J let out a snort at this. "We ain't got an elephant, in case you 'adn't noticed."

Thaddeus sent him a warning glance. "Dita, what do you mean?"

"So far, you have luck," she said. "People in circuses speak languages. But down there?" Dita shook her head. "No one speak English. I speak it — you see?"

"I do. And do you speak French, too?"

"*Oui, tres bon.* And Deutsch. And Spanish. So — I can earn my keep. You have room. If you don't want me up here, I will sleep down there." She pointed at the hatch in the floor.

"Not likely," muttered J. "First chance you 'ave, you'll be off with that ruby and we'll be stranded in Frenchie land without a pot to p—"

"Then perhaps you should sleep there," suggested Dita, her eyes flashing, "so we do not have to smell you."

Thaddeus sighed as the pair began to yell at each other, and wondered whether there was something aboard he could make into earplugs.

{Chapter 25}

SWIFT PROGRESS

The ruby airship flew south all day, over landscape that bucked and sprawled between patchwork fields and the curlicues of towns and villages. Dita was fascinated by the chance to see the earth from the air. Leaning beside Thaddeus's elbow at the controls, she pushed herself up on tiptoe to see through the window to the land below. She pointed out towns she recognized — Angers, Saumur, and others — displaying a sense of direction that Thaddeus found remarkable. J merely huffed and sulked, constantly telling the girl not to touch this and that.

"There's Poietiers," Dita piped up. "We are in Vienne now. I think we reach the mountains by sundown."

"You can't possibly know that," J scoffed.

Dita looked at him. "In *ordnung*. We find out soon enough," she said, serenely.

The landscape grew rockier as they flew on, chunks of gray granite littering the ground as if a giant had been playing jacks and grown bored. J and Thaddeus took turns at the controls, guiding the airship ever south. As the day drew onward, a mountain range rose over the horizon to loom ahead of them. Dark rain clouds twisted around the peaks. They gathered with the dusk, turning the sky from blue into an indigo-blackened bruise, full of foreboding. With them came a strong wind that buffeted the airship. Below spread a forest that seemed to go on forever. It pooled around the feet of the mountains, blocking out the ground in an endless sea of deep green. Here and there between the thick branches, they glimpsed a road meandering slowly between the ancient trunks, but more often it was invisible beneath the weight of leaves.

"Look," said Dita at one point, leaning past J to stare down at the road. "What is that?"

J and Thaddeus leaned over, too. Through the trees came brief flashes — shafts of sunlight glinting on something beneath the leaves.

"It must be people on the road," said Thaddeus.

- THE RUBY AIRSHIP -

"Looks as if there many," Dita remarked, as the forest parted for a second, to reveal a column of uniformed men riding quickly along it on horseback. *"Sie sind soldaten.* They are soldiers," she said.

"Well, if they carry on in this direction, they're going to get wet," said J, nodding at the horizon. "I don't like the look of that." A slash of lightning burst like a white-hot whip crack over the trees and shortly afterward, a roll of thunder rumbled after it.

"I don't suppose flying through a thunderstorm will be very healthy for this rig?" Thaddeus asked.

"Not very healthy for any of us, truth be told," the boy said grimly, as he glanced at one of the dials and pulled the left rudder around. "The wind's bad enough, but if we get swiped by a lick o' lightning, we're done for."

Dita craned to see out of the window. "There is nowhere to land. Just trees. I cannot see the road, or where it leads."

J pointed ahead, to a pass between two of the largest mountains they'd seen so far. "We'll 'ave to try and make for that," he said. "The road must go above the tree line and over — stands to reason. Let's just 'ope it's wide enough for us to land and that we can reach it before the storm does."

They stayed silent as J skirted the high edge of the storm, staying just out of reach. None of them had ever seen a storm from above before, and Thaddeus watched, fascinated. It was like watching some kind of battle. The clouds roiled around each other, spitting out fury and bellowing at the ground. The airship shook, J's knuckles white on the controls as he fought against the winds pounding them. The ship dropped lower as the boy guided it toward the pass. The trees still hid the road, and for a while Thaddeus thought that J must have been mistaken — there was no pass, or at least no road that carts could cross over. But then, there it was, snaking out from beneath the forest canopy and up over the rocky incline.

"Yes!" J whooped in relief. "We're nearly there! Now, I think I can hold her just as long as that storm doesn't change direction . . . but hold on to your hats, ladies and gents, we're in for a . . ."

A huge *crack!* sounded from above. A flash of white light filled the portholes. The airship jerked and hummed. Something hot raced along the metal bands that held the ship together. There was a groaning sound as if the craft itself was screaming in pain. They began to pitch into a spin, sinking toward the ground as a hissing filled the air.

"We're hit!" J yelled, his arms juddering with the effort of pulling back on the controls.

The ground was rising toward them fast. Thaddeus looked up, seeing the hatch that led on to the roof. He wrenched at it, pulling it open to let the lashing rain cut across his face like icy knives. Through the open square above him, he could see the balloon, a ragged hole torn in its side.

"We're losing gas!" he shouted. "But we're not on fire!"

Thaddeus clambered on to one of the top bunks and then pushed himself out through the hatch. Outside, the storm had shifted, sucking the airship into its grip like a creature pulling food toward its maw. The dark clouds pressed down on them from above, spitting rain and fire. The wind raged, wild and angry, making it almost impossible to breathe. He stuck his head back inside, already out of breath.

"There's a tear in the balloon," he gasped, wiping icy water from his cold-stung face. "If we could reach it, we might be able to patch it. But I can't. I'll never be able to steady myself long enough."

"Do sumfin', Thaddeus," J said, his arms shaking as he tried to hold the rapidly sinking airship steady. "Do sumfin', or we're done for!"

"*Lassen sie mich*," said Dita. "I can do it."

"No," Thaddeus shook his head, "you'll fly off into the storm. There's nothing to hold on to, Dita."

"Then you hold on to me," the little girl ordered. "My legs, yes? Come on, quick, quick!"

"If she can do it, better let 'er," J said grimly. "Ground's not coming up any slower while we stand around and chat!"

In a second, Dita was beside Thaddeus on the bunk, and in another she had clambered through the hatch into the roaring maelstrom beyond.

"Legs," she shouted back to Thaddeus, her voice almost torn away by the storm. "Hold my legs!"

Thaddeus leaned out of the airship as far as he could, until his arms and shoulders were exposed to the fury of the sky. He grabbed the girl's ankles as she scrambled across the wet wood. Above her, he could see the balloon's hole, small but rapidly billowing gas through the flapping scraps of fabric torn by the strike. Dita reached for them, pulling the ragged edges toward her and winding them around in her hands to close the gap.

"Refill," she screamed over her shoulder. "The balloon — tell the *knabe* —"

Thaddeus understood her at once. "J," he shouted

over the howling wind, "can you deploy the ruby? Refill the balloon?"

"Ain't never done it in flight before," J yelled back. "I ain't sure it can be done!"

"Try it, J — now!"

The boy did as he was told, winding the ruby machine's handle as fast as he could. Thaddeus watched as Dita was buffeted by the storm. She was already soaked through, her old dress sticking to her. Her hair had fallen out of her headscarf and was plastered over her face, but she clutched the balloon valiantly, the girl's small hands seeming even tinier against the huge contraption. More lightning strikes lit up the raging sky around them, the thunder an incessant drum roll right above their heads.

Thaddeus heard the hiss as J refilled the balloon. He watched as it swelled away from Dita. She had to battle to keep her grip as it struggled to jerk away from her with every new puff of gas. Thaddeus held on to her, feeling his legs beginning to cramp. His hands were numb with cold. He couldn't see for rain, and several times he felt the hot crackle of electricity as the clouds continued to hurl spears of lightning. He felt Dita move, and blinked the rain from his eyes long enough to see that she had something in her mouth.

He realized in a flash that it was her headscarf. Dita struggled to wind it around and around the torn fabric that she still clutched in her hands, tying it off in a complicated knot. The balloon was full now, bobbing and struggling to get away from her. She let go.

Thaddeus held his breath, but the knot stayed fast. All it had to do was last until J could bring them into land.

Dita was scrambling backward when the airship gave a tremendous jerk. The little girl screamed as she was flung flat against the slippery wood, only Thaddeus's grip stopping her from sliding off the roof.

"Dita!" Thaddeus yelled over the storm. He tried to pull her toward him, but she was a dead weight. His hands were so frozen he could hardly feel them.

"What's happening?" J shouted.

"Just get us down, J!" Thaddeus bellowed. "I can't hold her . . ."

A moment later, the ship touched down with a jaw-crunching jolt. Thaddeus's icy hands gave up and he lost his grip on Dita. She disappeared from sight, slithering down the rough side of the airship.

J appeared in the hatch. "Thaddeus! Are you —"

Thaddeus jumped to his feet, feeling the rain sluice down his neck. "Dita fell," he yelled. "Get out there!"

J uttered a curse and vanished, Thaddeus struggling after him. He followed J out of the gangplank and into the pouring rain, both of them running for the huddled figure. Thaddeus dropped to his knees beside the girl, feeling for a pulse.

"She's alive," he told J with relief. "But I don't know how badly she's hurt."

"We gotta get 'er inside!" J shouted over the noise of the storm.

"I don't know if we should move her!"

"We can't leave 'er out 'ere!"

Thaddeus nodded, pushing his hair back again, feeling the icy water cascade down his neck and into his sodden shirt. He lifted the little girl up. She weighed almost nothing.

"Put 'er on my bunk," J said, when they got inside.

Dita groaned and opened her eyes as Thaddeus laid her down. "There you are," he said in relief as her green eyes blinked at him, pained but at least clear. "Where does it hurt?"

Dita was silent for a moment, a look of concentration on her pale face, as if she were working out the answer to Thaddeus's question.

"My . . . my arm," she said. "I think it's just my arm . . ."

Thaddeus rolled up her torn sleeve as gently as possible. Beneath was a nasty wound, open and bleeding. It gaped its ugliness at Thaddeus, who took a deep breath and forced a smile.

"I'm sure we can sort that out in no time."

Dita smiled faintly, and then fixed her gaze on the ceiling. Thaddeus could see she was biting her lip. Against the pain or to stop herself from crying, he couldn't tell, but either way the policeman was astounded by the little girl's silent bravery. He'd seen grown men wail over far less.

J had vanished to one of the wooden cupboards at the other end of the cabin as soon as Thaddeus had revealed Dita's injury, dragging out a tin box and scrabbling around inside. He returned a moment later with a needle, thread, and roll of bandage.

"It ain't much," he said in a hushed, apologetic voice, "but it's the best I can do. Be careful wiv the needle, too — we're going to need it to fix the balloon later."

Thaddeus nodded grimly, taking the offered items. "Have you got any alcohol, J?"

J looked shifty. "A quart of cheap whisky, but don't ask me where it came from."

"I don't care where it came from, bring it here."

"Really? Is now the right time for a tipple, Thaddeus? I mean, I know we're all in shock and all, but . . ." The boy nodded at Dita, pale and still and trembling.

"It's not for me," Thaddeus snapped. "It's to clean this needle. Hurry!"

J scurried away again, coming back with a small bottle of clear, amber-colored liquid. Thaddeus grabbed it from him and uncorked the bottle, splashing the contents over the needle and thread, as well as his hands. He heard J stifle a squeak as a good deal of the whisky ended up on the floor.

"Right, Dita," said Thaddeus, as the crack and roll of thunder went on overhead. "This is going to hurt, but it's got to be done. I'll be as quick as I can, all right?"

Dita nodded and then raised her arm across her mouth. It took Thaddeus a moment to realize that the girl had taken the thin fabric in her teeth and was biting down against the pain.

He splashed whisky across the girl's wound, hoping to clean the worst of it. She shuddered, squeezing her eyes shut. After that, the first stitch was the worst — pushing the needle through the skin and out the other side. Thaddeus felt sick, but as he'd told Dita, it had to be done — the wound was too bad to heal on its own.

"Bleedin' 'eck," J muttered, slumping to the floor, white as a sheet.

Thaddeus sewed quickly and as neatly as he could, pulling the torn skin together. Then he splashed his hands with more whisky to clean them a little and wrapped the girl's arm in a bandage. Dita had passed out toward the end. She lay still and quiet in J's bunk.

Once the wound was wrapped, J and Thaddeus stood looking down at her. "She's a braver soul than maybe I's gave her due for," J conceded. Thaddeus was inclined to agree.

Exhausted and drained, they just managed to stay awake long enough for J to stow the balloon's remaining gas in the storage canisters. Then they collapsed into two of the remaining bunks, sleeping despite the storm raging on above their heads.

{Chapter 26}

REGRETS

$\mathcal{T}$he storm had raged all night, the cold rain pelting Rémy and Yannick hard until they eventually decided to find shelter under the trees. They turned off the road and secured the horses under the leafiest branches they could find before huddling, wet, bedraggled, and hungry, inside the tattered remnants of a dead oak tree.

Yannick managed to doze, but Rémy could not. A nameless worry nagged at her, a notion that something here wasn't quite right. But every time she almost caught it, the thought was engulfed by a buzzing that seemed to come and go inside her head. Rémy wondered whether it was caused by the storm, which seemed to be powered by the fury of heaven itself. She toyed with the idea of getting out the golden cube again but resisted the urge. Rémy was still unsettled by the loss of her opal and the discovery that Yannick had stolen something — however insignificant — from the Professor's workshop. *Show it only to the one you trust most*, the old woman's note had said — and that definitely wasn't Yannick. Not anymore.

She wished Thaddeus were there to talk to about everything else she had learned in the past twenty-four hours. That she had met someone who had known her mother, and her father, too. That perhaps she had a brother. That she had lost her beloved opal. Now that it was gone forever, Rémy kept touching her throat where it used to lie and wondering what had seemed so important that she would take it off. Why had she never explained to Thaddeus and J what it could do, or even Claudette and Amélie, before they had left? If Thaddeus had known, if they could have been more open with each other, none of this would have happened.

Rémy shut her tired eyes, willing herself not to cry. All of this was her own doing, and she had no right to feel sorry for herself. She knew the real reason she had kept the opal's powers secret. Because telling Thaddeus the truth would have meant confronting what he had said in Abernathy's underground chamber. Now, Rémy couldn't even work out why that would have been a bad thing. What could he possibly have told her that would have made things worse between them than the way they were now? Had she been afraid that he'd say he didn't love her after all? No, that wasn't it. The truth was precisely the opposite. She'd been afraid that he did love her — she knew it, in fact. Rémy knew that he loved her, and knowing that scared her more than anything else in her life.

Yannick's scornful words rang in her head again. *What did you think you were going to do? Wed him? Become a respectable little London housewife?*

The answer was, in fact, no. No, that wasn't what Rémy thought she was going to do. But she was afraid it was what Thaddeus was expecting. And the circus girl knew, hopelessly and with absolute certainty, that she couldn't do that, she couldn't be that. It wasn't her, and it never would be. So she'd avoided any chance of him ever bringing it up, because that was better than losing him completely.

She'd done that anyway in the end, of course, thanks to her stubborn pride. Rémy had told herself her anger back in London was justified because

Thaddeus had chosen the easy route and shifted the blame for the burglaries onto her trusty old friend Yannick. And how dare Thaddeus imagine he knew this friend of her childhood better than she did? How dare he assume that because Yannick was of the circus, he must automatically be a crook?

What a rank fool you are, Rémy Brunel, she thought now, hugging herself and staring out into the rain. *Since when has Thaddeus assumed anything? Did you stop to ask him his proof? No. Would you have listened even if he had told you? Probably not. Your pride has always been your downfall, and so it proves to be again. And now here you are with a thief, just because you were too much of a coward to face up to the truth. Worse, you'll never see Thaddeus again, and he'll think you were a part of it after all.*

Still, there was nothing she could do about any of that now. The best thing to do was to put London behind her, find Claudette, and get back into the circus life. Things could be worse, after all. At least she knew a warm welcome would be waiting for her once they finally caught up with Le Cirque des Secrets.

With that in mind, the sun was barely up when Rémy nudged Yannick awake. The storm had finally burnt itself out, and the landscape was peaceful once again.

"Come on," she said. "Let's get back on the road. We've still got so far to go before we catch up. They must be at least two more towns ahead now."

Yannick rubbed the sleep from his eyes and then looked at her carefully.

"What?" Rémy asked, suspicious.

"Do you feel all right?" the magician asked.

"What, other than being soaked through and very hungry?" Rémy asked. "I'm fine, why?"

Yannick grinned, jumping to his feet. "Nothing. Just wondered. Come on, then — let's go."

Rémy looked after him with a frown, almost remembering something. It faded amid another bout of buzzing.

{Chapter 27}

REPAIRS

$\mathcal{T}$haddeus woke to the delicious smell of coffee and to sun streaming through the portholes. Two of the pigeons were pecking about the floor, looking for breakfast, the third was cooing softly from its hutch. He blinked sleep away as he turned over to look up at the curved ceiling, when suddenly the events of the previous night came flooding back. Sitting up, Thaddeus looked at the opposite bunk. Dita was still there and seemed to be asleep. Her skin was paler than usual, but her cheeks were rosy. He got up and laid a hand on her forehead, relieved to feel no signs of a fever. The little girl stirred and mumbled, but did not wake.

From outside came brisk whistling and the clatter of tin pots. Thaddeus ducked his head out of the open gangplank to see J fussing over a cooking fire, smoke rising steadily into the blue sky.

"Morning," Thaddeus said, stepping out. "Storm's passed on then?"

J looked up at him with a cheery grin. "Mornin'. Aye, looks like the weather's turned. Ain't it pretty out 'ere?"

Thaddeus had to agree. They had landed at the apex of a rough road that passed between two mountains. The thick forest that had forced them to fly on dwindled into scrub, and beyond the pass, the road wound slowly down to the base of a fertile, green valley.

"I 'ad a bit of a look-see earlier," said J, as he lined up three tin mugs and began to pour thickly-brewed coffee into them. "I fink there's a village on the other side of the valley. What a place to live, eh?"

Thaddeus turned as the boy offered him a steaming mug. "You're strangely happy after what happened last night."

"Ah, well," said J, "the little miss looks like she's going to be fine so, all fings considered, it could 'ave been worse. That's why I made the coffee — thought she could do with a nice way to wake up."

The policeman raised his eyebrows. "I actually meant the airship. The damage, from the storm? It wasn't just the balloon, you know — the wood up there's badly gouged, too."

"Oh," said J awkwardly. A faint blush tinted his cheeks and he turned away to pick up the last two mugs. "Well, fing is, it ain't like it's not fixable, or nuffin'. So like I says, all fings considered . . ." He trailed off, looking down at the two mugs he held. "Er . . . I'll be back in a tick."

Thaddeus smiled to himself as J disappeared into the airship, though his heart ached a little. J's abashed look reminded him of himself, and that made him think once more of Rémy. He sipped his coffee — which wasn't at all bad — and gazed down into the valley beyond the pass, wondering where she was at that moment. He still didn't really know what he and J were doing there, or what he was expected to do when — if — he found her. The further they got into their journey, the more Thaddeus felt he was on a fool's errand. If it hadn't been for his worries about the Comte and for Dorfmann's concerns over Claudette, Thaddeus would probably have told J they needed to give up now. He thought it very likely that Rémy would simply laugh in his face when she saw him here, in any case. What did he have to offer her back in London, compared to the freedom of this landscape he saw around him — compared to the country she called home?

"Little miss is awake!" J's voice shattered Thaddeus's melancholy thoughts. "She ain't getting up yet, but she seems hunky-dory. Apart from the old arm, o' course."

Thaddeus headed back to the fire. "I'll change her dressing in a little while, once we've all finished our coffee." Shielding his eyes, Thaddeus looked up at the pierced balloon, flopping over the side of the airship like an old sock. "Tell me how we can fix the airship."

J dropped to sit cross-legged on a smooth boulder. "I've got spare scraps of oil skin and more needles like the one you used on poor Dita last night. Won't be easy, but we can patch the hole. It'll take a while, though. Trust me — stitching old animal hide together ain't a job for the lazy!"

Thaddeus looked back toward the mountain pass. "I'm not too happy about being stranded here."

"Ah well," said J, "I'm afraid there's nuffin' I can do about that. We'll just have to be as quick as we can."

Thaddeus nodded, swallowing the last of his coffee in one gulp. "We'd best get on then. Let's take a look at Dita first, though."

The little girl appeared before he could reach the gangplank. She'd tied her shawl in half around her neck to make a sling for her injured arm.

"Dita," said Thaddeus, "I should take a look at that arm again, change the dressings."

The girl smiled and walked down the gangplank with a nod of her dark curls. "No need. J has changed bandage already."

Thaddeus raised his eyebrows and looked at the boy, who was staring at his feet with reddening cheeks. "Has he, indeed? Well, I'm glad he's being so attentive. How are you feeling otherwise?"

"I've had worse," Dita shrugged. "Thank you for the . . ." She paused, not sure of the word, and indicated stitching with her one good hand.

Thaddeus smiled. "You're welcome."

"Come on, you two!" J called impatiently. "Stop nattering. We've got things to do, ain't we?"

Dita blew a strand of hair out of her eyes with a puff of her cheeks. "Ah yes," she said with a cheeky grin. "And you boys must do all the work, no?"

{Chapter 28}

THE HOMECOMING

$\mathcal{B}$y lunchtime, Rémy and Yannick had made their way up and out of the lush valley that the magician had insisted was a shortcut. Beyond the narrow pass, the road wound down into another stretch of forest, this time punctuated not only by the road but also by a fast-flowing river. Not far in the distance, more great mountains reached their stony forms up to threaten the sky, clouds bumping against their height. Rémy urged her horse back into motion, and they trotted down the road, the magician following behind.

They hadn't gone far before a faint flash caught Rémy's attention. At first she thought it was merely the sun glinting off a menhir in the forest, but then she saw it again and stopped. It came again, a bright gleam that swelled into existence one moment and was gone the next. Rémy squinted, but couldn't make out what was causing the flash. It was definitely something in the trees, reflecting the sun's rays.

"There's something up ahead, just off the road, by the look of it," Yannick observed, coming to a stop beside her as his horse puffed and stamped.

"Yes, but what?" Rémy muttered. "And how far away is that?"

Yannick shrugged. "A good few hours' ride on these steeds, I'd say, perhaps more. We'll be fine as long as it isn't more of those bandits."

That was exactly what Rémy had been afraid of. Because it looked to her as if something was camped in the forest not far from the road, and who else would pitch camp in such a remote place if not bandits? There was no town as far as the eye could see. It seemed as if the forest was deserted, and who would choose to make their home here, even a temporary one, unless they were hiding from something? She glanced down at her ride. The animal was already showing signs of tiredness after the long climb out of the valley, and she knew that if they were attacked, they'd never escape — not on horseback, at least.

"Come on," Rémy decided eventually, resigned. "There's no other way back except the way we came, so we have to carry on. We'll have to be ready to try and lose them in the trees, that's all."

They'd been riding for an hour when Rémy began to think that what they were seeing was something very different. They were close enough to see flashes of color through the leaves — reds and yellows, bright blues and pinks. If these were bandits, they were ones who were fond of standing out. Rémy's suspicions were further aroused when she spied a large gray mass meandering among the trees. She wasn't sure at first, thinking that perhaps it was just the shadows playing tricks with her eyes, but then she saw it again and knew exactly what it was.

"It's not a bandit camp! It's a circus — our circus!" Rémy cried. "That's Constance the elephant! But what are they doing here? There can't be anyone nearby to come to a performance. Why aren't they in a town?"

Yannick didn't answer as they spurred their tired horses on down the slope. The nearer they got, the clearer the circus became. There was old Anita's cara-van, painted with all the flowers of her home valley in Andalucia, there was the lion's cage, with the two big cats lying sleepily in the leaf-dappled sunshine. There was, of course, no sign of Gustave's old home, but Rémy searched for and saw Claudette and Amélie's caravan, nestled in the shade of a large oak tree. Relief flooded through her. At least they were here. At least they were safe.

She frowned, though, as they drew closer still. Something definitely wasn't right. The Big Top was nowhere to be seen. All the colors she had spied were of folded tents, still stowed on their carts. By the sun it was well after midday, but there was no sign of the kind of activity that should usually take place on a performance day, and if the tent wasn't up now, there was no way they'd get it up in time for that evening. And yet the circus must have been pitched here for at least a day, perhaps two — otherwise they wouldn't have caught up with it so quickly.

"Something's wrong," she muttered, more to herself than Yannick. "What are they doing here?"

They drew close enough that they were spotted. A shout went up as one of the folk milling about the caravans recognized Rémy. It was the chief clown, Augustus, though he wasn't in costume and there was no trace of his usual absurd makeup. Rémy waved back, happy to see a familiar face, and soon a crowd had gathered by the road as she and Yannick approached.

"Little Bird!" exclaimed Augustus, clasping her in a bear hug as she dismounted. "We thought never to see you again! Grew bored of London town, did you?"

Rémy grinned as she pulled away. "Just thought I'd better check on you all, Augustus. I know you can't do without me!"

Augustus chuckled, but Rémy could see anxiety beneath his jolly features. His eyes flicked to Yannick, but instead of offering a greeting, he merely nodded a curt welcome.

"Augustus —" Rémy began, but she was interrupted as something small and scruffy fastened itself to her leg.

"Little Bird, Little Bird!" It was Rolf, one of the small boys charged with looking after the circus's various animals.

"Rolf!" Rémy hugged the energetic bundle. "And how are you? How is Constance? Is she behaving, or is she still as grumpy as ever?"

"Still grumpy," said the boy, letting her go. "She'll be pleased to see you, though, you're one of her favorites. And so will Dominique! She's missed you — doesn't like anyone else to ride her."

"Dominique!" Rémy thought of her pony, who had served her so well over the years. "I have missed her too, Rolf, so much. I will visit soon. But first," she said, looking up at Augustus, "where is Claudette? And what are you all doing here? Why aren't you at the Jamboree, or somewhere further north — or at least in a village?"

A hush fell over the bubbling crowd. "Best ask Claudette that yourself, Rémy," Augustus said quietly, his gaze flickering once more toward the still-silent Yannick. "These have been strange days for us all, believe me."

A new murmur rippled through the crowd. It parted as Claudette appeared, as beautiful as ever, her long chestnut hair loose and drifting in the valley breeze. She held little Amélie by the hand.

"Claudette! Amélie!" Rémy pulled Claudette into a hug. "I've missed you both so much!"

Rémy pulled away, confused when Claudette did not hug her back. She was looking over Rémy's head at Yannick, who, in turn, was studiously looking elsewhere.

"Claudette?" Rémy asked, "What is it? Aren't you glad to see me?"

Amélie stepped forward and wrapped her little

arms around Rémy's waist. Because Rémy was not wearing her opal she could not tell what the child was thinking, but she was so grateful for the hug that she could have cried. Rémy hugged her back as Claudette finally looked at her. Her face was grave, and Rémy could see lines on her pale forehead where before there had been none.

"What are you doing here, Rémy?" she asked, her voice low and careful.

"What do you mean, what am I doing here? You didn't write for weeks. We'd promised to write, remember? I was worried something had happened to you. And I missed you — all of you. So I decided to come home. Aren't you pleased to see me, *mes ami*?"

Claudette looked at her from tired eyes, as if she could not really comprehend Rémy's question. "You led him to us. Why would you do such a thing?"

"What?" Rémy asked, looking back to the magician, still standing silently behind her. "Don't you remember Yannick? He was a boy with the circus, many years ago. I bumped into him in London — he needs work, Claudette. He's a good magician. And doesn't every circus need a good magician?"

"He has lied to you, Little Bird," said her friend, "if

he told you that was why he wanted to join you on the journey here."

"What do you mean?" Rémy asked, still more confused. "I don't understand, Claudette. What is happening here?"

Claudette looked into her face, as if trying to decide whether she was telling the truth or not. The realization shocked Rémy. Claudette was her best friend, but right now it seemed she did not trust or believe her. The thought made Rémy sick.

"Do you want to tell her, Yannick? Or shall I?" Claudette said roughly.

"Claudette," Yannick said, his voice placatory. "Listen, there is no need for this."

"Yannick was with Le Cirque de la Lune as a child, that is correct," interrupted Claudette, ignoring him. "But did he not tell you that he returned to us several months ago, as soon as Le Cirque des Secrets had set foot once more on French soil? He was waiting at the docks of Calais when we arrived, with a desperate story of hardship and saying that he needed a position."

"What?" Rémy asked, her head spinning. She turned to look at Yannick, who did not meet her eyes.

"He joined us then," Claudette went on, "and at

first we were glad to have him. As you say, Rémy, a circus can always use a good magician, and Yannick is certainly that."

"You never told me this," Rémy said to Yannick. "Why didn't you tell me you had been with the circus again?"

"Because he left us . . . abruptly," said Claudette. "I told him I never wanted to see him again. And now you have brought him straight to us, Rémy."

"Aren't you going to tell her why, Claudette?" Yannick's voice was angry, and Rémy looked over to see that he was standing with his arms crossed defiantly. "Why don't you tell her, hmm? What my great crime was. Go on — see if she can understand it. She accuses me of lying to you, Rémy — you're supposed to be her closest friend. So why don't you ask the great Claudette Anjou who she really is?"

{Chapter 29}

TERROR IN
THE FOREST

$\mathcal{C}$laudette's face darkened further, fury alight in every clenched muscle of her face. There were a few moments of silence. Rémy stared at her friend, and suddenly it was like looking at a stranger.

"Very well," Claudette said at last, her voice calm and very quiet. "My real name is not Claudette. My real name is Arriete, Comtesse Cantal de Saint-Cernin. I am what the children's tale calls 'the Lost Comtesse.' This is the secret I have kept for many years, Little Bird, and until recently, this is the lie I have told you and all who travel with me."

Yannick, his arms still crossed, surveyed the assembled circus folk. "So you told them, but none of them saw sense, is that it?" He shook his head in disgust.

"Ah, but we are none of us as clever as the great Yannick, eh?" Claudette spat angrily.

"You — you are the Lost Comtesse?" Rémy repeated, dazed. "Surely not! I can't believe it . . ."

Claudette offered a faint smile. "Believe me, Little Bird, I wish it were not true. I have done my best to hide all traces of that lost child. But Yannick here found out the truth. I don't know how, and I don't care to know."

"So that's why you were so interested in Claudette," Rémy said hoarsely. "I thought you were joking. But you knew all along."

"Whatever he told you, it's a lie, Rémy," Claudette said. "He is interested only in the reward he'll receive for turning me in to the Comte."

Yannick made an exasperated sound and threw up his hands. "Listen to the woman! It's absurd. You make it sound as if you're some kind of wanted criminal. As if being found is the worst possible thing that could happen to you. I don't understand you, Claudette. You're rich! You've been rich since you were born. You don't need to scratch a living in the dirt of French roads, reading the worthless fortunes of people who should be changing your chamber pot. All you need to do is make yourself known, and your life — Amélie's life — will change overnight. Why would you want to run from that?"

"You are a fool, Yannick. A damned, blasted fool," Claudette roared. "Who put up the reward? Tell me, who did?"

Yannick blinked, taken aback by the strength of her outburst. "The Comte de Cantal."

Claudette nodded. "Cantal is the last remaining of my birth family's line, the one clear inheritor of all its remaining wealth. Do you know the stipulation my parents placed on the inheritance of their fortune? The reason why he hasn't inherited already? The reason he might need to find me, instead of wanting to see me stay lost forever?"

Rémy looked at the magician's face and saw a flicker of doubt pass through his eyes, though his jaw remained stubbornly set and he said nothing.

"My parents' will stated," Claudette told them, in a calm, cool voice, "that their wealth was to remain mine in perpetuity. The only way the money can be released from their vaults is if I make myself known and can incontrovertibly prove my identity. Or," here she paused, glancing down at her daughter as if not wanting her to hear. "Or if my death can be proved with the same certainty."

Silence followed Claudette's words. It weighed upon the gathered circus folk like a dark shroud.

"I am the only thing standing between this man and an inheritance said to be the greatest still remaining since before the Revolution," Claudette said into the void. "Without me — dead or alive — he cannot inherit. The money is the only reason he seeks me. Once he has me, who is to say what he will do with me or with my parents' wealth? Anyone who has heard of the Comte de Cantal knows his reputation. Money of that magnitude can be nothing but evil in his hands."

Yannick shook his head. "That's absurd."

"Is it?" Claudette's eyes glittered harshly. "You forget, magician, that I am a teller of fortunes. I have seen my own. It splits into two paths, just as my life did when I was taken. One path is peaceful, happy. The other is full of death and destruction. I know which I choose for myself, for my child. I don't want money. I want to be left alone to live my life in peace. Which I would have been had you not arrived. I told you before, I did not want to be found. I sent you away and tried to escape, tried to leave no trace of where we were going. And yet now here you are again, and I wonder what you have brought with you this time?"

Rémy spoke, her voice dry in her throat. "We are alone, Claudette. I swear. No one was with us, and no one followed us."

Her friend's face was grim. "Is that so? But surely you know by now that Yannick here does not always need to do his own bidding. He sent no messages?"

"No," said Rémy. "No, I don't —" Then she stopped, remembering the messaging device she discovered Yannick tinkering with on the road. Hadn't he been talking into it? He'd said not, but . . . The buzzing returned, filling her ears with distraction.

"You're wrong, Claudette," Yannick said, "about everything. All the Comte wants is his family around him. You're his last remaining relative, however distant the connection may be. I am here with Rémy because he and I thought she could talk sense into you. Because all the Comte is offering you is a better life. He didn't have to send me. He would have found you eventually. But he wants you to understand how kind and benevolent he is. I know Little Bird is clever enough to understand that, even if you can't. Tell her, Remy. Tell her that she has nothing to fear."

Rémy shook her head. "If Claudette doesn't want

to make herself known, who are we to force her? It's her life, not ours."

Yannick threw up his hands. "You're all fools! Give the money away if you want, Claudette. Look around you — there are plenty in need of it. But for goodness' sake, use it! What good is it doing where it is?"

Claudette laughed hollowly. "I would be free to do that, would I?" she asked scornfully. "What if I rode through Paris, throwing handfuls of gold from my saddlebags? Would your Comte be as happy then? You are a rare fool, Yannick, if you believe he would stand by and let me do as I wish with that fortune."

The magician shook his head. "You should think better of people."

Claudette shook her head. "Every time I do that, magician, I meet a snake in the grass like you. All I want to do is live my life as I always have done. But all you see is the money. I have a mute daughter, born out of wedlock. What family of prestige will welcome her? And do you honestly think I would risk finding out, even if I hadn't read the leaves and seen the truth?"

The magician barked a harsh laugh. "Well, it's too late, anyway. I've found you, and so the Comte has found you, too. Thank me or not, Claudette, you will inherit your money. Then we'll see who the fool is."

Before anyone could stop him, Yannick leaped back into his saddle. His horse smarted, dancing forward on tired legs, but Yannick pulled it around and forced it into a flat gallop, heading back up the road the way they had come. Rémy went to follow, but Claudette's hand on her arm held her back.

"Let him go, Little Bird," she said, staring after the fleeing horse. "The damage is done."

"I think he . . . I think he hypnotized me," Rémy murmured, the buzz still filling her head. "I remember . . . telling him he shouldn't come, and then . . ."

Claudette grasped her shoulders. "He's a skilled hypnotist and you wanted to find me anyway, Rémy. It's no surprise he was able to use that."

"But I — I brought him here. I betrayed you, and now . . ."

"It is not your fault," her friend reassured her. "But we have to leave. Now. The Comte's forces must be close."

"We are ready to move out, Claudette," said Augustus at her shoulder, "just as soon as you give the word."

"It's too late," Claudette told him, bending down to haul Amélie into her arms and holding her daughter close. "I must take her and go on foot. The forest may slow them down."

"You can't," said Rémy. "There are bandits in the forest, and it is almost dark!"

"Better that than what's waiting for me on that road," Claudette muttered. She held one hand to Rémy's face. "I am sorry to have spoken to you harshly, Little Bird. It is good to see you, but —"

A shout came from somewhere among the gathered performers. Rémy and Claudette looked up to see flickering tongues of flame pouring along the road from the valley pass in bobbing lines. From this distance it looked like a snake formed of fire, slipping quickly toward them.

"Horses, on the road," said Rémy. "They're coming fast."

Augustus yelled for the circus to move out as Claudette ran for her caravan. Rémy followed, dodging the whinnying circus horses as they began to pull the caravans onto the road. Claudette ran up the steps of her home, setting Amélie down briefly and snatching up a bag she already had packed and waiting by the door. She thrust a fresh loaf in on top and pulled a heavy dark cloak from a hook, throwing it over herself.

Amélie, her eyes wide with fear, came to Rémy and reached for her throat, looking for the opal, the only thing that had ever allowed her to communicate in her own words. Rémy put her arms around the little girl. "It's gone, little one. I'm sorry. I can't hear you. It's gone. But everything will be all right."

Claudette swept Amélie up again, pulling the cloak around her and slinging the bag over her shoulder. "We must go, now, while there's still time."

"I'll come with you," Rémy said.

"No, Little Bird," Claudette told her, pulling her close as they crushed Amélie between them. "You must stay here. The circus will need you."

"But you need me, too!"

Claudette was already out the door and down the steps. She turned back, briefly. "We'll find you, Rémy. I promise. We'll find you again — somehow."

And then she was gone, slipping through the darkest shadows and into the depths of the forest. Rémy felt sick, lost, and alone. Around her, the circus was leaving, most of the caravans already on the road. Standing on the steps of Claudette's, she felt it jerk forward as the caravan's panicked carthorse tried to follow its friends. Rémy jumped down and ran to the front, releasing the lock, jumping up onto the driver's ledge. The horse moved without urging, its ears back in fear as it followed the rest of the hurried procession.

Rémy stood on tiptoe to look over the roof and back along the road. The flaming torches were still bearing down on them, close enough now that the thundering of hooves could be heard echoing along the valley. There were many, and they were getting closer by the minute. There is one thing that no circus can do, and that is travel fast.

"Rémy," Augustus shouted, and she looked down to see the clown running toward her. "We'll never escape them."

"We just have to hope they leave us alone when they see that Claudette is not here."

Augustus nodded, but Rémy could see the fear in his eyes. Suddenly she was angry. How dared these people hunt them? How dared they make them afraid?

"Augustus," she yelled. "Tell everyone to get ready to fight if we have to. The circus is our home, yes? We have done nothing wrong. If they want a fight, we'll give them a fight."

The clown nodded, disappearing along the rows of caravans. Rémy heard shouts echoing down the line, along with the odd cheer. She smiled to herself. *Yes, we'll be ready.*

The sound of a trumpet echoed so closely that her horse started in fright. The snake of fire had caught up with them, and Rémy watched as two streams of riders slid past them on either side of the road. The circus horses screamed in fright, and Rémy heard the caged lions roaring as the smell of fear filled the air.

The column stopped as they were surrounded.

"We seek the woman you know as Claudette Anjou," shouted a voice, and Rémy saw it belonged to a straight-backed fellow atop a pure black horse. He was dressed in a uniform of very dark blue. It was ribbed in gold, and he wore a helmet, also tinged gold. Rémy held her breath and waited. Everyone was silent. "I'll say that again," said the rider. "We are looking for Claudette Anjou. She has nothing to fear, but we will not leave until we have found her."

"She's not here," Rémy shouted into a thick silence punctuated only by the nervous snuffle of animals and the hiss of hungry flame. "She does not belong to this circus. You are mistaken."

The uniformed rider wheeled at the sound of her voice. He came closer, his horse prancing on elegant legs. *An Arabian*, Rémy thought absently. *Must have cost a fortune, that horse. What a waste to use it for war.*

"And who are you?" the officer asked, staring up at her with shadowed eyes.

"I am no one," Rémy answered. "I look after the horses, that is all."

Another rider approached. This one had the same style uniform, but with none of the gold piping, and he wore a simple hat instead of a helmet. He stopped beside the officer, passing him a piece of paper. As the officer unfolded it, Rémy realized with dismay that it was the poster Yannick had taken from the station in Calais — the wanted poster with her face clearly painted in its center. The officer consulted it and then looked up at her with a squint.

"You lie," he said, his voice smooth. "You are Rémy Brunel, the jewel thief also known as Little Bird. If this is your circus then it is also the circus of Claudette Anjou. Where is she? I give you one chance to answer, thief, before I take you in."

Before Rémy even had time to think, she was in the air. She leaped at the officer as if she were leaping from Dominique to another horse, but this time she kept her lead leg straight and strong.

It hit the rider in the chest with enough force

to steal his breath and unseat him. With a shocked groan, the Comte's officer fell in the dust, taking his lit torch with him, where it guttered and went out. In another second she had the Arabian's reigns and was wheeling it around, kicking and pawing at the rider behind. Rémy's only thought was to keep them occupied for as long as it would take Claudette to escape, convinced now that everything her friend had feared was true.

She heard a cry behind her and looked back to see Jacques, the lead tumbler, leaping from the roof of his caravan onto the back of another of the Comte's horses. There was a great roar as all down the circus line, the circus folk saw what was happening. They began to fight, using whatever skills they had to break the lines of horsemen surrounding them.

The pandemonium was complete when Constance the elephant began to stamp her great feet, raising her trunk above her head and trumpeting to the heavens. The unfamiliar sound of her war cry sent the Comte's horses into a frenzy. They began to buck, their riders struggling to stay seated. Rémy saw their confusion, and thought for the first time that they may actually be able to see off their attackers. She shouted for the circus folk to rally.

"Don't stop!" she cried as she unseated another soldier. His horse fled into the night, disappearing into the forest. "We have them!"

She didn't see that the commanding officer had recovered until she heard his voice, hoarse but loud, rising over the melee.

"Burn them," he shouted to the soldiers that still had torches. "Raze the caravans! Set them alight!"

"No!" Rémy screamed as the men stepped forward. She saw one torch thrust through the open door of Claudette's home. In seconds the vicious flames were devouring it from within.

She heard screams and turned to see every caravan in flames, glowing in the darkness. The inferno illuminated the road and the forest around it, the terrified screams of the still-tethered horses mixing with the children's wails of fear.

"The horses!" Rémy screamed, rushing toward Claudette's old carthorse, which was standing confused and fearful between the burning struts of its load. "Free the horses!"

The fire was too much for Constance, too. Her trumpets became full of fear rather than rage. She reared up, her two hind legs still clamped in the irons that held her in train. The huge creature wrenched herself free and charged, scattering the reassembled line of soldiers and running into the night.

"Enough!" shouted the officer. "We have what we need. Leave them to their fates."

Rémy turned. The air was fogged with smoke, drifting from the burning caravans and obscuring the road. The Comte's men were leaving, forcing their horses to ride past the burning caravans and back up the road. For a second, hope bloomed in Rémy's heart. They were leaving. They had destroyed the circus, but they were leaving — and without Claudette.

Then she heard a scream, rising above the others and dousing her with unnatural cold. Through the smoke, Rémy saw two soldiers leaving the tree line. With them they dragged a cloaked figure who struggled and fought, her chestnut hair flying wildly around her head. Claudette.

Now Rémy could see little Amélie, bound in the strong arms of another soldier, who laughed as she kicked at him. Rémy yelled with rage and ran headlong at their captors.

"Oh, for goodness' sake," she heard the officer shout. "Someone put that mongrel down."

There was the sound like a whip cracking. Something hit her in the shoulder with such force that

Rémy found herself airborne. She was flung sideways, knocked from the road and into the solid trunk of a tree.

The sound of Claudette's screams faded as darkness overtook her.

{Chapter 30}

REUNION

It had taken Thaddeus and J almost all day to repair the tear in the airship's balloon. They had taken it in turns to sew while Dita looked on, nursing her damaged arm. J hadn't been exaggerating when he'd said that sewing oilcloth was hard work — by mid-afternoon, Thaddeus's fingers were bloodied and bruised from the effort of forcing the needle in and out of the thick fabric. Still, it was worth it when they were able to re-inflate the balloon.

"We're back in business!" J cheered from the control desk. "Come on then, little miss and gent, let's be having you. Time's a-wasting, ain't it?"

They took off as twilight set around them.

Thaddeus watched out of one of the portholes as the valley dropped away, the airship suddenly at a dizzying height.

"I'm just going to follow the road," J told them, pointing to where it snaked and curled straight across the valley and up to a pass directly opposite. "So we're heading for that there pass."

With the gathering darkness came a glow from the south that lit the sky like a bonfire. It rose over the mountains that edged the valley and grew even greater as they neared.

"I don't like the look of that," said J uneasily. "It looks like the Thames on Guy Fawkes' night."

Thaddeus had to agree. "It can't be a forest fire," he said. "The trees are still dripping from the downpour."

"What do we do?" J asked.

"Carry on, J," the young policeman decided. "Just don't get too close."

J patted the control panel. "Right then, old girl," he muttered. "Let's have a look-see, shall we?"

The airship bobbed, the propellers whirring quietly as J spurred the machine on toward the pass out of the valley. Inside the cabin, they all held their breath, waiting to see what would be revealed on the other side. Then something like the sound of thunder echoed down the road. They all strained to see through the darkness outside the airship's window, but a pall of smoke had spread with the glow and they could see nothing but a smudge of burning orange.

"What is that?" Dita asked of the rumble.

"No idea, little miss," J said, "but whatever it is, it's coming over that road with a vengeance!"

The smoke was suddenly split by the terrified whin-nying of horses. They poured over the narrow pass in a panicked stream, dashing beneath the airship and sending up a sharp clattering of loose shale that pep-pered the hull.

"Bleedin' 'eck!" J cried.

Dita ran to the back of the airship, looking through the rear porthole at the stampeding animals as they disappeared down the trail. "I count . . . five — no, six," she called. "No riders. Some look like . . . *zugpferd* . . . horse that pulls cart."

"Where the blazes did they come from?" J asked.

Thaddeus didn't answer for a moment, looking instead out the window and down the road into the forest beyond. "I think blazes is exactly where they came from," he murmured.

J let out a gasp of shock. Below them, illuminating the edges of the wooded road like a thousand torches, was an inferno of the like Thaddeus had never seen. It burned tens of feet high, and seemed to stretch out as if the road itself had been turned into a river of fire.

Dita came to stand beside them for a second, staring open-mouthed at the awful spectacle below. "What is it?" she asked. "What could burn so?"

"J," Thaddeus said, looking up at the airship's roof hatch. "Did you bring your night glasses? I didn't pack mine."

"Yep," said J, as he reached for the bag he'd brought aboard back in Limehouse and dug around inside. "Take 'em everywhere, don't I? What you want 'em for?"

Thaddeus caught the device that J threw him. At first glance it looked like the strangest arrangement of metal and glass one could imagine, but once you looked closer, it became clear that the gadget was actually a pair of glasses, albeit peculiar ones. Instead of the normal single lenses there were three layers, one coated in a peculiar green film so that once the wearer had them on, their sight took on a strange-colored hue. The edges of each single lens was set inside an adjustable circle of brass. This was all welded neatly onto a sturdy brass frame that tucked over the nose and behind the ears, just like any other pair of eyeglasses.

Thaddeus put the night glasses on, feeling the familiar sense of dislocation as the world immediately took on a weirdly unreal tint. Inside the well-lit airship cabin, he could hardly see a thing.

"What are they?" Dita asked in amazement, staring at Thaddeus.

"Night glasses," J explained. "Rubbish in daylight — make you see as good as a cat at night." He nodded at Thaddeus. "Good idea."

Thaddeus climbed up until he could lean through the roof hatch, fiddling with the glasses to get them to focus. The first thing he saw was another knot of horses charging up the hill toward them. They crested the pass and almost collided with the low-flying airship, screaming and rearing around it, so close that Thaddeus felt the airship rock in their wake.

He knew what he was looking at as soon as he got the glasses to focus. What else could it be with so many caravans in one place?

"J," he yelled, nausea and fear threatening to engulf him. "It's the circus! It's burning!"

He heard J curse and scrambled back down into the cabin again, removing the glasses. "We've got to help them."

"Thaddeus," J said, nervously, "remember what I

said about the ruby's gas? If we get too close to that fire, we'll go up in smoke ourselves."

Thaddeus cursed. "We'll just have to get as close as we can and then land."

"What if the fire spreads?" J asked. "What if —"

"We can't just leave them to it, J!" Thaddeus exclaimed. "There are people down there, a lot of them!"

"If we can help, we must try!" Dita interjected.

"All right, all right," J said, turning back to the control desk. "I ain't arguing about that bit, I just . . ." He trailed off as the airship sailed down, over the smoke-clogged trees. "Look, there," the boy said, a tense minute later. "See?"

He was pointing to a scrubby clearing just off the track, about half a mile from the burning line of caravans.

"Good, J — set us down there."

Thaddeus was opening the cabin's hatch before the airship had even touched down. It landed with a bump, the gangplank slamming onto ground that was still wet. Even from this far away, the policeman could feel the heat of the fire.

"J," he said, "stay here, with the airship. You too, Dita. If it looks as if the rest of the forest is going to catch light, don't wait for me, take her back up. Okay?"

"But Thaddeus —"

"I don't have time to argue, J," Thaddeus said firmly, jumping from the ship. "Just do it."

He ran down the road, which had been churned to mud by the rain and by what must have been hundreds of horses. Ahead of him, Thaddeus could see the circus folk, silhouetted in the darkness against the orange flames. Some had formed a line through the trees between the river and the road and were passing buckets of water, frantically trying to douse the flames. Others were rescuing what they could from the caravans that had already been put out, dragging from the wreckage scraps of clothes, cooking pans, and other odds and ends. To Thaddeus, it seemed as if there was precious little left and no hope for the caravans that were still alight.

He reached the first caravan, a smoldering wreck of wood and burned possessions. Thaddeus kept going until he reached the head of the water chain. Before he could speak a bucket was thrust into his hands. He turned and threw the water at the flames licking around yet another of the wooden homes. Farther down the line, the policeman saw a loose sheet of fabric flapping hopelessly as it was consumed by the fire. He recognized it as part of the Big Top. A flash of memory came to him, of the first time he had ever seen Rémy Brunel. She had been performing inside that very circus tent, flying through the air like a bird. Anxiety clutched at his gut. His eyes searched the line, trying to find her face, but he couldn't see her. Another bucket of water was pushed toward him and then another.

There was a shout, and someone shook his shoulder. It was the big man behind him — the next in the line. He was yelling and pointing to the next caravan in the train, indicating that Thaddeus should move so they could try to extinguish it. More water was pushed into his hands, and he threw it as hard as he could, trying to reach the center of the searing flames.

A scream of terror reached Thaddeus's ears. For one sickening moment he thought it was coming from inside the blazing caravan, but then he saw movement. It came from beneath the caravan, not inside it. Someone was trapped inside the ring of flames that circled the wooden cart wheels. He shouted, chucking the empty bucket back to the man behind and throwing himself flat to the ground to get a better look. There was another shout from behind him as the big man realized what was happening and did the same.

There was a child, trapped under the caravan. It was a little girl, cowering between the burning wheels. She was sitting in the mud with her knees pulled up to her chin, shaking and crying.

Beside him, Thaddeus heard the circus performer utter a curse. Thaddeus didn't need to know the translation to understand what he meant. The caravan was completely surrounded by fire — it was a miracle that the floor above hadn't yet caved in and fallen on top of the child. It could only be a matter of minutes before the inevitable happened and she was lost to the inferno.

There was no time to think. Thaddeus turned to the man beside him. "Give me your jacket," he yelled over the noise of the raging flames and then reached out to point at what he meant. "Give it to me, quickly!"

The man understood, hurriedly shrugging off his shabby coat and pushing it toward the policeman.

"Sorry," Thaddeus muttered automatically before pushing it down into the wet mud under their feet. The garment was immediately soaked, coated with a thick slime of wet dirt. Thaddeus pulled it up from the sucking mud and threw it over his head and shoulders, the cold sludge a salve in the face of the fire's heat. He took a breath, staring at the flames, and suddenly his confidence crumbled. What on earth was he doing? Did he really want to throw himself into those flames? Was eighteen years enough for a life, if his ended here? Thaddeus suddenly felt very young and very scared and very much as if he hadn't seen nearly enough of life to throw it away so easily.

But then the trapped girl screamed again, pure terror lacing her child's voice. Thaddeus's heart clenched. He pushed the wave of fear and doubt away. What was the point of being a policeman if he didn't help people, whatever the cost? What else was he for?

He sucked in a breath and plunged into the flames, launching himself directly between the two front wheels. The little girl screamed again as he threw off the coat and pressed it into the mud at her feet, killing the first licks of fire that had danced across it.

"Come," he yelled to her, over the sound of the inferno, holding out his arms.

She screamed again, too terrified to move. A creak sounded above them as the caravan's floor threatened to give way. With no time to be gentle, Thaddeus grabbed the child by the forearms, pulling her to his chest and flinging the coat over her. He took one look at the ring of flames, then ducked his head beneath the sodden fabric and lurched forward, hoping against hope that he'd picked the right spot and wouldn't collide with one of the caravan's burning wheels. The girl screamed in his ear, her arms wrapped around his neck as they surged into the fire. This time, Thaddeus felt the flames reaching for his legs, curling their heat around them like a thousand tiny, vicious whips. He tried to stagger forward a few more steps but collapsed to his knees. The child screamed on, still clutched against him.

Thaddeus only realized they had escaped the fire when he heard shouting. The burning coat was ripped away, and the child was pulled from his arms. Someone else grabbed him by the shoulders, shouting at him. That same someone pushed him to the ground and made him roll in the mud until the burning in his legs lessened. When Thaddeus stopped moving, he felt hands under his shoulders, helping him to sit. An unknown hand tipped a cup of water to his lips and wiped the mud from his eyes. The policeman blinked and realized it was his companion from the water line. The big man patted his shoulder, nodding and smiling grimly.

"The girl," Thaddeus managed. "Is she —"

His new friend moved a little so that Thaddeus could see over his shoulder. The child he'd pulled from the burning wreck was being cradled in a crying woman's arms. She was terrified but seemed otherwise unhurt. Around them, the water line had broken up. The circus folk stood, looking at the burning hulks of their homes, resigned to the fact that there was no more they could do to save them.

"Mr. Rec!" Thaddeus pushed his sodden hair back to see J and Dita rushing toward him. "We thought you was a goner, for sure!" said J, out of breath as they came to a standstill in front of him.

"You should be with the airship, J," Thaddeus said hoarsely.

"It's all right, don't you worry," said the boy. "It ain't reaching the tree line — look."

Thaddeus looked blearily to where J was pointing and saw that the boy was right. The big man who had pulled him out began to speak rapidly in French. Dita listened for a moment.

"His name is Augustus. He is calling you a hero," the little girl told Thaddeus with a smile. "And saying that from now on, you are family."

Thaddeus nodded, too exhausted to smile and too overwhelmed to think. He struggled to his feet, scanning the crowd for one particular face. He saw no sign of Rémy, not even allowing for the covering of smuts that masked every face. His heart sank.

"Dita," he croaked, his voice still full of smoke. "Ask him what circus this is — was. What was it called?"

Augustus looked at him, and even Thaddeus could understand what he said next. "Le Cirque de Secrets."

"Do you — do you know of Rémy Brunel?" he asked, a sick feeling rising into his throat. "Little Bird, she's called . . . Er — Petit . . . Petit . . ." He tried to remember what her stage name had been in French, but couldn't.

"Ah *oui*, *oui*," said Augustus, "Petit Moineau! — Rémy Brunel . . ." He continued in a gush of French.

Dita frowned as she translated. "She was here," the little girl said, her voice fraught. "With a magician called Yannick. It was he who brought the Comte's men."

"The Comte was here?" Thaddeus asked, a chill befalling him.

"Not the Comte de Cantal himself," Dita translated. "But his men came. For — for Claudette. They set the *feuer* — the fire. Rémy . . ." The girl glanced up at Thaddeus with worried eyes. "He doesn't know what happened. There was chaos. They were trying to free the horses and move the lions. But . . ."

Thaddeus looked at her as she trailed off. "But what?"

"Perhaps nothing," said Dita hesitantly.

Thaddeus placed his aching hands on her shoulders and looked her in the eye. "But what, Dita? Tell me."

"Gun shots," said the girl reluctantly. "No one saw Rémy after that. And they were too busy . . ."

". . . too busy to look," Thaddeus said hoarsely. He straightened up, ignoring the sting of the burns to his legs. "So now we look," he said, looking Augustus in the eye. "Yes?"

Augustus nodded, grim-faced. "*Oui.*"

★ ★ ★

In the end, it was Dominique who found her. Thaddeus recognized Rémy's circus pony. She stood quietly beside a tree, nosing at something on the ground. The little palomino had been let loose with all the other circus horses but, instead of running, she had found her long-lost mistress. Rémy was slumped, not moving, beside the tree.

Thaddeus spotted her a moment after he saw the horse. For a second, his legs turned to lead and he couldn't move. And then, almost without realizing it, he was by her side, dropping to his knees. There was a nasty gash across her swollen brow and her shoulder was bloodied.

"Rémy," he said, tipping her face toward him and taking in the strangeness of her short hair. "Rémy?"

The pulse beneath his fingers was weak, but it was there. Relief surged through him. Thaddeus ripped off his muddy shirt. Most of it was useless, but he tore the cleanest scraps into strips, wrapping the rags around her injured shoulder.

"I've found her," he shouted, his voice cracking as he lifted her into his arms. Oddly, he no longer felt pain. "I've found her!"

She stirred as they reached the airship, eyes fluttering open, bruised brow creasing into a frown as she tried to focus.

"T-thaddeus?" she muttered. "What . . ."

"Rémy," he said. "It's all right. I found you. Everything's all right."

She remembered something then, and tried to struggle free. "C-Claudette," she grated. "I have to —"

Thaddeus held her fast against him. A moment later, she passed out again, her head against his chest.

★ ★ ★

No one slept much that night. For one thing, the circus folk had nowhere to sleep, and for another they were busy trying to round up as many of the circus horses as they could. Some, like the ones seen from the airship, were far away and gone forever by now. But others had not fled so far, and these were the ones that were brought back, slowly, over the hours that stretched toward dawn. Constance the elephant came, too, lumbering hesitantly toward her relieved keeper.

Dita and J went out to help in the search, but Thaddeus stayed with Rémy. He had placed her in his bunk in the airship. As far as he could make out, the wound to her head was worse than the wound to her shoulder. It seemed as if the bullet had only grazed her, scraping the skin but breaking no bone. Thaddeus bathed and wrapped the wound, and then did the same with the ugly gash on her forehead. Leaving her to sleep, he stepped outside into the gathering dawn.

The dead hulks of the caravans were still smoldering. To Thaddeus, they looked like the carcasses of a great herd of strange beasts. He stared at them for a while, and then went to help Augustus, who was trying to calm a still-terrified horse. They nodded at each other, smiling through the language barrier until Dita and J returned, another tired pony between them.

"Right, Dita," Thaddeus said. "I want to know everything that happened here."

{Chapter 31}

A PLAN

$\mathcal{R}$émy woke to pain and the sound of murmuring. She opened her eyes and found herself looking at a curved wooden ceiling. Sunlight was streaming through an open hatch above her head. From somewhere above her came the sounds of bumps and scraping. Twice shadows passed through the sunlight, as if someone was moving around up there.

Rémy tried to sit up, wincing at the pain in her shoulder. There was a blanket tucked carefully around her. She realized with alarm that, apart from her underclothes, that was all she was covered by.

The murmuring stopped. Another shadow came nearer.

"Well," said a familiar voice, still speaking very quietly. "There you are."

Rémy squinted as she looked up, trying to focus. Her head was still fuzzy. The figure dropped into a crouch beside her.

"Th-thaddeus?" she croaked, through a throat as dry as scorched earth.

The policeman smiled gently, picking something up from the floor beside the bed. He held it out to her — a glass full of water.

"Drink," he said, "but slowly. How are you feeling?"

Rémy took a few sips, then handed the glass back to him. "I — my head hurts. And my shoulder."

"I'm not surprised," Thaddeus told her. "It looks as if you had an argument with a bullet. And you hit your head."

Rémy blinked again, still confused. She looked down at her bandaged shoulder, naked apart from the dressing. "Where is my shirt?"

"Ruined, I'm afraid. Your corset and trousers are all right, though." Thaddeus gestured to the end of the bed, where both lay. Her boots stood on the floor.

Rémy shifted, uncomfortable, and then saw Thaddeus glance away and offer a slightly abashed smile.

"Don't worry," he murmured. "We got Dita to undress you."

"Dita?" Rémy asked. "Who's —"

Thaddeus shook his head. "Never mind that right now. We'll introduce you in a little while. Right now, I think you need more rest. J and I are just there if you need us." He nodded to the light he had emerged from, and Rémy's eyes had cleared enough to see that it was some sort of doorway with a ramp. She could just make out J's back, turned away from her, and beyond him, blue sky over green trees.

It was the trees that did it. The memory of the previous night flooded her aching head and she gasped.

"The fire! Claudette!" She tried to struggle up, forgetting for a moment about her damaged shoulder.

"Easy," said Thaddeus, holding her back. "Rémy, take it easy. You're not —"

"But — but they took her! They burned . . . everything!" Rémy, said almost in a sob. "I have to go after them!"

"Not yet," Thaddeus said, his voice firm as he tried to get her to settle. "Rémy, you're not well enough."

"Pass me my clothes, Thaddeus."

"Rémy —"

"My clothes."

Thaddeus looked at her, and she looked back, summoning every ounce of defiance she had. After a moment he nodded and reached for the garments.

"You need to take some time before you go rushing off," he said, as he passed them to her.

"Turn around," she said curtly. He did, and she climbed gingerly out of bed. Standing upright was more difficult than she'd imagined. Her head swam, and she blinked rapidly, trying to fend off the pain.

"Are you all right?" Thaddeus asked.

"Don't look!"

"I'm not!"

She managed to struggle into her trousers and fasten them, but the corset was another matter. Rémy succeeded in pulling it on, but the laces were hard enough to tighten at the best of times, let alone with blurred vision and a throbbing arm.

"Rémy?" Thaddeus asked, after a few minutes. "I can call Dita . . ."

"No," Rémy said hoarsely. "I just need — can you —" she sighed. "You can turn around now. Can you do this up for me, please?"

She turned her back as he moved. There was a moment of silence, and then Rémy felt him step closer. Another moment passed, and then she felt his fingers slide under the laces, pulling them in. He didn't say anything.

"As tight as you can," she said.

It was strange, feeling his fingers on her back. Thaddeus seemed reluctant to let them linger there, jumping slightly every time they came in contact with her skin. Rémy's mind was spinning, replaying not only the events of the night before, but also trying to work out what he was doing here, this far from home. She hadn't thought she'd ever see him again, but here he was.

"Did you come looking for me?" she asked, her throat still dry. "All the way from London?"

Thaddeus finished tying the corset. He said nothing for a moment, and then she felt his fingers brush against the short-cropped hair at the nape of her neck. The last time he had seen her, her hair had been far longer, though always tied up. For some reason she found herself holding her breath.

"Of course I did," he said finally, so quietly that she hardly heard it.

Rémy turned around and looked up at him. Maybe it was because her head still felt as if someone had hit it with a mace, or perhaps it was because she was so worried about Claudette, but she felt her lower lip trembling as she tried to stop her eyes filling with tears.

"You were right," she whispered.

"About what?"

"Yannick." Even saying his name made Rémy feel sick. "You knew he was the thief. You knew he was rotten. But I didn't listen."

Thaddeus shook his head with a faint smile. "I didn't know," he told her softly. "I just suspected. But even if he'd been the best man on Earth, don't you think I would have come after you anyway?"

"He's not the best man on Earth," Rémy said, almost choking on the words. "That's someone else entirely."

Thaddeus ran his fingers lightly up and down her bare arms, smiling down at her. "I'm just so glad you're alive," he said. "There was a moment, when I found you, that I thought you weren't."

She laughed softly and then shut her eyes, because laughing hurt. When she opened them again, Thaddeus was leaning forward, and for a second, Rémy thought he was going to kiss her. Her heart jolted, and she realized that she wanted him to, more than anything she'd ever wanted before. She looked up at him, holding her breath.

Someone cleared their throat, cutting through the moment as surely as if it were a knife passing through butter. The intruder was J, who stood in the doorway, looking at his feet.

"Sorry, lady and gent," he said. "But Augustus and the rest are about to head out. Thought you'd like to know."

"Augustus!" Rémy exclaimed, stepping away from Thaddeus fast enough to make her head spin.

"Whoa," said Thaddeus, putting an arm out to steady her. She leaned on him as they headed for the door.

Even though she'd remembered what had happened, it didn't prepare Rémy for the sight outside. The road was littered with the blackened hunks of ash and wood; the only signs left of Le Cirque des Secrets. Rémy blinked, eyes full of tears again as she took in the ugly mess that the Comte's men had made of her friends' homes. Milling between them were the circus folk, some with bandages and slings concealing injuries, though others had mercifully escaped from harm. Some were on foot, but others were on horseback. At least none of them had been killed in the inferno. The folk on foot led horses or pulled handcarts loaded with whatever they had managed to salvage from the flames. Behind them, with her keeper, Constance the elephant stood calmly, waiting to be off. Farther away was the lion's cage, its two occupants pacing within, still disturbed by the lingering smell of the fire.

Augustus dismounted when he saw Rémy, a grin on his face.

"Little Bird," he said in French, "how glad I am to see you up and about."

Rémy tottered down the gangplank and into the old clown's arms, where she sobbed. "I'm so sorry, Augustus. This was my fault. You've all lost everything, and it was my fault."

"*Tsk, tsk*," muttered Augustus, pulling back to look down at her. "There is enough badness in the world without you taking the blame for something you did not do. We are all whole, and that is something to be grateful for."

"But Claudette — and Amélie! They —"

Augustus ticked one finger beneath her chin and smiled, glancing up at Thaddeus. "Claudette and her chick will be back with us before you know it," he said. "This policeman of yours has a plan, *ma cherie*, and that is why we must be off at once. We have a long way to go on horseback if we are to accompany this wonderful machine."

Rémy sniffed, confused again. "Plan? Machine?"

Augustus smiled at her again and then turned to remount his horse. "Thaddeus and J will explain everything." he said. "Meanwhile, we will take Dominique with us. She will be safe with the other horses."

"Dominique!" Rémy exclaimed, seeing her beloved pony among the gathered animals. Hearing her mistresses' voice, the little palomino whinnied and stepped forward. Rémy petted the creature's soft nose. "I will see you soon, girl. I promise."

Dominique whickered gently into her hand as Augustus began to lead the homeless circus folk out into the road. They turned toward the southern end of the valley — the direction the Comte's men had taken. Rémy watched as Dominique joined them, trotting off into the dust.

Rémy turned around, putting her hand up to her bandaged head. "So," she said, to Thaddeus. "What plan? And," she added, for the first time taking in the contraption behind him, "what on the good green Earth is that?"

Chapter 32

INTO THE UNKNOWN

Thaddeus watched as J showed Rémy around the airship. He'd thought the boy had the right to be her guide, given that he'd built it himself. Besides, though the burns to his legs weren't nearly as bad as they could have been, they were still causing him pain. Seeing Rémy, wounded but walking, made up for everything, though. He shouldn't have been surprised, of course. She was strong enough to weather anything — that was one of the things he loved so well about her. It was also one of the things that made her infuriating, but Thaddeus wasn't fool enough to believe that he could have one without the other.

He sat on a boulder a few feet away from the open gangplank, watching the circus procession as it disappeared up the long road away from the forest. The horses were now nothing but tiny moving points against the dust of the road and the incessant green of the trees. He admired these people's resolve in the face of everything they had already lost and everything they still stood to lose. Around him loomed the silent shells of their lives and livelihoods, and yet still they were determined to save Claudette and Amélie and willing to take his word for it that they would not be alone in the attempt. He hoped fervently that their trust was not misguided.

They had released the caged pigeon while Rémy had lain sleeping in his bunk. Thaddeus had no idea whether it would reach Dorfmann, or even if it did, whether the German would be willing and able to help them.

"Penny for your thoughts? There, that's one English saying I learned in London."

Thaddeus looked up to see Rémy standing over him, a faint smile on her lips. Behind her, J was clambering up to join Dita on the roof, where she was checking to see how well their repairs had survived. Thaddeus made to stand up, but Rémy waved him back down and crouched beside him, wincing slightly.

"How are you feeling?" he asked.

"Not too terrible, considering," she said lightly, though the dark smudges under her eyes told him she should get more sleep. Then she nodded over her shoulder at the airship. "Thaddeus — this ship is amazing. I can't believe you and J flew it all the way from England." She shook her head. "I don't know if you are both crazy, or just brave."

Thaddeus smiled. "I know. It still seems like a bit of a dream to me, too. But without it — and J — we wouldn't be here now."

"It's good to see that ruby finally found a good home, too," Rémy added dryly, evidently thinking about the argument they'd had about the jewel back in London.

Thaddeus gave her an awkward smile. "Great things are often born out of difficult beginnings," he told her. "That's what I like to think anyway."

Rémy gazed out over the scene of ruin before them, her look of sadness more shocking to Thaddeus than the vivid gash and bruise still marring her forehead. He was used to seeing her angry and defiant, but he'd never seen her so readily near tears as he had over the past few hours. He wondered if that accounted for the moment in the airship just after she'd woken up, when he'd almost felt as if they were standing across that blasted chasm again, yelling hopelessly to each other.

"Augustus said you had a plan," she said quietly, dropping to sit cross-legged on the grass beside him. "Please, Thaddeus, tell me it's a good one."

He sighed. "Augustus is an optimist, I'm afraid. It's not really a plan. Well, unless you call 'let's go and get our people back' a plan."

Rémy smiled grimly. "I'll take it. If it means finding Claudette and Amélie, I'll take it."

Without thinking, Thaddeus took her hand and squeezed her fingers. Rather than pulling away, as she may have done just days before, Rémy laced her fingers through his.

"While you were asleep, Augustus told me what he knew. Once Yannick had revealed that he knew who she was, Claudette realized it was only a matter of time before the Comte closed in on her. Even if Yannick hadn't betrayed her himself, she thought it likely that he'd tell someone else who would — the reward was too great to pass up. She came clean to the whole circus — they held a meeting, where she told everyone the truth — and told them that she and

Amélie would leave alone if that's what they wanted. But they didn't."

"Of course they didn't." Rémy said softly. "She's family. She always has been."

"They thought about sailing to Italy, but the circus couldn't afford the passage. So they settled on trying to get over the mountains into Spain. Claudette thought she'd be safe there, safer than going north with winter coming . . . as long as they got over the passes before the snow closed them. In Spain, the circus could carry on touring and earning money. The only snag in the plan was that this area here, where we are now, is the Comte's territory. They traveled as quickly as possible, and they also stopped all communications with anyone outside the circus. That's why Claudette stopped writing to you."

Rémy nodded, tears filling her eyes again. "But it wasn't enough. Because of me."

"Not you," Thaddeus said firmly. "Because of Yannick. As Claudette expected, he went to the Comte and told him who she was. But he didn't know Claudette's plan to get into Spain. Augustus thinks the Comte refused to pay out the reward until he had Claudette in his clutches."

"So Yannick had to find her," Rémy concluded.

"Yes. News about what had happened to Gustave and Le Cirque de la Lune was common knowledge, including the fact that Little Bird had disappeared but had last been seen in London. Knowing how close you and Claudette were, he came looking for you."

Rémy shook her head. *"Mon dieu*, and he manipulated me so easily, Thaddeus," she whispered. "I was just too pig-headed to see it."

"You weren't to know his real motives," Thaddeus soothed. "It does you credit that you would be so loyal to your friends, even ones you haven't seen for years."

Rémy looked up at him mutely for a moment, the expression in her eyes so strange that Thaddeus couldn't understand it. "I should have been loyal to you," she said eventually. "I just let . . . stupid things . . . get in the way." Her fingers strayed to her throat as she spoke.

"You're not wearing your necklace," Thaddeus realized. He couldn't remember ever seeing her without it.

She smiled wanly. "It was stolen."

"By Yannick?" Thaddeus asked in disgust. "I swear, when I find him —"

"I don't know if it was him or not," sighed Rémy. "He swore it wasn't. But then, he hypnotized me to get me to do what he wanted, so . . ." She shrugged.

"I'm so sorry," Thaddeus said. "I know it was a gift from your mother."

Rémy looked out over the forest, a slight frown creasing her forehead. "You know," she said softly, "I'm not sure that I am sorry it's gone anymore. Without it, we might not even have found ourselves in this mess." Then another flicker passed her face, something like a mixture of realization and fear.

"Rémy? What is it?"

"My pack!" she said. "I was wearing it when we were attacked. Where is it? Is it lost? Please say it isn't lost."

"Don't worry," he told her. "You had it when I found you. It's in the airship — I stowed it in one of the cupboards for safety."

She blinked, relief flooding her eyes. "Did you look inside?"

Thaddeus frowned. "No, of course not."

"No, I didn't mean —" Rémy stopped and started again. "I didn't think you would have, but I wouldn't have minded. It's just . . . there's something in it I want to show you. Something I want you to see, and talk to you about."

"Do you want me to get it for you now?"

Rémy was silent for a moment, frowning as if

considering the question. Then she shook her head. "No. I think I have to wait until all of this is done. But you're the one I want to show it to. And I wanted you to know that."

Thaddeus had no idea what she meant, but her words touched him. It made him regret that he had to turn the conversation to more disturbing matters. "Rémy," he said, "there's something more I have to tell you. About the Comte de Cantal."

He watched her face darken with concern as he told her of Desai's list and the meeting he himself had witnessed in London.

"*Mon dieu*," she whispered, once he had finished. "And I thought all of that was done with."

"So did I," said Thaddeus grimly. "All we can do is hope that he doesn't have many of Abernathy's devices already. And if we can stop him buying the submarine, then . . ." Thaddeus trailed off, seeing Rémy's thoughtful face. "Rémy? What is it?"

She shook her head. "Maybe nothing."

"Tell me anyway."

Rémy pulled a face. "A couple of days ago, I found Yannick with one of those message-sending machines that the Professor made. He said he'd stolen it from the workshop, but what if he'd actually had it all along? I thought I'd heard him talking into it. He said he wasn't, but what if he was lying? What if he did know how to use it — because it had been given to him by the Comte? It would explain how those soldiers knew exactly where to find us."

Thaddeus sighed. "It would. I don't like the sound of that at all. If de Cantal has devices like that, what else does he have?"

Rémy rubbed a hand over her face. "And this is the man who wants Claudette — dead or alive," she said. "What — what if we're already too late? What if he's done something to her? What if . . ."

Thaddeus shook his head. "He put out posters, didn't he? He made his search public, which means he wants her return to be public. I don't know what he's planning, but it's not to cut her throat in the dark. He couldn't just produce her body and use it to claim the inheritance — it'd be too obvious that he killed her."

Rémy shivered. "Those soldiers — the ones that attacked the circus. Thaddeus, we're no match for them. There aren't enough of us. And what if he has more?"

"I know," Thaddeus said grimly. "I know."

★ ★ ★

They waited until dusk had painted the skies first pink and then a faded violet before cutting the guide ropes and taking the airship skyward. Thaddeus was at the controls, Rémy leaning beside him to see the earth drifting away beneath them as they rose. The sensation was like nothing she'd ever felt before — a weightlessness without weightlessness, the pit of her stomach rising and dipping with excitement and a tiny lick of fear. The trees below looked like children's toys, the river and road like strips of discarded ribbon.

"Strange sensation, isn't it?" Thaddeus said, watching her face. Rémy nodded, wordless, eyes fixed on the horizon as they drew level with the mountain pass and then lifted above it.

Thaddeus turned them southeast and in the distance, glittering, she saw lights. They outlined a mountain that, in the darkness, seemed like a prism reaching for the stars. It was immense and intricate, a network of yellow stars that seemed to be harnessed to the Earth, as if some great power had pulled them out of the sky. She couldn't imagine what they were — how they burned so brightly or what had created them. She wasn't sure she really wanted to find out.

"What's that?" she asked nonetheless, her voice

hushed as if they'd wandered into a cathedral by mistake.

"That," Thaddeus said, his voice unusually harsh, "is Mont Cantal, and it's where we're going."

{Chapter 33}

A FEARFUL
DESTINATION

They flew on through the night, the darkness hardening around them like obsidian. Overhead, the stars battled to outshine the ones that grew ever larger in the airship's sights. The city of Mont Cantal loomed out of the landscape like a huge monolith to an unknown god. The lights, which Thaddeus could now see were great torches of yellow flame, had burned all night, and that achievement alone made him take a breath. *What kind of mind could have constructed this place,* he wondered. *What was the architect afraid of, that he made it look so spectacular, and yet so forbidding?* He thought of the underground empire that Abernathy had built beneath London. Here, the wonder wasn't hidden away: it was on the surface for all to see. The policeman couldn't decide if that worried him less or more.

Augustus had been right to describe Mont Cantal as impenetrable. Thaddeus himself could not imagine how anyone could ever enter its vast walls unbidden, let alone reach the castle itself. The city was such a part of the mountain that in some places it was difficult to tell where the rock ended and the buildings began. A great wall had been built at the base, between two huge natural cliffs that formed permanent stone sentries. Behind this wall, the city was formed of three distinct sections. The largest was at the foot of the mountain, directly behind the wall and between the two cliffs, a higgledy-piggledy collection of buildings that alone would look like any city. This one, though, was set around a deep, clear lake, filled from a fast-flowing river fed by a great waterfall that cascaded from above.

A winding path had been hewn out of the rock itself, just wide enough for two carts to pass, leading to the city's second level. Here there were fewer buildings, constructed so closely against the mountain that Thaddeus had no doubt that part of them must be formed of caves that led deep inside the rock. The houses here were white-washed and neat, clearly owned by more affluent citizens than the ones below. This part of the town had an elegant square with a clock tower circled by cobbles. Yet another road, narrower and more winding than the first, led from this city-hamlet to the great castle that oversaw it all. High above his people, the Comte had constructed a forest of gleaming white towers and spires. These were so tightly packed and bound so closely by another great wall that it seemed impossible for anything but a shaft of light to penetrate beyond the narrow windows that peppered their sides.

Flowing down from an outcrop jutting out above the highest of these spires was the waterfall. It splashed and thundered, running beside the castle and down a chasm cut by centuries of snowmelt and rainfall. It bypassed the second tier and flowed into the lake. From the lake flowed a river that shot deep and fast through a grilled archway that had been constructed in the lower wall. On either side burned another two of those great torches, the smoke from which smudged the night air with ash.

"*Mon dieu*," Rémy whispered, standing beside him as she took in the immense sight. "Whoever built this place is either a genius or a madman."

Thaddeus felt a shadow pass across his mind. "I've known men who were both," he said.

"What we going to do?" J asked, leaning over his seat and staring out at the sight before them. "I didn't fink they'd see us coming in the airship at night, like — but with those torches, now I ain't so sure. They could see a fly comin' at fifty paces."

"Go around," Dita suggested with a twirl of her finger to indicate what she meant.

Thaddeus nodded. "I think Dita's got the right idea. Let's keep our distance for the moment and do a circuit of the mountain before the sun comes up. See what's on the opposite side."

There was a general murmur of agreement, hushed as if those sleeping below in that fearsome city might somehow hear and look up, despite the distance. Thaddeus flew the silent airship in a wide circle, keeping Mont Cantal on his right. It soon became clear that the huge torches they had seen burned only on the south side of the mountain, where the city stood. Once the ship had drawn level with the north face, it became clear why — here Cantal was nothing but a sheer rock cliff, almost entirely smooth from the tip of its height to where it met the plain at its base. There was no path, nor even any way of climbing the expanse of stone by hand. It was as if, some time in pre-history, the mountain had been smote in two, leaving one side smooth and featureless.

"Cripes," muttered J. "There ain't no army going to make it up and over that way, that's for sure."

"Not unless they've got an airship," said Thaddeus, with a hint of grim triumph. He flew them closer and then rose up the sheer sheet rock until they crested the very top of Mont Cantal. Doing so made it evident that the great line of torches did not actually reach the mountain's highest point, but began their burning beneath a small plateau that jutted out just below the summit.

"Well, well, well," said Thaddeus, looking down at the narrow space. "I believe we've just found one advantage we have over the Comte de Cantal."

No one spoke during the landing. For all that the little plateau seemed flat, in reality it was as stony and uneven as any other part of the south face. Audible sighs of relief echoed through the cabin as the airship touched down safely. Everyone inside sat quietly for a moment afterward, looking out at the orange glow that rose over the edge of the plateau and hinted at what was waiting below.

"We have to try to climb down, into the city," Rémy said.

Thaddeus nodded. "We'll have to do it now, before the sun comes up," he said. "Anything moving during daylight risks being seen. Rémy, you and I will go. J and Dita should stay here, with the airship."

"Wait a mo," said J. "You'll never get down there, find the lady, and get back up here before sunrise. The sky's already getting pink over yonder."

"We'll have to stay in the city all day, until the sun sets again," said Rémy. "It'll probably take us that long to work out where Claudette is, anyway."

"If they see you, you'll be trapped," Dita exclaimed.

"We'll be fine," Thaddeus reassured her. "They don't know who we are. We'll blend in with the locals. Don't worry. As soon as it gets dark again, we'll head back."

"What about the ship?" J asked. "What 'appens if someone comes lookin' up 'ere in the meantime? I dunno — a patrol, or sumfin'? We'll be sitting 'ere in broad daylight for hours!"

"You'll have to keep a sharp eye out, J. But why would they send a patrol this high? If they were worried, the torches would be burning all the way up here, too, but they're not. Like you said, there's no way anyone's coming up the north face. They've no reason to think anyone would be up here. This is probably the safest place you could be."

"But what if —"

Thaddeus cut the boy off, laying a hand on his shoulder. "If you're worried, at all, for any reason, then you take off, straightaway."

"We can't just leave you two behind!"

"We can look after ourselves, J," Rémy said. "Anyway, it's not going to come to that. Trust us."

J looked doubtful, but eventually he nodded. "You'd best get going then, ain't yer?" he said. "No sense hanging about waiting for trouble."

Chapter 34

THE DEVIL'S LAIR

Outside the airship, the night air was chilled. Rémy and Thaddeus made their way toward the plateau's edge, stepping carefully over the uneven ground. Several times stones skittered away from their feet, the noise seeming to clatter as loudly as thunder in the silence. But there were no shouts; there came no stampede of booted feet. Up here, near the roof of the world, they were as invisible as ghosts.

The most difficult part of the passage down was getting over the plateau. They had no guide ropes, no safety net. Pausing at the edge, they looked over at the drop below. The ground disappeared, curving in below the outcrop's lip and only jutting out again many feet lower. Here was where the line of ever-burning torches stood, perpetual sentries standing testament to Mont Cantal's might.

Thaddeus leaned close to Rémy, until his lips were almost brushing her ear. "Are you ready?" he asked, voice barely louder than a breath. "What about your shoulder?"

"Let's go," she whispered back, ignoring the question just as she was ignoring the pain from her injury.

He nodded, and a moment later they were on the rock face, searching for handholds and scrambling down as quietly as they could. Rémy was faster, of course, but Thaddeus impressed her. He was not used to heights as she was, but he didn't hesitate. He was different, she realized; different than the 'little police-man' she had met all those months ago. He was more confident, stronger. She was glad he was there. Rémy couldn't imagine wanting to take on this monstrous mountain with anyone else.

By the time they reached the line of torches, the sky at the distant horizon was a deep rose color as the sun edged toward it. They were running out of time, but neither of them could stop themselves pausing beside one of the burning plumes, staring at it in amazement. The base was a metal cylinder as thick and as tall as a tree trunk. It had been plunged directly into the rock face, as if some giant tool had gouged a hole in the mountain itself. The fire that burned atop was so fierce that it shot several feet into the air like a fountain, its constancy never fading for a moment. Just one of these would be a wonder, but Mont Cantal had too many to count.

"What fuels them?" Thaddeus murmured, holding out his hand to the metal cylinder. "I can feel the heat from a foot away. It's as if the fire is shooting directly out of the mountain."

"I don't think I want to know," Rémy shuddered.

Sound rose up from below them. It echoed from the narrow track that connected each of the torches. Rémy grabbed Thaddeus's arm and pulled him behind a boulder. Two men were making their way up the track, their heavy boots scattering dust and stones from the path as they walked. Both bore the uniform and helmets of the Comte de Cantal.

"A patrol," Thaddeus mouthed, silently. Rémy nodded. They held their breath as the men drew ever nearer.

Neither soldier spoke. Apart from the heavy tread of their feet, they were utterly silent. They must have climbed all the way from the city itself — a long way, even for the fittest of folk. Yet there was no hint of them puffing breath into the cool dawn air.

Rémy looked at Thaddeus with a frown, unsettled, and knew from his expression that he was feeling the same anxiety. There was something off about these two, something strange. She risked peeking out from their hiding place long enough to see that they had solid visors beneath their helmets. Their faces were completely covered by a rounded gold plate. Looking at one of these soldiers was like looking at the blank curve of a goblet. Despite herself, Rémy shivered. Thaddeus gripped her arm, silently reminding her to keep quiet.

They stayed huddled behind the rock until the soldiers' footfalls had faded.

"How do they see?" Rémy whispered, her mind full of the disturbing sight of the men's blank faces. "Why are they covered so?"

Thaddeus shook his head. "I don't know. We've got to hurry, though — there may be more of them."

Rémy nodded. "We'll stay off the path. Come on."

They slipped from boulder to boulder, pausing every time they heard a sound. Another patrol passed, as silent and as strange as the first, but they were not detected. As Rémy and Thaddeus got lower down the mountain, they began to pass caves. There seemed to be hundreds of them — some were tiny, little more than mouse holes in the rock, but others were larger, snaking away into the unknown. Rémy was relieved to see them — they would make excellent hiding places, a useful thing in such a hostile place. But they also reminded her of Abernathy's lair, and she never wanted to find herself anywhere like that ever again.

The roar of the waterfall reached them long before they got to its birthplace. The path passed directly beside where it gushed from the mountain, but Rémy and Thaddeus detoured around it, still anxious to avoid any patrols coming the other way. There was no way across the river until it reached the second tier, though, so they gave up on the idea of trying to get directly into the castle. They stared up at its turrets as they passed, instead, Rémy wondering which one of them, if any, held Claudette.

The sun was up by the time they reached the middle city. They hid outside the main wall, waiting for a gaggle of market traders and their carts to pass, before slipping inside behind them. Once there, they both breathed a little more easily.

"So far, so good," said Thaddeus with a slight smile.

Rémy didn't smile back. "What do you English say about famous last words?"

Thaddeus nodded, acknowledging the point. He was about to say something else when a bell began to ring.

"Ah, there we go," said one of the market traders to another. "It's time for the Comte's proclamation. Better get up there before all the best places are taken, eh?"

There was a general murmuring as everyone around them left their carts and began to head for the road that led up to the castle. One by one, the doors of the white-washed houses opened, and people poured out onto the street. Young and old, rich and poor, servant and master — it seemed that all were destined for the same place.

"Come on," said Thaddeus. "We'd better find out what's going on."

They fell into step with the masses, carried along by the crowds heading up the mountain.

Chapter 35

THE COMTESSE'S RETURN

Thaddeus looked around uneasily as they slowly followed the crowds. It seemed as if every road, path, and stairway around them was now clogged with people. There were soldiers everywhere, too, though these soldiers had their faces uncovered as they scanned the throngs for signs of trouble with cold eyes. Thaddeus felt hemmed in. He kept trying to calculate how swiftly they'd be able to get out if they needed a quick escape. The answer did nothing to quell his anxiety.

They had finally reached the wall of the castle when a fanfare sounded. Thaddeus looked up, shielding his eyes from the morning sun, to see a quad of trumpeters, dressed in what he had come to recognize as the Comte's colors — royal blue, gold and white — standing in a tight line above the castle's gates. The crowd surged forward. Thaddeus passed through the gates in a flurry of arms and legs that were not his own, carried along by the press of eager bodies around him. Together, they all spilled into the courtyard beyond, and found themselves standing beneath a stone tower that dominated all the rest. Huge white steps led to another great wooden door at its base, but what drew the crowd's attention was the balcony halfway up its crowning spire. On it, two more trumpeters stood at attention, and from its balustrade hung another large flag, fluttering slightly in the wind. The fanfare sounded again, shorter this time, and a soldier stepped forward onto the balcony from within. He wore an elaborate helmet, plumed with white feathers designed to mark him out as more than a common soldier.

Thaddeus felt Rémy grip his hand, her angry gaze fixed on the balcony.

"That's the one," she whispered in his ear. "He's the one who led the attack on the circus. He took Claudette."

"People of this great city," boomed the officer. "Pray silence for Comte Cantal de Saint-Cernin."

The soldier retreated as another, longer fanfare played out across the castle keep. Despite the numbers of those gathered in the courtyard, there was absolute silence, as if everyone assembled was holding their breath.

The fanfare went on as a new figure stepped onto the balcony. Thaddeus felt his breath leave him. There stood the Comte de Cantal, the man who had mocked Thaddeus across Sir Henry's dinner table, the man he'd seen negotiating for the purchase of one of Abernathy's infernal submarines. The man who had been convinced that in just one month, he would have enough money to buy the wretched war machine out-right. And why?

Because he knew, Thaddeus told himself. *He knew, thanks to Yannick, that after that night it was only a matter of time before he found Claudette and her fortune.*

Rémy pulled on his hand. He bent down so that she could whisper in his ear.

"I've seen him before," she said. "On the train from Calais. He spoke to Yannick."

The Comte wore yet another well-cut suit over his broad shoulders and stood with an air of assurance that radiated from the balcony like heat. He stepped to the balustrade and regarded the subjects below with a smile, but even from this distance, Thaddeus could see this genial look was deliberate and calculated. The Comte de Cantal, Thaddeus decided, was a man made sharp by nature, and cruel by spirit.

When at last the fanfare died away, the Comte raised his hands.

"Valued subjects," he began. "We all know that this, our beloved city, is the greatest in all the land."

The silence shattered in a cheering roar that threatened to shake the very foundations of Mont Cantal. Around them, the gathered multitude exploded in applause and yelled in whoops of delight. After taking a few moments to soak up the adoration, the Comte raised his hands for silence. The applause echoed away.

"As you know," the Comte went on, "I have made it my mission to locate the lost daughter of my great family, my second cousin who has been known since she was a child as the Lost Comtesse. For too many years, we have been bereft of her presence. It was a difficult task, for we knew not where to look, or even if she still lived. But I would not be deterred."

There came more adoring cheers. Thaddeus looked at Rémy to see her jaw clenched, her eyes hard.

"And so," the Comte continued, as the sound of

the crowd subsided, "it is my very great delight today to announce that the Lost Comtesse is lost no more." The rest of his words had to carry over a storm of clapping and whooping that not even the Comte could quell, nor did he seem to want to. With a broad grin on his handsome face, he announced, "My lords and ladies, people of France, I present Arriete, Comtesse Cantal de Saint-Cernin."

Thaddeus felt Rémy grip his hand tighter as the Comte turned back to someone farther inside the tower. Rémy's lips were moving, as if she were trying to tell him something, but the words were lost beneath the thunder of the crowd. The noise reached a crescendo as a new figure stepped out onto the balcony, reaching for the proffered hand of the Comte.

Thaddeus had only seen Claudette Anjou twice before. The first time was a fleeting encounter when he had been in pursuit of Rémy as the thief of the Ocean of Light. The second had been when Rémy had brought her friend to see her new lodgings at the Professor's workshop before Claudette and the circus had returned to France. He remembered her as beautiful, yes, but even so the woman he saw now was as far removed from the one he recalled meeting as a peacock was from a sparrow. Her chestnut hair had been swept up into a complicated knot that glittered as if studded with jewels. She wore a dress of light blue silk, patterned with flowers and leaves in pale green and pink and edged with intricate lace, both at the open neck and at the sleeves, which tapered at her elbows. It was her face, though, that etched itself into Thaddeus's memory and made his heart clench in sympathy. Claudette's eyes were blank, as if they had been hollowed out. Her mouth was set in a line so emotionless that it seemed impossible she would ever smile again. She stared ahead, expressionless as a porcelain sculpture, as if entirely ignorant of everything that was happening around her.

"Arriete!" shouted someone in the crowd, and then another shouted, and another, and another, until the entire multitude was chanting a name the woman herself appeared not to recognize — "Arriete! Arriete! Arriete!"

The Comte stepped toward Claudette, who was as motionless as stone. He touched one hand to her back and leaned to whisper something in her ear. She blinked once, as if waking from a deep sleep, and then raised an arm to wave at the crowd, smiling widely and nodding. Her eyes, though, remained as blank as a painter's primed canvas.

"Show us!" someone else yelled. "The birthmark! Show us!"

"Yes," shouted another voice, "the birthmark!"

The Comte leaned toward Claudette once more, whispering something else in her ear. She hesitated for a moment, dropping her arm. And then she turned around.

Claudette's gown had been cut to leave her back bare to the mid-point, her pale skin almost translucent beneath the power of the sun. There, curling between her shoulder blades like a serpent lost from the sea, was a birthmark, several shades darker than the skin around it.

The Comte held out his arms to the crowd, as if to say, "See? It really is her," and the multitude cheered once more. Claudette turned around, her face settling back into a blank mask.

"My people," the Comte boomed, once the noise had died down once more. "I have more joyous news to impart. For I called you here not only to celebrate the return of the Lost Comtesse, but also for another reason. I am to be married."

There was a sudden hush, and in it Thaddeus heard Rémy draw in a harsh breath.

"Yes," went on the Comte, "the Comtesse and I are

to be wed, joining the two great wings of our families once and for all. Rejoice with us, for the next three days will be ones of great, great celebration!"

The crowd exploded once more as Thaddeus looked down at Rémy. She was staring up at her friend with huge, shocked eyes.

Cantal seized Claudette's hand and held it aloft as the crowd cheered. Then the Comte swept back into the tower, pulling Claudette behind him. The crowd whooped and cheered a little longer, and then began to filter away, excited chatter filling the air.

"That was his plan," Thaddeus said. "He's not going to kill her. Once they're married, he won't need to. Her money will be his. And the people love him because of it."

Rémy shook her head. "I don't understand. Why would she agree? She can't!"

Thaddeus touched her shoulder. "Rémy, I imagine she doesn't have a choice."

Rémy blinked, her eyes focusing on his. "We have to get her out of here. Now — tonight."

He nodded. "I agree. Which means we need to know exactly where she's being held." Around them, the square was emptying quickly. "Come on, we need to hide."

Thaddeus headed for one of the many narrow alleyways that snaked between the buildings of the castle. They had to conceal themselves away from the watchful gazes of the Comte's men, who were herding the rest of the townsfolk out of the castle's main gate and back down to the city's two lower tiers. He wove his way through the remaining crowds, keeping close to the high walls and out of sight. They had almost reached the passageway he'd been making for when Rémy grabbed his wrist.

"Wait," she hissed.

"What is it?"

"Look!" She pointed back toward the main gate to a small knot of soldiers who were conferring beside it. They seemed to be paying attention to one in particular: a tall, thin young man in a plumed helmet that denoted a higher rank. "It's him," Rémy hissed. "It's Yannick!"

Rémy was right. Her old school friend seemed to be a magician no more. Instead he had taken on the garb of the Comte de Cantal's army.

Thaddeus grabbed Rémy before she could run at him. "Let me go!" she growled, her face a perfect mask of fury. "Let me go, Thaddeus! *Mon dieu*, I will kill him, I will —"

"Rémy!" Thaddeus continued to hold her as she struggled, pulling her deeper into the shelter of the alley. "Go after him now and we're all dead! Think of where we are, for God's sake!"

His words seemed to bring Rémy to her senses. She stopped struggling and nodded. Thaddeus let her go, and they watched from their hiding place as Yannick and his group of men marched away.

"He's joined them," Rémy said, her voice laced with sadness now, as well as anger. "How could he do such a thing? If he had just been tricked by the Comte — misled, somehow . . . But he knows the truth now, and still…" she trailed off, shaking her head.

Thaddeus let the silence between them float for a moment before touching a hand to her back. "Come on," he said. "The sooner we work out where Claudette is and get out of here, the better."

Rémy nodded, though the fury did not leave her eyes. Together, they rejoined the last of the people and slipped out through the castle gates before they were shut and bolted at last.

It wasn't hard to get the people of Mont Cantal to talk about the Lost Comtesse, or their city. In fact, it was the only topic of conversation that seemed to be of any interest to anyone. In the bars and cafés that threw out their colorful awnings as soon as the sun touched the yardarm. In the market and even just on street corners, the talk everywhere was bubbling with the news of the Comte's coming nuptials.

"How lucky that woman is," said one smiling woman to Rémy, over a friendly lunchtime coffee. "Just think! To be plucked from the gutter to live in such a place."

"Yes," said Rémy, through gritted teeth. "She is indeed the luckiest woman alive. How I envy her the chance to see inside the castle itself!"

"Oh, I know! And to live there, too. I've heard," said the woman, leaning closer with the glint of conspiracy in her eyes, "that the Comte's given his betrothed his own room. Isn't that marvelous?"

"Really?" whispered Rémy. "That must be the grandest room in all of Mont Cantal, no?"

"Oh, I should think so," agreed the woman. "They say it's the highest, too, with the greatest view of all." She sighed and sank into a reverie as she finished her coffee.

And so it was that Rémy and Thaddeus filled their day — with many cups of coffee, a few glasses of beer, much gossip, and a slow understanding of the design of the Comte's castle. By the time they began to make their way back up to the airship, it felt almost as if they'd lived there themselves.

Chapter 36

IN AN IVORY
TOWER

*W*hen the sun had fully set, the ruby airship rose into the air as silently as a bird on the wing. J was at the controls, Dita leaning beside him as they left the relative safety of the plateau and sailed out over the city of Mont Cantal. The atmosphere in the cabin was tense. They all knew what was at stake — it would only take a single shot from one of the Comte's riflemen to down the airship and all who sailed in her.

Thaddeus had made a rough sketch of the castle and where they thought Claudette was being held to help J navigate the airship. Rémy sat on the cabin floor and looked at it by the meager light of a candle stub. She didn't even move as Thaddeus sat down next to her and crowded in close, looking over her shoulder.

"How are you, Little Bird?" he asked softly.

She looked up then, watching the candle cast a festival of shadows across his serious face. "You haven't called me that for a long time. I'm not certain you have ever called me that at all."

He smiled, though the look in his eyes was still serious. "Tonight you need to be Little Bird more than you need to be Rémy. Will your shoulder hold up?"

Rémy flexed her arm to prove that it was healed. In truth, the wound was still sore, but it was no worse an ache than some of the bruises she had sustained during practice on the wire, and they had never prevented her from performing. She was determined that this one would not stop her now.

"It is fine," she said, looking once more at the picture he had drawn. It showed four imposing towers, smooth but for the single, guarded door at the bottom and the narrow, dark spaces that had been allowed for windows. For all its gleaming white paint, in Thaddeus's drawing it looked as it truly was — more a prison than a home. How she hated the thought of her friends being caught behind those walls.

"Tonight I will fly as surely as this ship," she murmured, tracing a finger lightly over the paper. "Don't worry, my policeman."

Thaddeus sighed. "Your policeman," he repeated quietly. "Am I never to be anything to you other than that, Rémy Brunel?"

Rémy looked up at him, her heart thumping a little in surprise. He wasn't looking at her, was instead studying the paper in her hands. For a moment she wasn't even sure he'd said anything at all. Her fingers fluttered to her throat before she remembered her opal wasn't there.

"You're not," she began, and then swallowed and tried again, "I don't . . ."

Thaddeus cut her off with a gentle shake of his head and a brief smile. "Don't think of it now," he said. "But when this is over — one way or another — we must talk. So for now, tell me, are your shoulder and your head healed enough?"

Rémy swallowed. "Yes," she said. "They're better. Not perfect, but better."

"Strong enough for what you have to do?" he asked. "Because if not, I will do it. I don't want you risking your life any more than we already are just by being here."

"I am well," she said firmly. "I can do this. I will do this."

Thaddeus stared at her a moment longer, as if he could read her mind through her eyes. He moved his hand toward her, and for a moment Rémy thought he was going to touch her cheek. But then he dropped it again. He nodded and stood, holding out a hand to help her up. She blew out the candle, throwing the cabin into near darkness. They didn't want a sentry spotting a strange light floating toward them through the night.

Thaddeus let go of her hand, and they stood on either side of J and Dita, looking out over the looming city. The torchlights were burning still, and in their yellow flicker the castle looked sickly, its white walls flushed as if with jaundice. Rémy shivered.

They sank toward the castle from directly overhead. They dropped toward the central tower, J letting the ruby's gas out slowly enough for the hiss to be almost silent, even inside the cabin.

"Better get ready," Thaddeus said in a low voice as they sank still farther.

Rémy checked the rope that she had already coiled on the floor of the cabin beside the airship's main hatch. One end was tied securely to a metal ring that

J had driven straight through the ship's wooden hull. They had tested how much weight both the rope and the ring could take, and Rémy was confident it would be enough for what they had planned.

"Okay," said J, a few minutes later, taking a deep breath. "Countdown to hatch opening begins . . . now."

Rémy and Thaddeus calmly began to count, slowly and in unison as the airship sank still lower. Once the two of them had reached ten, it would be time to put their plan into action.

"Nine," whispered Rémy and Thaddeus together. They looked at each other, Rémy's hand on the lever that would open the hatch. Thaddeus gave her a tiny nod. "Ten."

Rémy pulled the lever. The hatch opened, jerking a little at first, but silent, and then swung down smoothly on its recently greased hinges. J had made some swift adjustments so that the gangplank would fold all the way down and away. Rémy leaned out, watching it disappear from view as the night breeze ruffled her short hair. She looked back over her shoulder.

"A little to the left, J," she whispered. She looked out again as the ship began to drift in the right direction. "More . . . more . . . stop."

J threw the rudder, and the airship stopped moving and hung in the air. Rémy tossed out the rope, feeling it pay out through her hands, uncoiling as it fell. She watched as it reached its full length, hanging exactly as they had planned outside the highest window of the tower they hoped was Claudette's.

"Bon." Rémy nodded and glanced at Thaddeus. He was breathing quickly, his gaze intense and fixed on her. She smiled at him, once, and then dropped silently out of the airship, slipping down the rope.

Far below, she could see the ring of soldiers encircling the base of the tower. From the lower two town levels there drifted the faint hubbub of evening — occasional notes of music, the rise and fall of chatter as someone entered or left a bar. Around her came the haunting caw of gulls, wheeling to and from their nests in the rock of the mountain. Rémy hoped these accumulated noises would be enough to mask any she made herself.

The end of the rope came suddenly. Rémy looked up, seeing Thaddeus's pale face looming in the dark hole of the airship's hatch. She glanced down once more, but the soldiers were oblivious, too intent on keeping a watchful eye front and center to realize what was going on over their heads.

Despite her careful directions to J, now that Rémy was level with the window, she realized it was farther away than she'd thought. She reached out, but her fingers were still inches short of the diamond-patterned window panes. She glanced up at Thaddeus, but he'd vanished. Thinking quickly, Rémy hooked one foot and twisted it around the rope to make a hold and then reached out with her free leg. The motion swung her just near enough to get a toe to the narrow ledge. This she used to pull the rest of her closer, until she was flush against the window.

Rémy tried to see inside, but though there seemed to be the remains of a fire — embers smoldered in a hearth — the rest of the room was in darkness. She made out the vague shapes of a bed and a mirror, but there was nothing to convince her that this was the right room. What if the rumors they had heard had been wrong? What if she woke the occupant, only to discover it was the Comte, rather than Claudette?

She swallowed, her heart thumping against her ribcage. Looking down to check that there was no movement from the guards, Rémy put two fingers in her mouth and produced a soft whistle, a little like a birdcall. It was like none she heard in the air around her, and she feared that one of the guards would immediately realize that something was amiss, but there was no shout of warning, no sudden clatter of footsteps. She took a breath and made the call again. It was a tune she hadn't called to her lips for a long time, and she could only hope that if it were Claudette inside this room, her friend would recognize it.

A face appeared at the window, large eyes full of shock. Rémy could have whooped with happiness, for it was Claudette herself, dressed in a long white nightgown. Her friend fumbled with the window, pulling it open quietly. Rémy slipped inside, pulling the rope with her.

"Rémy," hissed Claudette, a horrified look on her face. "How did you get here? What are you doing?"

"No time to explain," said Rémy, looking toward the rumpled bed, expecting a sleepy Amélie to appear at any moment. "We're here to get you out. Quickly, get Amélie and come — Thaddeus will pull you up on the rope."

Claudette looked mystified, going to the window and looking up. "What . . . ?"

"It's a ship that floats in the air," Rémy whispered, glancing toward the door of the room. A light flickered from beneath it, and she could guess that there was at least one guard outside. "Please, Claudette, we have to leave!"

Claudette turned to her. "No. You have to go, Rémy. Go now."

"What are you talking about?" Rémy asked, "Claudette, we can get you out. Both of you. Come on, we have to go!"

"No, Rémy. I cannot." Claudette stepped toward her, gripping her shoulders. "Amélie is not here with me. He has her. The Comte de Cantal has my little girl."

A sick feeling gripped Rémy. "Where?"

Claudette shut her eyes against the tears that had sprung into them. "He has dungeons. They are in the caves, deep in the mountain, between the castle and the middle city — level after level of cells to imprison his enemies. He spends hours there, doing God knows what to those poor souls. He has her somewhere there, but I don't know exactly where or how to get there. He won't let me go to her. He won't let me leave this room unless it is to see him."

Rémy shook herself. "We'll find her, Claudette," she said, pulling her friend to the window. "I promise. But we have to get you out now — we won't have another chance."

"You don't understand," Claudette hissed. "The Comte has a messenger, standing by. If I do anything to make him angry, he'll send word that she must be killed. No one disobeys him, Rémy. If he finds me gone, he won't hesitate. There won't be any time to find her."

Rémy stared at her friend. "But — I can't just leave you here! Not with him!"

"You can — you must! All he cares about is the money. That's all he wants. Once we're married, he'll have it, and he'll let me have Amélie."

Rémy shook her head. "But what then? What about you? What kind of life will the two of you have? He won't let you leave, Claudette. He'll keep you prisoner here. Forever."

Claudette closed her eyes. "But Amélie will be safe. What else can I do?"

The rope twisted suddenly and then disappeared from the window. Rémy ran to it, looking out to see Thaddeus making his way down the rope. Reaching out, she grabbed his hand and pulled him to the window, glancing down at the still heedless guards.

"I was worried," Thaddeus said, once he too was inside the room. "We have to go, now. Every second we hang there risks us being seen."

"Claudette won't come," Rémy told him. "The Comte is holding Amélie hostage."

Thaddeus narrowed his eyes in anger. "Ms. Anjou," he said. "I know what you must be feeling, but . . ."

Claudette cut him off with a shake of her head. "But nothing, Mr. Rec. I appreciate the efforts you have made, but I must do what I must do. This you understand, I think?"

Rémy watched them stare at each other for a moment. Then Thaddeus nodded sharply, once. "I do. Rémy, we have to go."

"What! We can't just —"

He gripped her arm with enough firmness to add urgency to his whispered words. "We'll find another way. But there will be no other way if we are caught. Understand? We must —"

A shout echoed from outside. Rémy and Thaddeus both fled to the window. Below, more shouts broke the quiet, wheeling up the tower walls as surely as a gull's call. Beside her, Thaddeus swore.

"They've seen the ship," he said, but before there was time to do any more, the door to Claudette's room burst open.

"Well, well," said the cool voice of the Comte de Cantal. He stood in the open doorway in black trousers and a white shirt that was open at the neck. Beneath his shoulder was a holstered pistol. Behind him was Yannick, still in full uniform. "What do we have here?"

Chapter 37

ESCAPE

"Comte de Cantal," Claudette said immediately, her voice full of fear. "It's nothing. These — my friends believed I needed help, but I have told them I do not. They — they're going now. Please, please, monsieur — please, let them go."

Cantal stepped slowly into the room, entirely unmoved by Claudette's pleas. The scar on his cruel face seemed like a vein of cold silver in the flickering torchlight that lit the room. He looked at Thaddeus with a slow frown that gave way to lazy amusement.

"Don't I know you from somewhere?" he asked. "Wait a minute . . . aren't you the little London gutter

rat who became a policeman — or should I say police-
boy? What on earth are you doing here?"

"Rémy, go," Thaddeus said tensely, stepping in front
of her. "Go now!"

"Oh no," said the Comte. "I don't think so . . ."

He went for the gun holstered on his hip, his eyes
fixed on Thaddeus. The policeman didn't hesitate —
he lunged for the poker leaning beside the hearth,
slashing it hard across the nobleman's forearm. The
Comte roared with pain, dropping the gun, and
Thaddeus spun back toward the fireplace, grabbing
the silver sword that hung in a sconce above it. It was
decorative and had probably never once been fought
with, but it was all there was.

"Why are you just standing there?" the Comte
yelled to Yannick. He nodded his head at Rémy. "Kill
her!"

Claudette uttered a short scream as Yannick belat-
edly drew his sword, but he was too slow. Rémy leaped
onto a small table that stood between them, rocking it
forward and using the momentum as it tipped to pro-
pel her toward him. She moved so fast that he didn't
even see her coming. Rémy landed her foot at the center of his chest, his ribs cracking beneath the force of
her kick. He crumpled back out through the doorway,

landing in a heap as Rémy ran to the door, crashing it shut and dragging the table she'd upended across it.

Shouts and footsteps echoed from below as more soldiers began to climb the tower stairs.

"Thaddeus," Rémy shouted. "We'll be outnumbered in seconds."

She ran to the window. The airship was still waiting for them, but below, she saw soldiers running this way and that, pointing up at the flying vessel as they discussed how best to bring it down.

The Comte and Thaddeus, meanwhile, were in the midst of a full-bore sword fight. Thaddeus knew enough to keep him at bay, but the Comte was by far the better swordsman. He slashed toward the policeman with a series of lightning blows. Thaddeus grunted, pulling low and slicing wildly at the Comte's thigh, but he was easily parried with a clang that made the policeman's teeth chatter. Thaddeus fought on, clenching his teeth harder and driving in again as the Comte curved in another slash.

"Stop!" Claudette shouted as the two men fought, "Stop it! I am not going with them — I'm staying! Do you hear me? I'm staying!"

The sound of running came ever closer as more soldiers made their way up the stairs. The Comte lunged forward as Thaddeus deflected another blow that sent him crashing backward against the bed. Thaddeus jumped onto it, his feet tangling in the bedclothes as he backed away. The Comte grinned, sensing a victory, but Thaddeus found his balance again, jumping to the floor as he brought his sword down in a sweep that almost caught the nobleman unaware. The Comte yelled in fury, slashing so wildly that he dislodged one of the flaming torches that lit the room. It crashed to the ground amid another scream from Claudette.

The flame bloomed against the bedclothes, which caught light with alarming speed. In a second, the hungry fire had consumed it, shooting up to engulf the ceiling in a fury of heat and acrid black smoke.

Rémy grabbed Claudette's hands and dragged her to the window. "Now," she screamed, over the sound of the inferno and the clanging of the men's swords. "We have to go now!"

Rémy scrambled onto the windowsill. "J," she yelled, hoping against hope that he would hear her over the melee. "J!"

The boy's face appeared at the open hatch, pale and worried.

"You have to bring it down," she shouted, her eyes

full of smoke. "The airship — you have to bring it level with the window."

"I can't," he shouted back, pointing to the flames. "One spark and she'll go up in flames herself! And look!"

Rémy followed the direction of his finger as he pointed down into the castle courtyard. To her horror, several of the soldiers were preparing bows and arrows. Even worse, one of them held a burning torch. If one of those hit the airship…

Rémy grabbed Claudette, dragging the end of the rope around them both. "Thaddeus!" she yelled, as she tied it off, but the fight went on, furious and insane. "J," she shouted, "lift us up!"

Rémy felt the rope tighten against her stomach as the airship rose. Claudette screamed as she was pulled from the window and into the air, but Rémy held her fast. She blinked the smoke from her eyes as the room disappeared from view, shocked to see that the flames had already bitten into the roof.

"What about Thaddeus?" Claudette yelled, looking down in horror.

"He'll get out," said Rémy. "He has to. He'll get out . . ."

A whistling sound shot past them and the airship

jerked, bouncing them on the rope like fish on a line. Rémy looked up to see a flaming arrow just miss its target thanks to J's lighting reaction. He tried to right them again, but the sudden course changes sent the rope — and the two women hanging from it — on a wild swing, straight toward one of the other towers.

"Hang on," said Rémy, through gritted teeth, as she saw a stone balcony coming fast toward them. She lifted her feet, planting them against the balustrade, crashing against it hard enough to judder her teeth. Claudette screamed, the rope around them loosening as the hurried knot slipped undone.

"Claudette!" Rémy yelled, as both her friend and the rope threatened to slip from her grasp. She grabbed the slithering rope with one hand, wrapping her legs around Claudette to prevent her falling to her death. Claudette reached for the safety of the balcony, just as the doors inside were flung open with a crash.

"I can't let you get away!" Yannick shouted, a mad fury in his eyes. "He'll kill me! Do you understand? You have to stay. You must stay!" He grasped Claudette and pulled her, struggling, over the balcony's edge.

Rémy felt the airship jerk again and looked up to see another fiery arrow shoot past, even closer this time. A strike from one of those flaming arrows and the ruby airship would explode. Rémy swung herself toward the balcony again as Yannick wrestled Claudette inside the tower, kicking the door shut behind him. Rémy's feet touched the balcony wall, and she teetered there for a second before righting herself and letting go of the rope.

"J," she screamed, as loudly as she could. "Go! Go!"

He must have heard her, because as another arrow shot grazed the balloon, the airship lifted up and away into the night. There was a shout of fury from below as the archers realized their quarry was escaping, but by that time it was too late. As Rémy rushed to the balcony doors, the airship was already out of reach.

{Chapter 38}

FIRE AND BRIMSTONE

Thaddeus stumbled, crashing against the wall, coughing as the smoke filled his eyes and lungs. There seemed to be no air anywhere in the room, and the heat from the fire was even worse. Still the Comte seemed unwilling to give up, lunging at the policeman like a demon, almost goring him with his blade. Twice Thaddeus tried to reach the Comte's discarded gun, and twice it was kicked farther and farther out of reach.

"Comte," Thaddeus yelled, over the roar of the flames, his arms burning with the effort of the fight. "This is insane! We have to get out of here!"

"Only one of us is leaving, English rat," the Comte yelled. "And I swear to you it'll be me!"

"I don't want to fight," Thaddeus said, coughing again, almost blind as he parried another blow. "Neither of us needs to die, but both of us will if we don't get out of here!"

"You don't want to fight," the Comte repeated with a sneer. "So, a coward as well as a fool. I should have known!" He drove right quickly enough to nick Thaddeus's thigh. He cackled with glee as the policeman yelped in pain and stumbled backward. The nobleman lunged again, cursing with annoyance as Thaddeus parried. "Enough of this," he hissed.

The Comte drove forward with added fury, forcing Thaddeus back toward the flames. Thaddeus bluffed a falter, drawing the nobleman to him. The Comte sensed victory and over-stretched himself in a lunge. It was enough to give the policeman the upper hand. With a grunt of effort, he pushed the nobleman against the wall hard enough to stun him. They both dropped to the floor, Thaddeus's left leg pinning the Comte's left arm, Thaddeus's sword against his throat.

The Comte de Cantal spat in his face. Thaddeus flinched, which was just enough for his opponent to get one elbow free, crashing it into the policeman's temple. Thaddeus, stunned, almost blacked out, and the Comte was on his feet again in a trice. He grabbed his sword, took one step backward, ready to go for the killing stroke.

There was a deep, creaking groan. The wooden floor beneath them shook and then gave way. One minute it was there, the next it collapsed, crashing to the level below in a flurry of sparks and flame. The Comte disappeared through the ragged hole, crying out. Thaddeus lurched forward, still on his hands and knees, catching hold of his enemy's arm and slithering to a halt against the ragged edge of wood. He scrambled to his knees, clenching his teeth as he braced his feet against the uneven floor, trying to keep hold of the nobleman. The Comte was still holding on to the sword with his other hand.

"Drop the sword," Thaddeus yelled as the flames grew and grew around them. "I can't hold you!"

The Comte swung himself toward the edge but wouldn't let go of his weapon, trying to use his elbow to gain purchase, instead. Thaddeus reached out with one arm to grasp his shoulder, but he still couldn't drag the man over the edge.

"Comte!" Thaddeus shouted. "You need both hands! Let it go, before . . ." There was another crash as the fire ate away a second part of the floor. Thaddeus felt it threatening to give way beneath him but still it held. "Comte," he tried again, his throat sore with the effort, "I can't . . ."

The Comte de Cantal screamed as he fell. Thaddeus tried to grip his shoulder, but the nobleman slipped away. A second later, he had vanished into the inferno below. Thaddeus rolled backward just as a tongue of flame burst through the hole, threatening to swallow him too. He staggered to his feet, searching for a way out. But the door was too far away and the floor had disappeared. Thaddeus felt the rest of the planks buckle beneath him, rising and falling like an ocean wave. They collapsed, sucking him into the black void below.

{Chapter 39}

ONE LAST CHANCE

*Y*annick grabbed Claudette by the hair with one hand, holding a knife to her throat with the other.

"Stop," Remy told him. "Yannick, just stop. You don't need to do this. Please, just let her go."

"I can't, don't you understand?" the magician hissed. "He'll blame me, for everything."

"Then — then come with us," Rémy said, thinking fast. Outside, the soldiers were still shouting, and the sounds of the fire were growing ever louder. "We can all escape together. Come on, Yannick — right now, let's go."

Yannick laughed, but the sound echoed hollowly off the chamber's stone walls. "And then what, Little

Bird? There's no place for the likes of me in your new circus, is there? You told me that already, remember?"

Rémy shook her head. "I changed, Yannick. You can, too. All you have to do is help us now, and we'll help you. Isn't that what family does? And that's what we are, isn't it, despite everything? Family, Yannick. We're family."

Yannick squeezed the knife tighter to Claudette's neck. A bright bead of blood appeared against her skin as the point pierced it.

"This isn't you," Rémy whispered. "I know it isn't, not really."

The magician shook his head, but a look of uncertainty crossed his face. He hesitated, lessening his grip just for a moment, and that was all that Rémy needed. She glanced up to where the servants' bell rope hung through a small metal ring that fastened it to the ceiling. Once a bird, always a bird . . .

She jumped, taking off as easily as if she were taking a step. Rémy hooked one finger through the ring and at the same time raised her legs into a split position, moving so quickly that Yannick had no time to react. Claudette, though, saw what was coming and slammed her hand into her captor's wrist, jerking the knife away from her throat. Rémy twisted in the air, turning her finger around the ring as easily as if she'd been holding onto a trapeze. Her other hand grasped the scarlet bell rope, sending it ringing wildly as she dragged it tightly through its mooring. A second later it was looped around Yannick's throat, and she was in the air once more, dragging him to the ground. His knife clattered to the floor beside him as he lay, gasping and coughing.

"Run!" Rémy shouted. She and Claudette reached the door together, flinging it open and crashing through it into the corridor beyond. Yannick roared with hoarse anger as he scrambled back to his feet and came after them, lurching into the corridor like a drunk.

Rémy and Claudette ran, searching for an escape.

"We can't go down," Rémy shouted as soldiers' yells echoed up the stairs.

"Over the roof?" Claudette asked.

"Can you make it?"

"If the fire hasn't taken it already. Let's find out, shall we?" Claudette said, raising one hand to wipe away the blood at her neck.

They crashed into a room at the end of the corridor to find another bedroom, with no balcony this time. Their only option was the narrow, diamond-leaded window. Rémy rushed to it, flinging it open as her friend slammed the door shut and searched for something to block it with. Looking out, Rémy was dismayed at the lack of handholds she saw. She could make it, but could Claudette?

"We don't have a choice," said her friend, reading her mind as she joined her at the window. "You go first, Little Bird — show me how." She bent down, grasping the skirt of her long nightdress and tearing it off at the knees.

There came the sound of splintering wood as Yannick hammered at the door behind them.

"Go," Claudette urged. "I'll follow right behind."

Rémy did as she was bid, first standing on the ledge and then turning sharply. She gripped the lintel above, pulling herself up, finding purchase difficult against the smooth, white-washed walls above. She braced herself, relieved that the tiles of the spired roof were close. Hauling herself up, she turned and sat on the edge, looking over at the tower that had been Claudette's prison. The fire had bitten hard and was flaming hungrily over the roof, sending up a plume of smoke thick enough to obscure the stars.

Don't think about Thaddeus, she told herself. *He's probably already out. Maybe J came back. Maybe . . .*

There came crash after crash from below as Yannick rained blows against the door. Claudette was perching on the windowsill just as she had done, but Rémy's heart quailed at the sight beyond her friend. The archers were gone: everyone was concentrating on fighting the fire. But if Claudette fell, there would be nothing but a hundred feet of air and then a harsh stone courtyard to break her fall, and Yannick could be behind her in moments.

"Okay," she told Claudette, more calmly than she felt. "First rule is, don't look down . . ."

Rémy felt something loom over her and looked up. The ruby airship sailed over the rocky outcrop, cabin lights blazing like the sun rising in the dead of night. She stood up, waving her arms as J brought the ship in lower.

"Claudette," she yelled, as Dita appeared in the hatch and threw out the rope. "Get Claudette!"

Yannick appeared at the window, screaming with rage as Claudette grabbed the dangling rope and was whisked away. Rémy waited until her friend was climbing the rope to safety, then glanced back over her shoulder at the opposite tower. If she dropped over the right side of the roof, Rémy calculated quickly, she could reach the narrow wall that connected the two closest towers. Once she was across that, all she needed to do to reach Thaddeus was —

A groan swelled into the night: strange, inhuman and terrifying in its magnitude. A fresh bellow of flame exploded up through the tiles of the tower's roof, splintering them as if they were matchsticks. The sound of a hundred glass panels shattering at once filled the air, and a wave of heat rolled over Rémy, so powerful it stole her breath right out of her lungs. There were hoarse screams from below. The Comte's men ran as cracks appeared in the tower's very walls, ripping through the bricks as if they were paper, huge belches of flames erupting from the tears.

Then the tower crumbled. It seemed to hang there in the flame for a moment before toppling like a child's toy, collapsing in on itself with a rumble as deep as thunder.

Rémy stared at the space where it had been, and she could think of just one word.

Thaddeus.

Shock rolled over her like a cold wave. The world turned silent as Rémy stared at where the tower had been.

"Oh, dear," Yannick's voice sneered in her ear. "Not

sure even your beloved policeman could get out of that, eh, Little Bird?"

The fury was like a white-hot pain. She spun so quickly that Yannick's knife didn't even have a chance to cut her. Blind with rage, Rémy struck out, slamming her fist into his throat. Yannick gulped like a fish, eyes bulging in shock, and she kicked him hard in the ribs. His knife clattered to the tiles and slid away down the roof. The magician slumped to his knees, gasping for breath and holding his abdomen.

"You tricked me," he whined. "You lied. You said —"

She spotted something hanging around the magician's neck. Leaning forward, she hooked her fingers under it and wrenched it free. It was a small opal pendant, hanging from a slim gold chain.

The rope tapped her shoulder. Above her, Claudette leaned out of the airship, urging her to climb. Rémy grasped the rope, shaking off Yannick's hands as they pawed at her legs.

The ruby airship lifted away and down the mountainside.

{Chapter 40}

THADDEUS

The tower crumbled around Thaddeus, level after level giving way as the structure disintegrated. Flames licked at him as he plummeted through the ruin of wood and stone. He grabbed at some of the remaining floor as he fell. The plank broke under his grip, but it was enough to slow his descent. His feet hit solid ground, hard. He collapsed, rolling on cold stone, winded, aching, and with fresh burns.

Thaddeus lay staring up out of the darkness. Above him he could see the flaming innards of the tower, the floors that the fire had eaten through starkly visible voids. More rafters began to fall toward him as the fire tore them from their couplings. He scrambled to his knees, flinging himself out of the way as hellfire rained down. Thaddeus screamed in pain as a burn on his left arm connected with rock.

Crouching against the rough wall, Thaddeus blinked as his eyes adjusted to the uneven light. There were passages around him, leading in all directions. He remembered the caves he and Rémy had seen during their climb down from the airship. Perhaps the entire mountain was riddled with them, he thought: a honeycomb of passageways beneath the surface. If that was the case, there must be a way out. Struggling to his feet, Thaddeus picked up a shard of burning plank to use as a torch and chose a direction.

He'd only gone a few paces when he heard something behind him. The sound echoed against the walls just a second before he felt something sharp touch his neck.

"I should have known," said the cold voice of the Comte de Cantal. "Only a peasant boy would abandon his sword."

Thaddeus turned, slowly, feeling the steel of the Comte's sword bite at his neck. The nobleman stood silhouetted against the burning rubble of his castle. He was bloodied and bruised, his hair unkempt, and his trousers and shirt singed and tattered. But he still clutched his sword, and his scarred face still bore an air of infuriated arrogance.

"Comte —" Thaddeus began, but was cut off.

"Look what you have done," hissed the Comte. "You will pay for this, all of you, I swear. Where is Arriete?"

"Her name is Claudette," Thaddeus told him, finding it hard to draw breath with the Comte's blade still pressed against his neck.

"Whatever," said the Comte dismissively. "She can call herself what she likes as long as she hands over her fortune."

"She's not going to marry you, Comte," Thaddeus told him.

"Well, it is up to her, of course," shrugged the nobleman. "There is still the other option — for me to provide her body as proof of her death."

"The lawyers would know that you killed her for the money," said Thaddeus. "They'd never let you get away with it."

"Oh, really?" The Comte turned to look at the burning wreck behind him. "You do not think they might believe she perished in the blaze?"

"Look," said Thaddeus, "It's too late anyway. She's miles away by now."

The Comte laughed. "Either you think I am an idiot peasant or you are actually one. She won't go anywhere without her little whelp."

"She doesn't need to," Thaddeus said with as much conviction as he could. "We rescued Amélie earlier. They've already been reunited."

The Comte laughed again. "Impossible. Come, we must go. I suspect we will find the Comtesse at the girl's cell. She will do as I say when she sees a knife at her baby's throat." He wiggled the sword, scraping at Thaddeus's neck. "Go on — move."

Thaddeus stumbled slightly as the Comte pushed him down one of the stone passageways. "Not even you would really harm a child."

The Comte made a sound of disgust in his throat. "She's a mute wretch conceived in some miserable circus hovel. Even if the Comtesse does as she's told to keep her alive, do you think I'd have that living as my own kin? No, I'll get rid of it one way or another."

Thaddeus swallowed the sick anger in his throat. Oh, how he loathed this man. When the moment came . . .

"I saw you," Thaddeus said, his words echoing off the tunnel walls as they passed swiftly through them. "In London — or should I say, under London. You might think it's a secret, but I know about Abernathy and what he tried — and failed — to do. It's what you need the Comtesse's inheritance for, isn't it? To buy his war machines. You're trying to make them work for yourself. You'll fail, Comte. Just as he did."

"Abernathy?" the Comte repeated with disdain. "Abernathy was nothing but a fool, a stuffed shirt who thought he could defy the cause and follow his own agenda. His achievements were nothing — a storm in a teacup, as you English say."

Thaddeus frowned. "The cause? What cause? What do you mean?"

The Comte laughed, the sound unpleasant against the stony backdrop of the passageway. "Ahh. So, you do not know everything after all. Of course you do not. A child like you cannot possibly understand any of what you stumbled upon in London — how big it is, how important. How laughable it is that you, a mere London street boy, could dare to think you understand anything."

Chapter 41

AMÉLIE

Claudette, Rémy, J, and Dita watched the pandemonium below through the airship's windows. The townsfolk from the two lower tiers were trying to flee the city as the castle burned above them. Clods of flaming brick and mortar were scudding down the mountainside, threatening to set their homes alight. All they could do was run.

"I have to get to Amélie," Claudette whispered tearfully, watching the continuing destruction below. "I have to at least try."

Rémy blinked dry eyes, trying to focus on what could be done instead of what couldn't. Thaddeus was gone, she told herself, but Amélie could still be alive.

"We have to go down again, J," she said quietly.

"What?" J asked, aghast. "Rémy, I can't!!"

"You don't have to go near the flames," she said, tiredly. "Take us down to the middle section of the city. You don't even have to land — just get low enough for us to use the rope. We have to do this, J. We have to. *D'accord?*"

J looked at Rémy, his young face grim in the shadows cast by the Professor's instruments. For a second it seemed as if he would argue. Then he changed his mind and, with a brusque nod, began to bank the ship. None of the soldiers on the ground took any notice — they were too intent on fighting the fires that were destroying the Comte's fortress.

Rémy peered out the window as they sank lower. Already, two or three of the tall townhouses on this level were smoldering. Soon the flames would take hold in earnest.

"This is close enough," she said, as the airship floated level with one of the houses. She looked at Claudette. "Ready?"

Her friend nodded, her face still streaked with tears. Rémy couldn't remember seeing Claudette cry before.

"Okay, then," she said, and lowered the hatch. "Let's go."

The air outside was thick with heat, the stench of burning, and the screams of the desperate townsfolk. The dungeons were not hard to find. As Claudette had said, they were carved straight out of the rock and thus stood behind the last of the once-proud townhouses now cowering in the face of the fire. Two huge, solid iron gates proclaimed the entrance. There were sentry boxes on either side, but they had been abandoned by their soldiers. The gates, though, were locked fast. Claudette shook them, but they would not budge.

"We will have to climb," Rémy told her. She pointed to the top, where there was a small gap between the gate and its rock housing.

"I don't know if I can," Claudette muttered, her face pale in the soot-smogged air.

"You can," Rémy told her. "You must."

The gates were as simple as a ladder for Rémy. She was up and over the top in less than twenty seconds, but Claudette took longer. The trapeze artist paused to help her friend, easing her through the gap, untangling her long hair when it became caught. By the time they had made it to the ground on the other side, one of the houses they had passed on their way in was fully aflame. The sick light of its destruction cast a patterned shadow through the iron gates, turning the ground to lace.

Inside, sound echoed like unsettled ghosts. Screams and shouts thrown up from outside ricocheted around the enclosed space. There were torches burning on the walls, which seemed almost sedate in view of the inferno raging above them. They lit the way, but that didn't help much. A dozen caves led into the rock from the entrance.

"Which way?" Claudette asked, her voice nearing a sob. "I don't know which way! Amélie!" she shouted, "Amélie!"

The sound of hurrying footsteps clattered toward them from the passage on their left. A flustered soldier, wild-eyed and sweating, appeared. He hesitated when he saw them, as if wondering whether to go for his weapon. Then another of the castle's towers crumbled, a distant whump overhead that shivered the mountain. Fragments of the cave roof rained down on them all in a flurry of choking dust. The soldier changed his mind about stopping them and went to charge past them instead.

"Not so fast," said Claudette. Together, she and Rémy grabbed at him, hauling him up against the wall.

"Hey," the soldier cried, puffing and sweating even more now. "I weren't going to stop you. Let me go!"

"Tell us where Amélie Anjou is," Claudette growled, thrusting her face close to his cringing eyes.

"Eh? Who?"

"The little girl!" Rémy shouted, "The little girl you monsters locked up in this unholy place! Where is she, or I'll —"

"Oh," interrupted the soldier, with a shrill laugh. "Her! She's down there." He pointed to the farthest cave mouth. Unlike the others, it was dark, with no torches burning to alleviate the gloom.

Claudette and Rémy looked at each other. As one they let him go, the soldier almost stumbling to his knees as they moved away. Rémy grabbed the torch above them from its sconce.

"You don't want to go down there," the soldier called, his voice fading behind them as they ran deeper into the passage. "No one who goes down there ever comes out. Not even us guards. It's the Comte's orders!"

Rémy and Claudette took no notice.

Chapter 42

A TERRIBLE REVELATION

Thaddeus's head was spinning. What was the Comte talking about? How could anything be bigger than what he and Rémy had battled in Abernathy's lair?

"If Abernathy was such a failure, why did you want his machines?" he asked as they turned down another stone corridor.

"So that some other poor, deluded idiot like him doesn't try to use them. That would only risk more failure. I told them," the Comte went on. "I warned them not to let Abernathy take the key, but they wanted someone in position in England. Water and air, that was what was needed on an island. And I must confess, Abernathy's engineer had a certain genius, indeed. That airship of yours, for example; I look forward to adding that to my army."

"A-army?" Thaddeus stuttered, stopping. The policeman had the sudden sense that he was standing at the edge of an abyss. "Key? What —"

The Comte shoved him forward roughly. He stumbled, steadying himself against the stone wall. The policeman coughed, his lungs stinging. There was now an acrid tang in the air, stronger than the stench of burning rubble they had left behind. It smelled like rotting eggs. He almost gagged as another wave of the noxious fumes rolled down the passageway toward them. Thaddeus heard a tearing sound and saw that the Comte was ripping off the front of his shirt, using the strip of fabric to cover his mouth and nose.

Thaddeus stared at de Cantal's bare chest. Over the honed muscle was an ornate tattoo of a short, curved sword — a cutlass. The hilt was shown with a cupped guard that crossed directly over the Comte's nipple, which had been pierced with a pale blue, faceted stone.

"Aha," said the nobleman, with an amused nod at Thaddeus's shocked expression. "Indeed, I imagine this is different from anything you have ever seen before, yes?"

"A — a sapphire?" Thaddeus asked, his voice hoarse with fumes.

"Well done," said the Comte, pushing Thaddeus in front of him again. "Now move!"

Thaddeus coughed again, staggering forward. It was becoming harder and harder to breathe. He held one hand up against his nose, trying to filter out some of the stench. Ahead of them, a bright glow lit the sides of the rocky walls. There were sounds, too, pounding loudly out of the semi-dark.

"Is that sulphur?" he asked of the gas, his eyes watering so much that he could hardly see.

"Again, you impress me, Englishman," the Comte said as they came to another corner.

He forced Thaddeus forward faster as the policeman coughed and spluttered. Thaddeus stumbled around a corner and found that the passageway ended on a lip of stone that jutted out over an open space. Half-blind, he almost walked straight over the drop, catching himself just in time. His heart pounding, Thaddeus threw himself back against the wall and then slid down it, his legs buckling beneath him as the fumes proved too powerful for his lungs. He could hear the Comte coughing too, now, the fumes defeating his makeshift mask. Thaddeus shut his eyes and rested his head on his knees, gasping in vain for air. He was surrounded by noise of all description — banging, hissing, creaking, whining, whistling — a conglomeration of sound that was too great to separate. Then there came another sound, much closer — the tinkling of glass as something smashed it.

Something tapped him on the shoulder. He struggled to lift his head and saw the Comte holding something out to him. Thaddeus blinked at it blearily. It looked like some kind of mask with a leather front beset with two circular glass panels to see out of and a metal disk peppered with tiny holes covering the nose and mouth. There was a pipe leading from it, connected to a small cylinder that the Comte held in his other hand.

"Put it on," the Comte ordered. He passed Thaddeus the contraption and then pulled an identical mask over his own head.

Thaddeus did as he was told — anything would be better than breathing more sulphur. He pulled the leather straps on around his ears so that the visor fitted into place over his face. It was tight, and his fingers fumbled around the edge of the mask, touching a cog he found there. Turning it, he heard a faint hiss, and cool air brushed against his skin. It was immediately easier to breathe, and Thaddeus gratefully sucked in a lungful of oxygen. He struggled to his feet, clutching the canister. His vision was clouded despite the viewing glasses. The Comte moved to stand beside him, still holding on to his sword. Over the man's shoulder, he could see what had caused the sound of smashing glass — a cabinet, screwed into the wall. The Comte must have punched through its doors in his hurry to retrieve the masks.

"You see, boy?" shouted the nobleman, lifting his arm and swinging it out in an arc over the drop beneath them. "You see how foolish your friends have been to cross me?"

Thaddeus looked. He saw, in the base of the cavern in which they stood, a great hole cut into the rock of the mountain itself. In it bubbled molten fire, a furnace so hot that it could never be quenched.

"It's a — a volcano," Thaddeus managed, staring at the sight below with horrified eyes.

"Many mountains have the potential to be a volcano," the Comte said, his voice muffled but the glint of insane pride in his eyes visible even through his mask. "It just depends how deep you drill into its belly. Get a move on, would you? These masks are so tedious."

Chapter 43

DARKNESS

"*A*mélie!" Claudette shouted, her voice echoing along the dank stone corridor and dying in its depths. "Amélie!"

There was no sound, no indication at all that there was anything alive in the tunnel. Rémy hated to think of Claudette's little girl being kept in such a place. Surely not even a man as cruel as the Comte de Cantal would do such a thing to a child?

It was impossible to hurry — there was no light to see by, only a dim, gray glow. No, it was not even a glow — it was merely a sign that somewhere far ahead, the darkness was not as deep as here. Rémy and Claudette edged their way along, their hands against the uneven walls, their feet striking loose pebbles and kicking up choking plumes of dust. *At least*, Rémy thought, *everything here seemed dry.* She didn't like being underground again, but it would have been far worse if it had been dank as the tunnels of Abernathy's lair had been. Here, at least, there seemed no chance of a flood — no sign of any water at all.

"Amélie!" Claudette shouted again, making Rémy jump. "Please answer, baby. We can't find you. Please!"

Rémy's heart went out to her friend. She had never given up hope that one day Amélie would speak to her — that one day, she would be able to talk to her little girl. Amélie's silence was perplexing and at times, frustrating. Here, it could also be the difference between her life and death.

Rémy's hand struck something other than stone. She stopped and reached out again to touch whatever it was. She found metal, rough and old — a thin bar.

"Claudette," she said, "wait a moment."

In the gloom she saw the murky figure of her friend pause and turn back. Rémy reached out with her other hand and found another bar. Crouching, she ran her hand down to where it met the stone floor, and then, standing again, reaching up to where it disappeared above her head.

"What is it?" Claudette asked, her lilting voice fractured by anxiety.

"A cell," Rémy told her. "I don't know how big."

"Amélie!" Claudette shouted, again. "Are you here? Please tell us! Please!"

They listened for any hint of an answer, but there was nothing.

"What if she's not here at all?" Claudette asked, tearfully. "What if the soldier was lying and we're just wasting time?"

Rémy couldn't answer that question — it was one she'd been asking herself, too. But what if the soldier had been telling the truth? Turning around and abandoning Amélie to this terrible place was too awful to think about.

"We'll go a little farther," Rémy decided. "See how many cells there are, yes?"

She saw a slight movement in the darkness — Claudette nodding. They carried on, arms outstretched, hands brushing against cell after cell. The farther they went, the harder it became to breathe, and Rémy became aware of a strange smell in the air. The faint reek of old eggs mixed with musty air.

{Chapter 44}

METAL MEN

The Comte hustled Thaddeus toward the edge, the point of his sword jabbing viciously at the policeman's back. For a moment Thaddeus thought he was about to be thrown from the edge, but then through the dusty eyeglasses, he saw steps hewn into the rock. Thaddeus lurched down them, putting one hand out to steady himself while the other clutched his oxygen tank. It was difficult to see properly in the mask, but he drank in the sights around him, the terrible power of what he saw sinking deep into his bones.

From the lake of liquid fire flowed small, carved channels, directing the lava from its source and into passages that vanished from view. Vast slabs of rock kept these smaller lava flows in check, redirecting and restricting their flow as required. Each of these was connected to a huge metal arm that was in turn connected to a massive metal chamber that Thaddeus assumed must hold machinery to control the arms. It had been built into the roof of the cavern, and at one end was a square metal cabin with glass windows. As Thaddeus looked up at it, he saw movement; there were men inside. In fact, he realized as he looked around, there were men everywhere, dressed in strange golden armor and with the same blank visors as worn by the mountain patrol.

"They don't have oxygen canisters," he yelled. "How do they breathe?"

The Comte laughed. "Look again. Why would they need air when they have no noses, no mouths?"

The policeman frowned. "But . . . but they must need ventilation," he said. "Unless . . ."

"Ah," said the Comte. "Now the truth of my brilliance occurs to you. Why employ human soldiers when you can build ones that will never tire, never disobey, never wear out?"

His heart pounding, Thaddeus thought back to the Professor's illustrations of mechanical soldiers. If this was true, if the Comte had somehow managed to turn sketches like those into reality . . .

"This is your army?" he asked, a chill creeping over him.

The Comte laughed again. "This? No, this is not my army, peasant. These are merely the workers. I will show you my army."

He bundled Thaddeus forward, following one of the smaller lava channels, its heat bathing Thaddeus in a thick sheen of sweat. The policeman flinched as he looked up and saw the giant machine overhead reaching down to grasp an impossibly huge slab of rock. As he watched, it lifted the stone, swinging it around and placing it into the path of one of the smaller lava flows. The burning stream bubbled against it for a moment before turning to flow into a different channel.

"Lava," the Comte shouted over the clamor of industry that seemed to emanate from every corner, "is the most extraordinary natural resource in the world. It is a fire that never goes out, yes? With its power, I heat my people's homes and warm their water, for which they love me. And," he added, pushing Thaddeus through the cave mouth, "it allowed me to build . . . this."

Thaddeus found himself not in a stone corridor, but in another adjoining cavern. The stream of lava they had followed cascaded down a short drop into a small pool that then fed into another channel like the ones in the first cavern. At the other end was a great door built into the wall, leading who knew where. What else he saw below him, though, made Thaddeus sick with fear.

"You see? That," said the Comte, "that is my army, Englishman."

The Comte was pointing at what was row upon row of silent men. Their bodies were formed of metal — smooth, lean, and indestructible — because what Thaddeus had taken to be armor was in fact their skin. Each of their faces were golden and as blank as a new sheet of paper. And there were hundreds of them. Perhaps it was because they were so silent and so very still, but the sight of so many automatons in one place was even more terrifying to the policeman than the sight of Abernathy's human army had been all those months ago. There was something particularly chilling about these soldiers: Thaddeus knew without touching them that their bodies would be as cold as the stone of this mountain in which they had been created. He remembered J's words about the sketch in the Professor's book; the way the boy had shivered as he'd imagined a soldier who couldn't think, couldn't feel, and never became tired.

"Your silence does you credit," yelled the Comte. "For truly, there is nothing to say in the face of this wonder. You must see, now, how useless it is to disobey me, yes?"

Thaddeus swallowed, pulling himself together. "How do they work?" he asked. "How did you even build them?"

The Comte pointed again, this time to the lava flow they had followed from the first cavern. It flowed toward a large metal chamber that sat over the boiling stream. The chamber was curved and set with a chimney in its roof. For the first time, Thaddeus also realized that he could hear water — a lot of water, crashing and rolling as its thunder added yet another sound to the riot of noise. He looked up, his vision still obscured by the mask, and saw that the noise came from a waterfall that splashed through the wall of the cavern, close to the ceiling. This, too, flowed toward the metal chamber. What Thaddeus had first assumed was smoke smudging the air was actually steam.

"It's a steam engine," he said aloud in amazement. "You're using lava instead of coal to heat the water!"

"Well done," said the Comte approvingly, as if he were talking to a promising student. "This engine is the most powerful ever built. It drives both the machine you have already seen and that one over there." He pointed to another large contraption that stood silently behind his gathered army. "When that is running, it can press out one of my soldiers every thirty minutes. Their armor is formed from a single sheet of metal, heated and molded into form. They are then assembled, insides and all, by other such soldiers who have been designed specifically for such work."

"And what about the men?" Thaddeus asked, his mouth dry. "How do they work?"

"A combination of miniature friction engines and clock work," said the Comte. "They have taken a long time — and my entire fortune — to perfect."

"Comte, I don't understand," said Thaddeus. "Surely, all you need to do is sell one of these mechanical men, and you will be the richest man on the planet! Why do you need Claudette at all? Why can't you just let her go?"

The Comte narrowed his eyes inside his mask. "I will never part with a single one of these soldiers," he hissed. "Not one. I can't risk lesser men getting their hands on my mechanical marvels. All my soldiers are needed, all necessary for what is to come."

"And what's that?" Thaddeus asked, his heart thumping. "Comte? What is to come?"

"We are wasting time," said his captor. "I begin to think you delay me deliberately. Move."

The Comte pushed him up a flight of steps and toward a wooden door. Thaddeus stumbled through it and found himself in darkness.

"Take off the mask," The Comte ordered, pulling off his own and dropping it to the ground. "No sense in wasting oxygen when it's not absolutely necessary, eh?"

Thaddeus did as he was told. The Comte's sword pricked his spine, forcing him forward once again.

{Chapter 45}

A CHINK
OF LIGHT

"*A*mélie!" Claudette shouted, again, and Rémy could hear the fading hope in her friend's voice as they continued along the passage. "Little one, if you can make a sound — any sound — please tell us where you are!"

There was more silence. Then a loud but distant clanging started up somewhere ahead, the sound of metal hitting metal. It echoed around them and then stopped as quickly as it had begun.

"Amélie!" Claudette cried. "Is that you? We're coming!"

The clanging started up again as Claudette and Rémy hurried toward the sound. They passed cell after cell, and as they did so, Rémy realized that the light ahead was getting brighter. It was easier to see what was around them — how small these chambers were, how miserably bare. The chemical smell in the air was also stronger now, making them both cough.

Ahead of her, Claudette disappeared around a corner and cried out, skidding to a halt. Rémy reached her and saw what had caused the cry. They had indeed found Amélie — but she was not alone.

The Comte de Cantal lounged lazily against the bars of her cell, a metal cup dangling from one elegant hand. His other held a sword, which was crooked around the neck of someone he had forced to kneel on the floor before him — someone Rémy had never expected to see again.

"Thaddeus!" Rémy couldn't believe her eyes. "But how did you . . . ? Where did you . . . ?"

The policeman looked up at her with a faint smile. "Don't ask."

"You're alive," she said, still trying to take it in. "I thought . . . I thought . . ."

"Yes, yes, yes," barked the Comte impatiently. "We're all very touched, I'm sure. Now do shut up, or I may be sick. You," he said, standing up straighter and jabbing the metal cup toward Claudette. "You're the one I want."

Claudette's tearful gaze was fastened on her daughter, who sat at the back of her cell with her arms wrapped around her thin knees. Amélie's face was streaked with dirt, her hair was matted, and her eyes were large with fear.

"It's all right," her mother told her quietly. "Amélie, I'm so sorry. But everything's going to be all right, I promise."

"Oh, really?" said the Comte. "I'm not sure you're in a position to promise anything of the sort. Ah, ah, ah," he said to Rémy, who had taken a step toward Thaddeus. "I don't think so. Stay right there."

"I told you," Claudette said tiredly. "I never had any intention of leaving you, Comte. My friends were mistaken."

"They destroyed my castle," said the Comte coldly. "I think that's rather more than a mistake."

"Take my money," Claudette told him. "Once you have that, you can rebuild it. You can make it twice, three times as big, if you want to. Just let my daughter and my friends go, and you can have it all."

"What makes you think I need to bargain with you?" the Comte barked. "I believe I will take exactly what I want, when I want it."

Rémy was staring at Thaddeus. He was looking

directly back at her, his eyes alight with a fierce internal fire, and she had a feeling he was silently trying to tell her something. The problem was, they had spent so much time actively avoiding looking each other in the eye that she wasn't sure what it was. It made her tense, though, that fierce look. Thaddeus still had the Comte's sword at his neck — if he tried to move, de Cantal would slit his throat. But Rémy had the feeling that Thaddeus was poised, preparing to act.

She glanced around. The walls were uneven but otherwise featureless — there were no handholds, nothing to cling to. The bars of Amélie's cage were rusted, but firm. The curved ceiling of the roof offered no suggestions, either.

Claudette stepped forward and dropped to her knees on the cold floor. "Sir," she begged the Comte, "dear sir, I know you have a wise heart in your noble body. Please — please — let these two take my daughter far away from here."

The Comte merely laughed, apparently amused by the sight of the pleading woman. "Oh?" he said, "and why on Earth would I do that, when I already have you all within my power?" He twisted the sword against Thaddeus's neck. Rémy winced as she saw the policeman flinch.

"You have no need to show us mercy, I know that," said Claudette in the same beseeching tone, scrambling closer on her knees. She was close enough now that her pleading hands could reach the Comte's legs. She scrabbled at them feebly, her dusty fingers brushing at his thighs, at his naked waist. "We are indeed in your power," Claudette went on, "which will only go to prove how great you truly are should you honor this one request. I will do anything you so wish, my lord, anything — but please, let my child and my friends go. This wish only you can grant, and in your great mercy, I beg you will do so."

Rémy watched her friend uncomfortably. She was about to tell her to stop, that this was accomplishing nothing but humiliation, when she realized what Claudette had done. Her heart leaped. Once a pickpocket, always a pickpocket. Rémy saw the movement, as quick and as light as it was — with one hand, Claudette continued to paw pleadingly at the Comte's body. With her other, her fingers slipped into the pocket of his tattered trousers. There was a flash of silver in the dim passageway as she deftly pulled the keys from his pocket.

"Enough," said the Comte, still laughing, "get back, woman, before I lose my patience."

"But Comte —" Claudette reached for his arm — the one that held the sword against Thaddeus's neck.

It was all the intervention Rémy and Thaddeus's needed. In the fraction of a second that Claudette pushed against the Comte's hand, the policeman lifted his own to intercept the sword. Rémy ran forward, aiming a kick high at the man's arm, while Claudette flung the keys into the cell.

"Amélie," she shouted, back on her feet in an instant. "Quickly!"

The little girl knew exactly what to do. She scooped up the keys and in the next moment was fitting each key to her cell's lock in turn, trying to find the one that would release her.

"Treacherous imbeciles," the Comte screamed in rage, realizing that he was no match for a combined attack from the three of them. "You will all die for this! You will die!"

He lashed out at Thaddeus with the sword, almost scoring the policeman a nasty gash across his stomach. Rémy responded with a kick to his sternum while Thaddeus went for the blade. The weapon tumbled to the ground as the man wrenched himself free, stumbling backward.

Claudette turned at the sound of the cell door

squeaking open — Amélie had freed herself. She threw herself at her mother, who picked her up and hugged the little girl tightly.

"Go!" Thaddeus shouted, "Claudette, take Amélie out of here, now!"

Claudette hesitated, looking at Rémy.

"Yes, do it!" Rémy nodded. "Go, quickly!" She watched as her friend fled back down the passageway toward the prison's entrance as she and Thaddeus blocked the way for the Comte.

"Fools!" the thwarted nobleman screamed, backing away into the darkness behind him. "You imagine you can defy me? You will rue the day you even tried!" He turned from them and ran, disappearing along the darkened passageway.

"Rémy, we have to stop him," Thaddeus told her. "What he's got back there — it's worse than Abernathy. A hundred . . . a thousand times worse."

Rémy was out of breath, but nodded. *"D'accord,"* she said. He was alive and Claudette and Amélie were free. Right then, she felt as if anything were possible. "Show me."

{Chapter 46}

NEVER ENOUGH TIME

*W*hen they reached the engine room, it was clear something had changed. The machine that made the mechanical men's armor had fallen silent. Rémy stared at the scene before them with a horrified look on her face, ignoring the hideous fumes.

"What are they?" she asked of the rows and rows of silent soldiers.

"Mechanical soldiers. The most fearful fighting men ever created," Thaddeus said. He looked around as the sulphur began to burn his lungs. He'd left the masks the Comte had discarded where they lay in the passageway, hoping to find new ones with fresh stores of oxygen. "Where are they?" he muttered and then spied a glass cabinet riveted into the rough stone a few feet away. Thaddeus smashed it, pulling out two of the breathing masks and canisters. He held one out to Rémy. "The fumes — you don't want to breathe them for long. This will help."

Rémy pulled it on. Thaddeus reached over and twisted the valve cog so that she could breathe. "I can't see him," she said, her voice muffled beneath the hiss of air. "The Comte, where did he go?"

As if in answer, there came a loud, booming screech that almost deafened them despite the leather covering their ears. Then they saw him, standing among his golden army. The Comte de Cantal was wearing one of the breathing masks. He was also holding a silver box beset with colorful switches and antennae.

"That looks like one of the Professor's transmission boxes," said Thaddeus tensely.

The Comte flicked a single switch, and it was if the mechanical army had been woken from a deep sleep. As one, the figures lifted their heads. It was eerie, the silence that accompanied the movement almost dreamlike. Then the Comte flipped another switch, and they instantly came to attention, lifeless hands stiffening at their sides, feet sturdily stepping apart to stamp loudly on the stone. A second later, they began to march. The relentlessly even tread of their boots echoed around the chamber as, in impenetrable lines of emotionless metal, the soldiers stepped forward and then turned sharply in tight formation. As Thaddeus and Rémy watched, the great gate opened in the rock wall. The men disappeared from view, four abreast until the cavern was almost empty.

Below them, the Comte spread his arms in triumph. "They are programmed to protect Mont Cantal," he bellowed up at them. "No one will exit. No one will enter. No one will be able to defeat them. Welcome to your graveyard!"

The Comte began to laugh, the sound echoing eerily around the great chamber.

"What can we do?" Rémy asked Thaddeus, looking around frantically. "How do we defeat them?"

Thaddeus grasped her by the shoulders, spinning her around to face him. "I was wrong. We can't. Listen to me, Rémy — we just can't. Maybe if we'd got to him before, but not now he's activated them."

"Then what —"

"You have to run. Go now, and you can make it before the metal men reach the main gates. Get out of here."

"What about you?" Rémy asked. "Why aren't you coming?"

"I'm not as fast as you," Thaddeus told her.

"That's not true!" Rémy protested. "We can both —"

"It is true," Thaddeus told her, "and anyway, there is something I must do. Go, Rémy. Save yourself. Please."

"No," Rémy said, her voice rasping inside the mask. "No, whatever you are going to do — I'm coming too."

"Rémy —"

"Thaddeus," Rémy answered resolutely. "Whatever it is, I can help."

"It's dangerous," Thaddeus warned. "Extremely dangerous. If it works, I don't think there's a lot of chance of me making it out of here."

"Good," she said, stoutly. "Anything other than extremely dangerous has a habit of being boring. Now come on, little policeman, get on with it. We're wasting time."

Thaddeus stared at her for a moment, and then grabbed her hand and pulled her down the short flight of rough stone steps. He hauled Rémy under the stone arch and into the connecting cavern where the stench of sulphur was at its strongest, even with their masks.

"Mon dieu!" Rémy exclaimed, when she saw the lava pool.

"Up there," Thaddeus said, pointing to the huge machine in the ceiling. Its arms were still moving, and inside the metal cabin some of the mechanical men were still at work. "It controls the lava flow. It's what keeps it in check."

Rémy looked at him. "You want to destroy it?"

"I can't think of anything else we can do," he said. "If we can make the lava overflow . . ."

She nodded without him having to finish. "Well," she said, with a sharp grin. "It's better than drowning again, eh?"

If she hadn't been wearing that damned mask and if there had been time, he would have kissed her then. But she was, and there wasn't. There never seemed to be enough time, or at least not enough of the right time.

"You take the stairs," she told him, pointing to the metal rungs sent into the wall for the soldiers to climb.

"What are you going to do?" he asked.

Rémy was already running. "What do you think?" she shouted back over her shoulder.

Thaddeus didn't have time to watch her. He ran to the ladder and began to climb. It was difficult to see in the mask, and he had to wedge the oxygen canister into what was left of his trousers in order to use his hands, but he struggled on.

Halfway up he turned to see what Rémy was doing. He paused for a moment in amazement. She'd climbed onto one of the huge slabs of rock. The machine had started to lift it, but that didn't deter Little Bird. Instead, Thaddeus watched as she began to climb the mechanical arm itself.

He reached the top of the ladder and found himself on a narrow ledge that led to the machine's control room. For one jubilant moment he thought the way forward was clear, but then he heard a shout from below. It was the Comte, still wielding the controls to his fearful army. He yelled something Thaddeus couldn't make out and then flicked another switch. Inside the control room, one of the metal men began to move. It stepped out onto the ledge and headed for Thaddeus.

{*Chapter 47*}

ACHILLES' HEEL

The metal soldier was shockingly fast and on him in a moment. Unlike the lumbering, unwieldy mechanical contraptions Thaddeus had seen in Abernathy's lair, this soldier was lean and graceful, moving fluidly as it tried to grab for his neck. The policeman ducked, feigning a left and then moving right before launching a kick at the machine's leg. It was like attacking solid rock — Thaddeus's foot simply slipped off the polished metal. The move unbalanced him, and the mechanical soldier launched another attack, this time punching at his shoulder with enough force to hurl Thaddeus against the wall, jarring his spine and winding him. Through his pain, the policeman saw the soldier reach for something at his hip. It was a cruel-looking knife, with a long, hooked blade of the sort he had seen down on the docks in the hands of shipmen arriving from the Orient. The soldier pulled it from a scabbard fashioned directly into its metal flesh, and plunged the weapon toward him.

Thaddeus's only advantage was the narrow ledge on which he and his apparently impervious foe fought. If he could find some way to make the monster miss a step — to stray too close to the edge . . .

He quickly looked the machine over, searching for some weakness, however small. The metal of its torso was forged from one smooth piece, and each joint in the arm and neck overlapped so that its inner workings were hidden. The legs, though, were slightly different — one hip housed the evil-looking knife, and so bore no such smooth overlap. When its knife was in use, that could be a weakness. Besides this, the ankle joints were exposed to show an assembly of cogs and gears, constantly turning as the monster moved forward.

Thaddeus lashed out, aiming a stout kick at the unprotected hip, but to no avail. The soldier anticipated his move a fraction of a second before the blow connected and turned slightly before slashing the knife at Thaddeus's shoulder blade, missing by a hair's breadth.

Instead of pulling back, though, the policeman forged forward, ducking under the soldier's arm so that he was, for just a moment, behind it. The advantage was only a split second — the contraption was already twisting its featureless face around to work out where he was — but Thaddeus used it fully. He slammed his heel into the gears at the soldier's ankle. It was enough to unbalance the soldier. It lifted its arms and splayed its metal fingers to steady itself, which was all the hesitation Thaddeus needed. Gathering his strength, he brought up one leg and propelled it into the soldier's featureless torso. The kick had enough force to make the metal man step back — straight over the lip of the ledge on which they fought. Thaddeus lunged forward as it fell, grasping for the knife. He grabbed it by the hilt and the soldier let it go. The policeman righted himself and kicked out with one last blow to make sure it fell. It did so in total silence, plummeting to its end without even a hint of emotion.

A bellow of fury echoed off the walls. It was the Comte, watching from the floor of the lava room.

Thaddeus watched as the soldier crashed to the floor, half in and half out of one of the molten infernos. It lay there, torso, arms, and head still operational, but it was too late. It's legs and innards melted into the river of fire, disappearing like ice back into a pond on a sunny morning.

The Comte bellowed his rage again, but the policeman was already on the move. He could see that Rémy was ahead of him — she'd made it all the way up the metal arm.

"Rémy," he shouted at her, "their ankles are their weakness!"

She turned at the sound of her name and nodded once before launching an attack on the glass windows of the control cabin. Thaddeus saw another metal man coming for him. It charged through the door of the cabin as the glass behind it shattered under Rémy's attack, falling like sharp rain to the floor below.

"No!" the Comte screamed again. He threw another switch on the control box, and the soldier running toward Thaddeus stopped abruptly. It turned on its heel and started back to the control cabin.

Thaddeus followed, slashing and stabbing wildly at the soldier from behind. The knife bounced off the sheet metal of its armor but found a chink beneath the overlap at the machine's shoulder. The blade slipped beneath, and Thaddeus wrenched it back again. There was an immediate whining, winding sound as something within broke. Black oil spilled out like blood, bringing with it a torrent of tiny golden cogs. The soldier's arm hung useless at its side, but still it didn't stop.

Inside the cabin, Rémy had plunged through the broken window and launched an attack on the two machines left within. Not even these inhuman contraptions were fast enough to catch Little Bird, who leaped and pirouetted around the cabin as they thumped and bashed their way after her, damaging the controls with far more efficiency than they did their prey.

"This place is the heart of his entire operation," Thaddeus shouted, looking around at the myriad controls. "If we can destroy it . . ."

Rémy didn't reply, too busy evading the jerking, stabbing reach of one of the metal men. She threw herself back against one of the control panels and then slammed out her foot against its arm. At the same time, Thaddeus used his knife to incapacitate it, oil spurting everywhere as he slid the knife under the armor at the back of its neck and wrenched upward hard.

With Rémy keeping the other two occupied, Thaddeus looked around. The control cabin was a dense forest of controls, none of which were labeled.

"Can you turn it off?" Rémy yelled, as she rammed

one of her opponents back against a large pulley that hung down through a hole in the ceiling. It flailed its arms uselessly, entangled in the chains, unable to free itself.

"That won't be enough," Thaddeus shouted over the sound of crashing metal. "We've got to make the lava overflow, somehow . . ." He looked up, seeing through the dirty glass circles of his mask the clamps that held the cabin to the rock ceiling. He realized now that the whole structure was hanging on two huge rails that crossed the cavern's roof. The machine must have been designed to slide so that the stone slabs could reach different areas when needed. Thaddeus leaned through the smashed glass window and looked down — at the moment they were almost directly over the main lava pool. If the machine was to fall, not only would every one of the stone slabs be unable to operate, the weight of the cabin might just be enough to crack the edge of the lava pool.

"I could really use some help here," Rémy shouted.

Thaddeus turned to see that the final mechanical soldier had managed to corner her. It caught one of Rémy's legs in midair, making her overbalance. She crashed back against the control panel, crying out in pain as the switches and levers smashed into her back.

Thaddeus leaped forward, slamming his knife up and into the soldier's left knee joint. It staggered, giving Rémy a chance to get up, but righted itself almost immediately. It swung around, smashing one clenched fist at Thaddeus's face and catching his jaw with a crunching blow. He heard Rémy yell, and the soldier slid sideways, off-balance enough that its next punch connected with one of the glass panels still intact. The panel shattered, showering them all in glass.

"Tip it out!" Rémy screamed. Together they grabbed the soldier's legs and lifted up and out through the broken window. It made no sound as it fell.

"Look," Rémy said, breathing hard.

Below, a fresh column of gleaming metal soldiers were marching into the cavern. The Comte was directing them toward the cabin in which Rémy and Thaddeus stood, his ranting and raving visible even from where they stood watching.

"What do we do?" Rémy asked. "Tell me you've got a plan, Thaddeus, because I don't think we can delay that many for long!"

Chapter 48

CONSUMED

The policeman looked around, suddenly feeling help-less in the face of so many unknowns. "Start pulling levers," he said. "It's all we can do. Quickly!"

Together, they began wrenching levers and throwing switches. Some did nothing; others caused audible whines from the machine. He threw one switch to the upright position and felt the cabin move slightly. Looking out, he saw one of the huge metal arms move. It lifted, taking its massive load of stone slab with it. Thaddeus flicked the switch next to it and another arm did the same thing.

"Rémy," he said, "quickly, help me with these."

Together, they moved all of the switches into the

upright position, lifting all of the metal arms so that every one of the huge slabs began to move at once. The cabin shook with immense strain of lifting so much weight at the same time.

Below them, the small lava channels — the ones that had been blocked or controlled by the moveable rocks — began to overflow. Thaddeus looked down to see the Comte stepping backward warily as one river of fire burst its hewn banks and crept across the floor toward him.

There was a creaking sound from above them as the clamps holding the cabin in place began to buckle under the strain. The creak turned into the squeal of metal as one of the four pinion points gave way. A second later, another broke, and one side of the cabin dropped completely, hanging down toward the pool of lava. Rémy lost her footing and was thrown against Thaddeus.

"We have to get out of here," she gasped, pushing away from him as he held her steady. They fought their way to the doorway and scrambled out onto the ledge.

From outside the cabin, they could see the Comte yelling frantically, waving his transmitter and trying to direct his column of metal soldiers. One of the lava flows had already cut off their route to the ladder.

Instead, he had ordered them to climb the rock walls, and so they were clawing their way directly up the rock face on the other side of the cavern, making for the opposite end of the narrow walkway on which Thaddeus and Rémy stood.

Another of the cabin's clamps began to give way, the huge metal screws holding it in place scraping loudly free of the rock. Dust and chunks of stone began to pepper the ledge, falling on Thaddeus and Rémy.

"We've got to get to the engine cavern before they cut us off," Thaddeus yelled over the violent creaking of the cabin. "We can get out through the cells."

"I'm running out of air," Rémy shouted back. She pulled the canister of oxygen from her belt and shook it.

"I know, me too," Thaddeus told her. "Go!"

The metal ladder that the policeman had used to get to the upper walkway was useless, the lower rungs eaten away by the flood of lava. To get to the second cavern, they'd have to make it to another ladder that reached from the walkway to the arch that connected the two stone rooms.

"It's too far!" Rémy shouted over her shoulder. "We won't make it before they do!"

Thaddeus looked to where she pointed and saw the first of the Comte's golden men complete his scramble up the wall to the ledge. In seconds the machine was on its feet and coming for them.

"We'll make it!" he promised. *We have to*, he added silently.

Below them, more and more lava was flooding out of the pool, creeping across the floor. It moved faster as the flow deepened. The heat radiating upward was phenomenal — Thaddeus felt as if his hair may begin to smolder at any moment.

Then with a final deafening scream of metal, the last clamp holding up the machine behind them failed. Thaddeus spun around to see the great machine crash to the floor of the cavern. It thundered into the pool of lava, sending the steaming hot liquid splashing over the side. There was a cracking sound as the machine crushed the edge of the pool, opening farther the hole the Comte had drilled. Waves of molten fire washed out in an unstoppable flood, engulfing the carcass of the machine, which had already melted into a weird, twisted version of itself.

A blood-curdling screech echoed around the cavern. Thaddeus looked down to see that the Comte had been cut off. His precious lava had surrounded him, leaving him one tiny, shrinking island of untouched stone that was disappearing fast. Thaddeus paused, watching in horror as the Comte fumbled with his control box. Obeying their commands, some of his soldiers turned back. They tried to return to the Comte, some stepping from the rock on which they clung, some striking out directly into the molten fire. None of them could reach him — their metal bodies, so impervious in the face of human attack, melted in seconds when they came into contact with the lava. More and more of the mechanical men sank into the burning flood, until all that could be seen of them were their golden hands, reaching hopelessly for their master. Then they too were swallowed up by the lake of fire.

The Comte's island swiftly disappeared. The lava's appetite was as unquenchable as its heat, and it consumed him as he screamed, still frantically fiddling with his useless control box. He vanished, burned up by the fires of his insane ambition.

"Thaddeus!" Rémy shouted at him. "Don't stop! Hurry!"

He looked back to see that she had made it to the ladder and was climbing down. The lava below was rushing quickly toward the archway, threatening to block them off the way it had done the Comte. Thaddeus ran to the ladder, slipping down it as quickly as he could. He narrowly avoided jumping into the river of lava as it snaked its way past the bottom rung, landing just inches from its burning flow. Rémy pulled him to safety.

"We're too late," she said, sounding breathless as she used up the last of her oxygen. "Look!"

Thaddeus saw what she meant — the lava was already sucking hotly at the stairs that led to the cells. Their escape route was cut off. They were trapped.

{*Chapter 49*}

OUT OF THE MOUNTAIN

"*There!*" Thaddeus shouted. Rémy looked up to see that he was pointing at the only high point the lava couldn't possibly reach — the ledge below the waterfall that gushed down the wall.

"Go!" she shouted, glancing down and dancing forward to avoid the lava's reach.

They clawed their way up the rough wall to reach the water. It cascaded through the ceiling and then split in two. Some of it flowed down into the man-made riverbed below, to provide the steam for the Comte's huge engine. The rest, though, disappeared back into the rock through a void worn smooth by time and the constant passage of water. Here the river ran in a raging torrent that vanished from sight, down into the pitch-black belly of the mountain.

She was standing close to it, and the sight filled Rémy with a dread she hadn't felt even when she saw the lava break its banks. She was rarely afraid, least of all for herself. She had spent so much of her short life risking it that to put herself in peril almost came as second nature to her. But here and now, when there was no option but to plunge into the icy waters before them, she felt afraid. A memory surfaced, of trying to breathe but being unable. Of darkness, and cold, cold water.

"We have to go through there," Thaddeus yelled.

"Where does it come out?" Rémy asked. "Do you even know if it does? Maybe it just disappears right down into the earth. Maybe —"

"What other choice do we have?" Thaddeus shouted to her over the quaking rumble all around them. "Look!"

Rémy turned to see where he was pointing. The lava had completely filled the archway and was busy pouring into the lower level. They were utterly cut off — soon the only thing not burning would be the ledge on which they stood.

The last of the oxygen in her canister gave out.

Rémy pulled off her mask and tossed it into the raging lava below. Thaddeus did the same. They stood before each other, coughing as the sulphur choked them.

"We don't have any more time," Thaddeus yelled. "We have to go now."

"*D'accord*," Rémy said, as her heart pounded in her chest. "Okay." *Pull yourself together*, she told herself silently. *It's only water. You can do this. You've done it before.*

Thaddeus stepped close to her, putting his hands either side of her face and forcing her to look him in the eye instead of at the water. "It won't be like last time," he promised, as if he'd read her mind. "This isn't like Abernathy's flood. I'll be right with you."

Rémy didn't push him away as she might once have done. She tried to smile instead. "You're lucky you're not stuck here with J, is all," she shouted. "You know how he hates to take a bath."

Thaddeus smiled at her affectionately. "I'll go first," he told her.

"No," she said, taking his hand. "No, we go together."

The water was icy cold after the intense heat of the cavern. It pulled at their feet as they clambered into the tunnel's opening. Ahead, the passageway sloped downward into darkness, the water gushing past and over them with terrifying speed. They tried to stay upright as they picked their way toward the abyss below, but it was impossible. Thaddeus was the first to slip, his drenched shoe striking a slippery stone. He lost his footing. He let go of Rémy's hand and flung his arms out to steady himself, but to no avail.

"Thaddeus!" Rémy yelled as he vanished from sight. She froze for a second, shivering in the cold dark, and then took another tentative step forward.

A moment later Rémy found herself on her back, the wet stone scraping at her spine as the waterfall rushed over her. She tried to push herself up out of the drowning torrent, but only succeeded in taking a single gasp of breath before being dragged under again. The water was so cold it had numbed her instantly, and she tumbled over and over as the water cascaded down, down, down, bumping and scraping her against the harsh rock until her body felt like a bruised apple. Time and again she thought she had breathed her last breath, and time and again the water lifted her up just enough to take another before dragging her back down again.

Then, suddenly, there was daylight. Rémy was spat out of the mountain like a mouthful of cold coffee and found herself slaloming down the great waterfall that cascaded through the three tiers of Mont Cantal. Struggling to right herself, she saw Thaddeus ahead of her. He clung to a rock, drenched, his hair plastered against his head as his eyes searched the water for her. She threw up an arm, and he saw her. Their hands reached for each other, found each other, grasped each other. Thaddeus pulled her to the rock, and she clung to it beside him, one of his arms around her as they both gulped for air. Rémy blinked the river water from her eyes and saw that Thaddeus was as bruised as she felt — one welt covered his left eye, and blood was trickling from his wet hair. She reached frozen fingers up to his cheek, worried, but he shook his head with a shaky smile.

"I'm fine," he managed, through heaving gasps. "We made it. We made it!"

{Chapter 50}

YANNICK'S REMORSE

*Th*ey struggled out of the water. The waterfall had carried them all the way down into the deep pool at the lowest tier of the city. Overhead, the night air was smudged with smoke and the orange glow of flames. The fire from the Comte's castle had spread all the way down the mountainside, burning the city in its entirety. The place seemed completely empty — there were no screams or shouts, no sound of running feet. Mont Cantal had been abandoned, its people fleeing their burning homes and crumbling city.

Thaddeus helped Rémy to her feet. The path on which they stood led from the pool to join the main thoroughfare in and out of the mountain fortress.

Here, the houses were alight, but the road was wide enough for them to walk between unscathed. They soon realized that the fire was not their biggest problem.

"Look," said Thaddeus, nodding ahead at the great wall that encompassed the mountain's split.

The Comte's golden army stood sentry along the walls and in front of the main gates. They were in pairs, one facing in, one facing out, so there was no way to approach them without having to confront their blank faces and fierce strength.

"I hoped that the Comte's death would mean they'd stand down," said Thaddeus. "But it doesn't look that way."

Rémy scanned the wall, looking for a way out, but there was none. The grille that shut off the river was intact, and other than the main gate, there was no other exit except possibly over the walls. "What about Claudette?" she asked. "Could she and Amélie have got out before they blocked the gate?"

Thaddeus shook his head, still catching his breath. "I don't know."

"Claudette!" Rémy shouted. "Amélie!"

None of the mechanical soldiers made any sign that they had heard. Then there came the sound of scrabbling. It echoed around the empty houses, above the crackling flames, finally resolving into footsteps.

"Claudette?" Rémy shouted again. "Is that you?"

There was no answer. Rémy glanced at Thaddeus, and for once they could both tell what the other was thinking. They began to look around, searching for something to use as a weapon. Thaddeus picked up a large rock, while Rémy grasped a chunk of fallen roof beam. The sound grew nearer. They braced themselves as it became apparent that the sound was of hurrying human footsteps.

"Claudette?" Rémy shouted again.

A ragged figure appeared from between two charred houses. It most definitely was not Claudette.

"Yannick?" Rémy cried in disbelief.

He was a pitiful sight. He had lost his military jacket and the rest of his uniform was blackened and torn. His face and arms were smudged with soot, and he looked exhausted.

"Please," he said in French. "Please, don't hurt me, Little Bird. You're the only other two people I have seen! You must help me get out. Those things . . . those things!" He pointed a wavering finger at the soldiers on the wall.

"What did he say?" Thaddeus asked suspiciously. "What does he want?"

"He just wants help. Speak English, Yannick," Rémy snapped at him. "Do you know any other way out of here?"

The wretched magician shook his head. "No. There is no other way. We are trapped! Either the fire will get us, or those monsters will." He brightened for a moment. "Unless you can call your airship back? Then we can escape the same way as Claudette and Amélie?"

"Wait," said Rémy. "You saw them? They got out?"

Yannick nodded. "Will it come back? For you — for us?"

Thaddeus shook his head, looking at the flames around them. "They'd be mad to. The flames are too high, too much of a risk."

Yannick sagged. "Then we're done for. It's hopeless!"

"Ach, be a man for once in your life," Rémy said scornfully. To Thaddeus, she said, "We don't have to fight the whole of the Comte's army. All we need to do is get through their lines — make them leave a gap so we can get over the wall."

Thaddeus nodded. "What's your idea?"

Rémy pointed to where the stones of the arch

across the river created the only features in the great
wall. "We aim for those. They will be easier to climb.
I will create a diversion — draw some of them away.
Then you climb. Once you are high enough, I'll lose
them and double back."

"No," Thaddeus said immediately. "I can't let you
use yourself as bait!"

"It's the only way," Rémy insisted. "I'm the fast-
est of us all — both running and climbing. I have a
chance. You two have none. You know it's true."

From his grimace, she could see that Thaddeus
did know, even if he didn't like to admit it. "I don't
think —"

She cut him off. "We don't have time to argue, little
policeman," Rémy told him shortly. "The lava we let
loose is not going to stop. It is coming. Isn't it?"

Thaddeus rubbed one hand over his eyes, and she
knew she'd won. "All right," he said unhappily. "What
do we do?"

Rémy led the way as they ran swiftly down toward
the wall. The soldiers took no notice of them at first.
Rémy split off from Yannick and Thaddeus, waving
with her hand to indicate they should hold back. She
picked up a stone and skimmed it through the air so
that it glanced off the shoulder of one of the golden

men. It turned, primed and ready for attack, as she quickly began to scale the archway. She got three quarters of the way up before the soldier above sensed what was happening. It reached for her in one strong movement, and she started back down the wall again, scrambling quickly backward, though careful not to go so quickly that it abandoned the chase. It followed her, and so did the second in the pair. The two mechanical sentries came after her down the wall, leaving a small gap in its defense.

"Go!" she shouted to Thaddeus, as she drew the two soldiers away. "I'll follow! Quickly!" They were faster now they were on flat ground, but she was faster still. Rémy headed for the streets of burning houses, hoping to lose her metal pursuers in the tangled, smoky alleyways.

She glanced back over her shoulder to see Thaddeus and Yannick on the wall, making for the gap. For a moment her heart leaped — it looked as if they were going to make it! Then the two soldiers pursuing her stopped dead. Rémy paused, too, out of breath and wary, but they didn't attempt to catch her. Abruptly, they turned and started back to the wall, heading for their posts.

"Thaddeus," she screamed. "Yannick — look out!"

Thaddeus had gone up first and was almost at the top. Yannick was several steps below him. They both hesitated, wondering if they could reach the top and begin the scramble down the other side. The answer was no. The two golden men were back at the wall in an instant. Yannick froze where he was, fear stilling him against the wall, blocking Thaddeus's only path back to the ground.

"Yannick," Rémy shouted, scared, "jump. Just jump!"

It was too late. One of the soldiers started climbing up the way Thaddeus and Yannick had used, cutting off their escape. The other leaped directly at the wall, launching itself several feet into the air and landing beside Yannick, clinging to the stone like a spider. Yannick screamed and tried to get away, but the soldier clamped its hand around his leg, pulling at him as the magician scrabbled desperately against the wall. The second soldier reached Yannick and began to pull at him, too.

Rémy saw Thaddeus start back down toward the fray, intending to help the magician, who was screaming fit to wake the dead. She looked around and grabbed a hunk of fallen wood, hauling it up and running forward.

"Thaddeus!" She shouted. He looked up and saw her coming. She used all her might to throw the wooden beam toward him. He caught it and swung it at Yannick's inhuman captors as Rémy searched for another weapon. Then she, too, joined the attack. The soldiers showed absolutely no reaction to their blows. Yannick struggled feebly in their grip as Thaddeus tried again and again to free him. Then Rémy saw one of them reach for a small panel on its side. It flipped it open and pressed a button on the plate within.

Instantly, four more of the soldiers on the wall turned and began to walk toward the scuffle.

"Thaddeus," Rémy screamed. "Look! Get out of there!"

But in the act of turning to see what she meant, Thaddeus lost concentration. He wobbled, dropping the beam to catch his balance. In that moment, one of the soldiers reached out and caught hold of his leg.

"No!" Rémy shouted, as he yelled in pain at the heavy grip on his burnt skin. The sight of Thaddeus both trapped and in pain opened up a well of strength she didn't know she had. Rémy hurled the chunk of wood she was holding. It hit the soldier square in the back, hard enough to knock it forward against the wall. The policeman yanked his leg free.

"Jump," Rémy screamed up at him. "Don't think, just jump!"

Thaddeus did as he was told, letting go of the wall and throwing himself down toward her. He sailed over the heads of the soldiers and landed hard in the dust below. Rémy darted forward, dragging him up before they could react. Together they stumbled away as swiftly as they could.

"Yannick," Thaddeus managed, winded.

Rémy turned back to see her childhood friend surrounded by the Comte's mechanical men. Each of them seemed to be pulling him in a different direction, like a pride of lions with a carcass. She drew her lips into a straight line and kept moving.

{Chapter 51}

FRIENDS IN NEED

The soldiers didn't seem interested in following them. They'd been ordered to protect the wall, and that's what they were doing. No one in, no one out. Thaddeus's body was smarting, both from his hard landing and from the soldier's frighteningly powerful grip. He leant heavily on Rémy as they ran to the shelter of the smoldering houses of Mont Cantal.

"Rémy, it's no good," Thaddeus said, doubling over to catch his breath. "There's nothing more we can do."

She settled beside him against the wall, breathing hard. "So we just give up?"

"Unless you've got another idea?" he asked, as he

straightened up. "I can't see any way over that wall,
can you? Not alive, anyway."

She hesitated, and then shook her head. "*Non.* I just
hate to let them — him — win."

Thaddeus smiled and then moved to put his arm
around her, pulling her close against him. "He hasn't
won," the policeman reminded her. "Claudette and
Amélie got away. We destroyed that awful place of his.
I choose to count that as a win."

She smiled, and then pressed her face into his shoulder, wrapping her arms around him. "You English. So
easily pleased."

Thaddeus pushed his nose into her short hair as
he stared at the wall of flame licking steadily toward
them. "Yes, well. It looks as if I got the girl in the end.
So there's nothing for me not to be pleased about,
really, is there?"

Rémy lifted her head, her lips parting as if to come
back with some smart answer. Thaddeus took the
opportunity to kiss her instead, firmly and as if it was
the only thing that mattered at that moment. Which
it was.

The ground began to shake. It was only slight at
first, but the tremors quickly grew until the burning
houses around them began to crumble. The stones

on the road shook and bounced, cracks beginning to appear in the ground as the quaking grew worse.

"What is it?" Rémy shouted over the noise.

Thaddeus looked up at the mountain. The waterfall had slowed to a trickle, exposing the cave mouth through which they had escaped. Steam and yellow smoke were gushing from the depths in great roiling belches. The smell of sulphur began to reach them.

He looked down at Rémy, holding her even closer even as they both trembled in the quake. "The lava," he said. "It's coming."

Another sound rose into the air. This one came from the wall, not from the mountain. At first it was indistinct, a raucous hubbub that bubbled under the grating of the quake and the roar of the flames. Thaddeus and Rémy looked out from their shelter just as a volley of large rocks appeared over the wall. They shot into the air, raining down on the golden soldiers. Most missed their targets, but some found them. One of the larger rocks even dislodged one of the mechanical men, hitting it so hard that it lost its footing and fell off the wall completely. There was an audible cheer as it disappeared from sight.

"People," Rémy said in amazement. "It's people! But what —"

A trumpeting noise filled the air, a harsh shriek of anger that would be enough to scare the unwary into the grave.

"Constance!" Rémy shouted, astonished. "That's the elephant! It's the circus! Augustus must have made it!"

As if on cue, a figure appeared on the wall. It was large and broad-shouldered, and seemed to have a pigeon perched on its shoulder.

"My God," whispered Thaddeus, blinking through the acrid smoke as the large man swung a fist at one of the Comte's soldiers. "That's — that's Dorfmann! He got our pigeon!"

More people began to appear on the wall. One was pushed up by the elephant's trunk, others looked as if they had climbed, but all were ready to fight. And as Rémy and Thaddeus watched, fight they did — but not in the way of any usual army. Silhouetted against the wall, facing off against the Comte's army, was the most unlikely fighting force Rémy had ever seen. She saw Erik, the great Danish strongman who rarely spoke to anyone. He had his huge barbells slung across his shoulders. As Remy watched, he swung them left and right, yelling obscenities as he marched along the wall, crushing the Comte's soldiers as he went.

There was Augustus, yelling as he barged bodily at one of the mechanical men, and there was Marcus, the fire-breather, belching in the blank faces of the soldiers. There were the Tumble Twins, using each other as catapults so as to rain blows on the men from above with their acrobatics. There was Angelique, the square-jawed Spanish knife-thrower, pelting one of the mechanical men with her blades hard enough to pierce it until it slumped to its knees.

It was the circus, in full attack. And it was winning.

"Come on," Thaddeus shouted, grabbing her hand. "They're giving us one last chance!"

They ran for the wall as the lava exploded out of the mountain behind them. It came like a torrent, a storm of liquid fire that devoured everything in its path. It ate up the dead waterfall, boiling the last water into steam and burning the riverbed to dry black ash. The heat was phenomenal, and it hit the people below like a wall. The mechanical soldiers, however, did not pause at all, even when the quake worsened as the mountain itself began to split in two.

Rémy glanced back over her shoulder as she ran. Everything was collapsing, vanishing into the great and terrible crack that tore toward them like a rip in paper. There was lava everywhere. It wasn't just flowing out of the waterfall, it was bubbling up from the rents left by the quake, sucking the houses down into the mountain's crumbling, burning guts.

Still the Comte's soldiers fought on, senseless, careless for nothing but their orders. There were gaps along the wall now, but none that were breachable, or at least not for an ordinary mortal such as Thaddeus.

"If you can climb it, climb," Thaddeus shouted to Rémy.

"I'm not going without you," she yelled back.

"I can find another way out!"

"No!" she shouted. "Forget it. I'm not going without you, so forget it!"

There was a ringing thump as something struck the great gates. The blow came again, and again — the circus folk were trying to force them open from outside. The huge wooden doors shook on their hinges, but they wouldn't budge and they didn't splinter.

The lava was gushing toward them now, crushing everything in its path. The sulphur in the air was choking, blinding.

"There's got to be a way out!" Rémy screamed in sheer frustration. "There must be!"

"There is — for you!" Thaddeus told her. "Climb the wall, Rémy. Do it!"

She shook her head, the tears in her eyes caused by more than the sulphur. "No," she said, her voice dropping to a whisper. "I will not go without you. I won't." Thaddeus pulled her toward him, wrapping himself around her so that her head was under his chin and she was snug against him. Rémy shut her eyes and pressed her face into his chest, hearing the roar of the lava roll closer and closer. She heard Thaddeus raise his voice to shout up to the circus folk on the wall.

"Go," he bellowed. "Run — the wall won't stop the lava. Get as far away as you can!"

There was a pause, and then a shout came back. It was a voice Rémy recognized. It was J.

She pushed away from Thaddeus and turned to see the airship rise above the wall as the circus folk scattered and disappeared. The policeman swore hard and waved his arms, trying to send them back.

"What are they doing?" he said. "The heat —"

"Come over," urged Rémy. The airship was hovering on the wall itself, letting down a rope just long enough to graze the ground.

They ran toward it. Thaddeus forced Rémy to go up first, and she did, faster than she'd ever climbed before. J and Dita stood in the open hatch, white-faced, to haul her in.

"Climb!" She yelled down to Thaddeus. "For God's sake, climb!"

J lifted away before Thaddeus had even got halfway up the rope. Rémy wrung her hands in fear as the policeman was scraped harshly against the stone, but he held on. The lava reached the last line of houses as Thaddeus's feet were dragged over the top of the wall. He had stopped climbing and was merely clinging on for dear life.

Chapter 52

A PAUSE FOR BREATH

The fear was that the lava would devour the walls of Mont Cantal and set fire to the forest outside, turning it into an inferno that would be impossible to escape. In the end, though, that was not to be. The mountain that had appeared so impenetrable from the outside had been weakened from within by the Comte's own folly. It collapsed, folding in on itself like a house of cards and taking the remains of the city down with it. The lava reached the walls, chewing on their stones and picking off the golden men with its hot tongue, but then it, too, was sucked down into the great sink-hole of what once had been the Comte de Cantal's glorious and fearful home.

- SHARON GOSLING -

The airship fled the flames, flying far enough to touch the far edge of the forest where it met a river that had not been starved of water. Thaddeus jumped from the rope, his arms aching with the effort of holding on, his leg painful from his earlier burns. It was dawn, the pink tinge of a new day spreading out like a brilliant flag of peace.

"J," said Thaddeus, once the ship was safely down. "That was insane. But thank you. We'd be dead now, if not for you."

The boy grinned, the relief plain on his face as he and Dita stood close together on the gangplank. "Well, I wasn't just going to let you two roast now, was I? Tell you what, though, I'm not keen to have that kind of lark again in a hurry."

Thaddeus nodded, the exertion of the past day settling on him. He felt more tired than he ever had in his life. "You and me both, J. You and me both."

He and Rémy looked at each other, and J cleared his throat.

"Ahem," said the boy. "Well, I reckon we'll go and see where the rest of the folk 'ave got to, eh, Dita? Let them know where we are, like."

"Yes," said Dita flashing them a bright grin. "We will . . . leave you two. Back soon, yes?"

- 478 -

J and Dita headed off down the path they had followed from above the trees, soon disappearing into the greenery.

"They were holding hands," Rémy murmured. "Did you notice?"

Thaddeus reached for one of hers, lifting it to his lips and kissing her fingers gently. "I suppose an experience like that makes people think about what's important," he said.

Rémy smiled, and they sat side-by-side on the airship's walkway, both utterly exhausted. She frowned suddenly, and dug into the pocket of her breeches. She pulled something out and dangled it from her hand — it was a thin gold chain with a pendant hanging from it.

"Your opal," Thaddeus exclaimed. "You found it!"

Rémy nodded. "Yannick did have it. He knew what it meant to me, but he took it anyway." She looked up at Thaddeus. "How could I ever have trusted him over you?"

Thaddeus smiled. "None of that matters now. Do you want me to put it on for you?"

Rémy hesitated, staring at the jewel in her palm, and he frowned. "What's the matter?" he asked. "Don't you want to wear it?"

Rémy grimaced. "I do, but . . ." she trailed off.

"But what?" Thaddeus asked.

She took a breath. "It's just . . . the opal. I never told you, but after I nearly died — back in London, with Abernathy . . ."

Thaddeus took her hand, holding it tightly. "Whatever it is," he told her, "you can tell me. You know that, don't you?"

"I hear other people's thoughts," she said simply, before she lost courage, and willed him to believe her. "I don't know how, or why, but . . . since that day, when I'm wearing it, I can tell what people are thinking."

He stared at her for another moment and then looked down at the stone. She watched his face as he frowned in silence.

"I'm so sorry," he said.

"You're sorry?" blurted Rémy in surprise. "What have you to be sorry for?"

Thaddeus sighed. "The robberies, back in London. That night you got the ruby ring, and I came to see you — you were upset because you thought I suspected you. But you didn't just think it, did you? I thought it, and you heard me. And I'm sorry. I'm sorry that it ever crossed my mind."

Rémy shook her head. "I don't blame you. I don't. I

didn't even then, I just . . ." She sighed. "Why wouldn't you have suspected me? Given what you knew of me, how could I be surprised? And I wasn't. But it made me think . . . it made me think that we just don't . . . that we just can't . . . that we'll never be able to . . ."

"Rémy, look at me," Thaddeus said, interrupting her. She did, and he smiled. "I don't think you need a mystical stone to tell what I'm thinking right now."

She didn't. He kissed her softly. Rémy reached for him, and Thaddeus pulled her against his chest. When they finally broke apart, they stayed like that, as entwined as a stone comfortable in its clasp.

"I love you," she told him. "I don't know why I find that so difficult to say. But I do. I just don't know how we're ever going to work."

Thaddeus kissed her again. "We already do," he said. "We just have to remember that. No matter how complicated things seem."

There was a rustle in the woods beside the caravan. Rémy sprang out of Thaddeus's arms, spinning around, imagining an attack. But it was Amélie who stepped from the leaves, followed by Claudette. Rémy rushed to her friends, pulling them close.

"Thank you, Little Bird," Claudette said huskily. "Thanks to you, the Lost Comtesse is finally dead for good. She's gone forever, and I can go back to being nothing but a fortune teller. And a pickpocket, if need be." She glanced at Thaddeus. "Sorry, monsieur. I am too tired for anything but the truth, and I do not know how else we will make a living with the circus gone."

Thaddeus shook his head. "No need. We are a long way from England and my desk. If I even have one anymore, of course."

"What do you mean?" Rémy asked, looking up at him. "Why wouldn't you?"

"It's not important now," he said. "But I left without taking proper leave. And with Yannick . . . gone, I'll never recover the jewels he took. I can't imagine my name will be anything but mud back home . . . again. And there are some who still don't trust me after last time. Not that I care," Thaddeus added. "I would have come whatever the cost."

"Well." Claudette looked from Rémy to Thaddeus, smiling slightly. "What a good pair you make. Odd, but then who among us is not?"

Amélie left her mother's side and surprised them all by wrapping her arms around Thaddeus's waist. He crouched so that he was her height, and smiled.

"Hello," he said to the little girl. "I don't think we've

ever been formally introduced, Amélie. But I am very glad to know you."

The little girl looked at Rémy expectantly and then pointed to her neck. She wanted her to wear the opal, it was clear. Rémy opened her hand, looking at the jewel with misgiving. She had missed it and missed the love that her mother had given with it, all those years ago before Rémy had even had a chance to know her. But she didn't want to wear it — she didn't feel she could. Not anymore.

"Claudette," she said. "I want you to have this. And I want you to wear it. I think it will change your life. And Amélie's."

"What?" said Claudette, startled, as Rémy moved forward and began to fasten it around her friend's neck. "No, Rémy — I can't! I know how precious it is to you. Why would you . . ."

"I was told once that the opal is a talisman when given in love," Rémy said, taking Claudette's hand. "I think this will work. Shut your eyes and think of Amélie. No," she said, before Claudette had a chance to say anything. "Please, just do as I say. If it works, you'll understand."

Claudette shut her eyes. For another moment or so, the confused frown stayed on her face. Rémy watched and waited. A moment later, Claudette's eyes flew open, shocked as she stared at her daughter. She looked at Rémy.

"What is it?" she asked. "I don't understand. How —"

Rémy shook her head. "Don't question it. Just listen. Listen. Amélie is talking to you."

Claudette's eyes filled with tears. "She says she wants you to know she is grateful, Thaddeus Rec," she said, smiling. "And that you are family now, just like Rémy. She's right, of course," the woman added, wiping her eyes before taking Amélie's hand.

The little girl hugged her mother fiercely. They pair stepped away, talking properly for the first time ever. Thaddeus walked to Rémy, watching them.

"Won't you miss it?" he asked, taking her hand. "And what if it really was a talisman?"

She smiled, squeezing his hand. "It's fine," she said. "I have a new one."

{Chapter 53}

AN IMPOSSIBLE PARTING

$\mathcal{B}$y mid-afternoon, the circus folk were all assembled again. Thaddeus shook Dorfmann's hand when he came to return both the pigeon and the homing device. The big German slapped him heartily on the back, introducing the performers he had brought with him.

"When your pigeon came, I had no choice, ya?" Dorfmann explained. "When one of us is in trouble, we are all in trouble. We are family, you understand?"

Thaddeus did understand. It became even clearer as he watched them all milling about, laughing and chatting, the relief of their victory — and that they were all alive — clear on their faces. Someone started to play a guitar, then someone else began to sing, and before anyone knew what was happening, there was a party taking place right there in the forest beside the river.

Thaddeus watched Rémy, talking to Claudette, hugging Augustus, dancing with the circus children. She seemed so at home here — she *was* at home here. She had even retrieved her pack from the airship and seemed determined not to be parted from it. The sight sunk something painful into the pit of his stomach: a lump of stone that was as cold as it was heavy. He had a feeling that the next time the airship took off, it would be without Rémy Brunel. For how could she leave these people, who had risked so much and lost everything but their lives?

The thought made Thaddeus feel ill, because as much as he might want to, he couldn't stay here. Neither could he return to London, at least not straightaway. He knew, somehow, that for him this unexpected journey was not yet over. An image of the Comte's tattoo floated into his mind — a cutlass set with a sapphire stone. What was it that Desai had said as he'd left? That he had to return home to India . . . to deal with the Sapphire Cutlass. What was the plan that the Comte had boasted of in his cavern of terrifying constructs?

Whatever it was, whatever the truth that lay at the heart of the madness that had taken over both Lord Abernathy and the Comte de Cantal, Thaddeus knew he couldn't simply return to London and forget about it.

J appeared at his elbow, rosy-cheeked and cheerful. "They sure now how to party, these circus types, eh?"

Thaddeus smiled. "You could say that." He was still watching Rémy, who, feeling the scrutiny of his gaze, disentangled herself from the dance and walked toward him, smiling.

J clapped his hands against his thighs as she approached. "Right then," he announced, with an air of decision. "I says we get some grub inside us, then sees about saying our goodbyes. If we take it in turns at the controls so I can get some shut-eye, we could be back at the Prof's warehouse before sun-up tomorrow. How does that sound?"

Rémy frowned, glancing at him and then away again, and this time Thaddeus's heart sank fully to his shoes. He knew then that she wasn't going to come with them. Of course she wasn't — her friends had an entire circus to rebuild, and they needed all the help they could get.

"J," he said quietly, "slow down a little. There's no rush. Let's — let's just stay here for tonight, eh? Get our strength back."

"Yes," said Dita, "and what about me?"

J looked at her. "What about you?"

"You aren't even going to offer to take me with you? After everything I've done for you?"

"What you've done for me?" J repeated, in his best "offended" voice. "What are you talking about? After everything I've done for you, you mean! Anyway, what makes you think you'd be welcome in London?"

"Agh," Dita shouted, her hands on her hips. "After all those stories you've told me about your amazing warehouse! There's room enough for a hundred people, so it sounds! You can fit me in! Me, who has no home and has risked her life over and over for this stupid contraption!" She nodded violently at the airship, her dark curls bobbing furiously.

"It ain't stupid!" J yelled back, incensed. "And anyway —"

"Thaddeus?" He jumped a little as Rémy spoke at his elbow. She was frowning up at him. "Can I talk to you for a moment?"

"Of course," he said, though he'd rather cut off his own ears than hear her say goodbye. He left Dita and

J to thrash it out between them, and followed Rémy into the woods.

"So much has happened," she said, walking ahead of him, pulling the pack from her shoulder. "And there's something I need to show you."

Rémy turned, and Thaddeus saw that she had unwrapped the object she'd taken from her bag. It was a golden cube, carved with intricate patterns. She traced her thumb over it before looking up at him and holding it out.

"What is it?" he asked, fascinated, taking the cube and turning it over in his hands.

"It's a puzzle box. I have to solve it — open it," she said. "And when I do . . . I think it will tell me how to find my brother."

Thaddeus looked up at her in surprise. "I didn't know you had a brother!"

"I didn't — I don't," Rémy said, her face a confusion of emotions. "I might not. But on the other hand, I might, and if I do, then I've got to find him, haven't I?" She bit her lip. "What if I asked you not to go back to London, Thaddeus? What if I asked you to come with me?"

"Come with you where?" Thaddeus asked. "Rémy, what do you mean? Where are you going?"

She didn't answer. Instead she stared out through the dappled forest leaves to where the airship's balloon drifted gently in the breeze.

"How far do you think the airship can fly?" she asked.

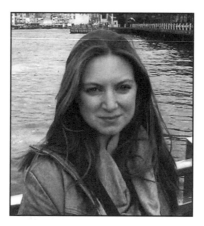

ABOUT THE AUTHOR

Sharon Gosling always wanted to be a writer. She started as an entertainment journalist, writing about television series such as *Stargate* and *Battlestar Galactica*. Her first novel was published under a pen name in 2010. Sharon and her husband live in a very small cottage in a very remote village in the north of England, surrounded by sheep-dotted fells. The village has its own vampire, although Sharon hasn't met it yet. The cat might have, but he seems to have been sworn to secrecy and won't say a thing.

ACKNOWLEDGEMENTS

The author would like to thank Laura Knowles and Julie Gassman for being such great editors and Liam Peters and Kay Fraser for creating such a beautiful cover. Thanks also to Julia Deppe for help with Dita's German speech and to Adam for unerring support. Most of all, though, thanks to the readers!